Legend of the Last vikings

–

Taklamakan

By

John Halsted

John Halsted

Legend of the Last Vikings

Copyright © 2006 John Halsted

Published in London by Abela Publishing Ltd.

Email: author@VikingLegend.com
Website: www.VikingLegend.com

ISBN 13: 978-1-907256-00-4

First Edition, 2006

Abela Publishing
Email: Books@AbelaPublishing.com
Website: www.AbelaPublishing.com

DEDICATION

This book is dedicated to my wife and children

who "lost" me to my research for two years.

John Halsted

Acknowledgements

In the main, the British Library and British Museum

and to all those academic staff at universities and institutions

around the world who took the time to reply to my unsolicited emails.

Prologue

1043AD

The rumble could be heard and felt long before it arrived. In the room everyone braced themselves as it rolled towards them. Then it struck. The building rocked and shook and centuries-old dust fell in a light rain from the roof. Outside roof tiles could be heard crashing to the ground.

"Ying, I fear this may be the last we can withstand. Already two of our four wells are dry and the other two are almost dry too."

"Before you admit defeat, tomorrow we must find out what has happened to the river."

Raising his voice over the noise, his companion shouted, "Yes, Ying, but the aqueduct bringing our water collapsed yesterday as well!"

Then as soon as it had started, the rumbling and shaking stopped. His voice sounded unnatural in his ears as he said, "It can be repaired."

"Yes, it can. But how long can we go on like this? All we seem to be doing is clearing sand out of the canal and repairing aqueducts. Already a good number of the people have left."

"I know. But when it's all over they will come back. They always do."

"They won't come back until the river does, and it left ages ago."

The two men rose and dusted themselves off and walked outside to see many others doing the same. An elderly woman lay in the street under a pile of slate tiles. A young girl stood over her wailing.

"Who is it?"

"I think it is Grandmother Chen."

"I am sorry. She was one of our most reliable citizens."

The two standing next to each other made for an odd pairing. One was short with straight black hair and a droopy moustache. The other had long, lean limbs and towered over his companion. Unlike his companion he was clean shaven and his blonde hair flowed down to his shoulders. They walked through the town to the outskirts and climbed a sand dune. The once thick green forest was showing signs of death. Instead of its former lush green, the undergrowth was now tinged with yellow and brown. A rim of chocolate-coloured silt ringed the lake, which had receded so far that the pier now stood orphaned in the fast-drying mud. Beyond that lay the ever present, ever creeping desert.

Wistfully the blonde one said "I could cry when I see it thus."

"I know."

"My Shambhala—being slowly reduced to a pile of mud and dust."

"From ashes to ashes… At least you were here when it was in its prime."

"Don't you start that Christian stuff with me, I get enough from my wife, thank you."

Quickly changing the subject, he said, "You know it would have been better if it had died suddenly and quickly, rather than this slow, painful strangulation."

After standing and considering their own thoughts for a moment or two longer, the two unlikely companions walked down the dune, back towards the town.

As they approached the town gate a woman waved and started towards them. Her hair, also shoulder length, was raven black and curly. Unlike the women of the town her skin was fair and, like her lover, her limbs were long and straight. Smiling and holding the hands of two fair-skinned children, she walked towards the two men.

Another rumble sounded in the distance. Its approach was marked by the fleeing of dogs and cats, and by birds taking to the air. People could be seen running for cover. One of the gate towers began to gyrate uncontrollably and large sandstone blocks, loosened by previous earthquakes, began to fall. The two children frightened by the earthquake froze and began crying. The woman stopped to comfort them.

Instinctively the two men began to run towards the woman and children, the tall blonde man outrunning his smaller companion. Before he could get to the woman, a falling block struck her neck and she dropped to the earth, at one with the block. While masonry rained down around them, the two children began screaming for their mother, who was now lying under a square-cut block of yellow sandstone.

As he sprinted towards the children, the tall blonde man screamed in a voice not often heard this side of the grave. He reached his children just as the capstone of the gate arch gave way and the whole structure tumbled inwards, crushing the man and his children. In a cruel twist of fate the very city he had fought long and hard to keep alive took his life and all that was dear to him. The short man arrived just seconds after the collapse, saved, ironically, by his short legs.

When the rumbling and shaking had ceased and the dust had settled, survivors began emerging from their safe hiding places in ones and twos. This time they looked not to the tall blonde man for leadership, but to him. He stood, silently staring at the pile of rubble while people gathered around. Eventually he said, "Now it is over. But first we dig them out and we prepare them for burial."

Someone asked, "Where are they to be buried?"

A puzzled look crossed his face, then he said, "In the crypt of the elders. Where else? Heaven only knows he fought long and hard enough to keep us and this city alive."

A voice from the crowd asked, "And then what?"

He stood silently for a while contemplating the question. The crowd stood and waited.

"And then we leave. Lou Lan is dead. There is not enough water to sustain us. While we have the strength and wherewithal, we will walk out of here."

John Halsted

1030 AD - 1066 AD

Standing night watch on an open ship in the middle of the North Sea is reason enough for anyone to take stock of their life; their past, their present, and above all, their future. But after the cataclysmic events of the past few days, I, of all people, had more than enough reason to consider my future.

My name is Ulf Uspakson, a grandson of Usvifer Spake. The story I am about to tell has unfolded over the past thirty-five years or so, with each event having an influence on the next.

In 1030 AD I had fled Scandinavia with my lifelong friends; the king's brother Harald Sigurdsson and Haldor, a son of the gode Snorre. The Norwegian army had been defeated in a fight for the crown of all Scandinavia at Stiklestad. Harald was brother to King Olaf Sigurdsson, who was later to become St Olaf. Harald Sigurdsson later became known as 'Hardraada', or 'Harald the Ruthless'.

It had all started in 1030 — or was it 1029 — when King Olaf of Norway called for the army to be assembled. Although Harald was only fourteen, his physique was already impressive, and no one could keep him from joining up. If they'd tried we would have probably stowed away and joined anyway, in secret. With reluctance Olaf decided that it was better to have him along where he could be watched and protected; the deal was that Haldor and I would come along too.

It had all come apart at Stiklestad when my king was killed in battle. His dying request was to keep Harald from being captured and executed, which would end the line of succession. With the battle having been lost, Ragnvald Brusason quickly assembled a crew and I, together with Harald and Haldor, fled eastwards using the back paths, eventually joining a remnant of our army in Svithjod. Who knew where the others fled to, or if they indeed survived?

Being the remarkable man that he was, the wounded Harald even composed a poem of his escape while wounded. It went thus:

My wounds were bleeding as I rode;
And down below the bondes strode,
Killing the wounded with the sword,
The followers of their rightful lord.

From wood to wood I crept along,
Unnoticed by the bonde-throng;
`Who knows,' I thought, `a day may come
My name will yet be great at home.'

As winter was now upon us we were forced to remain at Svithjod until the spring. This was as good a reason as any, as Harald was so badly wounded I don't believe he would have survived any more travel.

During the winter we gradually acquired ships. Repairing those we could, we worked and reworked them until they were ship-shape.

When the spring came, while a lot stronger, Harald was not yet back to his usual self. However we departed for Novgorod, where we sought and were given the protection of Prince Jarisleif, more commonly known as Yaroslav the Wise, who coincidentally was also Harald's father's half-brother.

With better medical care and long hours of sunshine, it wasn't long before Harald had recovered from his wounds and had started taking an active interest in "things military". His strength returned and he also began taking an active interest in the local female population.

By the end of that summer, Harald had distinguished himself in a number of skirmishes. He had grown to be a trusted captain in Yaroslav's army, and he had yet to have his twentieth birthday. Within another year Yaroslav had appointed Harald and Ragnvald Brusason to be heads of his Land Forces.

It was impossible to keep from Harald's ears the stories about Miklagaard and the merchants' fables of its gold, ready for plundering. After all, Novgorod was a major stopping point for Viking merchants travelling between northern Viking kingdoms and Miklagaard. It was also here that we first came across the brown, smooth-skinned Arabs, along with their impeccable manners and their incredible attention to personal hygiene.

Harald was itching to be "off a Viking" to Miklagaard. Between Prince Yaroslav, Ragnvald and myself, we managed to dampen his sense of adventure for a while longer by improving his education in the classroom, as well as turning a blind eye to his escapades with the local female populace.

I also improved my education by learning to read and write my native Runic, as well as Greek and the Roman language, Latin, and their strange texts. If my parents were alive now, I often wonder what they would say about me being able to read and write, and not in one, but three languages! On one hand my mother would state, "What's the use of reading?" and on the other she would nudge her friends at the women's gatherings, and proudly say, "He can read and write Norse, Greek and Latin!"

It was during those long winter days and nights that I became a slave to the beautifully illuminated manuscripts and documents in the great library in Yaroslav's palace. The documents were brought to life by magnificently illustrated texts and paintings—never before had I seen such beauty. Every day, from before sunrise, I could be found in the library poring over manuscripts. Harald and Haldor had to drag me out to practise my riding and swordsmanship.

Olaf, the court librarian, was at first suspicious of me, but answered my questions as best and politely as he could, considering he was under royal command to assist. He later became very helpful when he realised that he was in fact acting as my unofficial tutor. I soon found myself gravitating towards the historical documents and read through the accounts of Yaroslav's ancestors and how the Rus had come to be.

I was also becoming Harald's personal Scald. Because of our hasty flight, Harald did not have the luxury of the court Scald and someone would have to record the forthcoming events in the life of this bright and rising star.

During these library sessions I came across the account of Igor's ill-fated raid on the Kaspian port of Baku in 911 and of the 943 Volga Viking raid on Bredaa, the ancient Arran capital near Baku. Little did I know that Baku was to take a significant role in my future.

There was also mention of various other, usually unsuccessful, raids by the Volga Vikings into the Kaspian area in the late 900s.

I also read of Ibn Khordo Adbeh's accounts of Vikings travelling to Hind, Sind and Tianxia. What and where were these places? Olaf showed me the maps with their strange names and even stranger symbols, ranges of mountains and rivers that ran for thousands of miles across vast and open grassy plains and of deserts that stretched even further.

Eventually came the day when we departed for Miklagaard. We couldn't keep Harald at bay anymore. Over the intervening two years, remnants of our once proud army had filtered through to Novgorod in ones and twos and our ranks had slowly swollen so that we were almost a full regiment in Yaroslav's army. Yaroslav was soon feeding an army of thousands. It was he who eventually suggested that we embark on our journey south and east, and even provided the ships and provisions. In retrospect I think he was only too keen to get such a large force focussed on objectives other than on local matters — like maybe his throne, although that wouldn't have happened. After all, he was Harald's family and we had too much respect and admiration for him, especially after what he had done for us. We would have gladly laid down our lives for him.

Our adventures and service to the Royal Court at Miklagaard, where we became leaders of the Varangian Horde, are well documented and, allegedly, legendary. During our thirteen years we all amassed large individual fortunes, taken mainly from pirates, Harald more so than the rest of us. And why not? After all, he was our leader, and was considered by many of us to be "king in waiting". We had taken on and conquered forces from Arabia in the east, North Africa in the south and Italy to the Pillars of Hercules in the west. In the main we had ruled the Mediterranean in the name of Byzantium.

All the while, we had been sending our share of the booty we had earned back to Yaroslav for safekeeping. In the meantime Harald had risen to hold the third highest position in the Byzantine Empire.

He was refused the hand of Princess Mary, and was imprisoned for requesting it. It was then obvious that our time in Miklagaard was over; Harald had played his hand. So, in 1045AD we returned to our beloved Norway, paying tribute to Yaroslav on our return. Harald insisted on repaying Yaroslav, with interest, for the cost of the ships and provisions he had provided all those years before. Of course Yaroslav refused, so Harald insisted that the money be used to provide for the poor and orphans. So much treasure was deposited in Yaroslav's treasury that the poor and downtrodden of Kyiv could have lived like royalty for many a year.

Yaroslav, as wise as ever, cemented his link with Harald by giving the hand of his daughter Ellisif in marriage. He had already cemented ties with France and Hungary in a similar fashion.

It was my reacquainting with Olaf the Librarian that made me aware of the detailed journey of Ingvar Vittfarne, a Svea Scandinavian of royal blood. His 1041 journey record describes how he fought off dragons and serpents on his voyage down the Volga and across the Kaspian Sea, travelling to the east in an attempt to reach Samarkand, in Sarkland, and reopen trade links. It was thought that he died there, as he did not return from his last journey. It also mentioned his intention to travel on to the fabled Tavastaland. I wondered if he was still travelling and searching or if he had indeed gone on to Valhalla. What had he discovered on his journey? What sights had he seen that possibly no European had ever before seen?

Word had gone ahead from Aldeigjuborg. The Swedish King Olaf, uncle to Ellisif, had sent his nephew, Svein Ulfson, to invite Harald to sup with him in Svithjod. Harald and Svein entered into a pact of friendship and because of this pact, Svein accompanied Harald on his last leg to Norway. On the way we laid waste to Seeland and Feyn.

King Magnus Olafsson, then King of Denmark and Norway, heard of his uncle's arrival and wisely offered his legendary uncle half of his kingdom, to be ruled in league with him. Perhaps the thought of six thousand battle-hardened men suddenly arriving in his capital had something to do with it. Whichever it was, it felt good and right.

However, within two years Magnus Olafsson had died and Harald was asked to be king, a role he readily accepted. He was more than prepared for it. His previous fifteen years had taught him what it was like to be homeless and kingdom-less. It had also taught him leadership in both victory and defeat; but more of the former. Within two years Harald had earned the title of Hardradi or Hadraada—'The Ruthless One'. His experiences from 13 years "a-Viking" in the Mediterranean and half-running the Byzantine Empire stood him in good stead.

In the intervening years Harald waged a ceaseless war against the Swedes, trying to win that crown and make him king of all Scandinavia. I often wondered if it was it a subconscious response to Stiklestad all those years ago.

He even founded a new town in 1048, Oslo, which gave him a staging post and easier access to the Swedish mainland. Even so, Harald eventually made peace with the Swedes in 1064. For the first time in my life the knowledge that next summer there was not going to be another series of battles was a great relief.

August & September 1066 A.D.

It was one of those usual high-summer days in 1066. The court's agenda had been confirmed the previous day, so in reality there was nothing much to look forward to. Harald was insistent that we Vikings start keeping records as the emperors did in Miklagaard, otherwise our great military and seafaring feats would be forgotten, not to mention how we Vikings had trail-blazed trading routes across the world.

I had been conducting paper-making experiments using mulched pine bark and gum, trying to replicate the soft paper that was imported to Miklagaard from Sind, but I might say, with not much success. In frustration I had stopped just after lunch and was enjoying a mug of ale. I had dismissed my apprentices for the afternoon and it seemed that they disappeared before I had let them off.

Then it all changed in an instant.

The signal horn sounded from the hill tower, and men rushed about gathering shields, swords and battle-axes, and raced out to take their positions. The town readied to defend against an attack that never came. But the news that was brought was to turn our world upside down forever. Edward the Confessor, King of England had died!

The bringer of news was Tostig, brother of Harold of Wessex. Harold had cunningly outmanoeuvred his brother Tostig, had seized power and was now the self-proclaimed King of England. It was obvious that Tostig had fallen out with his brother when Harold had done this, and he was now asking Harald to raise an army and invade England with him. Bored with the necessary routine of court, this was something Harald was only too keen to do. But what was Tostig hoping to achieve? If Harald's invasion succeeded, Tostig would still not be ruler. I told Harald that he would have to watch his back with this one. He smiled cunningly at me and all he said was, "I know."

Harald claimed that his father and descendants had been promised the English throne by King Hardicanute, the last true-blood Viking king, who ruled England until 1042. So he, Harald, believed he should now be King of England. But who knows who had told him this? After all, he was a mere lad when his father was king. Maybe he had overheard something, or maybe his father or brother had told him this? It was such a long time ago and much had happened in the intervening twenty-four years.

Harald said summer was running out and that all haste must be made to assemble the army and invade England else the element of surprise would be lost. If only Tostig had been a few weeks earlier!

Tostig also told us that Duke William of Normandy was claiming the title. While the northern Frenchmen did have Viking ancestry, they were so intermarried with the local populace that they were, at the very best, only half Viking, if not a quarter or even an eighth. This claim was summarily dismissed by a confident Harald.

In early September some 300 ships set sail for England. Along the way we were reinforced by our Scottish brethren. On landfall we sacked Scarborough, and a few days later we defeated Morcar's army at Gate Fulford. Four days later we took York.

Unbeknown to us, on 25th September Harold's army arrived in Yorkshire after a forced march from the south. Buoyed by our victories and brimming with confidence, he took us by surprise at a place called Stamford Bridge.

It was a hot day and we had just taken off our byrnies ready to make camp for the night. Harold and his English troops waited patiently in the hot afternoon sun for this moment, then swooped in and devastated us. Our losses were considerable. Even worse, Harald and Tostig were killed, Harald with an arrow through the throat. This all seemed a little too familiar to me. Yet again I had been spared. Why? I could understand this happening once, but a second time? What plans did Odin have for me?

Of the three-hundred ships we had arrived in, Harold was gracious enough to let twenty-four return home. As the most senior remaining invader, Harold let me return to Norway as an emissary with a message that was all too clear. I had managed to persuade Olaf, Harald's son, to maintain a low profile and put myself forward as the most senior Viking. Had Harold uncovered our ploy, he may have kept Olaf as ransom or maybe even worse. However, I assembled our remainders and we headed the reduced fleet out into the North Sea.

During mid-morning on the second day at sea, Bijana Smedjrute's ship approached and he hailed me. Some crew had elected him as spokesman. He said they had been talking amongst themselves and did not want to return to Norway and to lives of so-called normality.

Was this the real reason? I asked myself. Did they really yearn for more adventure or was it that they did not want to return in disgrace after leaving with so many boasts of victory? I clearly had much to think about and told them I would give them my answer in the morning, knowing full-well that I did not have the power nor the inclination to stop them.

After the events of the past few days, I was not able to sleep and was awake most of the night. In the early hours and half-light of morning, I saw Bijana stand up in the bow of his ship. I knew he could see me, as he tentatively raised a hand and waved a farewell. I half raised my hand in return, knowing what was about to happen, and powerless to stop him. His ship, and a few others, then turned towards the Pole Star and headed north. I would not know the exact numbers until we took roll call after sunrise.

In considering their request I also realised that I too had a yearning for the old days, to "go-a-Viking". Well, more adventure-seeking than marauding. When thinking more about it, I really did not have a life to go back to. I had never married. My true love had died a lifetime ago while I was on my first English raid. We had intended to marry on my return. Since then most women who showed interest gave up when they realised that they were fighting a losing battle with a ghost.

Since then my marriage had been my duty to my king. In theory I now had no ties to Norway. Any ties and loyalties I had, had died at Stamford Bridge.

So, in the middle of the North Sea, in the half-light of morning, my future path crystallised before me in an instant. It was as if the sun had suddenly started shining brilliantly. I knew exactly what I was going to do.

Chapter 1

NIÐAROS

On the middle of the fourth day we arrived back in Nidaros. The populace lined the shore in a silent vigil as our eighteen boats rowed slowly into the harbour.

As soon as we had beached, I wearily climbed down from the prow of my vessel. The crowd, still silent and staring, parted as I strode up the beach. Haldor followed directly behind me.

There, standing stoically at the door of her long house, was Queen Ellisif with Magnus, the eldest of Harald's sons, a supporting arm around his mother's shoulders. Ellisif stood tall, regal and proud, knowing what was about to come. But I knew that on the inside she was crying, if not wailing, for the loss of her beloved husband.

The silent crowd followed, with only the sound of their footsteps crunching on the beach. To stop her seeing the tears in my eyes I went down on my knee and, keeping my head bowed, "My lady I bring…" I said, speaking more to the ground than to her, my voice breaking.

She stopped me before I could say anything further and bade me stand. "Ulf, we have known each other for far too long, and now is not the time for such formality. Tell me — no — tell *us* what happened," she said, raising her voice and including the gathered crowd with a sweep of her hand.

I recounted the events of our journey, skipping the unimportant details. Helped by Haldor, I also listed the dead. It was only at this point that the wailing started. Some of the older folk interjected with questions, which I answered as best I could.

When finished she immediately addressed her son, but it was more intended for the gathered crowd to hear. "Magnus, you realise that this now makes you king?"

"I do," he replied woodenly. The realisation that his beloved father wouldn't be returning was only too evident on his face.

"Send word for the Althing to gather in three days," Ellisif said to no one in particular, but knowing that the command would be out within the hour. This would ensure that no one would disturb her during the night with questions she could not answer.

"Ulf, Haldor, dine with us tonight, please?" The pleading and pain in her eyes were clear.

Haldor and I then walked slowly and wearily to our lodgings. We had not spoken much on the voyage back. Commanding separate ships made private conversation difficult.

All he said to me was, "For once I am glad that you're older than me." I knew exactly what he meant.

On returning to Ellisif's house later that evening, washed and in clean clothing, we were led straight to the long table. Magnus and Olaf joined us. No sooner had we sat down than soup and bread were put in front of us.

Ellisif said, "Ulf, I know you only too well. I know you will not have eaten for at least two days. So, eat first and then we will talk." She held up her hand, not allowing any objections. We ate slowly.

When I refused the offer of seconds, Cook shook her head in disbelief.

"So. What now?" asked Ellisif.

"My lady, you could return to Novgorod or Kyiv, to your nephew. He would give you shelter," I suggested.

"No," she said. "Norway is now my home, my country and my duty. I must stay and support Magnus. Besides, Norway needs leadership now more than ever."

Only a Royal Princess and Queen could have answered thus.

She raised a hand to her throat and asked abruptly, "Did he die quickly?"

Now the wife and lover.

"Yes," I lied. In truth it had taken Harald a full half hour to bleed slowly to death, while Haldor and I tried to get him off the battlefield. But there was nowhere to run to. The English were everywhere.

"Thank you," she said, looking at me knowingly. "It is good to know that he did not suffer. Did he have any dying command?"

"No, my lady. It was too quick," I replied, continuing the lie. Haldor glanced at me from under his eyelids, as he sipped a spoonful of soup. I'm sure the look wasn't missed by Ellisif, either.

"The body?"

"King Harold would not allow us to bring it back."

"I see."

"What will you do now?" she asked.

"I think I may do more study of the East in the new library in Kyiv," I said.

"You won't stay and help me, us?"

"I think it may be considered bad luck if I do. After all, I was at Stiklestad with Harald and now at Stamford Bridge. Many may consider the omens to be bad, which may have an effect on how they view the reign of the new king."

"I see. But you had thirteen years of success with Harald in Byzantium."

"Indeed. But that was Byzantium, this is Norway. Many will say that in Norway I bring bad luck, but that in Byzantium I bring good luck. You know how they are. So it will be better that I go."

"And what of you, Haldor?"

"I'm with Ulf, my Lady".

"Ah, Haldor. Always a man of few words."

"Yes, but consider—we will be seen as part of 'The Hard One's' reign, which was not liked by the chieftains and the people. Having us around may raise suspicions that you intend for Magnus to rule in the same way."

"I see. Your points are quite valid. A passing of the old… Are your minds made up? Is there any way I can change them?"

"Yes and no, my lady. But we will stay for the Althing and the proclamation of the new king," I offered.

"Oh. And why?"

"Ah, to ensure that no *mischief* is practised. We would hate to see the late king's lineage disappear after all we've been through with him."

"Thank you. I, we, would be most grateful," she said, giving a half smile.

After finishing our tankards of ale, we bade Ellisif and the princes goodnight and returned to our lodgings.

"And just what are you really intending to do in Kyiv, Ulf?" asked Haldor on the way back.

I told him of my North Sea revelation and the Legend of Ingvar the lost Viking.

"First off, I never heard of a lost Viking. But if'n he is, I guess we had better go and find him," he said firmly. It was good to have a focus, something to look forward to.

"We'll talk more about this in the morning."

"No, I fear it will not be for a few days yet."

"Oh. And why so?"

"Because, my friend, we have an Althing to oversee. And with a number of the elders now dead we will have to ensure that any ideas of mini-kingdom building are put to bed rather quickly."

"Oh. I hadn't thought of that."

"See you in the morning then."

And with that we entered our own houses, with sleep not far behind.

Chapter 2

A New Beginning

The Althing was assembled by mid-morning on the third day as requested.

Ellisif was her regal self in a full-length blue gown of shimmering silk, brought from Miklagaard by Harald. The silk was spun and woven in Sind and transported thousands of miles over the trade routes, passing hands who knows how many times, until it reached Byzantium. And now here it was, even further west, adorning the Queen of Norway.

On seeing her glide in, pan-faced with her back as straight as a rod, the throng stilled. Ellisif addressed the Althing and recounted the events leading up to Stamford Bridge and the tragic results thereof. Then the first order of business was for the remaining elders to pay their respects to Ellisif on the death of Harald. This went on for hours, with each elder trying to outdo the former with praise of Harald and his feats. At times this brought forth peals of laughter at others' silent solemnity as they remembered Harald, gracious to his friends, ruthless to his enemies.

The first order of business after lunch was the succession. The hush quietened, she then proposed Magnus be the next king, reciting his lineage and claim of birthright. She was regal and eloquent in her delivery, so much so that there was mute acceptance and no one challenged her or Magnus. Finally Ellisif addressed the gathering and stated that Haldor and I would be leaving for Kyiv, and gave our reasons for going. This raised more than a murmur but what was done was done.

On reflection I have to believe that there was an inner recognition and realisation that this was a time for change and for moving on. Because there were no objections to Magnus being appointed king, all present then hailed the new king and paid him homage. Once again, each elder was trying to outdo the former with speeches and orations that really revealed the hopes of the nation; the desire for peace and prosperity. I had to ponder; was the age of the Viking coming to an end?

All through this Magnus looked rather overwhelmed and at times bored. Two-and-half hours later it was over and a massive feast was laid on. This time I did not refuse Cook's offers of seconds, which brought a smile to her face. The feast lasted two days.

Word was out about my intentions to go east of Kyiv and search for Ingvar Vittfarne in Sarkland. Over the next few days more than a handful of men approached Haldor and me, asking if they could join us. Some we turned down, others we gladly accepted.

With October looming we had to get a move on and prepare for our voyage. Thankfully the greatest risk would be the first and most northerly portion of our journey. If we could make Novgorod before the first snowfalls, the rivers should be open long enough for us to make Kyiv. With minimal preparation necessary for the boats, we prepared, loaded and stacked supplies at breakneck speed. It was good to focus on something positive. We had our two knarrs ready within a week. We would not be taking longboats, as most of our voyage would be on rivers and we required vessels with a shallow draft. We re-jigged two four-oar knarrs to be eight-oared boats. We would not be trading, so the extra room was turned into rowing stations.

Then on an October morning in 1066 I stood on the shore of Nidaros again. I had a feeling in my gut that I would never again see Norway and this gathering of friends. I think they were thinking the same. Cook, as always, pressed a loaf of bread on me, but this time uncharacteristically gave me a hug as well, almost breaking my back. Despite her size, that woman was strong!

Then if that was not enough, Ellisif hugged me so tight she almost took my wind away. With tears in her eyes, she said, "Ulf, for so long you have been the foundation that Harald stood on and the anchor that kept him from doing foolish things. You have no idea how much you have meant to Harald and me, and to us as a family".

This revelation took me completely by surprise. I must have had a look of bewilderment on my face. I began to stutter, lost for words. She then said, "Yes, you were always there for us, always when we needed someone to talk a matter over with, you were there. I know you never thought of it in this way, but we know why you never married and you will never know how high we held you in this regard, for sacrificing so much for your King and country."

"My lady, I...."

"No more 'my lady', Ulf. I am now Ellisif again. My son is King and his wife is Queen. I shall now take the role that you filled for so long."

Magnus, whom I had bounced on my knee, now my King, approached and gave us his blessing. I could see that like me, he was holding back the tears. I said to him, "Keep that humility and you will make a great king. Remember you will have to be leader and servant at the same time. If you can do this, you will succeed."

We gave each other a hug and slapped backs. Then with that I turned and climbed aboard my ship and we were pushed off into the North Sea and steered for the Skagerrak and the Öresund.

Chapter 3

The Journey Back

Our first stopover was in Denmark. Thereafter we made our way through the Öresund, turning North into the Ostersjoen, heading for the Gulf of Vinland.

While the knarrs were built for sea and river travel, they were a lot slower than the longboats I was used to travelling and raiding in. Haldor made comment on this as well.

"Ulf, I fear that we are going too slow and may have to winter over in Holmgard. That is if we make Holmgard before winter sets in."

"Don't be so defeatist, Haldor. I have worked out that it may take us two days longer than usual."

"Ah—but just what is usual, considering that this is the first time we have travelled in knarrs and it is only the second time we have travelled this route in this direction?"

"You know what I mean. Anyway, what the knarrs lack in speed they make up for in manoeuvrability. This feature will help make up time on the rivers, so all should be equal by the time we get to Kyiv."

"Oh, Master, I bow to your superior intellect," he said mockingly. The crews laughed heartily for the first time since leaving Nidaros. Someone started humming one of our old rowing songs, and soon everyone was in full voice. This was more like it. We would need this spirit for the portages, which were ahead of us.

I made a point of stopping at Gripsholm, Södermanland in Svithjod. Gripsholm was allegedly the home Ingvar, and it was rumoured that stones had been erected in his honour, which also gave details of his route.

We were welcomed by a war party. Who could blame them? After all, we had been at war with Sweden for nigh on fifteen years. I jumped down onto the beach with no sword strapped to my waist.

The Karl addressed me. "I know you. You are Ulf Uspakson, chief lieutenant to Harald Hardraada, King of Norway. What do you want here? Have you now come to kill women and children?"

"I am Ulf Uspakson. King Harald is dead and I am no longer chief lieutenant to the throne of Norway. I come in peace, bearing no arms. My life is in your hands." With that I raised my arms to show that I was unarmed.

"And what of your men? Do they bear arms?"

"If you will allow them to disembark, they will do so without any weapons."

"We will allow them to disembark—weaponless. But first, what do you seek here?"

"I come in search of the stones erected in honour of Ingvar Vittfarne. I have made it my personal quest to seek out his resting place."

"You? A Norwegian, seeking out the resting place of a royal Swede? Why? What do you hope to gain from this?"

"Nothing but the satisfaction of knowing where he lies." I then recounted the story of my reading about Ingvar at Kyiv all those years ago. We were allowed to disembark.

I was shown the stones, and spent time taking detailed notes. The village scald also gave me a great deal more information, which I noted.

Late in the afternoon, my mission complete, I approached the Karl to offer my thanks and say that we would trouble him no more and would be on our way. During the afternoon he had obviously had a change of heart and invited us to dine with them and stay over.

That evening we had countless toasts to renewed friendship with our Swedish cousins and more for good luck on the journey.

In the morning we prepared to board and be on our way, with very sore heads to boot, and found we had gained four crew members, thrust upon us in the name of friendship. How could I refuse?

"Besides," the Karl said, "we couldn't let a Norwegian take all the honour for finding one of Sweden's most famous royal sons!"

So we gained Filip Brandsson, the twins Knut and Justus Ormsson and Ingvar Hallsteinsson. Ingvar had been thrust upon us with the skewed logic that having someone on the journey called Ingvar, from the same village as Ingvar Vittfarne, would bring us good luck. We would see. Initially I worried that Ingvar, at just nineteen, would be the youngest crewmember. I had to remind myself that Harald was in command of a regiment at his age.

With that we cast off and sailed back into the Ostersjoen and took a northerly bearing. After reaching the Gulf of Vinland we turned east and entered the River Neva. From this point on our world was almost entirely hemmed in by forests right down to the water's edge. Fortunately it was the end of summer and the rivers were slow flowing. We rowed into Lake Ladoga and set sail for the Volchov River. At Aldeigjuborg we stopped over for a night's well-earned rest. Sailing and rowing the knarrs in the open sea had been hard work. Had the rivers been flowing faster we most certainly would have had our work cut out for us.

We used tried and tested Viking river navigation methods as we made our way upstream. By observing the shape of the shoreline, the shapes of waves and the presence of river grass, it was easy to see where the current was weakest, and hence our headway was somewhat eased.

A few days later we rowed into Lake Ilmen and took a bearing on Holmgard. The sudden openness of the lake after the confines of the rivers was a joy to the senses. The entire area north of Ladoga to Holmgard and beyond was forested, although there was more evidence of man's handiwork than there had been twenty-one years ago.

Holmgard was almost entirely surrounded by swamps and the town was made almost entirely out of wood. Wooden houses and wooden churches, even wooden streets to lift the locals above the mud. Even letters had been written on bark. It was only in 1044 that the first stone building, the Detinets, was erected. Only the most powerful and richest of cities could afford stone fortifications. The following year the Church of Saint Sofia was built within the Detinets and it soon became the main cathedral of the North, due to its beautiful architecture and great size. But building with stone in Novgorod was expensive, as it had to be shipped in. This task was made harder as there was no good overland route. In summer the swamps thawed, which only left transport via water. But it is the swamps which give Novgorod its strength, for it can also only be invaded by water.

Therefore locals never saw the need to build with stone or brick, as cutting down another tree was easier than quarrying and shipping stone. It is this entirely wooden appearance that gives Novgorod its frontier town image. While the buildings remain wooden, the town gives a feeling that it is temporary, even after two hundred years. Until more brick and stone buildings are erected, and an air of permanence is established, Novgorod will always be a stopover.

We steered for Jan Ullrichsson's place. He was standing on the dock, his right foot on a keg of ale and his hands on hips. He threw his head back, guffawed and said, "Well, I never thought I'd see the day when the great Ulf Uspakson and Haldor Snorresson would arrive at my dock in knarrs!"

I jumped to the dock and we embraced each other, slapping backs.

"Jan, it's good to see you. I never thought you'd stay in the hospitality and goods business, especially after our adventures in the Mediterranean."

"Ah, Ulf, like I told you then — the blood lust had gone and there comes a time a man realises that he has to settle down."

"Aye. I know what you mean," I replied.

Just then a very pretty young girl brought out a tray with three tankards filled with ale. She had plaited blond hair and a full breast. Her arrival brought wolf whistles from the crew.

Jan raised his voice. "Just so we get this straight now — that woman is MY DAUGHTER! Anyone who fools with her answers to me."

"YOUR daughter?" I asked incredulously. "Jan, a businessman and now a family man as well! The world is full of surprises. You must have married soon after setting up business here."

"Aye. A young buck with his pockets bulging with gold from Miklagaard would make a woman a fine catch. And believe me, I had them

lining up. But this tavern and the store was up for sale by a recently widowed mother with a young family. She saw me coming. Not only did she sell me the business but got me married to her daughter as well."

"So she got you both ways, eh?"

"Yes, she did. She got my money for the tavern and store and she got it all again when I married Olga. Come, let's go in and meet the family. Our tankards are empty."

Jan's wife Olga was beautiful, even in middle age and after four children.

"Now I see the real reason why you stayed," I said. Olga blushed.

"Like I said, Ulf, there comes a time a man must settle down. It will happen to you one day as well."

"No, Jan. If it was meant to happen, it would have happened already."

"Says who? You're not dead yet. Least I hope you're not!"

Laughingly I replied, "I hope not either."

"Well then, there's still hope." Our tankards drained, Jan said, "Ulf, your quartermaster is hovering. Let's see to your supplies."

Over our evening meal I filled Jan in on the purpose of our journey.

"Ah, I see the bloodlust has left you but the wanderlust hasn't."

"You could say that," I replied. Jan had not lost his talent for being able to see what was really within a person's heart. His insights had come in quite useful on our campaigns.

After the meal I was besieged by his sons, regaling me to tell them stories about their father's adventures as part of the Varangian guard. I had to keep a close eye on Jan and Olga, as some stories were strictly off limits.

The following morning we cast off and headed on up the Volchov back into our hemmed-in world of forest and river. Jan, Olga and their whole family rose early to see us off. Jan had given us our supplies at cost and hadn't charged for our accommodation and meals.

We branched into the Lovat River and at the portage point we beached the boats. The long haul began. Oh, how I hated this part of the journey! Mind you, the exercise would keep us warm.

Because this was such a well-used route, a portage station existed here on the Lovat, another
on the Dvina and yet another on the Dniepr, with half-way stations at the mid-points between each. Local teams, assisted by the crew, would haul the boats to the mid-points, swap boats, and haul back to where they started from. A very sensible arrangement.

In a moment of reflection on one of the frequent rest stops during the portage, I thought how it is not until you leave a land of great natural beauty and see lands that are bleak and featureless that you can truly appreciate what you have seen. This flat open landscape with its open plains was stark and featureless and made me really appreciate the beauty of Norway's fiords. I thought that I could never see myself hauling boats for a living—especially along the route month in and month out—but still, there were worse jobs a man could do.

The portage eventually over, we rested overnight before re-entering our river and forest world. It would be like this all the way to Kyiv, with a few small exceptions along the way. In the morning we recommenced our journey down the Dniepr towards Kyiv, but first we called in at Smolensk.

Haldor and I were ushered into the court of Valdimir II Vsevelodovich, son of Vsevelodovich I Yaroslavavich, son of the late Prince, Yaroslav the Wise of Kyiv.

I knew his father well from the time Harald, Haldor and I had spent in his grandfather's employ in Novgorod on our first journey to Miklagaard after the fiasco at Stiklestad.

He greeted us warmly. "Welcome, Lords Ulf and Haldor. I fear you have been absent from the Kyivan courts for far too long. How is your King Harald and my Aunt Ellisif?"

Haldor and I glanced at each other; a glance that wasn't missed by Vladimir.

"Your Highness, I fear we bring sad tidings."

Valdimir's left eyebrow rose. "Oh?" he said

"Your Highness, King Harald was killed in battle in England but a few weeks ago."

"This is indeed sad news. Who is now King of Norway?"

"You cousin Magnus was proclaimed King but two weeks hence."

"And my aunt, the Queen?"

"She is as well as can be expected. I believe that her new role as advisor to the King will keep her mind off her loss."

"Yes, it may do. Well, it had to come sooner or later."

"What had to, sire?"

"Harald's death, of course. What else? Live by the sword, die by the sword. It's a wonder it did not happen sooner. So, what will you do now?"

"We are on our way first to Kiev and then to Sarkland."

"You've become traders?"

"Not quite, sire. We are on a quest to find the lost Vikings."

"You are? Tell me, have you ever heard of a lost Viking? I certainly haven't. No. If your Viking wanted to be found, he would have been by now. I fear you are chasing a shadow."

"Nay, sire. His journey is well recorded. I first read of the account in your father's library in Novgorod a long time ago. On the way here I have made detailed recordings of the stones erected in his honour in his home town in Svithjod."

"Svithjod? It's a wonder they let you in."

"It was touch and go for a moment. But we patched up our differences and even have four of them along with us."

"Ah, ever the diplomat. So, now you've become a *varjager*, eh?"

"Aye, sire."

"Oh well, I wish you luck. Although I could do with your services here."

"Sire, the bloodlust, like our youth, has gone."

"So you say. It happens to all of us sooner or later. Give my regards to my brother when you get to Kyiv."

"We most certainly will, sire."

With that the audience was over.

At least Iziaslav and Vladimir were still on speaking terms, which meant that the Dniepr should be open and quite safe to travel.

Chapter 4

The SAVING of KYIV

Our arrival in Kyiv was not noteworthy in any way whatsoever. After all, to anyone watching, we were just another two Viking knarrs on our way south to trade, albeit late in the season. We were intercepted in mid-river by a customs boat and directed to a dock by a young official and told to make ready for inspection. The crew looked at me in amazement. Didn't this young upstart official know who he was talking to? I gave a brief shake of my head, which was noted by the crew, who began to realise that a game was afoot.

We tied up and a senior customs official started walked down the quay towards us. He paused briefly, staring at us, and then began running, gesticulating and shouting all at once, "Boris, you fool! Don't you know who this is? This is the great Lord Ulf Uspakson and that is the great Lord Haldor Snorresson! They should have been directed to the ROYAL dock, you fool! The Prince will have your guts for garters because of your insult to these great men."

The young official's face dropped and his complexion took on a deathly pale hue. He started stuttering "But, but, but...."

By this time the crew were rolling in the gunwales with laughter. I too was struggling to hold back my mirth.

"Karl, it is good to see you, old friend. Do not worry, we are not here on official business."

"Nevertheless, My Lords, you should have sent word ahead, and we could have prepared a suitable welcome for you."

Boris looked decidedly paler.

"No, Karl. That is all over. King Harald is dead. We are no longer officials of his court. We are here as visitors only."

"My Lords, you could never be *just visitors* to Kyiv. You played a significant part in the establishment of Kyiv. The people will forever be in your debt."

"Yes, yes, yes. Until we're dead and buried. Then we'll be forgotten."

"NO, my Lords! Never. Always."

By this time a crowd had gathered, some of them recognising us and pointing, despite it being years since we had played any part in Kyiv's ascendancy on the central European stage.

The crowd suddenly parted and out from the throng strode Olaf, surrounded by a guard of honour; older, balder, greyer and definitely fatter, but twenty years stuck in a library can do that to a man.

"Ulf! Haldor! My friends, it is so good to see you." There was much hugging and slapping of backs in the Slavic style. "How are you both? What moron made you moor here?"

"Oh, it was Boris over there. What are you going to do to him for making us moor *here* with the riff-raff of the world?" we asked mockingly.

If Boris could have shrunk to become an ant, I'm sure he would have. Olaf did not hold an extremely high or important office, but for the Prince's personal librarian to be here on his dock, with the Royal Guard of Honour and on first name terms with these two men was simply too much for Boris to bear. Not to mention his boss calling them Lords! Boris fainted.

This raised raucous laughter all around.

"Karl," I called, "see to Boris. It's not his fault he does not know who we are. He couldn't have been born when we were taming central Russia. Oh, and Karl—send him to Olaf in the morning. He'll be studying history."

"Yes, yes, My Lord," stammered Karl, only too happy to have been let off the hook so lightly.

"Now, my friends," said Olaf, "the Prince awaits you."

"He knows we're here—already?"

"Yes. He saw you coming."

We looked at Olaf in amazement.

"No, no. He does not have the eyesight of an eagle, but he does have a new toy sent to him from Arabia, called a spyglass. We were having an audience on the balcony and he was testing his new Arab invention and happened to see you on the river. He monitored your progress, recognised who you were when you were closer, and sent me to, ah, request you join him for refreshments."

With that, Haldor, Olaf and I marched off to see the Prince. It was just like old times. Only, I had to remind myself it wasn't.

Kyiv had certainly become a city worthy of note, almost rivalling Miklagaard for its beauty and architecture. It was hard to believe that Yaroslav had taken a trading post of wood and mud huts and turned it into a place of such beauty in just twenty years.

The city consisted of two parts. The lower part, the Podil, and the upper fortified part where the Prince and his retainers and bodyguard lived. The docks were in the Podil, and we were being conducted to the Upper City.

Haldor and I recognised some of the older buildings and wanted to stop and explore. But royalty does not like being kept waiting. Compared to Kyiv, Novgorod was a hovel. I mentioned this to Olaf.

"Yes," he said, "but it is all likely to be lost if Yaroslav's heirs don't sort out the line of succession."

"I had heard about the problems, but did not realise they were that bad."

"Oh, you don't know the half of it! When is a civil war not bad? Just a warning — Prince Iziaslav is likely to ask you to take up arms with him against the pretender. Consider yourselves lucky that he saw you first. If he had heard of your arrival without seeing you first, then it is likely that you would have been locked up as spies."

"That bad, eh? Thanks for the warning."

On entering the royal palace, I could not help but notice the double guards at almost every entrance. This infighting must have been costing the Prince.

"Well, the Lords Ulf Uspakson and Haldor Snorresson. Why did you come to my Kingdom disguised as traders, when in fact I know your true vocations?"

"Your Highness," I replied, "your brother Valdimir II Vsevelodovich of Smolensk sends greetings."

"Oh, you've seen him, then?"

"We have indeed, Your Highness."

"He is well?"

"In very good health, sire."

"So, what is the purpose of your being in Kyiv?"

"Sire, we bring sad news. Harald of King Norway is dead and his son Magnus is King."

"Harald DEAD! How?" This was obviously news to the Kyivan court. "Go on."

"King Harald died in an attempt to wrest the crown of England, promised to him by King Hardicanut, but usurped by Harold of Wessex."

"When did this happen?"

"But two months ago sire."

"Ah. And what of my sister, Queen Ellisif?"

"Her majesty requested that I, we, that is Lord Haldor and I, stay, but we both thought it best that Magnus, your nephew, becomes King in his own right, and that all connections with the past are broken. Sire, Harald's rule had been harsh, even for us Vikings. His battles for the crown of Svithjod were long and hard, with an even harder toll on Norway. Norway now needs a time to rebuild her strength and her economy. We believed it would be best if it was done without the shadow of Harald hanging over the throne."

"A long speech indeed, Lord Ulf. So, just what are your intentions in coming to Kyiv?"

"Your Highness, we are in search of the Lost Vikings who were led by Ingvar Vittfarne on a journey to Sarkland about thirty-five years ago. He was also planning on going to Tavastaland, but never returned. I read about him in your father's library when I first visited Kyiv."

"This is true, My Prince," interjected Olaf. "Over the years I have made this a personal project of mine and have amassed a great deal more information, which Lord Ulf will no doubt be more than glad to review."

"I see," said the Prince. "My Lords, would you be interested in joining my army?"

"With respect, sire, we have been fighting non-stop for nigh on thirty years. We have come to that point in our lives when neither of us is young anymore, our bones are beginning to creak, and to be frank, sire, we have had enough of fighting. The bloodlust is gone."

"And just how long do you intend staying in Kyiv?"

"Just the winter, sire."

"I see. Your bones are not so creaky that they can stop you travelling to the far and distant lands. Porting a ship cannot be so easy either, eh?"

The Prince thought for a moment or two, then said, "Very well. The price of staying the winter in Kyiv and the price for using my library and the services of Olaf, is that you will train my army. You will not have to fight, only train them. Olaf, see to it that the appropriate arrangements are made."

With that our audience was over.

The library had been rehoused and had grown considerably over the last twenty years. After I had left for Miklagaard all those years ago, Olaf's imagination had been sparked by my interest in the far-flung reaches of the world, and in particular in Ingvar Vittfarne. He made a point of questioning just about every ship's captain that passed through Kyiv. It soon became common knowledge amongst the trading fraternity, and some military as well, that the librarian of Kyiv, Olaf, wanted information about Ingvar and how far east the Viking traders had travelled. And so I began reading and absorbing the mass of information that Olaf had gathered over the intervening twenty-one years. I now had twenty years' worth of reports, documents and maps to absorb in just a few months.

Olaf's quest for information had even made it as far as the Seljuk Kahnate, as had the reputation of Kyiv, its librarian and its library. The Sultan had sent an ambassador to study at the library in order to share knowledge and improve relations between the two empires. This ambassador had been at the library for three years now. His name was Ibn Rashid al-Arslan, a widely-travelled prince of the realm and noted scholar of Islam and of the peoples of the world. The three of us formed a working party and divided the information into three groups, spanning seven years apiece. We established a standardised matrix under which all information was to be recorded and started the long, arduous task of cataloguing the reports.

I soon made a point of stopping work in the mid afternoon. By then my head was stuffy and I needed some fresh air in my lungs. I usually went down to the training grounds and sparred with whichever officer was keen to test his hand against me. This way I could not be accused of not spending time training the army. After all, I was training the officers in the finer skills of swordsmanship. Ibn Rashid al-Arslan began to join me on my afternoon sojourns and soon was considered a part of our crew.

Our absence in the afternoons also allowed Olaf to catch up on his work as librarian, a task that was getting harder and harder due to the reputation he had earned for the establishment. In an ordinary week he would field at least ten requests for information or reports. However, now that a civil war was in progress, this had doubled and wasn't showing signs of slowing down. He now employed a host of researchers and spent most of his time directing them and reviewing reports before they were sent out to their requestors.

It was on one such dark, midwinter afternoon that Ibn and I were making our way through the market place to the training grounds when we came across a worrying sight. A large crowd had gathered outside the granary. They were beating on the door demanding grain.

An immediate effect of any civil war is a shortage of food. In this case it was an acute shortage of grain. Only the shortage was being felt now, early in the middle of winter, instead of the usual end of winter. The situation had all the hallmarks of an impending riot. I told Ibn to rush and get the army. I gave instruction that they were to be led by Haldor and were to divide and approach on all the major streets leading into the market square, but that they were not to attack on any account without my signal. Understanding my thinking, he rushed off.

I forced my way to the front of the crowd, turned over a box, drew my sword and stood on it with both arms raised. My sword pointed skywards, plainly obvious.

"Citizens of Kyiv," I shouted over the throng. "My name is Ulf Uspakson." The crowd began to quieten, so I raised my voice even further. "I served under Harald Hadraada, who served Yaroslav the Wise. Together we quelled the Pechenegs and brought the Kazars to heel."

The crowd was now quite, but still restless. This had to be contained and dispersed quickly, before it got out of hand.

"We remember you, Lord Ulf," a voice cried out from the crowd.

Good. This was the credibility I needed to manage them.

"Citizens, appoint a few spokesmen to speak to me, and I promise you that I will take your complaints to Prince Iziaslav himself."

"Oh, and how long will that take?" asked another raised voice.

"Too long," another shouted. "By then we shall all be dead from hunger."

"Citizens," I shouted, "believe me — it is far better to die hungry and warm in your bed, than it is to die hungry and cold with a sword through your gut or an axe in your head."

The army had started to arrive and checked just where I had told Ibn I wanted them.

"Look around you," I called. "The army has ALL the exits blocked. If you resort to violence now, you WILL - BE - SLAIN!" I accentuated the last three words on purpose. "Do you want to die now, in the dark, in the snow? Will this be your last few moments of life? Will it be your blood that stains the snow red?" And pointing with my sword arm to a woman with a babe on her hip, I said, "Or will it be the blood of babes, the blood of your children staining the snow red?"

This seemed to have a sobering effect. Taking the high ground, I continued, "Who among you will speak for the people of Kyiv? I exhort you now, come forward and I WILL take you grievances to Iziaslav myself in the morning, if not sooner! Your names will remain secret with me."

This seemed to satisfy the massed crowd and a few men were pushed forward. I called to the troop leaders to let the crowd disperse, but to maintain ranks.

After the crowd had fully dispersed, I ordered patrols to ensure that any small groups were moved on or dispersed, not giving them time to regroup and storm the granary. I also posted a large guard at the granary.

Ibn approached me. "That was close," he said.

"Yes," I said. "Too close for comfort." Despite the cold, I was drenched in sweat.

Ibn ushered Haldor, the spokesmen, and me inside the granary.

Sitting on bags of grain, the spokesmen told us that the people were on half rations and the army on full. The granary supervisor confirmed Iziaslav's command. He said Iziaslav wanted his army to be fully fit at the beginning of spring, ready to march immediately after the snows had melted, not weak from a winter of inactivity. Our arrival must have seemed like a godsend.

His logic made sense, but it did not make sense that the people were starved. What would there be left to defend or rule if the people starved and died? Buildings? I kept this conclusion to myself, but I knew Haldor and Ibn would have come to similar conclusions.

A captain of the Royal bodyguard put his head through the door, and seeing us he then entered.

"Lord Ulf, His Royal Highness, Prince Iziaslav, would like to see you immediately!"

"I'm sure he would," I replied. "Come, Haldor. Ibn, you're in charge."

"But he's an ARAB!" exclaimed the captain.

"Yes, he is. And just how many Arabs do you know who happen to be the son of a King and can read, write and speak Arabic, Greek, Slavic and Latin? Plus, he has my confidence and the respect of my crew," I retorted. Bowing slightly to Ibn, I said, "Your Highness, you're in charge. Understood?"

"Yes, My Lord. Understood," said Ibn, bowing. I raised an eyebrow at his use of my title and smiled inwardly. The captain led us off.

We were led into a room adjoining Iziaslav's bed chamber.

"It seems that I have you to thank for averting a riot tonight," he said.

"Yes, your Highness. So it seems."

"Tell me what happened?"

I recounted the events of the afternoon.

Iziaslav was visibly troubled. After a few minutes of silent thought, he turned to me and asked, "In the circumstances, what would you do?"

Unlike some rulers I had met, this man was not stupid. I had had time to think of reply.

"My Lord, if you maintain the current orders, very soon you will be fighting a war on two fronts. Internally and externally. This will considerably weaken your ability to fight the Pretender in the summer. Your soldiers will be more concerned with their families' welfare than the defence of the realm. They will begin to desert, first in dribs and drabs, and then en masse. In short, you will have lost the war before it has begun."

"This I have already worked out for myself. I asked what you would DO?"

"My Lord, I would put the army on three-quarter rations and increase the rations of the people but not quite to three-quarter rations."

"This sounds interesting. Go on."

"Use the option of increasing to three-quarter rations as bait for joining the army or becoming engaged in activity that would support your build up. This way you will engage just about the whole of Kyiv, if not all of Kyiv, in the war effort. After all, who is going to turn down extra rations of food? Women and children can become involved in leather work, some of the basic wood-turning activity, stoking the blacksmiths' fires, uniform making and so on. The men will train either as battlefield soldiers or as defenders of Kyiv. Plus, anyone not drawing three-quarter rations could be considered as possibly disloyal to the crown and should be watched carefully."

"I now see why you were an advisor to the throne of Norway. First you quell a riot, then you give the people what they want and you get me what I want. All in a single act. Most commendable."

"You are most kind, sire."

"Don't flatter yourself. But it is you that I must thank for saving my Kingdom. What is left of it, anyway. GUARD! Send word for my ministers and the scribes, we have work to do tonight."

"Your Highness, may I also be so bold as to suggest that I first let the spokesmen know of your decrees, before you make the proclamation?"

"Oh—these are MY decrees now, are they? And why?"

"It's a matter of protocol, sire. These men were pushed forward by the people." I was careful not to say 'elected' by the people. I went on, "It is clear that they are held in good stead and are respected by them. May I also suggest using them as leaders in this winter's enterprises?"

"You're pushing your luck, Uspakson, but it not the first time you've made sense tonight. Very well. It will be so."

The ministers and scribes arrived, led by the prime minister, and we settled down for a long busy evening.

And so in the morning with bleary eyes and an unshaven chin I met with the spokesmen at the granary again. Ibn and Haldor had acted as messengers.

"I have good news," I said, and proceeded to tell them of my discussions with Iziaslav and of the offer of increased rations. I did not omit to mention my part in the decision-making process. I hoped this would subdue any cynical comment about Iziaslav. I was right.

Not long after our meeting, criers went out to all parts of the city with activity rosters, and in the winter of 1066 Kyiv was mobilised and became an industrious city.

I was amazed at the ease of transformation. The ministers and their clerks had just about every detail of every citizen at their fingertips. Years ago Yaroslav had divided the city into segments and each segment was divided again and again. Each segment and sub-segment had a person in charge.

Through this system Yaroslav managed the city. He said he took guidance from this from the Biblical book of Exodus where, once out of Egypt, Moses established a similar structure for leading the Israelites.

After an initial period of involvement in the mobilisation, as it came to be called, we once again settled down to studying and examining the Vittfarne documents.

By the time spring approached, we had catalogued and categorised every report and map received, and had begun to develop a journey plan. Ibn's knowledge of Asia, west of the Himalayas and Pamir mountains, proved to be invaluable in putting the journey plan together. Being a scholar he had recorded his travels to these places, over land and water. This in itself was priceless, but what made it even more valuable were his observations of the people who lived there. I believed that we had never been better prepared for journey. If only we had had similar intelligence before our disastrous attack on England. But, if we had, we would have probably won and I would not now be in a library in Kyiv fulfilling a life-long dream.

Chapter 5

RATS

As the weather improved we began working on the ships in dry dock, preparing for the journey that now lay before us.

About this time we gained an extra crew member. Yurii Vartinen was a lanky blonde-haired son of a Vinnish ship's captain. He had completed three round trips from Vinland to Miklagaard by the time he was eighteen. On the return leg of the fourth trip, his father's ship was attacked in the Black Sea by pirates, and only he and three other crew members had survived. They made it to shore and walked for weeks to the mouth of the Dniepr scrounging food from local fishing villages. At the Dniepr they were given a working passage to Kyiv. The other men had secured working passages home, but Yurii decided to stay on in Kyiv because he preferred his options there than on a farmstead back in Vinland.

He had found employ at the granary as the resident guard and rat catcher, and was apparently good at his job. He had witnessed my handling of the near-riot and had been watching me ever since, waiting for an opportunity to show his usefulness. He seemed to appear out of nowhere and started helping to prepare the ships without being asked. That he knew his way around ships worked in his favour and soon he was eating meals with us as well. He and young Ingvar seemed to be creating a close friendship.

About a week before we were due to leave, we were applying the finishing touches to the repairs we had carried out, and the crew was packing stores, when suddenly Big Sven Johansson cried out, "Cursed rat! I'm going to kill you!"

But before he could move his great hulk, Yurii shouted, "Stop where you are!"

At which Sven froze. This was followed by a swooshing sound and a loud ker-thunk of metal embedding itself in wood. The rat was firmly skewered to a bulwark. It had died so quickly, it hadn't even made a sound.

"YOU COULD HAVE KILLED ME!" Sven screamed.

"No chance," Yurii replied. "My knife blade is too short. It would never have hit a vital organ through all your blubber."

At which the crew, in silent amazement until this point, burst out laughing.

"I'll show you, you little whipper-snapper!" cried Sven, leaping the freeboard.

"Not if you can't catch me!" challenged Yurii, and the chase was on.

Round and round the ship they went, making us all dizzy. We laughed so hard that tears were streaming down our faces. Soon Sven was out of breath and had to concede to the youth.

"That was some throw, Master Yurii," I said. "Just where did you learn to throw like that?"

"On my first journey to Miklagaard. I had pestered my father so much he eventually agreed to take me along. But he knew I would not be able to hold down a job as a full member of his crew, so he appointed me as ship's storesman. One of my jobs would be to ensure that rats did not get to the food and cargo. Catching rats on land is hard enough, but have you ever tried doing it on a boat that is rocking on a sea or travelling down a river? Anyway, one of the crew taught me how to throw knives, and it seemed I had a natural aptitude, for I learned pretty quick. When we got to Miklagaard, my father paid the men their wages and me mine. He took me to an ironmonger and had him make me a set of balanced knives. When we were attacked I lost all but one, this one," he said, holding up the knife. "The long and lonely nights in the granary have enabled me to further hone my accuracy."

"An interesting story," I said, not giving anything away, but already having made my mind up to invite him along on the journey. I would discuss it with Haldor and Ibn later that day when we were alone.

We all returned to our work. It was obvious on the crew members' faces that Yurii had earned his place on the crew. As a peace offering he offered to help Sven clean up the mess the mouse had left; a marksman and a diplomat. Yurii's value to our project had suddenly been raised a few notches.

Later, over our evening meal, I made the proposal to Haldor and Ibn.

"I don't know what's taken you so long to get to this point," said Haldor.

"What do you mean, 'so long'?" I asked him.

"You tell him, Ibn," said Haldor.

"Ulf, we have been watching you and the boy for a long while now."

"Oh…" I interjected.

But Ibn raised his hand and continued, "Let me finish, please? You are more than fond of the boy. Whether you have realised it or not, you have taken him under your wing, just as a mother hen does with her chicks. Is it possible that he is like the son you never had, for you treat him like he was your own?"

"I, I…" I stammered, "I had never consciously thought of him like that."

"No. You would not. But it is in your nature to lead. A good leader always protects those he leads. And in protecting, sometimes the leader grows more than fond of one or two of his crew."

"Like now?"

"Like now," Ibn and Haldor chorused.

"I'll tell him in the morning."

"No," said Haldor.

"Oh. And why, may I ask?"

"Because the crew want to do it. They have something planned," he replied.

"You're ALL in on this?"

"We are most indeed all in on this," said Haldor.

"Then, may I ask a question?"

"Go head," Haldor said with a silly grin plastered on his face.

"Just who is leading this expedition, then?"

"Why you, of course!" he replied with mock respect.

"And just what else have you got planned?" I asked

"Well, we have another crew member to welcome aboard as well."

"We do?" I asked incredulously.

"Yes, we do," Haldor said. The silly grin hadn't left his face.

"And just who might that be?"

"Well, Ibn, of course," he replied.

"Ibn?" Turning to him, I said, "You didn't tell me you wanted to come along. What about your tenure at the library?"

"Oh, three years is a long time to be sitting and studying. I need some action. Besides, I would rather have the heat of Asia than the cold of Europe. Figs, grapes and mulberries plucked from the tree as you pass, and eaten fresh. Not stale, dry and weeks old, like you get here. Clear blue skies, fast-flowing rivers and snow-capped mountains. Aaaah."

I sat stunned and amazed. I had been working with this man for four months, day in and day out, and I had never heard him speak thus.

He looked at me and smiled. "Besides, you will need a scribe, or a scald as you call them, to record the journey. You will be too busy leading and won't have the time to fulfil the role of scribe as well."

"Well, that's that, then," I said. "Is there anything else you haven't told me?"

"Oh, not as yet," Haldor grinned.

This turn of events was indeed a good omen for the journey ahead.

The following day was the first sea trial for the boats. Just why they were called sea trials when we were on a river nowhere near sea mystified me. However, Yurii, as keen as ever, was first on the boat. Taking it out to mid river, the crew concocted a story whereby Yurii was to perch high up on the prow of the boat with the remainder of the crew in the stern. The aim of the exercise was to rock the boat back and forth to test the freeboard. This was indeed a unique test, a veritable first in Viking history — probably the last as well.

Once the boat was rocking like a cradle, to the amusement of many on the quay, on a downswing the crew in the stern all simultaneously jumped, thereby upsetting Yurii's rhythm, throwing him off balance and into the freezing Dniepr, to howls of laughter from the crew and the shore.

Hauling him on board, someone said, "Now he looks like a drowned rat," which brought more peals of laughter.

"The rat slayer has himself become a drowned rat," commented another.

"Yurii *Rat-Slayer* Vartinnen. Has a sort of ring to it, don't you think?"

"It certainly does. I think we should call him Rat from now on. It makes sense. First he slays a rat with a single throw, then he avoided capture from Big Sven, escaping like a rat, and now he looks like a drowned rat. So Rat it must be."

The knarr was rowed back to the quay with Yurii shivering amid ships.

On arrival at the quay side, I welcomed Yurii as a fully fledged member of our crew and gave him his new name. Seeing his face light up was a sight to behold. I then said to the crew, "You realise that Yurii is not the only new member of our crew?"

They looked at me with frowns on their faces.

"Our other newest crew member is Ibn Rashid al-Arslan. I think he should be "formally" welcomed into the crew as well."

The look of panic on Ibn's face was hilarious. He started backing away down the quay, saying, "No, no. You can't do this to me. You can't, you really can't."

His exit from the quay was blocked by Haldor. The men swept him up and carried him to the end of the pier amid cries of protest from Ibn. On a count of three they swung him out into the Dniepr, which he entered with a great splash and a flailing of arms and legs.

The crew stood there cheering and guffawing. Ibn didn't surface.

"What's going on?" I asked

"The Arab is playing games. I think he's seeing how long he can hold his breath underwater."

"Yeah. He said something about not being able to swim. I guess he would say anything to get out of being thrown in."

Slowly the realisation that maybe Ibn couldn't swim dawned on the crew. Within seconds all had jumped in and were searching for him.

Haldor and I commandeered a rowing boat and rowed out to mid stream. Just when it seemed that all was lost, Big Sven surfaced with a spluttering Ibn in his arms. Fortunately they were downstream from us and it did not take us long to row over to them. We hauled them aboard and rowed back to shore with Ibn lying in the bottom of the boat panting for breath.

"How many people, do you think, who grow up in the middle of a desert, ever learn to swim?" he spluttered.

"I never thought of it that way," I said.

"Me neither," said Haldor. "I guess you had better learn really quickly, as our journey is liable to involve quite a bit more travel on water."

Slowly, one by one the crew emerged from the freezing river. This had been a sobering experience for them. But not sobering enough for them to realise that Haldor and I were the only two dry members of the crew. So we were dutifully marched to the end of the pier and at the point of a sword were each persuaded to take a swim in the Dniepr.

The whole spectacle of these mad Vikings swimming in the Dniepr, still freezing with snowmelt, had drawn a crowd to the dock. The keeper of the tavern where we usually ate brought out tankards filled with mulled wine, which warmed us all the way down to the bottom of our guts. We then made our way to our lodgings to change our clothes. I also informed Rat that he had better inform his supervisor at the granary that he would be leaving.

"And when will that be?" Yurii asked.

"Oh, sunrise tomorrow," I replied nonchalantly.

"TOMORROW? Tomorrow — we're going tomorrow!" His face was showing joy and anticipation at once. With that he dashed off to the granary.

That night we said our goodbyes. Prince Iziaslav had held a feast in our honour, after which we had been invited to at least three other farewell feasts, each seemingly more sumptuous that the previous.

Iziaslav, knowing our intended route, gave me personal letters of introduction, for which I was most grateful.

Under Islamic law, Ibn was not allowed to drink alcohol made from grain. So we had introduced him to honey mead, to which he took with relish.

So in the early hours full of food and ale, Ibn, Haldor and I stumbled into our lodgings.

We were all on the dock before sunrise, and to my astonishment so was Olaf.

I said, "Olaf, my good friend, you should be in bed where it is warm. The docks in the cold and dark are not a place for you."

"I know, I know. But I have something for you." And with that he pulled a long oblong-shaped box out from under his cloak and pressed it into my hands.

"If the Prince knew he would kill me. Good luck and send me as many reports with detailed descriptions and whatever books as you can for my library."

"We will, we will," I promised.

Uncharacteristically, he gave me a hug, kissed me on both cheeks and said, "My friend, I have never been a physical man. I therefore experience the far lands, have many adventures, see it and do it all through you and your eyes. Hopefully my gift will enable you to see with more clarity," and with that he was gone.

So as dawn broke we cast off and headed down the Dniepr towards the Pontus Euxinus. Soon the dome of St Sophia's and Kyiv's silhouette were hidden from view and the steppe slowly wakened as the morning light crept across the land. This was truly a magical start to this leg of our journey.

Chapter 6

The CATARACTS

We had decided to leave before the spring flotilla departed along the same route to Byzantium to trade their cargos of mainly furs, honey and slaves. I did not want to be held up by the slower-moving merchants with their cargo-laden boats. I had visions of spending hours, if not days, rescuing and mending merchant vessels all down the cataracts. We needed to be quick and agile. So, taking a chance, we departed a week ahead of the flotilla.

I knew that we had a few days of easy sailing before we would have to negotiate the Dniepr cataracts. There were seven in all. During this time, in return for being taught how to swim, Ibn began teaching the crew Arabic. For most of the older crew this was a re-acquaintance with the language, having learned it in Miklagaard. For the younger members, it was learning from scratch. Ibn said it was harder un-teaching the colloquial Arabic of the older crewmembers than it was teaching the younger ones from scratch.

Unlike the upper Dniepr region, where forests grew right down to the river, the mid Dniepr was a mix of steppe and heavy forest. Approaching the cataracts the river banks began to grow higher, and in some places were vertical granite. More than a few of the crew thought that they had seen people watching us, flitting and darting between the trees and peering down at us over the precipices. We were now in the middle of Pecheneg territory, and if my hunch was correct, then our friends the Pechenegs were up to their old tricks again. Until quelled by Yaroslav, the Pechenegs were a fearsome barbaric warrior tribe. They struck so much fear into an early embassy from the Hanseatic and Rus Kingdoms to Byzantium that the ambassadors chose to return home the long way via the Mediterranean, France and Germany. Now with the country in the grips of a civil war, they had returned to type.

If I was correct, then they would wait for us to beach, approximately halfway through the rapids, then attack. We would be tired and weary from "feeling" our way through the cataracts. We used a combination of a crewmember walking ahead in the freezing water and everyone standing and feeling the river bottom with long staves, guiding the boats through the rocky cataracts. If we had waited until June, we could have ridden the rapids from top to bottom on the high waters of the Dniepr without fear of striking a rock and holing a boat. But waiting that long meant wasting almost half of the summer, which I did not want to do.

I commanded the crew to make ready their weapons, for we knew from past experience that the time and place for the attack would be when we beached at the head of the fourth rapid, Aifur—the impassable rapid, at which point we would have to port the boats six mil downstream. What the Pechenegs did not know was that we had a tried and tested plan for such situations. The older Varangians knew it well. It was the brainchild of Harald, and we had used it many times before all over the Mediterranean, and it worked well. Haldor and I briefed our crews, allocated responsibilities and prepared for the beaching.

As soon as I saw the standing stone marking the start of Aifur, I gave the signal to start turning for the beach. Swords were quietly drawn from their scabbards and placed alongside shields out of sight, but where they could be snatched up for action in an instant.

We had run the ships up on the beach and were making out as if we were about to haul the boats up for portage, all the while pretending not to notice the barbarians creeping ever closer.

Under his bushy brow Big Sven Arnkelsson was keeping a watchful eye on them.

"How many do you reckon?" I asked him under my breath.

"'Bout fifty. No more than sixty," he said.

"Then with our thirty we're about even. Where do you reckon the largest concentration is?" I asked him.

"Over there in the thicket. Like a herd of bloody elephants, they are."

"What's elephants?" Rat asked.

I started to answer "They're...." But then checked and said, "Now's not the time, Yurii. I'll tell you later."

Facing away from the thicket, I said to Haldor, "As soon as they attack, take five men and loop around the back of the thicket, cut off their escape and drive them back towards us."

"Yessir," said Haldor in his usual manner of mock respect, but knowing my exact intention. His frivolity belied what we were planning. After thirty years of fighting together we no longer needed to ask each other why.

We beached the boats alongside each other, but ensured that none of the crew was between the boats. This way we would all be on the outsides and all the crew would be brought into action simultaneously and in a single line of attack.

Then they attacked. The Pechenegs sprinting in waving their weapons in the air and emitting bloodcurdling screams. It would have driven any untrained soldiers to flight. But they had a surprise coming.

From a seemingly chaotic milling-about, the Pechenegs were suddenly faced by a wall of well armed Vikings screaming back at them as loudly, if not louder. To make matters worse the Vikings advanced as one unit, causing the Pechenegs to check their ragged advance.

I quickly surveyed the Pecheneg force, which more resembled a group of bandits than a well-trained fighting force. I quickly spotted their leader, who was wearing a gold armband and was directing his force from the back.

I signalled Big Sven, who with Rat and Ingvar started circling around the rocks in order to get behind the Pecheneg leader. My strategy was to capture the leader and the fight would go out of them.

Weeks upon weeks of drill during the winter in Kyiv were paying dividends in a way that I had not predicted. The advance took on a rhythm of its own. Cut, parry, thrust. Cut, parry, thrust. It did not take long for us to gain the upper hand and soon we were driving them back. Steel rang against steel and the Pechenegs started falling back. More than a few of their number fell and you could see the panic start to form in their eyes as they looked around to see that they were not the only ones being driven back. Some of their more able wounded had already retreated from the scene. We maintained our line and steadily we drove them back until they were almost back to where they had started from. For all their outward ferocity, the Pechenegs were only adequate fighters, not well trained in the art of warfare. Their strategy was obviously to paralyse their victims with fear on the initial attack, not giving time for an organised retaliation. Only this time, the tables were turned.

Legend of the Last Vikings

Then two things happened at once: Big Sven captured the Pecheneg leader, and flanked by Rat and Ingvar Hallsteinsson, was holding him in a headlock; then Haldor trotted into the open leading a herd of saddled horses.

On seeing this, the fight went right out of the Pechenegs, and they started to flee in all directions. Of their original group, we had killed twelve and captured another seventeen. Almost half of their force had been neutralised. Add in the wounded and possibly two-thirds would have been taken out of action.

The captured leader would guarantee our safety at least to Baruforos, the fifth cataract, when we would re-enter the water. I hadn't made my mind up on whether or not I would keep him prisoner until we had cleared Strukun, the seventh and final rapid. Plus, the horses would do well as beasts of burden for the duration of the portage. Not that we were carrying as much as a normal Svear trader. I also decided to use a few of the horses as scouts. The extra height and extra speed could prove invaluable if the Pechenegs ever decided to regroup and attack. But I didn't think this would happen—well, not anytime soon. My reasoning, and hope, was that they would spend time squabbling about either who was going to be leader or what the plan of attack was going to be, or both.

While Ibn prepared the medicine kit, Haldor and I conducted a roll call. We had some wounded, mainly from arrows and a few cuts from swords. But nothing that couldn't wait until the next centre of civilisation. Rat was safe. Haldor, Ibn and I then dressed and washed the wounds with what little medicines we had. The fresh freezing-cold water of the Dniepr cleansed many wounds. The coldness of the water helping stem blood flow. I made comment that we needed to have a larger stock of medicines for the size of our force. They both agreed.

We decided that the wounded would ride the horses and take care of the baggage train, while the Pecheneg prisoners would assist the rest of the able-bodied crew with the portage. As we had no archers, Rat was under instructions to bring down any prisoner who attempted to escape. I couldn't have the Pechenegs thinking that we were soft targets.

It was obvious that the Pechenegs were taking advantage of the lack of local law and order caused by the internal strife at court. Before we made it to Baruforos, the Pechenegs made two further attempts, both at night. I think these were less attacks against us and more attempts to regain their lost horses, a most valuable possession in their environment. We suffered no casualties, but by our bloodied battleaxes and swords we knew that they had gained more wounded. This was turning out to be a very costly raid for them.

53

At Baruforos I put Big Sven in charge of a party and gave them instructions to ride the horses and baggage down to Strukun, but not to get too far ahead of us. This would mean that the boats could ride higher in the water, reducing our risk of holing. It also meant that the boats would be more responsive to the currents and that bit harder to control.

If we couldn't stop the Pechenegs, then we could at least hinder them. And without their horses their ability to raid would be severely curtained, for a while at least.

While we loaded the boats at Strukun, Big Sven led the horses a few mil out to the west and set them free. He then rode back and joined us. At this point I set the Pecheneg leader free, minus his gold torque, which I pitched into the river; the ultimate insult. We pushed off and sailed the calmer waters towards the Pontus Euxinus.

It wasn't long before we noticed the speed of the river slowing as it entered the delta. We stayed in the central stream and soon had to hoist sail to maintain our speed.

I couldn't help but wonder if we would face any worse hazards on our quest to find Ingvar Vittfarne?

Chapter 7

Korchev

On entering the Pontus Euxinus, we didn't turn directly south east, which would take us across the southern point of the Korsun isthmus, and bring us close to Korsun itself. Instead we initially maintained a southerly course. We had purposely taken a wide berth around the Byzantine port of Korsun and stayed out to sea while we made for Korchev. The last thing we wanted was Byzantine bureaucracy poking its nose into our affairs. Besides, we could be mistaken for pirates and it could take months to sort out, which was time we did not have to spare.

Vikings were not uncommon in Korsun, but not as common as the Arabs and Byzantines. The violent activities of our forefathers had imbued a lasting distrust of Vikings and the Rus by the Byzantines. As a result we were never allowed into any of their cities in large groups and never with our weapons. This made us feel naked and it also made us easier prey for those who were armed.

Our tactic involved sailing a day on each of the three sides of a square. We sailed south, then east and then north. This would keep us away from Korsun and give us a wide berth around the Korsun Isthmus before we headed north into the Yenikale Strait and into Korchev. Our wounded were not so bad that they required immediate attention. Ibn reckoned a few extra days of rest and sea air would do them more good than any doctor could just now. The sea was not living up to its classical name and the going was easy. So on we sailed.

On our northerly leg into Korchev, along the Yenikale strait, the peaks of the Korsun peninsula rose majestically on our west flank, seemingly right out of the sea. They appeared larger and more dramatic than they actually were, as there was not much else of similar stature in the area to bring them into proportion. The forested slopes had grey and weathered rock breaking through on the upper reaches. The peninsula also has labyrinths of caves, which Haldor and I had explored when we were last here some twenty five years ago. No one knew why they were made, which gave our explorations an air of mystery. The locals grew wheat, grain and barley on the plain, which was amply fed by streams and rivers. In all it was a most productive area. I could see why the rulers of Byzantium and Kyiv wanted to rule this area.

On our eastern flank, the Caucasus Mountains were mere foothills and rolling pasture.

The Yenikale Strait, like the Bosporous Straits, gives whoever controls the Strait absolute control over sea traffic, and hence the opportunity to make a great deal of money through taxes, as Yaroslav had done with Novgorod and Kyiv. The strait was like a giant funnel, 9 mil wide at the southern point, 2 mil wide at the northern and only 25 mil long. It enabled an easy defence of the area in the case of sea-borne or land invasions. All the defenders had to do was wait for the invaders to come to them. Over the past few thousand years the area had been ruled by Greece, Rome, Byzantium, Kazahria and now the Kyivan Rus. No doubt the conquerors of the future would want to control this area as well.

Approaching Korchev, you could detect a faint odour of rotten eggs.

"Phew. What's in this place that smells so bad?" asked one of the crew. "You sure this place doesn't have the plague?"

Ibn answered, "Quite sure. What you can smell is the Sivash, or the Putrid Sea."

"Wassat?" grunted another as he pulled on his oar.

"Just east of the northern end of the Yenikale Strait there are a number of, uh, pans cut off from the Sea of Azov by a long spit of land called the Arabatskaya Strelka. These are but smaller versions of the Kara-boghaz Gol in the Kaspian sea, which we will see, and smell, in due course. What happens is the hot sun evaporates the water, leaving a residue that has high concentrations of sulphur and sodium. It is these which give off the smell."

"Who would want to live here with that smell?" asked someone.

"Well, eventually when all the water has evaporated, the sodium and sulphur crystallises and can be mined and sold."

"Sounds complicated to me," another said, which raised a chuckle. "How do you know all this?"

"Because this is the way I came to Kyiv. Up the Kaspian sea, across Armenia, across the Sea of Azov, past the Sivash and overland to Kyiv."

"A most unusual route," one commented.

"Not if you were coming from where I came from. Going via Byzantium held more risk, was longer and was more expensive," Ibn replied.

We made Korchev just before the port chain was raised for the day. In Korchev it seemed you couldn't turn a corner without coming across a Viking trader. This was because Korchev was controlled by the Prince of Novgorod, who of course was allied to the Prince of Kyiv, who in turn had close relations with the Nordic Kingdoms through marriage mainly by and through Yaroslav. We knew there would be less questions asked and less bureaucracy if we sailed into Korchev with a bunch of wounded Viking sailors, plus our letters of introduction would silence any inquisitive parties.

Immediately on landing I set about finding a doctor and Haldor and Ibn lodgings.

Nevertheless, a few hours later I eventually found myself hammering on the door of the Governor's mansion as the sun set. Not a good time to start calling on a Governor. The guard was not too impressed at my demands for an audience with the governor, especially at this time of the evening. Not sure if he should throw me out, he called his sergeant, who was not impressed at being called away from his evening meal.

The sergeant eyed me up and down as if I was a vagrant, and before I could speak, asked, "And just what do you want at his time of day? And before you ask—NO, you can't see His Excellency now. Business is closed for the day. Come back in the morning."

"If I come back in the morning, by midday tomorrow you'll be court marshalled. And if I have my way, drawn and quartered as well."

His eyes betrayed his true feelings, I could see him wince internally. Nevertheless, he said, "Ooh! And just who do you think you are?"

"My name is Ulf Uspakson, Lord Lieutenant to Harald Hadraada, King of Norway, formerly of the Varangian Guard." He didn't need to know that Harald was dead. I went on, not giving him a chance to interrupt, "And until two weeks ago in the employ of Prince Iziaslav of Kyiv in the defence of the same city. Here are my letters of introduction."

The sergeant stiffened slightly, not knowing if I was serious or not. He took the letters and started to read them. It was taking him so long I offered to read them out for him. Just then the guard captain came down to find out what was happening, obviously having sent the sergeant while he finished his meal. I thought to myself *the privileges of rank*.

He looked at me with a puzzled expression, took the letters off the sergeant and began to read them, somewhat quicker than the sergeant, then briskly snapped to attention. "Let him in. NOW, you fool! What's taking you so long? Don't you know who this is? Please forgive me, Lord Ulf, I didn't recognise you at first. It's been a long time. I served under you when Prince Yaroslav the Wise was based in Novgorod. It's very hard to find good soldiers nowadays. Especially ones WHO CAN READ," he added. The latter remark was pointedly aimed at his sergeant, who was now trying to make himself invisible by standing in the shadows.

"Thank you, Captain...?" I let the question hang.

"Oh. Verenka, sir. At your service," he said, half-bowing.

"Alright, Verenka. I need to see His Excellency right away." I changed my mind about Verenka as quickly as I had been to judge him.

I was ushered into the governor's office with due haste.

"Ah, Lord Uspakson, I don't believe we've had the honour?"

"No, Your Excellency, I don't believe we have," I said curtly.

"I do apologise for my guard's demeanour. But I do receive calls from all sorts at all hours of the night. They are trained to sort out the chaff from the wheat, so to speak."

"So I have found out," I replied, not hiding my impatience.

"Now what can I do for you?"

"I have just arrived from Kyiv. We were attacked by the Pechenegs on the cataracts. I have wounded men and can't find a doctor to treat their wounds."

Without a moment's hesitation he said, "Captain, call my personal physician, and send some men with litters to bring Lord Ulf's wounded men to the barracks."

"Thank you, Your Excellency. You are most kind."

"Not at all, Lord Ulf. Anything for a defender and friend of Kyiv. Now can I get you something to eat, maybe a drink?"

"Thank you, Your Excellency. No. Not just now. I must see to my men first."

"Of course. Would it help if I had the kitchens opened for a meal a little later?"

"It would indeed, sir."

"Then it shall be so. Guard! Tell the cook to open the kitchens and start preparing a meal for Lord Ulf and his men." The guard hurried off.

"Sir, you honour me," I said.

"No, Lord Ulf, it is I — we, Korchev — who are honoured."

He knew that such an act would be reported back to Iziaslav in Kyiv and was probably hoping it would earn him a few extra points towards a promotion and possibly even get him a posting back home. With that I hurried off to see to my men.

We rested for four days in Korchev while the men recovered their strength and their wounds healed, the subtropical climate being very agreeable for recuperation.

During the interlude, I spent time with Governor Poznyakov, giving him a report on the attack, which he said would be dispatched to Kyiv with all haste. He confirmed my suspicions that the Pechenegs were taking advantage of the civil war and had increased their raiding activities on the Dniepr again. The majority of his men had been transferred and the garrison strength was at its absolute minimum. He asked if I would lead a raid against the Pechenegs. I informed him that what was needed was a permanent solution to the problem, not a holding action. He agreed with me but said that he had had to try.

On the afternoon of the third day I was working on the boats with the crew when Ibn came aboard. He fiddled about with a few things, which seemed odd, then sidled over to me and said, "Don't look now but we are being watched."

"Oh. By who?" I asked, keeping my head down.

"I think it is the Black Scorpions."

"The what?" I asked.

"The Black Scorpions. They are a sect that tried to merge Zoroastrianism with Manechism, with disastrous results."

"Merge what with what?" I asked, my head coming up.

"Keep your head down," Ibn hissed, "and keep working. It seems your education is not as complete as I originally thought."

"It seems not," I said.

"I think the whole crew should hear what I have to say about the Black Scorpions. If we all leave now it will seem suspicious, so tonight at meal time will have to do," he said.

"Well then, it seems we have a lecture planned for this evening. Mind you, it will also be an opportunity to give more details about our planned route."

"I agree," he said.

"Good. Now just where is the person watching us?"

"Over there, the man sitting on the quay pretending to mend a net."

"How do you know he's pretending?" I asked.

"Not being a fisherman, I didn't at first. Then I watched other fishermen mending theirs and realised he was just fiddling. I also realised a more fundamental issue—his dress. He is too well dressed for a fisherman. Not over dressed, but when did you last see a fisherman go to work with boots like those? Also the cut of his shirt is wrong. You see his sleeves? Well, they're too long. My guess is they're long on purpose to hide his tattoo."

"Tattoo?"

"Yes, of a black scorpion, usually found on the left shoulder blade—with his membership number."

"They sound organised and sinister."

"Believe me, they are."

"How do you know?"

"My father interrogated one in Gorgon when I was a boy. I sneaked into the torture chamber and watched and listened. But come, we're finished here now. Let's go and eat."

"Some childhood you must have had," I commented.

That evening we hired a private room and Ibn began with his lecture on the Black Scorpions.

"Approximately five hundred years ago, after the time of the Romans, a man was born in Bactra. His name was Zarathustra. He went on to become a great teacher and his teachings eventually formed into a religion which was called Zoroastrianism."

"Zoro what?" asked one of the crew.

"Zoroastrianism. In short they were fire worshipers, and I will give some more details in a moment. Zoroastrianism was the religion from Byzantium, through Bactra, Sogdiana and Tianxia. All along the Silk Road."

"What's the Silk Road?"

"It's a network of trade roads that runs from Byzantium through Merv, Herat, Bactra, Maracanda, Kaxgar, Wulumqi and into Tianxia. One arm goes from Bactra to Bulgar, where your fellow Vikings have their main contact, another goes down into Sind.

"Moving on. In the year 240AD another man was born in Babylon to a Christian mother and Zoroastrian father. His name was Mani. Like Zarathustra, his teachings became a religion and began to rival that of Zoroastrianism. While Zoroastrianism placed great emphasis on the laws of purity and sacredness of the seven creations, and don't ask me what the seven are because I don't know, they take their beliefs in purity to the point that they will not allow the dead to poison the ground and they leave them out on towers for vultures and other birds of prey to eat. When the bones are picked clean of dead flesh, they are then gathered and buried.

"Manecheism, which is what Mani's religion came to be called, taught that Evil was not a perversion of Good, but rather an alternative form of Good.

61

In other words, you could never do any wrong or Evil. Everything was Good, but just in different forms. By the time Manechism spread throughout the Silk Road countries, it was taught that Evil had already won on earth. But this was contrary to the teachings of all the major religions, Zoroastrianism, Christianity and Islam. As a result Mani was put to death in 277AD and his followers exiled to an arid area in Tianxia near the Taklamakan Desert.

"Some of these exiles reasoned that Mani had become confused because of his dual-religion upbringing. They then tried to merge Manechism with Zoroastrianism with disastrous results. The group had no respect for anyone or anyone's property. Their symbol is a black scorpion with three eyes, eight segmented legs and a tail with nine joints. The mathematics gives the number fifty-two, which is the number of weeks in a year. They use this to claim that their beliefs are divinely ordained. The scorpion used to be coloured blue, green and red to stand for three of the five elements — space, air and fire. I know not why or when it changed to black, but black it now is."

The Black Scorpions were themselves exiled by the Manechists, which says something. They became a secret society of cutthroat thieves and defrauders, whose only aim was the amassing of wealth. Their secret sign is called the forefinger-scorpion-gesture, which is made up from a fist with the forefinger and little finger extended.

Each has the scorpion tattooed on his left shoulder with their membership number."

"Membership number?" someone asked.

"Yes. They use an ancient form of counting designed by the great Ferghani mathematician Abul Aabas Akhmad Mukhammad Kasir al-Farghani, more commonly known to your European mathematicians as Alfaraghanus, or to us from the east as Khasib."

"Phew. For a moment I thought you were going to ask us to remember his name in full," I said.

"Not on your life," Ibn replied. "To finish off, the numbering system uses a disused algebraic numbering system to the count of six. So no one, except the Black Scorpions, know the system and order of digits.

However, if you kill a Black Scorpion, you become a marked man for life. They will hunt you down anywhere in the world. They have become adept at disguises and have ingratiated themselves into communities from the land of the Frank, Rome, Byzantium and all major cities east into Tianxia."

Standing up, I said, "Well, I hope you remember all of that. It may come in useful someday." Just how many true words had been prophesied in jest, we were to find out—unfortunately sooner rather than later.

We broke for some refreshments and then I stood up and started my briefing.

"Some of you will be wondering why we are here, up in the north, when Miklagaard is down in the south. Well, the answer is because we are going to Bactra. A lot of the reports on Ingvar Vittfarne originate in Bactra, some from Byzantium and some from Tianxia."

"Tianxia?" someone half asked.

"Yes, Tianxia. So my reasoning is, as Bactra is halfway along the Silk Road, we start there and depending on the information we receive, we can work our way either East or West from Bactra, which will save us a great deal of time. Plus, like all of us, with the exception of Ibn, we've never been to Bactra, so it will be a new experience for us. In order to get there we have to travel up the Tuoni River and portage across to the Volga."

This raised a lot of moans.

"The good news is that the portage is only about sixty-five mil, unlike the Lovat-Dniepr portage, which is about one hundred and fifty mil. Then we sail down the Volga to Hardzhy-Tarkhan. From Hardzhy-Tarkhan we cross the Kaspian sea and sail, or should I say row, up the mighty Oxus to Bactra."

"Sounds easy," someone said.

I continued, "Even better news, we leave the day after tomorrow," which raised some cheers.

On the morning of the fifth day we departed Korchev just as soon as the harbour chain was lowered and took a north easterly bearing across the Sea of Azov.

Because there is so much fresh water flowing into the Sea of Azov, and such a restricted outlet, the sea's water had a much lower saline content that the

Black Sea, or any other sea for that matter. In some places it was completely fresh and the men took great delight in being able to drink "fresh" seawater.

Chapter 8

The FORTRESS at SARKEL

A few days later we entered the Gulf of Taganrog and we saw the coast of ancient Thanais on the north shore of the Sea of Azov, and were soon approaching Rostov. The artfully decorated ceramics from Rostov could now be found as far away as Byzantium, Kyiv, Novgorod and even in the Nordic kingdoms.

Rostov was given to Yaroslav by his father Vladimir Svjatoslavovich in 988AD, after conquering the area in 965AD. Yaroslav ruled it until 1010AD. True to form, he even founded a new town in the north, Yaroslavl. But Yaroslav didn't plant towns for nothing, there had to be gain in it for him. His reasoning was that Yaroslavl would be the buffer for Rostov against any Bulgar attacks from the upper Volga.

We stayed the night in Rostov, preparing for our push up the Don to the fortress at Sarkel. The locals informed us that it was about 200 mil, or about four days' journey. However I knew it would be more like four days' hard rowing against the Don's current. I also knew that I couldn't expect to raise the sail as the prevailing wind was from the north east, the direction in which we were heading. So four days' hard slog it would be.

I was pleasantly surprised when we arrived at the fortress city of Sarkel in just three days. The Don was wide and relatively slow flowing, which made our going easier and quicker, and the crews performed magnificently. I relished my turn on the oars. There is nothing like a group of men singing a stirring song and working in time. We seemed to fly over the water.

On day three an undeclared race developed. After pulling out from our overnight camp we were at first in the lead. Then Haldor's knarr pulled even and then ahead of us, and then our crew responded, and so it went on. I should have stopped it in order to save the men. But a little competition every now and then, even between crews, helps keep a sharp edge.

Eventually we were going so fast that the knarrs began planing, their bows rising and the wake now a white froth and not the normal gurgle. At each change of the lead the singing got louder. Haldor and his crew took the bait and the race was on. We came racing around a bend and upon seeing Sarkel for the first time on the north bank, I cried out to Haldor, "Last one to the first quay buys the ales!"

"You're on," he shouted back over the now roaring crews.

We were so absorbed in our race that we didn't notice the armed guard rushing out of the fortress and down to the docks. Haldor's crew pipped us by a hair's breadth.

Thinking we had a guard of honour I ordered oars up and, using our speed, our helmsmen expertly swung the boats in parallel to the shore, both beaching at the same time. It was a totally unrehearsed manoeuvre, but was executed with a flourish that only expert seamen could muster.

The speed of our approach and our singing had been taken for an attack and the guard rushed out. When it was obvious that all it was was two Viking knarrs having a race, there were the typical anonymous cynical comments from within the ranks

"Kutarev's got it wrong again."

"Yeah. It's always 'Hurry up and wait' with him."

"Not a-bloody-gain."

As the guard captain approached the comments died down.

"You, Viking!" he boomed, pointing at me. "What the bloody hell did you think you were doing?"

"Having a race. What else did it look like to you, Captain....?" I left the question hanging. Not receiving an answer, I turned and started tying up the boat.

"Look at me when I speak to you," he screamed at me.

Oh no. One of those, I thought to myself. I had come across his sort before. He was a bully not a leader. I turned to him and said, "But you were not speaking. Just standing there with your hands on your hips..."

The men were still in the boats with the oars at attention. Ignoring the flustered Captain, I turned back to the men and ordered them, "At ease, disembark."

"NOT BEFORE I SAY SO!" he screamed.

Turning again, I calmly said, "Oh. And why is that?"

"DON'T patronise me!" he shouted.

"And why not?" I calmly asked him, knowing he would become even more flustered.

"Because I SAY SO."

"Uh-huh. And just WHO are you?" I asked.

He began spluttering, his face as scarlet as an emperor's cloak. His men were enjoying this, so were my men, and so were Haldor and Ibn, and so was I.

I was about to answer when a voice boomed out over the assembled troops, "His name is Ulf Uspakson. That is Lord Uspakson to you, Kutarev. And with him is Haldor Snorresson. And that is also Lord Snorresson to you, Kutarev. I served under these men when Yaroslav the Wise, God rest his soul, tamed the Pechenegs. I also served under him when we were Byzantium's feared Varangian Horde, serving under Harald Hadraada. We ruled the Mediterranean from Jerusalem to the Pillars of Hercules."

The "voice" sat astride a magnificent white gelding and belonged to Commander Barjik Chernetsov, who had served under me with great distinction. It was no surprise to me that he was now the commander of Izaislav's Eastern army.

The captain stood rooted to the spot, his face still scarlet, amid sniggers from his troops.

Cernetsov asked, "Captain Kutarev, just who called out the guard?"

He stuttered out his reply, "I - I did, sir."

"And, pray, may I ask why?"

"Well, these two longboats approached the fort at speed…" and before he could say another word we all burst into laughter. Kutarev went redder still, knowing he was the butt of a joke but not knowing what the joke was. His mouth opened and shut like a fish in a pond.

"Kutarev, you idiot. These are not longboats. They are knarrs, used for trading. Anyway, did you really think that we could be overrun by a raid of just TWO boats? No offence to you, Lord Uspakson."

"Well, sir, they were making so much noise, I thought it was a much larger force, when I heard them I called out the guard straightaway and came straight down here."

"And you obviously did not check the size of this invading force with your own eyes before ordering the guard out." He threw up his hands in frustration and said, "Why am I not surprised? Dismiss the men. Lord Ulf please disembark your men ashore and join me for refreshments."

"It would a great pleasure, Barjik. Although, I think maybe not as great as the fun I've just had."

Barjik Chernetsov roared with laughter, and we brought the boats ashore.

Rat made to come with us, but Big Sven placed a hand on his shoulder and shook his head ever so slightly. I did not miss Sven's gesture.

I found out that Sarkel actually means "White Fortress", given its name because of its white limestone bricks. The fortress was built in the 830s by the Greeks and Khazars and was the capital city of Khazaria. Ibn was furiously noting this in his book. We later found him outside making a sketch of the fortress.

Barijk said, "We normally arrest Arabs who make sketches of our fortress."

"Rest assured," I told him, "he's not a spy."

"If that came from anyone else I wouldn't believe him."

That evening over a meal Barjik Chernetsov filled Haldor, Ibn and me in on his life after we left Byzantium.

"On returning to Kyiv I was quickly absorbed into the army. Yaroslav needed every able-bodied man he could get his hands on. My experience under you and Harald came in useful, but my experience of command even more so. So I was quickly promoted, had a few campaign successes and here I am now, defending Iziatslav's Eastern front."

"Why aren't you on the Volga?" I asked. "Surely that is the front?"

"Theoretically speaking, yes. While we have a nominal force at Gorodische, we don't have a fort as large and strong as Sarkel anywhere forward of here. And at the moment Iziaslav can't afford to build a large fort at Gorodische. Besides, we know the territory well and prefer to use the strip between the Don and the Volga as buffer territory. The plan is that we will fight a rearguard action all the way across, harrying and pricking whomever the enemy may be, all the while drawing them into a well-laid trap. At the same time a force will come down from Kalach-na-Donu and cut off their retreat. The only way out will be south, and if we so desire we can cut that off as well with our forces based at Korchev."

"I see you have the bases covered," I said.

He complimented Haldor and me by saying, "I was taught by the masters."

"What about your men? How often do you train them? An idle force grows fat, lazy and weak."

"I rotate the men in and out of the three sites on a regular basis. I also rotate the commandants, the captains and the sergeants. This way I always have a force on the move somewhere in the region, which gives the illusion of presence. Plus, the men get to know the country they may have to fight in some day."

"Very smart. But are all your captains as, ah," I paused, searching for the correct word, "competent as Kutarev?"

"Ha, ha. Yes, even more so. Kutarev was bumped up for saving Iziaslav's daughter from drowning at Kyiv many years ago. He was and always will be sergeant material. He believes he is an exceptional officer, which is why he is always based at Sarkel. The truth is, I couldn't afford to let him out of my sight. He would have the troops mutinying within a week."

"Very wise, Barjik, very wise."

"As I say, I was taught by the masters."

"Is Verenka one of your men?"

"Oh, yes. One of my most trusted. He keeps an eye on Poznyakov for me. He is under instructions to imprison Poznyakov should a force attack, and he, Poznyakov, decide to surrender before a sword is lifted in Korchev's defence. You know what these politicians are like."

"Only too well, Barjik. Only too well." I was tired and wanted to sleep. The exercise of the past few days was catching up with me now that I had had one glass of wine too many.

"Which is why you are now a Varjager instead of a courtier, eh?"

"Yes."

"Now, please excuse me, it's time for me to do my rounds. Must make sure Kutarev hasn't stuffed up the rosters. Please stay and enjoy the food and wine as long as you like. I won't be back for a few hours yet."

Haldor and I had another goblet of wine and we retired to our quarters.

The next morning we said our farewells. Barjik Chernetsov requested that I deliver a batch of letters to the garrison at Kalach-na-Donu which I agreed to do. We rowed up the Don for a further two days, eventually reaching Kalach-na-Donu.

Like the run up the Lovat River, which seemed like a lifetime ago, there was a great deal of forestation and where it wasn't forested, the land was gentle, undulating and green for the most part. Not the most inspiring landscape I have seen on this earth.

"Kalach-na-Donu," I said as we approached the town. "Kalach on the Don. I wonder what the history of this place is?"

Ibn replied, "It is undoubtedly a Khazarian settlement."

"And why would that be so?" I asked.

"Well, the Khazars settled this area because no one else wanted it. It is believed that they chose Judaism because it solved the problem of not being allied to the Islam of the south and east, nor the Christian states of Byzantium and Kyiv to the west and north."

"So it was a religion of convenience."

"It may have been so in the beginning. But like all these things, after a generation or two, the people forget the original reasons and really start to believe in it."

"I know what you mean. We had a similar 'conversion' in Norway, Sweden and Denmark, from the old beliefs to Christianity."

"And are you a true believer, Ulf?"

The question took me by surprise.

"Ah, I would say that I have been a nominal believer. Harald's brother Olaf has been made a saint, but Harald was anything but. Had I served more under Olaf than Harald, I might have had a stronger belief."

The town consisted mainly of wooden houses, so typical of a river-crossing and frontier town, not dissimilar to Novgorod.

We landed and I went off to find the garrison commander while the men prepared the boats for portage.

The commander was a bit taken aback when a Viking marched into his compound and introduced himself. Realising that Chernetsov wouldn't have given these dispatches to anyone he didn't trust implicitly, Captain Zukyov invited me to share a pot of cha, which was brewing in his office. He explained that the cha had been introduced by the Arabs, and he found it refreshing in the heat of summer and warming the cold of winter. He had secured a supply for his troops which they had with their morning, noon and evening meals. The difference was that he added goat's milk and honey, which took away the bitter flavour. I knew it was not uncommon for lemon and honey to be added to cha in Byzantium, but the addition of milk gave my taste buds an altogether new and pleasant experience.

I was then given a tour of the garrison. The wooden structure was slowly giving way to stone and brick. Zukyov believed this to be absolutely essential if they were ever to survive an attack. Stone and brick would still be standing after the roof had burnt out, but after a fire a wooden stockade would leave a great big gap, making a retreat inevitable. Barjik had a good man here.

Chapter 9

Hardzhy-Tarkhan

On the way back to the boats I purchased a bag of cha from the local store, and by the time I made it back, the crew had the boats unloaded and out of the water. Learning the lesson from our portage on the Dniepr cataracts, Haldor had arranged a train of mules to carry our goods and extra help for the portage. A system similar to the Lovat-Dvina-Dniepr portage existed here as well. And so we set off for Gorodische on a warm spring afternoon.

The portage was not spectacular in any way, just damned hard work. There was a steady stream of travellers en route going in both directions. The route was the shortest distance, with the least amount of vertical travel, between the two towns. When looking at a map, the route we travelled made a large letter S. First we travelled south, then turned back on ourselves and headed north east, before turning south again on our final leg into Gorodische.

We arrived at Gorodische in the early noon and could have set sail for the Kaspian straight away, but we rested, stayed overnight and sailed at first light in the morning. Olaf had received reports from a Hardzhy-Tarkhan merchant, who claimed his family had first-hand knowledge of Ingvar and his movements, so we were keen to press on. We pushed hard through the 250 mil, making Hardzhy-Tarkhan in just four days. The sandy-clay bleakness of the surrounding steppe lands did not entice us to linger. Rowing with the current sped our journey along. Although the river was wide, and hoisting sail would have given us more speed, the twists and turns of the braided river would have meant a lot of hard work with the sail up. This would have taken a lot of concentration and I did not want to miss the telltale signs of a rock and risk our venture by pushing too hard at the wrong moment.

On the portage and on the journey down, Ibn had been briefing the men on the required standards of behaviour when in a Jewish environment. In his words, "Our barbaric northern ways would not be tolerated," which made us all laugh for we didn't consider ourselves as barbaric at all.

We bypassed the ruins of the city of Itil on the east bank of the Volga and soon entered the delta area. When Yaroslav's father Svjatoslavovich sacked Itil, he also destroyed the Khazar empire, but he did not destroy the Khazars. No longer the major force in the region, they simply moved slightly east and north and continued to do business and exist as before.

We followed the detailed directions, which were to guide us through the myriad of channels and streams to the city, which lies on just eleven of the delta's many islands. On seeing the many bridges, canals and waterborne traffic, Haldor remarked how like Venice it was. In some places the city was obviously below the high flood levels and dykes had been built to prevent these areas from flooding.

Hardzhy-Tarkhan is a Jewish city. After Itil's destruction it was now the Khazarian capital of the remains of the great Jewish Khazarian empire. A true cross-roads of cultures, the city could boast a Greek Catholic archbishop, an Armenian Christian archbishop and a Lamaist monastery, not to mention a host of synagogues.

On sailing in, we saw fishermen hauling a large, long fish out of the river, and instead of gutting it, they bashed it with large wooden clubs.

"Odd way of killing a fish," said Haldor.

"They are in the first stages of harvesting caviar," said Ibn. "They do not kill the fish yet, as it would spoil the caviar. So they only stun it. When they get it back to their huts, they will kill the fish, slice it open and harvest the caviar from the roe sacks."

"And the fish? Do they eat it?" I asked.

"Only the poor eat sturgeon," said Ibn.

"What a waste," Haldor said. "There must be a use for it."

"It's even more of a waste, because it takes a female sturgeon twenty years to mature, only to be killed for one sack of roe. But to answer your second question, Hardzy Tarkhan is so wealthy they couldn't care less."

"They will when it's all gone," said Haldor.

"I fear you are correct, Haldor. Unfortunately it's the way of mankind to be like this," said Ibn.

The city's leaders had signed a peace treaty with Yaroslav in 985AD shortly after he became Grand Prince of Rostov. Being the intelligent man he was, Yaroslav recognised the city and the people for what they really were. Not just a cultural crossroads, and a buffer between Kyiv and the Arabs, but the kick-off point for the northern arm of the Silk Route. It was through this city that the Silk Route trade came into the Kyivan princedom. Therefore peace was essential to ensure stability and profit.

As we floated along, we passed the ruins of Sarai-Batu on the north shore of the Volga, the city's original settlement. Ibn informed us that Sarai-Batu was now inhabited by the poor, downtrodden, beggars, thieves and cutthroats.

We were headed for the Bolshie Isady, the town's main market square. We threaded our way through the myriad of canals and dodged the local river traffic. After an hour we had to admit that we were totally lost. I chuckled at the thought of being lost. It was only a few weeks ago that Prince Valdimir II Vsevelodovich of Smolensk challenged me by stating that Vikings could never get lost.

Seeing this, Haldor said, "Pray, let us in on your private jest, Ulf?"

"I was just reflecting on Valdimir Vsevelodovich's assertion that he had never heard of a lost Viking. And here we are now — not in the middle of nowhere, but lost in the middle of Hardzhy-Tarkhan." This raised a few chuckles all round.

We hove to at a quay and Ibn asked for directions to the Bolshie Isady. The local rolled his eyes and shrugged, his thoughts obvious, but gave us directions. Within twenty minutes we rowed into the Bolshie Isady. The area was teeming with boats and people. Vendors were selling wares on the quay, from tables, from market stalls and from boats of all different shapes and sizes. A wide canal ran through this section of the town. We tied up at the first available space and Haldor lashed his boat to ours. Fish, caviar, sugar, salt, naphtha, cottons, wools and spices from all over the orient were on display and their aromas gave off a pleasurable, heady fragrant mix, one that I have found only to be present in Eastern city markets, and nowhere in the West.

Ibn, Rat and I set off in search of Balgichi Simantov, while Haldor and Big Sven set about reprovisioning the boats. After asking around, we eventually arrived at his store after passing down a row of gold and silver smiths. To have accommodation in this part of town gave the impression that he was a man of means.

Balgichi Simantov was a merchant of books and manuscripts—and information. He was a short man with typical Jewish features. Being a Jew, he wore a skullcap, which had thin wisps of greying hair protruding here and there. Khazar skullcaps are unlike the skullcaps I have seen in Jerusalem and Byzantium. They are more like small hats and are exquisitely embroidered. His was dark blue and had an intricate pattern of brilliant blues, reds, greens, gold and silver. I later found out that they have different caps for winter and summer. The winter caps are just as exquisite but are fur-lined to keep out the cold and biting winds that blow in off northern Siberia.

On entering his shop, he said, "Ah, Varangians, *and* an Arab? Most interesting companions. I was wondering when you were going to come."

Taken aback, I said, "You were expecting us?", not knowing if this was his standard way of greeting customers to his store.

"Yes, for a long time now. I thought you might have been a bit younger though."

"How so?"

"Well I have been in correspondence with the Librarian of Kyiv for a number of years now. I have sent him much information. No one asks such specific questions if they don't intend to follow up on it. He is with you now?" he enquired, avoiding the latter part of my question.

"Alas, no. He was unable to travel."

"Ah, I am sorry. I would have liked to meet him very much. I think we are kindred spirits."

"Well, what is stopping you from going to him?" I enquired.

"I fear that, like him, my books keep me here."

"Yes, I can see that," I said, taking in the store's interior for the first time. The walls were lined with bookcases from floor to ceiling. The floor space was taken up with twenty uniformly arranged tables; five across by four deep. While the tables were neatly arranged in rows, there were books piled up on the tables and piled under the tables. Everywhere you looked there were books and roles of manuscripts and maps. But, surprisingly for a town on the edge of a desert, no dust nor cobwebs. Olaf would have been proud.

I asked him, "I assume you have everything catalogued and, ah, shelved in the correct place?"

He smiled and said, "Oh yes. Couldn't find a thing if I didn't. Anyway, I am ably assisted by my daughter. Serakh!" he called. "Come and meet the gentlemen I have been telling you that we have been expecting for a long time."

A young woman of medium height entered the room. She wore a floor-length red silk gown. Her hair was auburn and, although tied back, was waist length. Her face was ordinary but here eyes were cobalt blue and shone with life. On her feet she wore the traditional decorated ichigi slippers. Rat's mouth dropped open and she gave him a knowing smile. I had to give him a sharp nudge in the ribs to bring him back to reality.

She said rather silkily, a bit too silkily for it not to be put on, "How do you do, gentlemen? Can I get you some refreshments? You must be parched after such a long journey." She was working Rat like a puppeteer.

"Serakh!" barked Simantov. "Leave the boy alone and brew us a pot of cha."

"Yes, father," she said demurely and glided out of the store.

"I'm sorry," said Simantov. "She has this ability, a power, and she works it well, especially on the unsuspecting. Her mother had it as well. She could have me eating out of her hand at any time and I wouldn't even know I was doing it. It is good to see that at least you two gentlemen have some experience of life. Now, let me show you what I have."

We adjourned to Simantov's office and workroom for privacy while Serakh watched the shop. We pored over maps and reports that Simantov had acquired from his many contacts along the Silk Road. He had more than one report from various sources confirming that Ingvar had made it as far as Bactra, and had then gone further east. There was an information gap of about fifteen years and then reports started filtering through from further east of a white tribe in the area of Korla and Lou Lan, far along the northern branch of the Silk Road that runs around the north side of the Taklamakan Desert, at the east end of the Tarum River basin. But these reports were unsubstantiated.

We explored, confirmed, discounted, cross-checked and accepted many of the reports. Simantov had done an excellent job of categorising them into possibles, probables and unconfirms. We examined the reports from just about every aspect, thinking of the contingency plans that would be necessary should they be true or not. Slowly a plan began to form in my mind and the final stage of our journey plans began to be laid.

On the way to the store I had seen many store signs in Arabic as well as some with runic symbols. Curious, I asked Simantov about the unusualness of finding runic in Hardzhy-Tarkhan. I had only ever come across runic in the northern lands of my birth.

He said, "Up and until just one hundred years ago, the Khazars used the runic alphabet in everyday life."

"But it is almost exactly the same as the Futhark runic alphabet as we Vikings use. We are thousands of mil apart. How is this so?"

"This is something I have also wondered about. In researching this I have read and been told that many, many years ago the Svea tribes migrated north and west from this area, eventually settling in the area of your birth. They took with them the same alphabet. Understandably there are a few differences, this occurs over time, but it is essentially the same. I am not alone in this theory. Your friend Olaf and I have had much correspondence on this subject, as I have had with other sources in Rome and Byzantium. Without exception, we have all come up with similar explanations. It becomes even more obvious when you examine the map. Look here," he said, unravelling a map. "It is not that far between Norway and Kyiv. Neither is it that far between Kyiv, Sarkel and Hardzhy-Tarkhan. Consider, the journey from one end to the other, and back, is now made by not just one, but hundreds of your kinsmen, every year. You yourselves are proof of this."

When explained like this, it suddenly became easily explainable.

"I see. But how come I don't understand what they say? The words are incomprehensible," I said.

"Ah, you have overlooked one important aspect. The alphabet may have remained almost the same, but the language has changed. In the Western countries, is not the same Roman alphabet used to write Latin and Frank? You see?"

"And what about the Arabic writing?"

"Ah well, that is also simple. Sad, but simple. The majority of our trade is with and through the Arabs. No one in this part of the world, apart from us, can read runic. So about one hundred and fifty years ago, in about 920, we started using the Arabic script and over the years it has gained more and more prominence, to the extent that most of our contract law is now written in Arabic. But now, my friend, I fear you know too much. So we'll have to hang you."

My head snapped up, and then I saw the sparkle in his eyes. He said, "Ha ha. Caught you out. It's an old Khazarian proverb, 'If you know too much, they will hang you, and if you are too modest, they will trample on you.' So you see, now we will have to hang you."

This man had a wonderful way of making complex matters simple. If this is what comes from spending a life reading books, assimilating cultures and languages, I wanted to spend the rest of my life doing it. But first I had to find Ingvar.

All the while, Serakh keep us well supplied with leavened bread, spicy dips, caviar and sweet cha. What we didn't notice was that Rat had slipped away as well.

It was well after dark when we were brought out of our literatic revelry by a loud and persistent hammering on the shop's door. When Simantov opened it Haldor stood there, hands on his hips, and said, "I was beginning to wonder if you were still in this shop or if the Black Scorpions had already got you."

Standing aside to let Haldor in, Simantov demanded, "What do you know about the Black Scorpions?", a sudden harshness appearing in his voice, in stark contrast to the joke he had made earlier.

"Well, we saw one watching us at Kerch before we departed," I said. "Ibn here knows of them and gave us a briefing on what signs to look for."

"Oh my, oh my. I fear that you are marked men."

"Why?" I asked. "We have done them no harm!"

"It's not what you have done to them, it's what Svear Bolgars did to the people of Baku during the raids of 914 and 942. They still carry the grudge. Thousands upon thousands were massacred at Baku, which is just over halfway down the west side of the Kaspian Sea. It is also said to be the headquarters of the Black Scorpions. I fear that because of your ancestry and your openness,

Black Scorpions now know of your journey plans. You will have to be very careful from now on."

With no more to be gained, I said, "Balgichi Simantov, you have been most helpful and generous to us and you have freely given us adequate warning about the Black Scorpions. How much do we owe you for your hospitality and your invaluable information?"

"Ulf Uspakson, you can pay me back by finding the resting place of Ingvar Vittfarne. You see, one of my forefathers joined Ingvar on his journey when he came through here. And then my great grandfather joined Igor on his raid. Neither came back. Near on five years ago, my only son, Pesakh, went in search of them. I have received unconfirmed reports that he fell foul of the Black Scorpions. Find my son and the grave of Ingvar and you will have paid me in full." This was a very real and sobering request from Simantov. We were about to walk out of the shop when we realised that Rat and Serakh were still engrossed in conversation.

"Still working her magic on him, I'm afraid," said Simantov.

"Rat!" I called "It's time to go."

"Coming," Rat replied, without turning.

"Oh, Lord Ulf," called Serakh in her put-on silky voice, "please promise to bring my Rat Slayer back to me. Please?"

"YOUR rat slayer?" Haldor asked incredulously.

Haldor, Simantov, Ibn and I looked at each other with amused expressions on our faces.

Putting on a serious voice, I said, "Of course I will. But first you have to let him go before I can bring him back."

Rat was trying to detach himself, their hands touching and lingering, their eyes locked; both held halfway between eternity and the present.

"RAT!" I snapped.

"Yes, yes, I'm coming," he said, turning and walking to us.

Just as we exited, Serakh rushed forward and pushed a bundle into Rat's hands, kissed him on the cheek, and dashed back inside. As the door was closing Rat strained to have a last look at his newfound love. I gave him a playful shove, started walking down the now dark street, and said, "When we get back you'll have the rest of your lives together. That is, assuming that she doesn't work her magic on some other poor unsuspecting youth while we're away."

"Don't say that! She wouldn't. She couldn't. She'll wait. You'll see," cried the half boy, half man.

I winked at Haldor and said, "Aah, true love, and in only one hour. Now we're going to have a love-struck youth writing reams of poetry about the moon and stars on our boat. Haldor, would you be partial to swapping Rat for Ingvar?"

"Not on your life," he said. "I want the rats skewered. I don't want him thinking of his true love, throwing his knives and missing. I mean, he could hole the boat, or maybe even hole one of us. No, far too dangerous. You keep him."

Ibn joined in the fun and said, "You realise that it could become even worse? In his newfound tenderness he may start to LIKE rats. Can you imagine our boats being overrun with rats? I propose we make him swim behind the boats until he has overcome his infatuation. Besides, it will make the boat lighter — and faster!"

Rat started, "It's not funny. What would you know about being in love? You don't even have a woman or a wife."

Defiant in defence, his outburst cut close to the bone. Haldor placed a firm hand on Rat's shoulder and said in a most authoritative voice, "Don't even think about going any further along that road, dear Rat," and with his hand still stuck firmly on Rat's shoulder, he left it at that. I knew that when the right moment arose, Haldor would fill Rat in. Never could I have asked for such a true friend.

The frivolity gone, I didn't ask what was in the package, but I found out later that it was a traditional white silk towel with the same exquisite embroidery that I had seen on Simatov's skullcap.

Sensing the embarrassment, Ibn quickly changed the subject and said that we were fortunate to get all that information without being charged. He said that the Khazars were re-exporters of foreign goods. As middlemen, inspectors of trade, goldsmiths, and silversmiths, they exacted a minimum ten percent tax on all trade, which is how they made their money. With the exception of caviar and naphtha, the region was not rich in natural minerals, well none that had been found as yet. So just about all raw materials were brought in, reprocessed and sold at a profit. Processed goods were sold on with a straight mark up.

This had been the way of the Jews since they had been evicted from Egypt all those centuries before. To give credit where credit is due, they were extremely good at doing business this way.

That evening we had a feast. This had become a tradition before Viking sea voyages of any kind. The tradition arose out of the knowledge that anything could happen at sea and that every extra ounce of energy could be vital to survival in extreme circumstances. In other words this could be our own last supper, so to speak.

Despite the late hour and despite the tonne of ale we consumed, we finally got to sleep. Ibn had sourced some honey mead and had consumed as many tankards as we had of ale.

The next morning we were up before daybreak, carrying out the final preparations before heading south. As before in Kerch, Ibn sidled over and said, "It's happening again."

"What is?" I asked him

"We are being watched again. I think by the same person."

"Where is he this time?"

"He is pretending to be one of the labourers loading the boat, just three along."

"How did you spot him?"

"First, he was not as active as the others, and I thought I recognised him. He has grown a beard, but it was those boots again. He must be really partial to them. I mean, how many fishermen or labourers have such good boots?"

"He can't have much upstairs."

"No, not too much. But then that's probably why he is on observation duty and not at Scorpion headquarters making important decisions. I wonder how many of his victims have actually come back?"

"Well, maybe this is going to be a first for him."

"Let's hope so."

"I wonder how he got here?" I asked aloud, to no-one in particular.

Ibn provided the answer. "Probably overland from Kerch. If he rode hard, he could have arrived at least a few days ahead of us."

"Makes sense. This way he can confirm his intended victim is in the vicinity, which enables him to set a definite trap."

With that Haldor called his readiness to sail and Big Sven called ours. I gave the order to cast off. On seeing us cast off the Scorpion stood upright and looked straight at us. His mistake. I hefted a battleaxe and stood with folded arms and the axe resting over my shoulder. I looked him straight in the eyes. I think he got my message, as he stopped what he was doing, turned and briskly walked away from the dock.

Once on the Kaspian proper, we took a south-easterly bearing and headed for the mouth of the mighty Oxus, about four hundred and fifty sjømil away.

On the morning of the second day on the Kaspian, we awoke to find we were shrouded in bright mist.

"A good way of hiding," Ibn said.

"Not if your mast can be seen out the top," I replied. "Rat, you're the smallest, up you go and tell me if and when you break through."

Rat shimmied up the mast and at about ten fot, he called down, "I'm through. It's amazing. A whole sea of cloud, like a carpet. I feel as if I could just step out and walk on it."

"Well, don't try!" I called back. "You may be madly in love and may also believe that you can do anything. Believe me when I say you can't. Look right around and tell me where the sun is, and if you see anything else."

"I see the sun, it's over there! Wait — I also can see another mast about two mil away."

This worried me. It could be the Black Scorpions.

"Is the mast moving?"

"Yes, slowly. It's going South."

"Is it ahead of us?"

"Not yet but it soon will be."

"Alright. Note the position of the sun again and come down now."

Haldor's boat was lashed to ours. I called to him and said, "Drop your mast now! They can see us with the masts raised."

Big Sven swiftly organised our crew and the masts were down in record time.

"Now, Rat — where is the sun?"

"There — " he pointed in a direction that was just off the port beam.

"You had better be right, otherwise we will be aground in no time at all."

"Listen up, men," I said. "The other mast may or may not be the Black Scorpions but I'm not willing to take that chance. So until the mist burns off we row and we row quietly. Muffle the oars with cloth. We will try and throw them by rowing due west."

I discussed the situation with Haldor and we decided to sail down the west coast for a day in case the vessel was indeed looking for us and doubled back to find us. We decided to execute a reverse plan on the next day. It would slow us down a bit, but not by much. We would be eating cold meals for the next few days, as a fire — especially at night — could be seen from ten mil away. Smoke could also be smelt at an almost equivalent distance, especially at sea, where there was a smaller variety of smells than on land. So any thought of hot meals was scuppered.

With that the crew got busy. We had quick cold breakfast, muffled the oars and began to row. Three hours later the mist burned off and we found ourselves in the middle of the sea with no land or other vessel in sight.

Once the sun had burned the mist off there was no point in trying to hide. We had a following wind so we reset the masts and hoisted sail. We kept a watch during the day but saw nothing untoward, even with my new spyglass.

That night we hove to just off the west coast and dropped the masts and hunkered down for the night.

In the early hours Big Sven shook me awake and signalled for me to be silent. Once again we had a low mist, but it was lighter than yesterday's. He whispered that he had heard another vessel not far off and they were using muffled oars as well. Knowing that another vessel was not far off was one thing, but one using muffled oars was definitely suspicious. I had done enough sailing with Big Sven to trust what he said without questioning his judgement. We quietly woke the crews of the two boats and prepared for the attack.

I had Haldor relash the boats so that they could be separated at a moment's notice. I also had the men eat something quickly and then lie down and pretend to sleep. Big Sven kept an eye and ear open for the impending attack. We knew it would have to be soon, as the sky was lightening and they would soon be visible. Big Sven lay his sword on the deck and used it to show the direction from which the attack was coming.

We saw and heard them at the same time. Big Sven pretended to be asleep at the tiller. We waited while they drew nearer and nearer. Just then I saw an archer stand up in the bows of the pirate boat with a flaming arrow drawn, ready to fire.

"NOW! HALDOR, NOW!" I cried.

Big Sven tugged on the rope lashing us together, and the men jumped to their oars and started pulling hard. Haldor's boat aimed straight for the starboard side of the pirate while we cut across their bows and circled to the port.

The move surprised them and in the confusion the archer's aim was thrown off by the sudden manoeuvre. I recognised the boat to be a Greek Ousiako Dromon. Because of our manoeuvre, the archers, drawn up along the starboard side of the galley, had to split ranks. I could hear the complaints once the order had been given to have half move to the port side to counter our possible attack. This meant having to carry the cauldrons of hot oil across the deck of a moving ship; a risky business.

I wondered how on this earth they had they managed to get a Greek galley into the Kaspian. It couldn't be sailed in. Porting our boats had been hard enough, but a galley seemed all but impossible? Nevertheless, it was here and it was now.

The deck of the Dromon was crowded with archers and other men milling around, which I took to be boarding parties. A good galley captain would never have allowed so many on deck at this time of an attack. It also meant that we could never hope to board and win a deck battle with our meagre arms and numbers. But if we didn't fight now we would have to fight later.

The galley captain was using a fixed double bank of rowers and I concluded that with so many men on deck he was not intending to disengage his top bank for fighting. Using a double bank would give him more speed and manoeuvrability, but it meant he could engage less men to fight. If this was indeed the case then I gambled that his rowers were all probably slaves. If they were slaves then our best bet was to start the attack from within the galley and use the slaves' hatred for their masters in our favour. The crowded conditions could also work in our favour. All we needed was a few good men to break in and set the slaves free, then mop up the mess afterwards.

On seeing Haldor's charge, the galley's helmsman started to correct his course and steer away from his knarr. But in doing so he steered directly toward my boat. He corrected again and was obviously trying for a central line to give his archers optimum time and angle to set fire to our boats. He was soon receiving the ire of the archers, as the course corrections were upsetting their aim.

Just as we started coming into range, Haldor and I veered away from the Galley, leaving their archers with nothing to aim at. They had to shoot their burning arrows into the sea as the arrows' shafts would soon start to burn as well. Unless extinguished with all haste, burning arrows could have disastrous consequences for the galley.

We then swung in behind the galley and attacked from the stern. This meant the archers had to move their cauldrons of oil to the stern, which bought us time to close in on the galley. It also gave the archers a smaller target to aim at and the crowded conditions at the galley's stern also meant that fewer of them could be brought to bear at one time, thereby reducing our risk of fire and failure. I put a few men in the bows of our boats to fend off the arrows as best they could with their shields. A few arrows started falling amidships but were soon brought under control by Ingvar and Rat. And so we closed on the galley.

As soon as we came under the stern's overhang, Big Sven hurled an axe with a rope attached, which stuck fast in the stern. Hand over hand, he then started drawing us in. One of Haldor's crew executed a similar throw. Our lack of archers was beginning to tell, but I couldn't let that shift my focus just now. If we didn't sort the galley out now, we would have to later. Better it be now with all my men than later with fewer and wounded men.

Big Sven managed to secure another rope in similar fashion, and was soon scrambling up. Instead of going up and onto the aft deck, which would have meant certain death, Big Sven, and those who followed, went in through the officer's living quarters half a deck down. Their objective was to get to the rowing slaves and set them free. Our only hope was their weight of numbers and the pandemonium they could cause. I was also gambling on the slaves not being so emancipated that they would be unable to assist us. But hatred can drive a man to perform amazing feats, even when emancipated. I had seen this when Harald, Haldor and I had attacked the pirates on the Barbary Coast all those years ago and we had set slaves free in a similar manner.

The cramped quarters below decks could also work in our favour, in that fewer of the galley's fighting men could be brought to bear at any one time, and I would not like to be the one to face Big Sven wielding an axe and a sword in a narrow passageway. I concluded that they obviously had had easier pickings in the past and had never considered an internal attack by experienced seamen.

Big Sven had apparently succeeded in his objective, as the galley's oars came to a dead stop and a roar went up from within the ship. The deck officers were screaming commands and pointing all over the place. Some of the archers disappeared from the stern, I assumed to fire on the freed slaves. Then suddenly the decks were awash with slaves taking their own retribution on their former masters. Some officers who were still alive chose to jump ship rather than face a bloody and awful death at the hands of the men they had so obviously maltreated.

Then the action was suddenly over. It had taken less than half an hour, but felt as if a lifetime had passed. A rosy red sun broke over the horizon.

I boarded the Dromon and came across the scene of a massacre. I had hoped to never see one again. The decks were awash with blood. Haldor led me over to the body of the Dromon captain, now a lifeless corpse. The captain's tunic was ripped and his left shoulder exposed. It had the unique black scorpion tattooed onto it, with its curious number. The remaining bodies of the officers and archers had the same. I conferred with Ibn and Haldor and we decided to sew all the Black Scorpion bodies into weighted sacks so that they would sink to the bottom of the Kaspian, never to walk this earth again. I reasoned that while it would be less suspicious for a slave to wash up on the shore of the Kaspian, it would be raise alarm bells if a Black Scorpion were to do so.

I then turned to the remaining slaves. Many had been Viking traders taken captive while trading on the lower Kaspian. Others were Khazars, and some were Rus, Bolgars and even Arabs. All welcomed us with hugs and kisses. I instructed that they be given a decent meal.

I conducted a roll call and we counted seven of our own dead or missing, including Justus Ormsson the Swede. Ingvar Hallsteinsson had sustained a serious abdominal wound and Ibn wasn't hopeful of his survival. Rat had had his right shoulder nicked and burned by an arrow. He assured me that it wouldn't harm his throwing or his aim. Big Sven had a wound to his left forearm, obtained in the close hand-to-hand fighting on the way to free the rowers.

The battle won, I called a mini-council to decide what we should do next. Haldor suggested returning to Hardzhy-Tarkhan with the freed crews. While it was the most logical option, it would also take a great deal of time and I wanted to get proper medical attention to the crews as quickly as possible. Ibn suggested sailing for Gorgan at the south eastern tip of the Kaspian where his eldest brother Malik Shah, proclaimed heir and future Sultan of the Seljuks, was the governor. Ibn assured us that he would guarantee us doctors and treatment. This seemed like our best option.

After their first decent meal in years I informed the freed slaves of our plan to sail for Gorgan, and explained why. I organised them into two shifts so that only half were rowing at one time, leaving the others to enjoy the fresh air and sun on deck.

Big Sven took charge of the knarr while I stayed on board the Dromon.

That first night most slept on the decks under the stars, stars that some hadn't seen for months. Over our meals they informed us that they had been based at the port of Baku, which had become the headquarters for the Black Scorpions, just as Simantov thought. The Scorpions were not liked or wanted in Baku, but no-one dared cross them nor ask them to leave. They had taken over the old Zoroastrian Maiden Tower and there in the seven levels they carried out their warped and perverse practices from the torture of victims to enforced virgin orgies. Baku, they told me, was becoming a ghost town.

On the spur of the moment I asked, "Does anyone know of a Pesakh Simantov?"

There was a shuffling and a thin arm was raised and an even thinner voice said, "I am Pesakh Simantov. Why do you want to know?"

"Because your father sent me to find you."

"My father? Sent you? He is still alive?"

"Oh yes. We were with him but three days hence."

"And my little sister, Serakh?"

"Well, she's not so little anymore. She has already sunk her talons into Rat over there. He thinks he is going to be your brother-in-law someday."

Pesakh Simantov was now in tears, crying tears of joy and relief, his body wracked with sobs as his crewmates consoled him.

There was no point in trying to get more information out of him just now.

"We will talk more later," I promised him and carried on questioning the other freed slaves about the activities of the Black Scorpions.

As we approached Gorgan I suggested we weigh anchor out of sight of land. Ibn was to go in and make contact with his brother. I didn't want his brother paying the price for harbouring the Black Scorpions' boat. Ibn agreed to this and said we were to run up white flags on all our masts. This would signify that we had come in peace and did not intend to invade.

My plan was to ferry the freed slaves to the port and then set fire to the Scorpion Dromon. This way it would seem to have disappeared without a trace.

When the first images of Gorgan appeared in my spyglass, I ordered the boats to heave to. We then transferred all weapons to the second knarr. The last thing I wanted was a misunderstanding and more bloodshed, least of all mine.

When we arrived at the dock, an armed guard was already present. When Ibn was recognised, the demeanour changed from one of threat to one of joyous welcome. We were ushered up to the palace where the brothers, who hadn't seen each other for years, embraced and slapped backs. Ibn gave a quick account of what had happened and his brother started snapping orders in Arabic, and troops began scurrying all about the place. Here was a man used to command. The crew were instructed to row back and commence the ferrying operation, bringing the sickest first. By the time they had all been shipped ashore, the dock resembled a makeshift hospital of the kind I had seen only once before in Byzantium after the city was attacked. Doctors and townspeople all worked together to tend to the wounded. While most only required rest and feeding, some were in failing health and would probably never recover.

Little did we know that this would probably be one of the last times that Europeans and Arabs would work together in harmony to alleviate human suffering. For, within five years the first crusades would start, driving a wedge between the two peoples that would last for centuries to come.

At lunch on the third day the senior doctor gave us a report on the men. "Your Excellency, most men have made a remarkable recovery, with the exception of eleven or so, who will require a while longer."

"How much longer?" asked Malik Shah.

"Sire, with the human body, who can tell? Already some men, who I did not think would be able to walk for weeks, are up and about. I can only surmise that the activity through rowing on the galley has helped keep them strong."

"Either that or you have improved as a doctor. Very well. Thank you for your report."

I picked up the thread. "Your Excellency, will the remaining men be allowed to return to their homelands?"

"Well, why not? They have been unwilling slaves long enough, don't you think?"

"Sire, passage for eighty-five men will cost a great deal, plus the cost of the medicines and feeding them…"

"ENOUGH!" he boomed, raising his right hand. "Lord Ulf, if all men were as honest and honourable as yourself, we would all live in a very pleasant world. The pirate ship has been a thorn in our side for a long while now, and has caused a drop in trade, which has not been good for this part of the empire. Your removal of it will more than pay for all that you have mentioned, and more. No, there will be no cost to you. Let us say that the account has been paid in full."

"Sire, you are very generous. The men will be very pleased when I give them the news."

"What are your plans, Lord Ulf?"

"Sire, we plan on journeying to Bactra, wintering over there and starting afresh in the spring."

"And you, Ibn?"

"My brother, I will go with him. Our fates are intertwined."

"Yes, I see this. This will be good. Before you go I will give you letters of introduction. The Oxus is our northern border in this area. You must be careful. You will require the necessary travel authorities. The letters will also instruct the governor to accommodate you over the winter. You, my brother, and Lords Ulf and Haldor in the Imperial Palace, and your men in the soldiers' quarters. Is this satisfactory?"

"Your Excellency, how could we say no?" I replied.

"Good. Your men—do they speak Arabic?"

"Yes, Highness. Your brother has been instructing them. Plus, the older men learned in Byzantium."

"Ah, even better." He addressed his secretary, "Ibrahim, make it so and bring the letters to me for signing as soon as possible, as these men will want to be away in the morning. Now come, I have some justice to attend to"

We were led onto a balcony overlooking a square, in which hundreds of people were gathered.

Malik Shah explained, "This man has been a constant thorn in my side. He is the son of a fairly wealthy merchant. At twelve he was caught stealing from the poor baskets, so we gave him five lashes. He was caught again within a week, so he was given twelve lashes, one for every loaf of bread he stole. A few months later he was caught stealing, this time jewellery, so I had his little finger cut off. At this point he left Gorgan. On his return here he had a thumb missing. I found out later that he had been caught stealing and punished accordingly. Now he has robbed a widow of her life savings and her daughter of her maidenhood. Although we can't prove the latter was robbery, we can prove the former. So today we will cut off his right hand as the ultimate punishment befitting a thief under Islamic law."

At this point the thief, a man of about twenty-five or so, was led into the square, blindfolded with his hands tied in front of him, and his feet shackled. A large fire was burning, into which a number of metal rods had been thrust.

In the centre of the square stood a man with a large battleaxe. He was using a whetstone to apply a fine edge to the blade.

I asked, "Why his right hand? Is he right handed?"

Ibn chipped in, "Ulf, you were obviously not listening when I was giving instruction on this. In Islamic custom you eat with your right hand and do your, ah, ablutions, with your left. As a result you always greet people with your right hand, never your left. To do so is an insult."

"Ah, I see. So the lack of a right hand means he has to eat with it as well as perform his ablutions. Which makes him, unworthy…?"

"Unworthy, yes. But more importantly, unclean."

"Ah, I begin to see the logic. This sort of punishment wouldn't work in my land, as we don't have the same sense of justice that you do. Although, the lack of a right hand would severely curtail his ability to earn a decent living."

"Yes," the Governor replied. "Ibn has apprised me of your customs.

"Ah, now for the sentence."

The thief's right forearm was tied to a block, just above the wrist, by a soldier, who then stood back very quickly.

Quick as a flash of lightning, and in one fluid action, the axe man stepped up and swung his axe. It bit through the wrist, completely severing it. The scream was gut-wrenching. Even the Governor winced. The axe man then walked over to the fire and took out one of the tongs, which was heated almost to white-hot. He applied the tong to the bloody stub, quarterising it, and the thief screamed again. The Governor winced again.

I could see he was going to be a fair but firm Sultan one day. Here he had given the thief more than one chance to prove himself worthy of a place in his society. The thief obviously did not want this and so was denied his place in society according to their law.

The thief, still writhing and crying in pain, was led away to the city gates to begin his expulsion from society.

Chapter 10

Chorascoia

The Governor had requested that the galley not be seen in the waters around Gorgan. Understandably he was fearful of Black Scorpion reprisals. So Big Sven, Ibn and I, with a few eager volunteers of freed slaves, made one last return journey to the galley. We set fires and sailed back to port. The burning vessel made a spectacular sight, black smoke billowing, against a setting sun.

However, I thought that by now a message would be well on its way to Baku, and I wondered what sort of retribution it would bring. But then I countermanded my thought pattern with one of logic, in that we would be long gone by the time the Black Scorpions had started to perform any acts of retaliation.

Being in an Islamic town, I was hoping that the men would not be able to source any alcohol and let slip our intended destination, for just a few days longer.

I was on a mission to replace the men I had lost by inviting some of the stronger and fitter of the freed men to join us on our mission. I came across Pesakh Simantov at a tavern, drinking sweet Arabic cha. He had already begun to look healthier and was fast losing that gaunt look that all emancipated people have.

"Pesakh, there you are," I said upon finding him.

"Lord Ulf," he greeted. "Yes, you did say we would speak again. I was wondering if that would ever come about, especially as you are leaving tomorrow."

"I hadn't forgotten my promise, Pesakh. The way I see it you have two choices. You can go home, where your father and sister will be more than pleased to see you, or you can come with us and complete your mission."

"When do you leave?"

"Tomorrow, first light."

"You know, Lord Ulf—I've sat here looking at this cup of sweet cha for about an hour now."

The change of subject took me by surprise.

He went on, "It was my favourite drink. Now I can't stomach it. After so many months of a bread, water and bland lamb stew, I can't handle any food or drink with too much spice or flavour. So here I sit trying to decide if I should drink a cup of cha. For if I drink it, I will surely bring it up."

"Well, that's a decision only you can make," I said. "Besides, if you don't drink it your teeth won't rot and turn yellow. Or does it happen the other way 'round?" I said.

He laughed. "Lord Ulf," he said firmly, "I will be there before sunrise."

"Good man. And no more Lord Ulf. Just Ulf, like all my other crew. Alright?"

"Alright—Ulf."

"That's my boy. See you on the dock," I said, slapping him on the shoulder. I wish I hadn't done that, as I could still feel his bony condition under his newfound clothes.

I carried on with my mission.

On departing from Gorgan, we deliberately sailed north and slightly west, so that anyone watching would think we were returning to Hardzhy-Tarkhan. This was only a feint, for as soon as we were over the horizon, we changed course and sailed due east for the mouth of the Uzboi River. On this leg we sailed through some of the debris of the now sunk galleon.

The Uzboi is the overflow from the Sea of Aral, which is fed by the Araxes River and the mighty Oxus River. Ibn told me there was a time, not so long ago, that the Oxus used to flow directly into the Kaspian, but irrigation works had seen it redirected to the Aral Sea to provide water for increased crops and the burgeoning population of Urgench.

The redirection of the Oxus also served as a security measure for the Khorazem rulers of the area. Any invading force would have only the Uzboi channel to use, whereas previously they had used both the Oxus, the Araxes and the Uzboi, and therefore any land-based forces would have had to split in order to defend the land.

At the end of the second day we weighed anchor just off the mouth of the Uzboi in plain sight of land. Although we couldn't make out any movement at all, even with my spyglass, we kept the white flags flying from the mast to indicate our good intentions, should anyone be watching. The following morning we started rowing up the Uzboi, which was low and heavily braided. We made a few bad choices of channel and had to backtrack. At the end of the day we had only made about 20 mil, despite the sluggish current. I recorded it as our worst day's travel so far.

At mid-morning of the second day we saw a group of riders on a distant hill. They stopped and watched us for a short while and then rode away.

In the mid-afternoon a mounted troop galloped across the sandy plain towards us. I ordered the crew to tie up on the east bank.

"Tie up to what?" Big Sven asked. "Which grain of sand would you like me to tie up to?"

"Alright, alright. Less of the funny stuff and let's get the boats beached before those horsemen get here."

"What's the hurry?" Big Sven asked.

"Impression," I told him. "First impressions count for an awful lot in this part of the world."

I watched the dust cloud grow ever closer. I had a few of our trunks stacked near the mast and climbed up. When I judged them to be within visual range, I struck a nonchalant pose, leaning against the mast, all the while watching the horsemen ride in.

They were dressed in clothes of a deep purple colour. Their hats were conical in shape and matched the purple of the dress. They were rimmed with black fur, which had a gold twine twisted through it. The peak of the cone had a gold bauble. Their shirts were baggy and gathered at the waist by a black sash, from which hung curved Arabic sabres. The sleeves were gathered at the wrist in a similar fur to that lining their headgear. The pants, also baggy, were gathered at the ankles with the same fur and gold lining. On getting to the bank, the riders reined in and their leader trotted forward.

"You are the leader," he addressed me in Latin.

"I am," I replied in the same language, still leaning lazily against the mast.

"What is your business here?"

"I am en route to Bactra," I replied.

"What is your business in Bactra?" I was asked.

"To seek lost friends," I told him.

"You require this many men to seek a lost friend?" he asked, his eye falling on Ibn.

"Lost friends," I corrected him. "More than one."

"I heard you," he said.

"Ah, good. I thought your Latin may not be as good as my Greek."

"You speak both?"

"But of course," I told him. "Rus, Norwegian, Danish and Swedish, as well."

"What are these Norweegeean and Sweedeeish?" he asked

"They are the languages of my people. We come from lands to the north and west of Kyiv."

"Ah. I thought there was only snow and ice north of Kyiv."

"It is obvious your education is somewhat lacking." He did not appreciate this remark and pursed his lips. "The land north of Kyiv has as much forest as there is sand here."

He turned to his men and spoke to them in Arabic "Hah! He expects us to believe that. More forest than there is sand in Arabia!" He laughed again.

I continued in Latin, "I don't expect you to believe anything and everything I tell you. But would you believe it if Ibn Rashid al-Arslan told you?"

"Yes…" he started replying in Arabic, and then realised that I had addressed his comment, but in Latin not Arabic. This realisation obviously caused him to miss my comment about Ibn's royal heritage.

He said, "You didn't tell me you spoke Arabic."

"You didn't ask," I snapped back.

"Where did you learn Arabic?"

"When I was chief lieutenant to the general of the Varangian Guard in Byzantium, oh, sometime between about fifteen or twenty years ago," I told him.

His face darkened as soon as I mentioned the Varangian Guard. Straightaway he asked a question I knew to be rhetorical, "You were at Jerusalem?"

"And you were inside the walls," I replied.

"Yes," he said. A range of emotions showed on his face. He obviously wanted revenge for the siege of Jerusalem, but we were also under a white flag and he dared not harm us. One of his men trotted forward and whispered in his ear. The leader's head snapped around. "You have His Highness, Ibn Rashid al-Arslan with you?" he asked, wide-eyed.

"Yes, I've just said so. Don't you hear anything I say?"

"I am here," Ibn replied, stepping forward, before the troop leader could reply and the situation could worsen.

"A thousand pardons, Your Highness," he said, bowing from his waist while still in his saddle. His men did likewise. "I did not recognise you."

"It would seem that not only are you blind but that you also hear only that which you want to hear. What is your name?" Ibn demanded with a timbre in his voice we had never before heard.

"A thousand, thousand pardons, Highness. Please forgive me. I am Suwayd al-Khawalani, Captain in His Imperial Highness Sultan Alp Arslan's Northern Army, Border Guards." The tribute was growing.

Now that the decision on whether or not to let us travel any further was a foregone conclusion, al-Khawalani said, "Safwhan here will be your pilot to

Kunya Urgench. He will guide you through the river. We will ride ahead and prepare for your arrival."

"Captain," Ibn said, "you may ride ahead but you may not warn of my arrival. You will tell your masters of the two boats of Varangians, but not of me. Understood?"

"Yes, Highness. But may I ask why?"

"My brother Malik Shah, the Governor of Gorgan and the Northern Provinces, the future Sultan, has asked me to conduct an inspection of Kunya Urgench. What better way to see things than as they really are? Do you understand?"

"Yes, Highness."

"Do your men understand?"

"They will, Highness."

"Very well. You may proceed."

They reined their horses around and rode off in the direction of Urgench.

Safwhan was a fine pilot. He did not take any wrong channels and we made good time. He told me that they often purposely silted the channels and dug new ones so that any regular visitors would not be able to sell information on the channels to any enemy of the state, thereby making an invasion harder.

We continued up the Uzboi and into the Saka Tigrakhauda, a small lake formed in a depression on the Uzboi, where we stopped for the night. The following day, with the Aral Sea in sight, we took a wide channel to the north, which cut across the delta and took us straight into the Oxus without entering the sea. I could now see why Ibn and others had called it the mighty Oxus; it was comparable in size to the Dniepr, Volga and the Nile, and must surely rank as one of the great rivers of the world. To have such a river in such a dry and arid land must be regarded as a godsend. I could see why the river was worshipped in ancient times as the giver of life. The desert sand was not lifeless at all. Add water and you could grow almost anything, which is what was being done here, much like the Egyptians and the Nile.

About five mil before Kunya Urgench we came across the deserted ruins of a massive fortress and temple on the left bank of the river. I roughly calculated its base to be about one thousand eight hundred fot. I wondered aloud what it could have been. Safwhan answered my question.

"It is the remains of Toprak Kala. A mighty fortress-city of ancient times, it was the capital city in this area. The Khorezm architects placed the city in an ideal situation and built a city so strong and magnificent that its walls were never breached. It was part of the Achaemenid Empire before the time of Mohammed and before your Christ. It was ruled by Darius the Great after he subdued Chorasmia almost two thousand years ago. It later regained its independence but was subdued again about eight hundred years ago by the Kushans and then later taken over by the Hephthalites."

"The who?" I interjected. I had heard of and read about the Kushans and Darius the Great, but not this last lot.

"The Hephthalites, also known as the White Huns. A race of fair-skinned people who ruled Sogdiana, Bactra, Chorasmia, Sassania, including Merv and Heart. They expanded eastwards into the Tarum basin and had some conquests there before they invaded, conquered and ruled northern Cush as well. They were eventually defeated by a combined Persian and Turkic army."

"Well, I never—a race of white-skinned people in Asia. Who would have thought it? Please forgive me—do go on."

"Then in about 710AD the area was attacked by the Arab general Kutejba. When the invaders realised that they would never breach the walls, they damaged the irrigation systems beyond repair, thereby forcing the city into submission. However the irrigation system was never successfully repaired, and the city had to be abandoned. In time a new settlement at Kunya Urgench sprang up, and over time Toprak Kala was left to be reclaimed by the desert."

"A sad story for such a mighty city. How come you know so much about it?" I asked.

"This river is my home, no matter who rules here. The story of Toprak Kala was taught as a fairy tale when I was a youth and then given as a lesson in strategy and preparedness when I did my military service."

"Still, a sad ending for such a magnificent place."

We rowed up to Kunya Urgench, the seat of the old Arab Emirs, expecting the captain to have let slip that a royal personage was aboard one of our vessels, but were surprised to find that he had not. We tied up and Ibn produced our "papers", which we had had "approved" at Gorgan.

I let Ibn do the talking, preferring to let the port official believe that we were ignorant and unable to speak Arabic. After the papers had been inspected and found to be in order, Safwhan was permitted to return to his unit. As he departed he caught my eye and gave me a knowing wink. I returned the compliment.

Ibn, with Haldor and me in tow, went through the routine of haggling for accommodation with the dock-side tavern keepers. He explained that we would have to sleep with the general populace for at least a day or two while he went on a cursory inspection of the city. This was something only he could do, as the appearance of Vikings in certain parts of the town would be certain to raise suspicions, something he was keen to avoid for the meantime.

While Ibn was off inspecting the city, Haldor, Pesakh and I asked at the port official's office in broken Arabic how we could find out if Ingvar Vittfarne had ever come through Urgench. The port official was sceptical but said to try the Hall of Records in the administration building in the town centre. On arrival at the Hall of Records, we approached the guard at the door who, when he eventually understood what we were after, called a clerk.

The clerk was a short wiry little fellow dressed in traditional Arab garb. On hearing us out, once again through our pretend broken Arabic, he sucked in a breath through pursed lips and said in perfect Latin, "You will have to submit your request in writing, and it must be in Arabic. Come back in a few weeks and we may have something for you."

"A few weeks!" I exclaimed. "We need to be firmly ensconced in Bactra for the winter by then."

"I'm sorry, Efendi. But those are the rules. I don't make them, I only apply them."

"What if I said you were to have the information for me before first prayers on Saturday?"

"Impossible," he said.

"Oh," I replied, with my left eyebrow raised, "We'll see about that! What is your name?" I asked. He started to answer then thought better of it, at which point he turned and walked away with a dismissive gesture, muttering under his breath about mad Varangians. I later related the story to Ibn, who said nothing and only nodded.

Two days later, with Ibn's inspection complete, Haldor, Ibn and I walked up to the palace gates and Ibn declared his real identity. The guard guffawed. Fortunately Captain al-Khawalani had seen us approaching and came out to meet us.

"Welcome, Your Highness. May I escort you to the Governor's chambers?"

The look of disbelief and awe on the guard's face was indescribable.

"Yes, please lead the way," Ibn said, giving the guard a look that could have turned wood to stone. His royal training was now beginning to show through. We were impressed.

al-Khawalani said, "I have taken the precaution of sending Safwhan ahead to give warning of your arrival. The Governor will have at least, oh, five minutes to prepare."

We all laughed. al-Khawalani was truly entering into the spirit of our journey.

Not waiting to be announced, Ibn burst straight into the Governor's office with Haldor, al-Khawalani and myself in tow. The Governor was struggling to get into his robes, as were a few young women.

In a very level voice Ibn said, "It would seem that the reports my brother were receiving about you were correct. Not so?"

"Yes, Your Highness. A thousand pardons, sire. It will never happen again."

He fixed a steely glare on the Governor, "You are correct. It won't happen again. You will have your personal belongings packed and you will be out of this town by sunset."

"But, sire. There is no way to obtain…"

"SILENCE! If you're lucky you will be spared by the elements, but not if my father finds out. If I were you I would rather risk the elements than my father's wrath. And, if I had my way you wouldn't be allowed to risk either! How can you permit such personal laxity in a frontier town? If you can't guard against your own weaknesses, how do you expect to guard the borders of the Empire? The battlements of the city are crumbling in places, some of the guards are drunk and prostitution is rife in the garrison."

The now ex-Governor tried to start speaking again.

"SILENCE! Not another word. Guards, escort this piece of filth out of the city!"

With that the ex-Governor was dragged out of the room.

"Well, I'm glad that over," said Ibn, obviously relieved.

"Me too," Haldor said. "Remind me never to get on your bad side."

Ibn laughed. "I sometimes surprise myself. Did you see his knees trembling? It was all I could do to stop laughing. But no, he had to go."

"You're quite right," I said. "Neither Harald nor Yaroslav would have tolerated such laxity. You were quite right in dismissing him. I sometimes wonder if shame is not a more appropriate sentence than death."

"Spoken like a true Arab," said Ibn. "Now, I will have to ask you to go on to Bactra without me, while I wait for the replacement governor. I will join you as soon as I can."

"I thought you may handle it this way," I said. "Can we take Safwhan with us as a pilot for the remainder of the journey up the Oxus?"

Ibn was about to answer when al-Khawalani interjected, "A thousand pardons for interrupting, Highness."

We all turned and looked at him.

"My troop and I would be honoured to escort Lord Ulf and the Varangians to Bactra."

Ibn sat for a while in thought, and then said, "It would seem that I am about to lose one of my most effective troops to the search for Ingvar Vittfarne."

Suwayd al-Khawalani was beaming from ear to ear at the compliment.

"Captain al-Khawalani, you and half your men will remain here with me. The other half, and the pilot Safwhan, will go with Lord Uspakson to Bactra. Once the replacement governor arrives, you will escort me to Bactra."

I said to al-Khawalani, "This is when you are supposed to beg His Highness to excuse you so that you can go and inform your men of their impending journey."

Flustered, al-Khawalani began, "Of course, of course — a..."

"Yes, yes, I know — a thousand pardons. Away with you."

We all roared with laughter.

"Oh and before you disappear, al-Khawalani, inform the garrison commander that I would like to see him, at his earliest convenience, of course."

Bowing and bobbing al-Khawalani backed away then almost ran out of the chamber, which made us laugh even harder.

When some semblance of order had returned, Ibn said, "Right, now for the next order of business. Guard! Get me the records clerk."

The word had obviously got out that a new broom was sweeping clean the governor's palace. The records clerk entered the chamber bowing and scraping. His nervousness becoming more apparent when he saw Haldor and me standing beside Ibn.

"Ah, the records clerk. What is your name?" Ibn asked.

"I am Hurmuz al-Ukbari Your Highness."

"Well, al-Ukbari, you have met these two gentlemen." Not giving the clerk time to confirm nor deny, Ibn continued, "They have a request for information. I will expect you to have the information they require before they leave tomorrow for Bactra. Understood?"

"Yes, Your Highness," al-Ukbari said. His look of resentment and near hatred wasn't disguised in any way at all.

When he had gone I said, "I think we've made an enemy."

Ibn agreed, "Yes. We'll have to watch that one — closely."

Chapter 11

BACTRA the BEAUTIFUL

At least the Oxus was deeper than the Uzboi and was in places canalised. I was not sure that we really needed Safwhan as our pilot. Although, he did once or twice place a hand on my arm and point in the direction we should be taking. The river was swifter than the Lovat and the Tuoni, and made rowing all the harder. Where we could we hugged the banks and the slower flowing water, the midstream current being too swift to row against for any extended length of time.

Here we were rowing through the ancient land of the Parthians and Sasanians, those magnificent empires that had ruled this area for centuries. It was disappointing to see that the land of the Parthians was really nothing more than scrub and desert. From the accounts of history I had imagined rich lands with rolling plains of wheat and groves of fruit trees. But no, it was just sand and rock.

Midway through the short journey to Bactra, we smelt the fabled city of Bukhara wafting westwards across the plain. Safwhan said it was about fifty mil east of our current position.

A few days later we rowed up to the port area of Bactra. Safwhan muttered the phrase, "*Bakhdhim Sriram eredhvo drofsham*", which he translated for us as *Bactra the Beautiful with banners flying*, and flying they were. Like Kunya Urgench, the city was located on the Oxus River, and was awash with colour. The white and cream hues of the buildings were accentuated by the late summer sun. The multitude of colourful banners flying from the many buildings and poles added vibrant splashes of colour to the whole spectacle. And all this against the backdrop of the magnificent snow-capped Hindu Kush mountains. I could see why the Arabs called Bactra the "Mother of Cities". It was truly a magnificent setting.

The wide alluvial plain surrounding Bactra had an intricate irrigation system. Probably along the same lines as the ancient, but now deserted, Toprak Kala. Safwhan informed me that the water was channelled through a system of underground channels, which he called qanats. He said that some of the qanats were large enough for a man to walk through. These qanats were covered over to prevent evaporation in the heat of summer and freezing in the cold of winter. I had thought the Romans were good engineers; these feats of engineering impressed me even more so.

This system obviously worked well, for the river plain was green with crops and the trees were laden with the fruit of late summer, and the rivers, like the Dniepr, were teeming with fish. This city had no need for food imports. If Toprak Kala had been anything like this, then I could see why kings and sultans would have looked upon it with envy.

Safwhan informed me that trees growing pistachio nut trees and mulberries grew wild here, as did wild carrots. This, with the plentiful fish, meant that even the poor need not go hungry in Bactra.

Scattered throughout the mountains were mines that produced gold, silver and lapis lazuli. Gold and silver tiles were supplied to the temple of the goddess Ananita at Ecbatana, where teenage girls prostituted themselves in her honour. I couldn't but help compare this with the virgin rapes that the Black Scorpions enforced on young girls in Baku. I thought it strange how values can differ so widely even over relatively short distances.

Upon tying up at the dock a port official came toward us. I noted an altogether more relaxed approach to security here. I mentioned this to Safwhan, who said, "Yes it is. The main checkpoint is Kunya Urgench. If you can get past that, then you're either security cleared or you've succeeded in subduing Kunya Urgench, in which case there's no point in trying to resist. Anyway, we're only two boats and our approach would have been seen from a distance away. They would also have seen members of the border guard on both boats, which would have allayed their fears."

Safwhan greeted the official and gave him our papers. The official read the papers, with many glances from the papers to me and back again. He asked Safwhan for confirmation of the orders. Safwahn said to him,

"Why don't you ask him yourself?"

"Does he speak Arabic?" the official asked.

"I most certainly do," I said rather firmly. This was beginning to become a ritual every time we made port. While initially fun, it was beginning to become tiresome.

"Lord Oos-park-sun," the official said, battling over my surname, "I do beg your forgiveness. My name is Mustapha al-Jaziri, Port Captain of Bactra. It's just that the last time we had people of your, ah, kind here, they did not speak any Arabic, which caused all sorts of problems and, ah, misunderstandings. Once again, my apologies."

"You have had Norwegians here?" I asked him. "When?"

"Nor-wee-geeans? No, no. They called themselves, now let me think, Swa, Swae?"

"Svear," I offered.

"That's it! Sweer."

"Svear," I corrected him. "More accent on the second syllable. When was this?" I asked, my interest now sparked.

"Oh, a few years ago. They caused a ruckus right here where we are standing now. A misunderstanding over port fees. They were requested not to return."

"I see," I said. My earlier hope that it may have happened earlier and possibly been Ingvar faded fast.

"You were hoping that it may have been something or someone else?"

"Yes I was. But he was here a long time ago," I said.

"Well. You will have to visit the records office. Despite the changes in rule here over the past few hundred years or so, the records office has remained, for the most part, remarkably intact."

"Oh, good. Well, you raise my hopes. Unfortunately the records clerk in Kunya Urgench was not so helpful."

"Ah, so you've crossed swords with Hurmuz al-Ukbari."

"You know him?"

"Most certainly we do. He was the Head of Records here in Bactra but was caught selling information to rival political factions in the city. This is not unusual for records clerks to do to supplement their income. So long as it's to

Arabs and not the enemy. But he was playing both sides against each other and was eventually caught. Unusually he was given the choice: demotion or loss of a hand for theft. He chose demotion. In his case it may have been better to lose a hand. Alas! I fear I have kept you here on the doc with idle chatter when I should have been escorting you to the Governor. Come, we must make haste."

Our boats were attracting an audience, only because these were probably only the second and third Viking knarrs ever to be seen in Bactra. I set a combined guard of my men and the border guards. While my men could do the job more than adequately, the border guards gave legitimacy to any action of defence, should it be required.

Governor Abu Bakir greeted us with all the formality he could muster. He was so attentive that it was overwhelming. I hoped Ibn would get here within a few days or I thought I would go mad. Haldor and I weren't sure if the servants who were assigned to us and trailed us everywhere were genuine servants or spies. Nevertheless we used them to find our way around the city. After a day or two of viewing the sights, we got down to the business of searching the archives for any mention of Ingvar. We found a few oblique references to Ingvar having been in Bactra, which was more a record of his arrival, a short description of his personage, and of his departure towards the east and the Kaxgar oasis. Thereafter there was no further mention of him. Disappointing, but nevertheless we had a confirmed record of him having been in Bactra and we knew in what direction he had travelled.

With our formal research activity over, we concentrated on getting the boats out of the water and prepared for winter storage. We noted that the local boats were coated with a black tar-like substance. Mustapha informed us that it could be found locally and that it seeped out of fissures in the rock and in some places bubbled out of the ground. They had found it to be an excellent sealant and he recommended we use it to waterproof the boats.

So the boats were unpacked, and we began to prepare them for a winter of storage. The governor was appalled when he found out that I was intending to tar the boats alongside my men. I informed him it was our way and that if I did not I would lose the confidence of my men. This really intrigued him for his men would lose his confidence in him if he did as I was intending to do. However he laid on soap, hot water and towels for us so that at the end of every day's work, we could scrub ourselves clean before dining with him in the palace.

Haldor and I were given silk towels, much like Rat's personal gift from Serakh.

109

While Rat was over his mooning phase, it was clear he was still madly in love with Serakh and his eventual return to her had become his primary objective.

We became firmly ensconced in our winter quarters. We had to ask Mustapha if it was custom that we had to dine with the Governor every evening, for it would make a change to go down to one of the taverns and dine and be merry with the crew. But it was not to be.

A letter arrived from Ibn, delivered personally by Safwhan, informing us that the new governor had arrived in Kunya Urgench and that he would be departing for Bactra early the next week after completing the handover.

Now that the boats were tarred and dry-docked for winter we had run out of things to do, as it had been done sooner than I expected. I had purchased some jewellery with mainly lapis lazuli stone inlaid. I thought that a combination of lapis and amber would make for very attractive jewellery. The Governor, seeing my purchases and sensing our boredom, suggested we visit some of the mines before they closed for the winter. We agreed to this and he began to make the arrangements for us.

In my conversations with Mustapha, I found out that the Bactran winters were short, and I mentioned that if this were the case then I hoped to be off again in late February. This was advised against as, while the winters in Bactra were short, they were not as short in the eastern Ferghana Valley, nor on the south side of the Tien Shan mountains. The first caravans only left the Kashgar oasis in late March, and even then at some risk to themselves, for it was not uncommon for blizzards to blow through the region at this time. I was told many a caravan had been found in late spring fallen where they had frozen.

I asked Governor Bakir to assign someone from his border guards cavalry to assist with the purchase of horses for our journey east. At first he wouldn't hear of it and wanted to give us horses from the royal stable. I said I couldn't possibly permit this as it was a personal quest and shouldn't be underwritten by Sultan Alp Arslan, even if his son were on the mission with us. Then Ibn arrived and settled the matter. He, Haldor and I would be given mounts from the royal stable and we would buy the balance for the crew. Governor Bakir would assign someone from the cavalry to help us choose the best horses for our journey. I was informed that the Bactrian horses were of a breed to be desired. The Han Chinese Emperor Wudi sent his armies West in the first century AD to obtain the Heavenly Horses of Bactria for his cavalry. I was also led to believe that the worst Bactrian horse was still better than best

Khazarian or Arabian stallion. A proud boast indeed, for it was obvious they had not seen and fought against the massive Saxon shire horses. I tried to explain how big a shire horse is to the officer assigned to help us source our horses. Either he couldn't comprehend their enormity or simply didn't believe a horse could be that big. However, having our own horses to train over the winter would allow us to refresh our riding and equine care skills. It would also give us a level of mobility we previously did not have.

Chapter 12

ENTOMBED

A week or so later Governor Bakir advised that a visit to a lapis lazuli mine had been arranged. The beautiful blue gemstone had held a fascination for kings and queens down the centuries. The Egyptians used it for the eyes of their pharaohs' statues and their women used the powder form mixed with water and gum as facial makeup to cover their eyelids. They also carved it into the shape of an eye and set it in gold and used it as a focus during meditation. Mystics believed it would eliminate old and negative spirits and would project thoughts or emotions. Doctors in some countries used them as healing stones and in Cush they were used to create mantras. And here we were, in the land of its origin, about to see how they were released from the clutches of mother earth.

We were told to wear warm clothing for the mine was high in the mountains.

We left Bactra at mid-morning and took the road towards Charikar, crossing the Bactria River, heading directly east towards the Hindu Kush. This was an ideal opportunity for the men to get used to their mounts and vice versa. Not only that, it would also help toughen up their rears and thighs for the long rides ahead. There's nothing worse than being saddle-sore from a day's riding and having to mount up again the next day for another day's riding. Those first few days feel as if they will never end.

In mid-morning we bypassed the town of Mazar-e Sarif and stopped at Tašqorgăn for lunch. At first the going was easy, and then we turned off the main track and began to climb off the plain. We entered a long valley, which, while fairly wide at the mouth, narrowed considerably as we progressed. A stream gurgled and bubbled its way along the valley floor. The track was then reduced to a path, precariously stuck hard against the valley wall, the centre ground held by the stream. Now the strength of the Bactrian horses began to show through. Sure-footed they walked on up the path carrying us as if they had been born to it, which of course they had. We had to dismount to negotiate our way around a pack-train of horses loaded with raw lapis lazuli coming down the track, destined for the jewellers of Bactra, Bukhara and Maracanda, where they would be processed before being shipped to the far corners of the world.

The mine was incredibly high in the mountains and I wondered what logic would have driven a man to come up this high, bleak valley looking for the gemstone. The answer could only have been one of two things, necessity or greed. Even though we had done a fair deal of exercise, we were noticeably short of breath. At first I thought this was from the cold, but Ibn informed me that it was the altitude.

We arrived at the mine in the late afternoon and the mine owner was on hand with a welcoming committee to greet us. He was a large man with an even larger toothy smile. I thought he smiled a little too easy. Too many thieves have given themselves away by only smiling with their mouths. The ultimate betrayal is done with their eyes.

Haldor must have been thinking the same, for he caught my eye and a knowing look passed between us.

"Welcome, Your Highness," he said, bowing to Ibn and touching his heart, his lips, and his head in the traditional Arabic greeting. He continued, "Welcome, Lord Uspakson and Lord Haldor," bowing towards us, "and welcome men of the North."

"I am Sulaym al-Marhani. Welcome to Orlameš Mine, one of the oldest mines in Bactria. We have been mining lapis lazuli here for over a thousand years."

"And you've been here all this time?" teased Ibn.

"No, no, Your Highness. Ah, I see you jest." His smile grew even toothier and wider.

"Yes I do, but can we have the speeches inside? I do not jest about the cold, especially with the sun about to sink below the line of the hills."

"Of course, sire. How thoughtless of me. Yes, please do come inside." The smile had never left his face. The horses were led away by a stable boy.

It was incredibly cold, and few of the men, who thought that they had experienced the coldest weather on earth while sailing on the Nord Seë, found themselves borrowing clothing from the mine store.

Being so remote the mine had to be a home away from home for the mine staff. It had its own stables, administration block and living quarters. On entering the administration block, al-Marhani ordered a round of the sweet, hot cha that the Arabs are so fond of. It couldn't arrive quickly enough, for my extremities were frozen. Over tea al-Marhani asked if we wanted a quick tour or if we would like to wait until the next day. We chose the latter.

Dinner consisted of a specially prepared lamb stew with added spices, served on a bed of saffron-flavoured rice. During the meal the miners entertained us with song, dance, comedy and drama; not at all dissimilar to life in Nidaros or Opslo during winter. It all made for a very entertaining evening, with much laughter and joviality shown by all. All the while Sulaym al-Marhani smiled.

At the end of the evening we were shown into a gallery, which contained many pieces of polished and carved lapis lazuli. While interred so far away from civilisation, the miners were permitted to select a piece of lapis lazuli, within reason, and could work on it over the months in the evenings. This ensured that pilfering was kept to a minimum and that the miners were kept busy. The final product was theirs, which could be sold or kept as a gift. Invariably they were sold on to augment their meagre earnings. The quantity and quality of the carvings were amazing. There was everything from intricately carved horses, busts, polished eggs of all sizes, ceremonial daggers, and even a rendition of the Alexander's Frisian knot.

At the end of the evening we were given a last round of sweet cha and our good health was toasted yet again. I suddenly felt inexplicably tired. al-Marhani assured me that it was the effects of the altitude and that rest was advised. He assured us that we would feel fine in the morning. Too tired to argue, we were shown to our quarters.

In the morning I awoke; cold, damp, in the dark and covered in dust. I fumbled around and Ibn's voice came out of the dark

"It would seem that the warnings we had about the Black Scorpions were correct. They will not stop until we are dead."

Not having fully awoken, I replied with a grunt. "Huh? Come again?"

"We are entombed in a cave of sorts."

"Entombed? I don't like the sound of that word."

"Neither do I. But nonetheless we are entombed."

Haldor began to stir.

"Why didn't you wake me earlier?" I asked.

"I tried but you were still unconscious."

"Must have been in the last round of tea last night."

"I agree. I have come to that conclusion myself."

"Are we all here?"

"No, there are just eight of us."

"Who?" I asked, my eyes slowly becoming accustomed to the dark. I began to make out various shapes—some still prone, one or two propped up on an elbow, lying silently listening to our exchange.

"You, me, Haldor, Big Sven, Rat, Pesakh Simantov, Knut Ormsson and Larz Völundarson."

"Why us?" I wondered out loud.

"Because we are the leaders," Ibn replied. "Remove us and the rest are, in reality, just followers."

"Yes, I suppose so. Stupid question, really." Now fully awake I asked, "Alright, just how do we get out of here?"

"I have been examining the ground. I believe the front of the cave to be this way," Ibn said, pointing at a wall of fallen debris, "and the back to be that way," pointing in the opposite direction.

"Why?" Haldor asked.

"Because the ground is more trampled at that end, and less so at the other."

"Alright, supposing your logic is correct. If we try and tunnel our way out, they'll more than likely be waiting for us, and our tunnelling will be in vain. Agree?"

"Agreed," chorused Ibn and Haldor. The others, now awake, listened in silence.

"Alright then. Our way out is via that pile of fallen debris behind us."

"How do we know if the fall at the rear is not a collapsed rock face?" asked Knut.

"We don't," I replied. "But if we tunnel out the other way, and do make it out, our efforts will have been in vain, for we have to conclude that we didn't get here by ourselves." The message went home.

"Also, consider this. If they were mining a rock face with potential returns, and it had caved in, it would more than likely be cleared. No, I think this is a caved-in tunnel to an area that's been mined out.

"Alright, let's start moving rock. I suggest we start about two thirds of the way up the right, so as not to take from the top nor from the bottom. We'll take turns in being the front man. No point in all of us being at the front, we may cause a greater cave in. I'll go first. The rest of you form a chain to help clear the debris I clear."

And so we started.

Not being able to judge the time of day made it difficult to know just how long we had been at it. We had shifted a great deal of rock and sand and had come across a massive rock blocking the path we were clearing. It was also beginning to get hot and stuffy. I then changed our plan of action and divided us into two teams, one working each side of the stone. I reasoned that this would double our chances of escape. Our exertions had begun to warm us up. As I worked, I began to think out loud. "Was Governor Bakir in on it, I wonder?"

Ibn replied from the other side, "We will have to assume so."

"Why?" I asked.

"Because, why did it take so long to arrange a visit to a mine?" Haldor chipped in.

"True," I said.

"But is he a Scorpion or is he under their control, being blackmailed by them?"

"Either way, one is as bad as the other," Ibn said.

"True," I repeated.

It was beginning to become even more stuffy in the enclosure.

"We've been at it a while. Let's take a rest," I suggested.

Rat, being the youngest of us all, continued to work the left flank of the stone with Big Sven, while we rested. My head began to throb with an ache I had never experienced before. The last time I felt this bad was as a boy when Haldor had bested me with a wooden practice sword and whacked me on the head. My head was sore for days, not to mention the lump.

I closed my eyes to ease the pain.

I awoke to find my face being slapped by Rat.

"Wake up, Ulf. Wake up. I've broken through."

"Huh?" I replied, still groggy. "Oh! Good. How long have I been asleep?"

"I don't know. Maybe a few hours, it's hard to tell. Just about everyone else is as well. Only Big Sven and I managed to stay awake and that was hard. Anyway, we broke through a while ago. I have never smelt air so fresh and so sweet."

I stumbled over to the gap and sucked in a breath of fresh, sweet icy cold air. Rat was right—never before had a breath of air smelt so good. I still had a splitting headache.

As Big Sven, Rat and I worked the hole grew ever wider. Life-giving fresh air began to flow freely into our cave and the others slowly began to come around and join in. Like me, all complained of headaches. Curious, I thought, we all have the same symptoms. Why did it not affect Big Sven and Rat in the same way?

About halfway through the excavation we came across the skeleton. The rotten cloth wrapping crumbled at a touch. After what seemed an age we finally had an opening large enough for us, or should I say Big Sven, to fit through. Rat was going to go first, but Big Sven held him back, and went through first himself. A few moments later a muffled voice called through the opening that it was safe to come through. Rat went next, followed by Haldor, Larz, Ibn, Knut, Pesakh and finally myself.

When I scrambled through, what we found shocked us. There were about thirty or forty skeletons, draped in working clothes, lying about the place. Most were neatly lined up against the cavern wall, others were in various postures.

"These were the first to go," said Haldor, pointing at the neat rows of skeletons. "And those few over there the last."

It was clear that they had been trapped when the large rock had fallen. They had obviously tried digging their way out, and it was their efforts on the far side of the fall that had enabled our breakthrough, for more had been dug out this side than the other.

What was sinister was that there was no evidence of an effort to dig them out from the outside.

The breeze was decidedly cool. "Well, they didn't die from a lack of fresh air," I said. "They must have starved to death. What surprises me is that there is no evidence of cannibalism."

"Cannibalism in Muslims? Never!" said Ibn. "But how can you tell?"

"No scattered bones. They're all complete skeletons." I had seen the results of cannibalism in North Africa. "Now, cast around and see what you can find. Maybe we will be able to make some torches. I don't fancy fumbling and stumbling my way through here in the dark."

We all got to work. Pesakh and Rat found half a container of naphtha. Ibn and Larz ripped the old clothing into strips, dipped them in the naphtha and wrapped the strips around shovel handles. All we needed was a spark to light the makeshift torches. Ibn and Larz continued to search the skeletal miners for flints but found none. The rest of us crawled around on our hands and knees searching the ground for flint. I instructed them not to discard any stones, but to pile all candidates in the middle of the area. After a while we set about striking the stones, looking for that telltale spark. We had just about exhausted the pile when Pesakh leaned back and exclaimed, "Ow! Curses — that was sharp. I think I've cut myself. Ow!" he said, sucking his hand.

At first we did not register the significance of Pesakh's outburst. Then as the realisation dawned, Haldor, Ibn and I stopped our efforts and our heads rose in unison and we all three exclaimed, "FLINT!" and scrambled over to where Pesakh was sitting sucking his bleeding hand.

"Show us where your hand was when you cut it, Pesakh," I instructed him.

"Why, just here," he said, pointing to the spot.

We dug around and Haldor prised a sharp rock from the wall of the cavern. Using an iron shovel he struck the rock against it. The sudden spark was blinding, and left us with hues of colours and spots in front of our eyes.

"Rat, Sven, Larz, bring the torches over here. How many do we have?"

"Eight," said Sven. "One each."

"Good. We'll only light two at a time, and keep the rest in reserve, for we don't know how long we will be down here."

Haldor struck the flint a few more times before we managed to get the first torch lit. Lighting the second was a lot easier.

What we saw was a large cavern with a tunnel sloping downwards. What was amazing was that the seams of lapis lazuli were evident all around us. The area hadn't been mined out. The miners had been sealed in here and no attempt had been made to rescue them. This was becoming more and more sinister all the time.

"Well, no point in standing around here," I said. "Let's get going."

We trudged off down the incline. Big Sven's stomach rumbled and we all laughed, only too aware of the hunger pains that were now beginning to reach out from our bellies.

The tunnel carried on down, twisting and turning. In some places we went up short inclines, but in the main we continued downwards. In some places we crossed rivulets of water that ran out of the rock on one side of the tunnel, and back into it on the other.

"Looks less like a mine and more like an access tunnel," said Haldor. "Rather like the caves at Korsun."

119

"Yes. I was trying to think what they reminded me of," I said.

In some places we crossed bare rock worn smooth by feet in times past, which was further evidence that this tunnel had been well used. In other places we trudged through thick powder-like soil, which raised clouds of dust, making most of us cough. We trudged on, stopping every now and then to drink from the underground streams whenever someone was thirsty. Sweat dropped into my eye, stinging as it did so. The further we descended the warmer it was becoming.

Just when I thought we must surely be approaching the centre of the earth, the tunnel levelled off and then started sloping upwards. I took this as a good sign.

"Ah, good," I commented to no one in particular. "I thought that if we descended any further we'd end up in Niflheim."

"What's Niflheim?" asked Pesakh.

"In Norse legend there are three levels in which the nine worlds reside. Mankind lives in Midgard, which is at the top of the middle level. Niflheim is the lowest of the nine levels. It is the place of the dead."

"I really needed to hear that just now."

"You asked."

Everything beyond our pool of light was a mystery waiting to be discovered. Just as I was beginning to run out of hope the walls of the tunnel disappeared and we found ourselves in a cavern, off which ran three further tunnels. We stopped and I held my torch aloft and saw that this was not just simply an intersection of tunnels. The tunnel roof was vaulted in a fashion similar to the great church of Byzantium. These tunnels hadn't been built by miners, they had been engineered by masters of construction. My hope was given a life-saving boost.

"A veritable underground crossroads," I commented.

"More like a rabbit warren under the mountains," said Haldor.

"Definitely the stuff of Norse legend. Hey, Ulf, do you think we'll find a few Dolgthvari or Dori down here?" asked Sven.

"Why? Do you want to eat them?" asked Lars jokingly.

"No. But maybe they'll have some food," said Sven. The pains of hunger were not hidden from his voice, acutely reminding us of our predicament.

"Unlikely. I would have thought we would be more likely to come across Garm or Svartalfar."

"No, thanks. Those we could definitely do without."

I asked rhetorically, "I can't help but wonder who built these?"

Picking up the change of subject, Ibn said, "That's easy. The ancient Buddhists were very adept at scouring monasteries out of the sides of mountains. This area is riddled with them."

Equally tuned to my change in direction, Haldor asked, "Oh. And just how do you know this?"

"When my Uncle Tughrul Begh was building on his empire…"

"As one does every week," chipped in Haldor, which brought about a few chuckles.

"Yes. Thank you," said Ibn impatiently. "As I was saying, when he was building his empire, the forces he was fighting in this area would suddenly vanish. Later he discovered amazing networks of caves and tunnels. He also found out that these had, in the main, been constructed tens, hundreds, if not thousands of years ago by the Buddhist monks."

"That long? But for what purpose?"

"That remains the mystery."

"Alright, enough of the history lesson. Which tunnel do we take?"

"The most trodden one, I would have thought," said Haldor.

"Good thinking. Now we have to find it. We'll start with that one. Rat, you stay here so that we know which one we came out of. In fact, you can all stay here while Ibn, Haldor and I check them out."

With that decided, we walked to each tunnel entrance and examined the ground. In the dim light of our torches we did this in silence, saving our concentration for the ground around each entrance. In one of these silences I had just started to talk, when Lars said, "Shush."

We turned and could see him, head cocked, straining to hear in the dark. Waiting a moment or two longer, I asked.

"What is it? What can you hear?"

"It sounds like a river."

"Don't be foolish," Rat replied, "a river here?"

"Why not?" Larz said. "How many rivulets have we crossed on the way here?"

"I suppose," shrugged Rat.

"No. It's bigger than that. It sounds more like a waterfall."

"Which way?"

"That one, I think," he said, pointing to the tunnel to our left.

We all stopped what we were doing and strained our ears.

"I think he may be right," said Haldor.

In the flickering light and over the popping and spluttering of the torches, we stopped and stood in silence, straining to hear the telltale sounds of a river. Faintly, very faintly, I could hear the sounds of water running over rocks.

"Larz, I think you may be right," I said. "If it is a running river, it must run in somewhere and out somewhere." Our hopes of escape were raised. I hoped and prayed that they wouldn't be dashed.

"It's just as well—we couldn't tell which tunnel was the most used. That one it is, then."

As we progressed down the tunnel, the sound of falling water grew louder. Just as suddenly as we'd come across the vaulted crossroads, we entered a large underground cavern. A fast-flowing stream fell over a number of rocks into a large underground lake, which stretched away into the gloom.

There were hundreds of pointed pillars reaching up from the ground and down from the ceiling; pinks, yellows, creams and browns were reflected back at us and in the water. It was truly a place to behold. Places like this littered Norse legend and children's fairy tales. And up until now that was all they were to me — legends. But here we were standing in such a cavern, deep underground with a running river and a lake, still as a mill pond in spring.

"Mimir's well. The spring of Jotunheim," murmured someone behind me.

"What?" asked Rat.

"More Norse legend," replied Sven.

"Oh."

"I guess that's our way out," said Ibn, pointing across the lake.

"It does look that way," confirmed Haldor.

"I don't see a way that doesn't go via the lake," said Sven. The dry areas only proceeded for about one hundred fot on our side of the lake and a little more on the other.

"Well, we can stay here and die, or we strip off and swim," I said.

"Wouldn't it be better to build a small raft to carry our clothes and the spare torches?" Knut asked.

"Now that's a good idea! Divide into two teams and cast around and see what you can find."

On the far side of the cavern, we came across an altar. A few copper and bronze trinkets were scattered about looking like they had been knocked off the altar. Rat uncovered a ceremonial dagger in the dust and Larz and Knut found a stash of tools and old crates in the rear of the cavern near where the river emerged from its dark opening. We sorted the good wood from the rotten and carried our finds back to a flat area. On my command we stripped off our undershirts and using the dagger to cut them into strips, which we tied together. The strips were used as ropes and we lashed the wood together to form a raft.

123

"I know what I'm going to do," said Sven. And with that he started stripping. We all followed suit. We rolled our clothes into bundles and using our shirt sleeves tied the bundles together. Ibn had by now overcome his initial modesty and was not afraid to strip off in front of the crew.

"Now I bet you're glad you've learned to swim," I said to him.

"Yes. But what am I swimming into?" he asked. That was a question on all our minds.

"Keep those torches out of the water. We need the light and I don't want to have to try and light wet torches. Walking in the dark is bad enough, but swimming in the dark…" I left them to finish the sentence.

"You don't want your boots on, as they will become waterlogged and may even drag you under," I said. With that I placed my boots on the raft and naked as the day I was born I waded in to the ice-cold water. The others followed in line astern, audibly sucking in their breath as they entered the water. Rat and Sven took the raft between them.

After about three hundred fot it looked like the cavern had come to an end. But as I had come this far I wasn't going to stop until I had examined the whole lake. As I swam closer to the end, I saw that it didn't just end; the exit from the lake was hidden behind an outcrop of rock, unseen in the dim and flickering light. The way forward was through a tunnel that looked to be manmade rather than natural. The tunnel roof was an almost perfect semicircle. I paused briefly to check that everyone was still together. It didn't take much to see that we were all getting very cold and needed to get out of the water as soon as possible.

I then said with false bravado, "Can't be far now. See the roof of this tunnel? It's been shaped by a chisel, so the quicker we get through, the quicker we'll be out of the water and back into our warm clothes." No one spoke as we paddled forward.

The tunnel roof was a good ten fot above the water level and was smooth and semi-circular. Smooth from having been fashioned by chisels in the hands of men. There were none of the telltale signs of natural erosion.

The first section was relatively short and made a sharp turn to the right about thirty fot in. It straightened out then turned sharply to the left after about the same distance. Was it made like this so that no one could see through? The water level stayed constant, although it was noticeable that there was a current here.

Soon after taking the left turn, we entered a massive chamber, obviously manmade, the centrepiece being the pool in which we were now swimming. Steps led down to the water on three sides. The fourth side had caved in. A ray of sunlight lit the chamber from a high aperture. I led the men over to the steps and climbed out of the freezing water. We stood, naked and dripping wet, and marvelled at the smooth grey and pink walls and pillars. Surrounding the pool were arches, passageways and rooms all carved out of solid rock. The shining smoothness of the polished rock was in stark contrast to the natural rock face. Inscriptions in an unknown text had been carved into some of the walls. Others had frescoes of various scenes painted on them. Some of the frescoes were embossed with brass, silver and gold. We were silent in awe, our cold temporarily forgotten.

"What manner of place is this?" I asked in wonder.

Larz tapped me on the shoulder, "Ulf, turn around," he said.

Startled by this intrusion, I turned. There lit by the beam of sunlight, sitting astride the tunnel we had just come through, was a statue of a giant golden Buddha. It was covered in dust, but nevertheless golden, set in a carved recess.

"By all the gods of this world and the next," Rat said in astonishment, "I have never seen anything like it!"

"Me neither," said Sven.

I said, "I have seen many things in my life, but never anything like this."

Our reverie was broken by Ibn, who said, "Well, this confirms my suspicions. A hidden Buddhist temple. Long abandoned but a Buddhist temple nevertheless. I guess that when we Muslims drove out the Buddhists, they couldn't take all this wealth with them and sealed the entrance to prevent it falling into our hands."

"Either that or the Black Scorpions sealed them in when they wouldn't part with their Buddha. Just imagine what that gold is worth."

"The alternative is that the Buddhist monks sealed this place off, themselves inside, to ensure that the Black Scorpions, or anyone else, didn't get their hands on the fat guy."

The effects of the cold were beginning to take effect and we began to shiver. I instructed the men to get dressed as quickly as possible and then search for anything that would burn. We had two torches left and needed to get a fire going as soon as possible to warm our bodies.

We moved into and out of the many rock-hewn rooms and chambers. Eventually we found what must have been the living quarters, most of which had wooden pallets strewn on the floor. Some pallets were covered in lice and bug-infested straw mattresses, in an advanced state of decay. We shook these off and dragged the pallets to the main hall. Our frozen hands made this difficult, for at first we could not grip the wood. Added to this, the cold water had sapped our energy, making what should have been an ordinary task very difficult.

Eventually enough wooden material had been stacked and we tossed one of the remaining torches into it. The tinder dry wood caught almost instantly and within a few minutes we had a roaring, almost smokeless bonfire. I had to pull Rat back from the fire, as his frozen hands wouldn't feel the heat and I was sure he would burn himself.

As soon as we were warm enough I instructed the men to dress and retrieve more of the pallets. After the exertion of the swim, we needed to rest and recuperate. Food would have been good right then, but we would have to make do. Too tired to make conversation, we let the fire burn down to a bed of coals, and fell asleep.

I awoke suddenly and immediately saw that we were in total darkness. The shaft of light had disappeared. I concluded it must now be night outside. It was good to have a point of reference again. All around me were asleep. I arose, broke up some wood, and put it on the fire. Ibn and Haldor stirred.

"What's up, Ulf?" Haldor asked.

"Just putting some more wood on the fire," I said.

"Must be night. There's no sunlight," he said.

"I guess," I said noncommittally.

"You worried about where to next?" Haldor asked.

"Well, Haldor old mate, we've come this far and there is no obvious way out of here," I said.

"Well at least we will have died in a beautiful place," he said rather macabrely. "Anyway, why don't we talk about this when we have had more sleep and have some light to explore this place by?"

"You're right. Go back to sleep," I said, still worried about just how we were going to get out. I took a burning stake and walked down to the caved-in temple entrance and began to explore. With the dim light I could just make out part of the outline of a sunken boat, crushed under the fallen rock, but not much more. It then dawned on me that there were no skeletons in the temple, nor had we come across any in the living quarters. I concluded that Ibn's quick assessment was correct. In my heart hope sprang to life again. On returning to the fire I added some more wood and lay down again. We would do a more thorough investigation in the morning.

Haldor shook me awake. "Come on, sleepy head. Sun's up. It's time to start exploring."

I had not been in a heavy sleep and came awake almost instantly. The shaft of light was back.

"What did you find on your midnight ramblings?" he asked.

"Not much. A sunken boat under the fallen rock," I said, sitting up.

"No way out?"

"No, none as yet. The first priority will be to find where the water exits."

"What about the window?" Ibn asked.

"Too high and the walls too smooth to climb," I said.

Checking around, I saw that everyone was now awake.

"All awake? Alright. This is what we're going to do: Rat, Larz, Knut and Pesakh, your job will be to find more wood. Bring back as much as possible. Sven, Ibn, Haldor and I will scout around and try and locate where the water exits. When we have found it, we'll have to decide on a plan of action. But first let's get some warmth into this place. It must have been terrible living here during winter."

We then set about our tasks. The four of us took a burning stake and started climbing across the fallen rock. At the extremity of the fall we came across a whirlpool. I stripped off and dived down. The cold was a shock to my system and I almost surfaced immediately. I overcame my shock and continued the dive. At about ten or fifteen fot down, I could see that a few slabs and pillars had fallen across the exit and were lying almost horizontally, resting on the far-side steps. These were obviously supporting the debris above. There was a gap of about three fot between the slabs and the water drained through here. I thought I could see a faint glimmer of light but I wasn't sure if it was real light or if it was the effects of running short of breath. I pushed for the surface. Ibn and Haldor dragged me out and we hurried on over to the fire. As I dried off and dressed, I reported on what I had seen.

"I think that I should go down and have a look as well," Haldor suggested.

"I agree," I said. "I would also like Rat to dive and have a look too. That way we will definitely know if I was mistaken or not." They all agreed.

We all made our way over to the whirlpool and Haldor and Rat stripped off. Haldor went first and surfaced shortly after.

"Curses, it's cold!" he exclaimed as we pulled him out. "Yes, I think you're right, Ulf. I also saw a glimmer of light. Now I'm going to get warm."

Rat went next and reported the same.

I addressed the group. "Considering that there is a window up on high that lets in sunlight I have to conclude that we are close to the outside. Also, the building of a temple such as this almost certainly means that it was built fairly close behind the rock face. Building any further in would have been an astronomical task. Also, the existence of fatso over there—" I said, pointing to the golden Buddha, " —would imply that the front door was not too far away either. Agree?" They all agreed.

"We now have a choice—we can stay here and die not knowing how close we are to finding our way out, or we can try getting out by swimming under water. This is a risky venture. I will not pretend to say that we will make it. But so far we have proven the Black Scorpions wrong. We simply didn't sit down and die in the cave. We have overcome, and, I for one, do not want to stay here and die, but would rather die trying to gain my freedom. And just think of the stories you'll be able to tell your grandchildren if we make it, not to mention the look on al-Marhani's face when we present ourselves."

"Well said!" said Haldor. "Do we have agreement that swimming for it is our way out? All in favour say aye."

A chorus of ayes rang around.

"Alright," I said. "We'll have to strip — again. Tie your clothes in a bundle and tie them around your waist with the bundle against your stomach. This way, if it snags on anything it will be easier to free than if it were on your back. And hope and pray there's no young maidens on the outside. It could be rather embarrassing."

"Who for? Them or us?"

"Ha ha, Sven."

We stripped and prepared for the dive. As Ibn hadn't done any great amount of swimming, never mind underwater swimming, we arranged for him to go in between Haldor and myself. Rat would go first, Haldor, Ibn, me, Pesakh, Larz and Knut, with the rear being taken by trusty Sven.

Chapter 13

BREAKOUT

Not wasting time, we entered the water in quick succession. Following the whirlpool down we then swam frog-style under the pillars towards the patch of light. Towards the end the gap narrowed considerably and my clothes squeezed my stomach, almost forcing me to exhale precious air. I wondered how Sven would manage through here. No sooner had I passed this point than the pool of light suddenly grew large and bright and I was bursting through the surface, gulping in great lungfulls of air.

A few shepherd boys stood in amazement, wide-eyed and open-mouthed, as white-skinned, naked men started popping up out of the water. When Pesakh emerged they ran off screaming and wailing, leaving their sheep and goats unattended. We all burst out laughing. Knut surfaced, and I counted seven. There was no Sven. I untied my bundle and dived back under. Sven was jammed in the narrow opening near the exit. He was flailing and getting nowhere. I knocked him gently on the jaw and signalled to him that I would give him a breath. He nodded his acknowledgement and I moved forward, placed my lips against his and just about had all my breath sucked away. I then signalled to him to try and move back and untie his bundle. He couldn't move at all. I shoved him and he budged a little. Then I felt a hand on my shoulder and Haldor moved in to repeat the exercise while I returned to the surface. As soon as I surfaced, Larz dived down. We were running out of time. Larz was down longer than expected. Haldor was about to return when Larz surfaced, dragging an unconscious Sven with him. He had somehow managed to free Sven and drag him through.

We all dragged the dead weight of Sven onto the bank and somehow managed to get him into a kneeling position. His great torso was upright, his head forward, chin resting on his chest. Rat and I thumped his back. After what seemed like an eternity, he hadn't responded. Not knowing what to do, I grabbed his hair and pulled his head back. Rat and I gave one last almighty thump, which would have been hard enough to break a normal man's ribs. Sven, head still back, took an almighty breath and started coughing and spluttering. He dropped to all fours and vomited vast quantities of water. He then rolled over on his back, too exhausted to move, and heaved fresh air into his lungs.

A few minutes later he said, "There I was, on my way to heaven just then, and here I am back with you lot. What does a man have to do to get some peace and quite around here?"

We all howled with laughter, more out of relief because our trusted and dear friend was still with us. His bundle of clothes bobbed up into the middle of the pool, driven out by the current. Pesakh waded in and retrieved it.

We had just finished putting on our sopping clothes when a crowd of people, led by the shepherd boys, came tearing over the rise towards us, waving sticks and shouting.

My immediate thoughts were to flee, but Sven was in no condition to go anywhere and we had no armament with which to defend ourselves, should we get caught, which in our weakened state was an almost certainty. So we stood and waited for the crowd to arrive.

When all the shouting had died down and a semblance of order had been established, the village elder introduced himself. "I am Kalas al-Tolem, elder of the village of Aybāk. Who are you?"

"We are travellers who were entombed by a group called the Black Scorpions in the Orlameš Mine. We have travelled here via underground passages and swam out via an underwater tunnel."

"I see. The last person to exit the monastery was over three hundred years ago, which is why your sudden appearance has caused great anxiety among my shepherds. It's not too often that three-hundred-year-old people suddenly rise out of ponds in the mountains."

We all laughed, for the twinkle could be seen in his eyes.

"I assure you, none of us is three hundred years old."

Then it struck me — his eyes were blue! How could this be?

Ibn's next question provided the answer. "Kalas al-Tolem, that is not a very Arabic name?"

"No it is not, and you are quite correct. Our tribe can trace our ancestry back to the time that Alexander the Great conquered this area approximately one thousand, three hundred years ago. Hence the Greek - Arabic mix of my name. You will also see a prevalence of blue and green eyes, and even red and blonde

131

hair. But come, we must get you back to the village and get you warm. This way, please," he said, indicating with his crook and walking off in the direction from whence he had come.

Considering the time it took for the shepherd boys to return, the village could not have been that far. Nevertheless, the half mil that it was seemed to take forever. We were so sapped of energy and in need of nourishment that it took an almighty effort to cover the short distance. The shepherd boys were taken in with Big Sven's size and did what they could to assist him to cover the distance, which in reality was nothing really.

In the true Bactrian hospitable style, a feast was laid on for us and half the village crowded into Kalas's house.

Ibn took charge of the introductions. "These men are Varangians from a far and distant land and I travel with them to seek out one of their forefathers, who passed this way many, many years ago. I am Ibn Rashid al-Arslan, named after my grandfather, al-Rashid, the great Abbasid Caliph of Baghdad. I am the fourth son of Sultan Alp Arslan, Sultan of the East and the West and of the Seljuks, protector of the Abbasid Caliph of Baghdad."

At this our hosts' eyes grew wide with horror and they fell to their knees.

"No, please," said Ibn. "You have saved my life, our lives. You opened your homes to us, you offer us refuge, food and drink. You have slaughtered your best sheep and goats, broken open your larders and offered us your best food and cheeses, all for strangers, whom you have never before met. No, it is we who should kneel before you. Besides, I have relinquished my claim on the throne of Baghdad."

"Sire, you honour me and my family."

"And you honour me and mine," Ibn said, bowing.

Ibn then launched into our story and the village listened to it, captivated by the tale of adventure and heroism, while we sat around a blazing fire, drying off, eating and drinking. While we ate Kalas told us that, yes, he knew of the Black Scorpions and touched a silver pendant at his throat, which contained verses of the Koran in miniature. This act would apparently ward off any evil jinns that might be lurking. Yes, there had been a Buddhist monastery here in the time before his father's father's father. Yes, the Buddhists had been evicted by the Muslims, and the temple later taken over by people claiming to be Zoroastrians. But no fire was ever lit to honour Ahura Mazda, so no one really believed that they were true Zoroastrians. When trying to make the entrance larger for the removal of the Buddha, there was an earthquake and the entrance had caved in. This was taken as a sign from the gods that they were not pleased and the site was abandoned for fear of further annoying the gods and risking falls or cave-ins. And, no, no attempt had ever been made to gain re-entry for fear of displeasing the gods again.

Our questions answered and our hunger sated, we fell asleep around the fire. Not being a heavy sleeper I was woken by a chorus of snores during the night. I heard the sound of shuffling about, and saw one of the young village girls putting more wood on the fire. I gave her a smile and a wink. She giggled and blushed.

In the morning, we were preparing to depart but our hosts insisted we stay one more day to recover our strength. On reflection their insistence was a blessing because it gave us time to think out and plan our next moves.

Ibn said, "If we go back to Bactra, we will be showing our hand to those who want us dead. So I suggest we find another way of getting word to my brother and a way of keeping a low profile in the meantime."

"I think he's right," said Larz. Haldor was unusually quite.

For the moment I was prepared to let them do the thinking and speaking and only make my mind up after I had heard all opinions.

"But we can't keep a low profile here," said Larz. "Think about it. Seven white people and a Turk who emerge naked out of a pool of water. One of them a veritable giant with long yellow hair and a beard to match. How long do you think the shepherd boys can keep that quiet?"

"You're quite right," I said. "We can't stay here. But where do we go to?"

Out of the corner of my eye, I had seen the village elder's wife nudging and urging him, whispering in his ear, as if to say, *Go on. Tell them.*

Haldor suddenly said, "Ibn, how did the previous Sultan, Toreg whatever his name was, die?"

"He was assassinated," Ibn said, ignoring the slight on his great uncle's name.

"Yes, you told us. And now that you are for all intents and purposes dead, what will your brother do?"

"Why, he would come to find me... You don't think it's an elaborate trap to lure my brother in and assassinate him?"

In response Haldor raised his eyebrows.

"We must warn him. Immediately!" cried Ibn. He turned to Kalas. "I have to write a letter to my brother Malik Shah, Governor of Gorgan and the Northern Provinces. Do you have any writing materials?"

Kalas said he had, and sent his wife off to get them. While the parchment and quill were being retrieved, I quickly made some ink from the ash of the fire. I darkened the light grey liquid with some scrapings off a charred piece of wood. It was a bit lumpy, but it would have to do.

Haldor spoke again, "Before you start writing—what means of transport will your brother take to get to Bactra?"

"He will ride, of course. He hates ships. He gets seasick. Even on land," said Ibn.

"Alright," said Haldor. "We have to assume that the assassination attempt will be made in the palace at Bactra, when he is thought to be safe. Assuming that your brother can be intercepted on the way to Bactra. Picture this, a shepherd boy, or a stranger, comes galloping across the desert at speed towards his entourage. What would happen? If the messenger lived, would he be allowed anywhere near your brother?"

"No," said Ibn.

"I thought so," said Haldor. "Now, who would be best placed to get a message to your brother?"

"I would say Captain al-Khawalani or Safwhan."

"And if they, for some reason, are not with your brother?"

"Then... Mustapha al-Jaziri, the port official at Bactra."

"My thoughts exactly. I think that he may be your best bet," said Haldor. "The messenger may miss your brother for whatever reason. The desert is a big place and say he has overcome his seasickness and travels on the river? No, the best person is Mustapha al-Jaziri. The distance to Bactra is shorter and he has access to the palace. He also knows Safwhan and al-Khawalani. We need a letter for him and a letter that he must pass to your brother."

Haldor hadn't finished. "You had better tell your brother that we will go into hiding for the remainder of the winter, so he must not start searching us out until spring. Anyway, he'll have bigger things to worry about over the next few months."

Ibn said, "Yes, you are correct. I will make it so." He addressed Kalas as he wrote, "This letter... must be...delivered...to al-Jaziri...to him personally... placed... into... his hands." He paused. "Do you have someone who can deliver it?"

"Yes, sire. Of course."

"Good."

"The rider will leave now, sire. They will be delivered."

Ibn asked, "How will you get into Bactra? The gates will be closed by the time he gets there."

Kalas smiled slyly. "We have our ways and means, sire. You must remember, my people built Bactra — over a thousand years ago."

The significance of this statement was only too obvious.

The letters sealed and dispatched, Kalas approached us. "My wife and I could not but help overhear what you said about needing not to be seen. You are quite right. This is not the place to be unseen. But we know of a place where you can go and be safe, away from prying eyes and ears until you are ready."

"Where is this place?" Ibn asked.

"It is a week's hard ride from here."

"Yes, but where?" insisted Ibn.

"I am sworn to secrecy and may not tell," our host replied.

"Then how do we know you are not leading us into an ambush or more captivity?" Ibn said.

"Then I give you my dagger," he said, reaching into his tunic and drawing out a sheathed and bejewelled dagger, offering it to Ibn. I saw the men tense, ready for an attack.

"If we are attacked or ambushed, then you can take my life with my own dagger, for my honour will have been ruined."

We were quite taken aback by this offer of entrustment. However, if ever there was an act to gain our trust, then our host had just given it. We all sat there staring at the proffered weapon, lying openly in the palm of his hand.

"Ibn, I think you should take the dagger," I said. "It's been offered to you."

"What? Oh yes," said Ibn, coming out of his private world of thought. He took the weapon and pocketed it.

"Now, this place you're taking us to?" I said.

"Ah, yes. It would be better if we travelled at night and rested during the day. We must also disguise you, as if seen, even at night, your white faces and dress would give you away."

Ibn said, "You are correct, of course. Do you have dress they could borrow for the journey?"

"But of course. Sukaynah! Instruct the women to bring forth a garment from each of their husbands. Tarifa, bring some soot from the fire and mix it with water. We will need to make their faces darker. Also, bring my razor and a bowl of hot water, we must shave their beards as well. I urge you to make haste. We must leave as soon as it is dark."

Chapter 14

ACROSS the ROOF of the WORLD

We left Aybāk as soon as it was dark. Kalas's prompt organisation of the journey made me think that this was something he had done more than a few times before. Speed being the essence of our journey, we travelled light, with only a day's rations each. Kalas explained that we would be sleeping under a roof on every second day, hence there was no need to carry a lot of food, the weight of which would only slow us down.

Initially we kept away from the main routes. Staying well to the north of Kunduz, we travelled extra distance around the back of a small range of mountains. Night travel was cold work, but Kalas never missed a turn and the sure-footed Bactrian horses never put a foot wrong. Just before sunrise we came out of the valley and onto a wide and open plain and soon cantered into the ruins of the ancient Greek town of Ay Hanom. The town had been abandoned by the Greeks after the fall of their empire about a thousand years before. I wondered why no one continued to live here, as the town provided easy access to the fertile ground. Kalas informed me that when the Greeks were defeated, many were slain after safe passage had been guaranteed. Due to this dishonour the locals believed the spirits of those slain still haunted the ruins and that they wandered through the streets by day and night—a belief Kalas was not going to prove incorrect. On the contrary, it was one he fostered, as it gave him a safe stopover on the way to wherever it was we were going.

No fire was lit, as it may have attracted unwanted attention. As such we ate a light meal of dried meat, pistachio nuts, unleavened bread and cheese, washed down with icy cold, fresh spring water. I had never felt so alive.

The following evening we set out again, still travelling north. We crossed the Konkce River and kept well to the east of Yangiqala. We eventually crossed the Panj River to the north of the town just as the river starts to braid. Not wanting to be seen and challenged, we had to be ever so careful here, as the braided river created many islands on which people now lived. After crossing the river we cut west around the base of a mountain and then turned north into the Kyzylsu Valley. Even in the dark I could see that we were on a wide plain with mountains that seemed to touch the heavens on either side. Light from the half moon bathed the landscape a palette of blues, greys, blacks and purples,

137

with the high snow outlining the ridges and peaks in silver, in stark contrast to the black night sky. The river was a silver ribbon snaking down the valley floor.

Once again we made our destination, the village of Kurbanšam, just before sunrise. Instead of going into the village centre, Kalas led us around the outskirts and we trotted into a dilapidated and disused caravanserai on the western edge of the village. Kalas informed me that it belonged to his family. It was built more than five generations ago when the Silk Road used to pass this way. The ascendancy of Maracanda and Bukhara had meant a shift in the route of the road. Whoever was the head of the family had obviously made a bad decision in not relocating the caravanserai to the new, more northerly route. However, a cousin and his family still lived in the remaining buildings, which came in handy, especially on occasions like the one we were presently in.

Exhausted after two river crossings and a night of riding, we declined the offer of food, preferring the option of a bed and a day's sleep. We awoke later and within minutes our host had plates of steaming hot lamb stew in front of us. Ravenous, we wolfed the food down and were on seconds in no time at all. Our body clocks were slightly disoriented by our night travels, for it was now daylight outside, and we spoke for a while before heading back to bed.

We were woken from our slumbers by Kalas with bowls of water for washing. I was not sure if I would ever get used to the Arabic habit of washing before and after every meal. I noticed Pesakh followed similar practices. I concluded that it must be something to do with the desert lifestyle.

Washed and fed, our third night of travel took us further up the Kyzylsu Valley. Initially the valley had been a wide corridor but had now started to narrow. Towards the top end of the valley, the route criss-crossed the river, making use of the best routes forward. Fortunately up here the river was shallower and not as fast flowing. However it was even colder, as only a few mil away were the glaciers from which they were born.

We came upon a confluence of three streams and branched to follow the left tributary, all the while climbing. At the head of the valley we began to climb very steeply and crossed the boggy cirque of the stream's head. Soon the slope was too steep to climb vertically and the path turned into a typical alpine zig-zag. Despite our horses being fit and well fed, they soon began to puff and pant in the rarefied air. Just as it was becoming apparent that we would have to get off and walk, a few stone buildings appeared out of the gloom, stuck fast to the side of the mountain.

"This is where we stay for the rest of the night," said Kalas. "At daybreak we will walk over the pass and down into the Vakhsh Valley on the other side. Rest now, for it will be hard work."

Kalas led us to an enclosure for the horses. It was not a proper stable because it had no roof, but the ancient walls provided shelter from the cool wind. Remote as it was, it was nevertheless stocked with fresh hay.

"Let me guess, another cousin?" I said to Kalas.

"You are not slow to learn, Ulf Uspakson. Yes, I have many cousins along this route. To reduce suspicion, the route is used infrequently. But when we do use it, it is usually for an important reason," he said.

"Like now?" asked Ibn.

"Like now," our guide repeated.

With the horses bedded down, we went to a ramshackle-looking building. It was in fact a building within a building. The outside was made to look old and run down, while inside it was double walled, warm and waterproof. I was sure that our host had more similar surprises in store for us.

It seemed that I'd only just closed my eyes when I was shaken awake by Kalas. He had brewed some sweet tea from melted snow. We had this and unleavened bread and cheese for a quick breakfast.

The pass was seldom used, and then only by experienced locals; it was considered safe to travel in daylight. The pass, in reality a saddle, looked like it was only a couple of hundred fot above us. We started off at a brisk pace leading our horses, and almost immediately crossed the snowline. Just as soon we were puffing and panting as heavily as the beasts we were leading. The path was all but obliterated by the snow and if it hadn't been for Kalas's expert eye and knowledge of the area, we would have surely fallen to our deaths within the first half hour.

Kalas was patient and instructive. Our foodless underground excavation days and our underwater escape exertions seemed like a lifetime ago. But the effects of these events, just a few days ago, were beginning tell.

We stopped twice on the way up and a third time in the saddle, which we made in time for a short lunch. The view from the top was magnificent.

Stretching away to all four points of the compass were snowcapped mountains. It was as if someone had thrown a crumpled blanket across the face of the earth and dusted it with a covering of snow. Looking back down the valley, from which we had just climbed, it was clear that we were more than just a few hundred fot above the buildings, as they were now specks on the mountainside. If you didn't know they were there you would miss them completely. I could not get over the similarity to my own Norway; steep-sided forested valleys with streams running down the middle. Glancing around, I could see that all the Norsemen were probably thinking similar thoughts. However, looking forward, the change in scenery was drastic in the extreme. From what I could see of the Altai Valley, it was a treeless area with nothing but scrub, mountains, rock and snow. Kalas said to me, "When I was a boy, my grandmother would tell me the story of the fabled city state of Shangrila. When I first crossed this pass as a boy of fourteen, I thought I was about to enter that place."

"I can see why," I said. "It is a most spectacular sight. In my homeland we also have mountains and valleys, with the sea filling many of them. I have been across the top of them. We call it the Roof of Norway. If that was the Roof of Norway, then this must be the Roof of the World."

"What is this "sea" you speak of?" asked Kalas.

"Have you seen the Kara Kum Desert?" I asked him.

"Once, when I was a young man. It is to the north of here."

"Well, imagine replacing the sand with water. If you go out far enough and stand up in your boat, you will not be able to see anything but water to the four corners of the earth."

"So much water," he said in wonderment, "one would never have to go thirsty again."

"It's not that simple," I said. "The water tastes of salt. Instead of quenching your thirst, it makes you thirsty."

"Ah, it sounded too good to be true. Have you sailed on this sea?"

"I have sailed half the world on the sea. From Byzantium to Rome to the Pillars of Hercules and back. On the Nord Seë, the Black Sea, the Sea of Azov and the Kaspian Sea as well. There can't be that many seas left for me to travel on."

The descent was even trickier than the ascent, and we had to concentrate on our balance. Leaning too far back you would fall on your rear and start sliding. Too far forward and you would topple uncontrollably, head over heels, to your doom. More than once a firm grip on the horse's reins and the sure footing of our Bactrian mounts saved us from entering Valhalla that day.

Once we were below the snowline, we remounted and walked off down the valley towards Rogun and the Vakhsh River. As before, we sheltered for the remainder of the day at a house outside the village away from prying eyes. Because of the almost back-to-back legs of the past two days, we stayed a day and a half in Rogun, before resuming our nocturnal meanderings.

Kalas informed us that we were now on the Silk Road proper. It followed the Vakhsh River valley in a south-west to north-east direction. To the west was Maracanda and in the east the fabled oasis own of Kaxgar. He said that by now the caravans should be closing in on either end of the valley in preparation for wintering over. This should leave the middle section we were travelling on relatively free of traffic. Even so, he did not want a chance encounter to destroy the secrecy we had taken so much care to maintain. So our ride down to Gharm would be as before — by moonlight. Whenever we saw the telltale signs of a campfire we circled away from it. When this was impossible we rode through as quickly as possible, keeping our faces covered, eyes to the front and not stopping to speak.

On this section of the river, the valleys were steep sided and the bottoms narrow. Here the river was channelled and flowed through with great force. Further up the river, just after Gharm, the Vakhsh River was renamed the Surkhob and closer to its source it was called the Kyzylsuu.

I asked Kalas why this was so. He said it was a combination of the river having been called all three names at different points in history and the three different tribes that had settled along its course over these periods.

From Gharm the valley widened out considerably and we followed the course to Ocajilgan, and then on to Kara-Kavak.

On an unusually warm day we departed from Kara-Kavak, the ninth day of our journey. We turned north and with the Kyzylsuu at our backs started up the Taldyk Valley. All Kalas would say was that by the end of the day we would have made our winter sanctuary. While the valley was wide it was also bleak and windswept. The area reminded me of some of the Ukrainian steppe. The grass was short and had little colour. There were few trees and rocks were strewn all over the place. The grey rock, white snow and the lack of vegetative colour added to the impression that this was a place uninhabited by man and beast.

The temperature continued to rise as the day progressed. By late morning we were sweltering in our garments. The previously clear blue sky had taken on a dirty reddish brown hue. Kalas said, "It is the samoom. Come, we must hurry."

Picking up pace, I trotted besides Kalas and asked him, "What is a samoom?"

"It is a sandstorm off the Kara Kum Desert. They usually occur in the region around Bactra, Bukhara and Maracanda. I have never seen one this far east and never in this region. The rising temperature is the preceeding hot air coming off the desert. If we don't get to the caves before the wind arrives, we could be buried in sand. We MUST hurry!"

Chapter 15

The Warning

Two days after we left, our messenger, Kalas's son Dhu Nun, arrived at Bactra and immediately sought out Mustapha al-Jaziri in the port area. He was in luck; there was not much river traffic that day and Mustapha was in his office doing his paperwork.

On his arrival, the messenger asked to see Mustapha in private.

"What would an important person like the port captain want with a low-life sheep herder like you?" scoffed the senior clerk.

Keeping his composure, Dhu Nun replied, "It is of vital importance that I see the port captain in private. I have a personal message to deliver."

He waved the note in front of the senior clerk. Not being able to ruffle the shepherd was annoying the clerk, who tried to grab the note. Dhu Nun stepped back out of reach. Not liking being shown up in front of his juniors, the senior clerk advanced on Dhu Nun. "Give me that!" he shouted.

"It's not yours to see and it's not mine to give. I am but a messenger."

Now more irate that he had been outmanoeuvred by a sheep herder, not to mention the lack of respect he was being shown, the senor clerk advanced again, snatching at the note. Dhu Nun whipped out his dagger and plunged it right through the clerk's hand, pinning it to the counter. The clerk's screams brought Mustapha out of his office.

"What in Allah's name is going on here?" he demanded.

Dhu Nun quickly pushed the letter into Mustapha's hand, extracted his dagger and sprinted from the building. Mustapha chased after him, but then the realisation of what had just transpired dawned on him and he ceased chasing. He looked at the sealed envelope, pocketed it and returned to the office. He arranged for the two junior clerks to take their senior to the doctor to have his hand seen to, and gave them the rest of the day off. He closed the door behind him and retired to his office to read the letter.

On first reading the letter he was ecstatic that his friends were alive, but by the time he completed the letter his face was indeed sombre. "Oh my, oh my," was all he could mutter.

A week later the samoom hit. It was later recorded as the worst in living memory. So much sand had been dumped that small animals simply disappeared; unprotected cows and horses suffocated through inhaling too much sand; and houses had to be dug out from the hills of sand that had formed around and over them. Both the dead and the living were found in some of these.

Crops were obliterated, as were the roads, and the qanat system was so choked with sand it was in danger of collapse. The Oxus River had had so much sand deposited in it that the small dams that had formed along its course were in danger of overflowing onto the plain and changing the river's course away from Bactra permanently. Teams of men left their jobs and armed with shovels were assigned to clear parts of the city, the river and the qanat system.

Malik Shah arrived in Bactra almost eleven days after the samoom had wrought its devastating effects on Bactra. On hearing of his brother's demise, he had departed almost immediately and ridden hard for Bactra. Ibn's guess that his brother wouldn't sail proved to be correct.

He arrived in Bactra three weeks after the fateful cave in, delayed at Kunya Urgench by the samoom that had affected the whole of central Asia, from the Kaspian sea to the Pamir mountains.

Immediately on hearing of his arrival, Mustapha made an excuse to visit the palace in the guise of having to take an update report on the river condition to the Governor as the senior clerk was in no condition to do so. This raised a few eyebrows, as update reports were usually delivered by the senior clerk, leaving the port captain to get on with what he was supposed to do. Added to this, the river was all but clear of the debris left behind by the storm.

Being a regular visitor to the palace, Mustapha was waved through the palace gates by the guard. To approach Malik Shah direct would be too suspicious and he would probably be treated with contempt. No, it had to be done more discreetly, so he sought out his old friend Captain al-Khawalani instead. He found him pacing in the corridor outside the Governor's chambers.

"Mustapha, my friend — how are you? What brings you here?"

Ignoring the questions, he pulled al-Khawalani to one side and said in an urgent whisper, "Suwayd, listen to me now. Ibn Rashid al-Arlsan and the others are alive."

"This is good news! We must tell Malik Shah immediately," al-Khawalani said and started to go.

Mustapha grabbed him and pulled him back. "No! Not yet. It wasn't a cave in. They, the others, were captured by the Black Scorpions and entombed at the mine. They have broken out and are in hiding. Ibn Rashid al-Arslan believes it to be an elaborate trap to assassinate Malik Shah."

"Then we must warn him."

"Yes. But don't burst in. It must be done discreetly and subtly. Here, read this letter to me from al-Arslan and you will see his instructions are quite clear."

al-Khawalani read the letter carefully, not one but twice. Mustapha then gave him the second letter addressed to Malik Shah.

He said, "Alright, leave this in my hands. I know what to do." With that he knocked on the chamber doors and said, "Excuse me for interrupting, Your Highness. An important letter has just arrived by messenger from Gorgan. I thought it important enough that you receive it immediately."

By now Malik Shah knew this captain of the guards well enough to trust him. He had planned the journey from Kunya Urgench and had explained the whole route to him beforehand, going over each of the risks and providing alternative options in case of attack. His conduct on the ride and the way he handled his men had left an impression on Malik Shah, so much so that he intended to arrange his transfer to Gorgan as soon as he got back.

"Ah, al-Khawalani. Oh well, yes. Bring it in," said Malik Shah.

Turning to close the door, al-Khawalani gave Mustapha a short smile and a big wink and closed the door behind him.

Realising that the matter was now completely out of his hands, Mustapha returned to the port office to complete his paper work.

The palace bathing room was built on the foundations of an old Roman villa, which in turn had been built over a hot spring. Being an active earthquake region, there was no shortage of hot springs and even less shortage of hot water. Inset into the floor, the pool was made from polished grey marble, quarried in the area. Its sheen was offset against the cream, matt sandstone of the palace. The bather could relax in a hot bath and take in a panoramic view of the Oxus Valley with the mighty Hindu Kush as a backdrop.

The attack came when Malik Shah had just stepped out of his robes and into the palace's private bathing pool. Because of the cooler air, there was more steam than usual. He and al-Khawalani had guessed it would either be here, when he was at his most vulnerable, or at the mine, which he was to visit the next day.

The assassin was one of the Governor's personal servants. He had been assigned to see to Malik Shah's every personal need for the duration of his stay at the palace. As was regulation since Sultan Toreg Beg's assassination, all people and equipment had to be searched prior to entering the presence of the royal family. The searching was done by Malik Shah's personal bodyguard, to which Captain al-Khawalani and his men had been temporarily assigned. He, al-Khawalani, and three other men had been concealed in wicker laundry baskets in the poolroom prior to Malik Shah entering.

Walking over to the curtains and reaching up to adjust them, the servant asked, "Would Your Highness like a little more light?"

"No thank you. It is quite sufficient."

Deftly, the servant retrieved a long, thin sabre-like spike from the centre of the curtain rail. He pushed a wooden stopper, from one of the many spice and salt jars, over one end of the spike, giving a hand grip. In short, he had made a makeshift sabre and the servant had become an assassin. Seeing the assassin's quick movements through the wicker basket, al-Khawalani shouted, "Highness!" and rolled out of the basket as fast as he could, as did the other three.

The assassin lunged into the pool and thrust the ad hoc weapon towards Malik Shah's right eye.

Knowledge of an impending attack had already heightened Malik Shah's senses. This, coupled with the shouted warning, was enough to enable him to evade the lunge. The assassin was thrown off balance, as the weapon did not meet any resistance. His feet being slowed by water resistance added to his plight, and he fell headlong into the pool. Floundering and weighed down by his clothes and boots, he was stared at with disdain and contempt by a naked Malik Shah. The four guards had sufficient time to pick themselves up and stroll over to the pool. Disarming the attacker, they dragged him out of the water.

With the failed assassin securely held between them, dripping water on the marbled floor, Malik Shah said, "Take him to the cells and lock him up with a treble guard on the inside; and the outside. If he dies before I can interrogate him, you will all pay. al-Khawalani, please arrange another servant and return here as soon as the prisoner is interred. Now I am going to finish my bath."

The aplomb with which the statement was delivered would be a topic of conversation in the courts of Baghdad and taverns across Persia for years to come.

The following day Malik Shah and his entourage, dressed in suitable mourning attire, departed Bactra to inspect the sight of the cave in, which had taken his dear brother's life.

Chapter 16

SAMOOM

The samoom whipped around our faces with the sound and the sting of a thousand bees. The sand stung our skin, blinded those foolish enough to open their head covers to it, and caked in the moisture around our nostrils and mouth. The sand invaded our beings through every opening in our clothing, no matter how small. Kalas was insistent that we push on. He assured me that our destination was not too far ahead. I, for one, was keen to find the best shelter we could and sit it out. Over the roaring of the wind, I could just hear Kalas say that sitting it out could take a week.

We covered our horses' ears, faces, nostrils and mouths with strips of cloth torn from the bottom of our robes. Most of us had our calf-length boots on, so our legs were, in a fashion, protected. But the driven sand found its way into our clothing and dribbled down the inside of our boots, making walking very uncomfortable. Before the wind hit us with its full force, we had hastily convened a method of staying together. Each rider would tie the reins of his horse to his left hand and hold the tail of the horse in front with his right; let go and you were alone against the elements. And so we plodded on.

What we had not considered was the mud. The warm desert air and sand quickly melted the lower lying snow and soon we were walking ankle deep in mud, which flowed like water. I managed to convey to Kalas that if we did not get off the valley floor, we would soon be waist deep in mud flowing from the upper reaches of the valley. He nodded his understanding and we turned left and I was pleased to note that we had begun to climb. Still the wind whipped sand against our faces and the mud flowed around our ankles. With the changing intensity of the wind came corresponding changes in colour and sound. More than once I thought I saw a figure materialise in front of me, only to disappear as quickly as it formed. Tricks of the light, I told myself. No wonder people in this region believed that these winds were inhabited by jinns and werma.

Then one of the spirits took form and grabbed my arm. It was hooded and I couldn't see its face and its hands had no fingers yet it was able to grip me. I fought it off and it came back to grab me again. I fought it off a second time and then a third and then it disappeared into the wind. Maybe the samoom was really inhabited by werma.

I then realised that in fending off the werma's attack, I had let go of the horse in front of me. I felt my way down the side of my horse to find that no-one was holding on to the tail of mine. I shouted the names of the men, but against the roar of the wind it was useless. I was alone against the elements.

I kept walking uphill, searching out a piece of high ground that was not flowing in mud. Eventually finding a spot, I lay my horse down and covering my head and the horse's head with yet another layer of clothing I sat down to sit out the storm.

A combination of starvation in the tunnel and caverns, and nine days of hard travel on light rations was taking its toll. Add the effects of the samoom to this, and I realise now that I must have been close to exhaustion. I started drifting in and out of sleep and battled to stay awake. After what seemed like an age, a regular consistent thumping, like a drum, began to invade my consciousness. At first I was not sure if was hearing correctly. Thump, thump, thump. I must admit its regularity in this situation was unusual, but I couldn't make my mind up if was manmade or nature playing a trick on me. Then the sound changed. It went from its regular slow single beat, picked up tempo and changed to a beat that I would have recognised anywhere. Thump, thump, thump-itty, thump. And again, Thump, thump, thump-itty, thump. The attack beat from our Greek galleys as we were about to row into battle—Haldor!

With my legs covered in wet sticky mud I climbed into a kneeling position. My horse, sensing that we were about to move, shook himself off and staggered to his knees as well. Holding tight to the reins, I was dragged upright. We ploughed our way through the treacle-like mud and roaring wind towards the sound. We eventually came face to face with a wall of rock. Realising that the sound must have been echoing off the rock, I worked my way along the face, feeling as best I could with my wrapped fingers. Slowly, but ever so slowly, the sound began to change. I stopped for a while, ankle deep in sticky mud, howling wind and stinging sand, and listened. I managed to identify a fainter sound, slightly offbeat to the one echoing off the rocks, somewhere off over my left shoulder. We started towards the beating again.

I'm not sure how long it took, but it seemed like a lifetime. I tripped and fell over rocks a number of times and by then was wet through. The sand chaffed my every joint and lifting each boot was a battle in itself. Suddenly out of the gloom more of the evil hooded figures emerged again, descending on me. Desperately I tried to fight them off. Then everything went black.

Chapter 17

The Mine

The group silently clambered their way up the mountain through the snow, using rocks for cover. Some had had their gloves torn by the torturous climb and their hands were bleeding. But still they continued climbing silently towards their objective.

Their eyes had adjusted to the dim light, and on a hand signal from their leader they simultaneously dropped into a crouching position.

Up ahead a brazier burned bright against the black sky, making the snow glow an unnatural yellow-orange. Two figures could be seen standing around it, warming themselves in the cold night air. With silent hand signals the leader indicated to his men to encircle the encampment. Their purple and black uniforms ideally suited to night operations, he watched them melt into the night.

After a while he stood up and started walking nonchalantly towards the encircled camp. Noticing that he had not been seen, he started whistling, at which the two men at the brazier snapped to life and scrambled to retrieve their weapons. Too late. Twelve shadows emerged from the darkness, one carrying an extra two swords. The two hapless guards were put to death at a nod from the leader.

For the first time in five hours, he spoke. "Now we sit and wait for the fun to begin."

The royal party was making its way up the long narrow valley up which Ulf, Ibn Haldor and the others had made their way only a few weeks before. They were about to enter the narrow neck when al-Khawalani galloped up to Malik Shah and reined in.

"Is everything prepared?" Malik Shah asked.

"As ready as we shall ever be, Highness."

"Good," Malik Shah replied. "It won't be long now."

Immediately following the episode in the pool room, Malik Shah put in a complaint to the Governor about the page assigned to him, who had mysteriously disappeared in the middle of the day. The Governor apologised most profusely and said he would immediately assign another. While he went about trying to get this done, Malik Shah and al-Khawalani planned an assault on the mine under the pretence of finalising the next day's travel arrangements.

Intelligence sources had revealed that there was a well-used back way into the mine. The approach to the back entrance was just as narrow and treacherous as the formal entrance route. Taking a queue from Alexander the Great's conquest of this area, al-Khawalani suggested that the attack party ride to the start of the valley and travel the last few mil on foot high along the snowline, which would first mean climbing the mountain. Who would think of an attack coming from above and from within the mountain range?

Although he could see the risk in this plan, Malik Shah eventually agreed, acknowledging that there was no other way to get that far up the valley without being discovered. And so the plan was set. A group of riders would return to Kunya Urgench immediately. The ruse being in response to Ibn's letter, which al-Khawalani had delivered earlier that day. Under cover of darkness this group would circle back around Bactra and ride hard up the Bactra River valley and make their approach by night, just as Alexander the Great and a few select men had done thirteen centuries before.

The hope was that they had made it thus far, or else Malik Shah, al-Khawalani and their small band of men would be riding into the jaws of a trap at a distinct numerical disadvantage. As no rider had come back down the valley to warn them otherwise, they had no reason to suspect that they had not achieved their objective. Either they had achieved their objective by now or they were dead or captured, or both.

On approaching the mine, there seemed to be an acceptable level of activity. There was the sound of steel hammers ringing against chisels and rock being hauled up from the depths by donkeys with laden saddlebags.

al-Marhani was on hand to meet them. The smile Ibn's letter had spoken of was stuck firmly on his face.

"I am Sulaym al-Marhani. Welcome to Orlameš Mine, Your Highness, although I wish it were under better circumstances."

"As I do, al-Mahrani, as I do," said Malik Shah.

"Please do come in for some refreshments," suggested al-Mahrani, gesturing towards the buildings. Remembering his brother's letter and the method in which they were drugged, Malik Shah refused.

"Not just yet. I would first like to visit the spot where the, ah, accident happened."

"But of course, sire, but of course. Your wish is my command. If you would dismount I will have your horse stabled and will show you to the spot."

"No, I don't care to dismount just now. I don't want to get my new boots too dirty. Lead the way, will you?"

"Very well, sire." A look of consternation crossed al-Mahrani's face as he led the party to the site. What he did not notice was al-Khawalani's deployment of his men. What looked like informal groups of twos and threes scattered across the compound courtyard was in fact a deployment of men at various strategic locations. Most of his men had already dismounted. The few who had led the horses to the stables had in fact already taken over the stables. The stable manager and grooms had been trussed up and tossed into an empty stable and were now under guard.

As soon as al-Mahrani led off Malik Shah to the site, al-Khawalani led a few men into the administration centre and started to round up the staff. Seeing the royal troops entering their premises, a junior clerk slipped out the back way and raised the alarm.

On hearing the alarm, Malik Shah immediately turned his horse and galloped back to the compound. Men were streaming out of the accommodation block; except these were not miners but well-armed and trained soldiers. They immediately engaged Malik Shah's men and the fight was on. Miners, not believing what they were seeing, initially laid down tools and stood and watched the battle in fascination.

Being the coward he was, al-Mahrani made for the stables. When he saw that they were already under guard he made his way on foot through the compound towards the rear exit. A few other Black Scorpions had started evacuating the compound as well.

"Come back and fight, you cowards," al-Mahrani screamed. "Come back and fight." Clambering up the steep incline after the escapees, he clutched at the boots of those already ahead of him and tried to pull them back, only to be kicked in the face.

"What for?" someone shouted back. "It was over the second the attack began. Couldn't you see that, you moron?"

He stopped his exhortations and joined in the flight.

The fleeing scorpions crested the ridge with al-Mahrani in the lead and were confronted by a single soldier in a purple and black uniform, standing in the middle of the track with his arms folded. They checked at the sight of this single soldier and stopped. Then someone screamed, "There's only one of him, charge!" and the group moved forward en masse. The coward al-Mahrani let the Scorpions advance around him. The remainder of his troop hidden behind rocks and boulders on either side of the track, stood on the troop commander's order, cocked their bows, took aim and let loose their arrows. The advancing front row fell and the group checked again. In an attempt to avoid capture, a few at the rear began scrambling up the near vertical face of the Hindu Kush. The archers picked them off with ease and they fell screaming to their deaths. The troop commander called out, "I suggest you lay down your weapons now, or suffer the same fate of those who have fallen."

They looked at each other as if wanting someone to say surrender or die. No one took the initiative. The troop commander gave the order, "Archers, cock your bows..."

Acknowledging defeat, the remaining Black Scorpions tossed their swords into a pile on the ground.

"Good," said the captain. "Now, kneel on the ground with your hands behind your heads."

Obediently they kneeled. He then instructed his men to search the kneeling Scorpions. When this was over he said, "Alright, now take off your boots. We don't want anyone pulling out a concealed dagger, or trying to make a run for it, now, do we?"

al-Mahrani began to complain about inhumane treatment. A soldier slapped him quite hard, which shut him up.

Boots now off, the captain said, "Alright, now start walking back down the pass. Anyone attempting to escape will be dealt with accordingly."

The subdued group turned and began to walk back down. Within a few minutes the hopping and jumping over stones and rocks stopped as their feet, numbed by the cold, lost all feeling.

In the compound al-Khawalani's men were being driven back down the valley. He screamed at the miners to join them. A few did, but in general most were more terrified of what would happen to them and their families, should word ever get to the Black Scorpions that they had fought against them.

Just then a shout was heard from across the other side of the compound as al-Khawalani's mountain men entered the fray. They had herded the escapees into the stables and placed them under guard. When the sensation returned to their bloodied and torn feet, they wouldn't be wanting to go very far. Freed of their burdensome task, they now joined in the main fight, catching the Black Scorpions in a pincer movement.

Seeing the battle swing in favour of the royals, more miners began to join the fight against the Black Scorpions. Soon the few remaining Scorpions were encircled. al-Khawalani called a halt to the slaughter and offered them surrender. They accepted and were duly imprisoned with the others in the stables.

During the post-battle site inspection, a miner led Malik Shah and al-Khawalani to a door that was never opened in the presence of mine staff, but which he knew al-Mahrani and other Black Scorpions used with great frequency, especially at night. Not able to find a latch, al-Khawalani ordered al-Mahrani be brought from the stables. On his arrival he said, "His Highness would like to inspect your, ah, private quarters. That is, the quarters behind this door."

"No. Please don't make me—please!"

"Ahem. You don't seem to understand. You are in the presence of royalty. This is not a request, THIS IS AN ORDER!" al-Khawalani barked at him.

"No, please. They will kill me."

"Well, then—it's either them or us who are going to kill you. If you open the door, we won't kill you."

"I can't, I can't," al-Mahrani wailed.

"Alright then, as you're of no more use to me or His Highness your life is forfeit. Guards, get this snivelling piece of shit out of here and behead him."

"NO!" screamed al-Mahrani. "I'll open it, I'll open it."

"Good, that's better. Well, what are you waiting for? Get to it!"

The door swung silently open and a stench wafted out from a passage cut into the rock. Dim light flickered from wall-mounted torches. Malik Shah, preceded by al-Khawalani, entered the tunnel. al-Mahrani followed behind, secured between four soldiers. They descended into the mountain. The passage, originally a mineshaft, took a number of twists and turns and terminated in a great underground cavern.

The party was shocked to discover twelve iron cages, each holding six prisoners of many origins. There were Sindese, Kushans, Arabs, Uighirs and the remainders of Ulf's Scandinavian crew. Extensive machinery dedicated to the art of torture lined the other side of the cavern with cubby holes cut into the rock containing hand-held torture devices. Along the back wall a row of smaller cages hung from the ceiling. Each held a body in various states of decay, with the leftmost containing but a skeleton. In front of the cages stood a large iron cauldron. An altar had been built along the fourth side of the cavern and a large polished bronze flame was attached to the wall behind it. A circular plinth was centrally placed in front of the altar. A fire burned in the plinth, the flames tinged with an eerie blue-green glow. The cave had an overpowering and oppressive feel of evil and reeked of death and decay.

Three of the cages held women, all naked, some pregnant. On seeing the party enter, the prisoners became agitated and cowered as best they could in the rear of their cages. Then a few realised that al-Mahrani was himself being held prisoner and their demeanour swiftly changed to one of aggression. al-Khawalani recognised a few of Uspakson's crew and ordered two of the soldiers to get the cages open and another to get clothing to cover the women.

All the while al-Mahrani kept his head bowed. As the prisoners were let free and led out of their living hell, more than a few had to be restrained from attacking him. al-Khawalami selected the most lucid of the prisoners and questioned them.

"Allah be praised," one said. "At last He has heard our prayers. You have captured the devil himself. It was he who tortured and starved us."

Another said, "He boiled some of us — always alive. He put us in those cages," he said, pointing to the back of the cavern. "And then immersed us in boiling water; others had the heat increased slowly, just to see how we would die."

One of Ulf's crew informed him, "The women were raped for their pleasure. Their babies were sacrificed to the fire god on the altar and they, the Scorpions, drank their blood. Others were tortured on the racks by him and his men," he said, pointing to al-Mahrani.

Another said, "Sometimes it went on all day, sometimes all night. The moaning and screaming never stopped. If he wasn't boiling he was stretching. If he wasn't stretching he was cutting. If he wasn't cutting he was raping. It went on and on."

"Where are you from?" Malik Shah asked.

"I am from Kaxgar, the oasis town of the Taklamakan Desert, at the base of the Tien Shan, the Celestial Mountains."

"How did you come to be here?"

"I was on my annual trade circuit from Kaxgar to Maracanda to Bactra. I stopped for the night just short of Bactra, at the usual traders' camp. Then I woke up here, in this cavern."

"Were you travelling alone?"

"No."

"What happened to your companions?"

"They were brought here as well. That is one in the third cage along," he said, pointing to a decomposing corpse. "The others were murdered in this hell hole a while ago now."

"Well, you're safe now. al-Khawalani, check that there are no other exits from this cavern. If there are, seal them. Then put all the prisoners in here. Prepare the cauldron. Be sure to have sufficient wood. We don't want to give him just a hot bath, do we?"

"Understood, sire," said al-Khawalani, his face beaming.

Malik Shah then turned to al-Mahrani and said, "You, I'll deal with later," and walked out of the cavern, leaving a wide-eyed al-Mahrani to consider his fate.

After the captives were transferred to the dungeon and locked in the cages, Malik Shah returned to the cavern. He had had a chair placed in front of the altar and had al-Mahrani brought before him in chains.

"You have been found guilty of crimes against Sultan Alp Arslan, against humankind and, above all, against Allah."

"I don't believe in your god," retorted al-Mahrani. "What sort of god is He that requires people to pray on command at a set time every day? Where is the meaning, the passion? Where is the feeling? And what crime have I committed against the Sultan?"

"A good try, but you're still guilty," said Malik Shah. "Do you remember my brother? The one you had entombed, in the tunnel and made out it was an accident?"

"How…" al-Mahrani began. He then realised that what he thought was impossible had occurred.

"Yes… that's right. He escaped. As did all the others you entombed. That is the crime against the Sultan. You tried to kill one of his sons—and failed. Then you tried to kill another of his sons, and more importantly, the heir to the throne—me! And failed again. How does it feel to be such a failure?

"The crime against humanity is the depravity you have practised in here and the entombment of guests of this country. My guests."

For the first time al-Mahrani could see how limited his future was and began to tremble.

Looking him in the eyes, Malik Shah said, "Now you know just how those you killed felt. The one part of your experiments you could never understand. But now you do. You are going to suffer the same fate as those poor men in the cages at the rear."

"NO, NO, NO!" al-Mahrani screamed as he was dragged to a cage. "Not that, not that, any other, but not that!"

"And why not? How many did you kill this way? Lock him in a cage and immerse him in the water."

al-Khawalani's men dragged a kicking and screaming al-Mahrani to a cage and forced him in, watched in silence by the imprisoned Black Scorpions. The cage was then raised, swung over the cauldron and lowered into the water. Malik Shah lit the fire. He watched while it took. When it was burning brightly, he walked from the dungeon, followed by his troops.

On his orders the tunnel was collapsed, but even that did not purge the death screams of al-Mahrani from their ears. With all hope of salvation extinguished, Malik Shah gave the order that the door was to be sealed and the mine was to be closed, never to be reopened.

Chapter 18

The Hidden Kingdom

I awoke in a large candlelit room with no windows. Startled at my surroundings, I tried to sit up. I was gently pushed down and someone spoke, a woman's voice. At first I couldn't understand what she was saying; I then realised she was speaking Greek. Not the Greek I knew, but an older more classical style.

"Shhh. There, there. You're alright. You're safe now."

"Wha….." I started, not recognising the language at first. "Oh, Greek. Where am I?"

She answered, "In the Hidden Kingdom of the Hephthalites."

"The where? The who?" I asked disjointedly.

"The Hephthalites. You were lost in the samoom, and were found with the drums."

My eyes adjusted to the gloom and I saw that she had waist-length pitch-black hair tied back off her face. Her eyes were a mesmerising pale, washed blue. While they were big and round, they had a hint of the oriental about them as well. The contrast between her hair and her eyes was remarkable. Our eyes connected and it was as if I looked right into her soul and she into mine, and the two became interlocked. I don't know how long we held each other's stares, but it was the most magical experience of my life.

"…Ah, yes," I said, returning to the present. "The werma, the storm spirits. What happened?"

Her face was oval and nicely proportioned, and those eyes… "The storm is still raging. The spirits weren't spirits. They were people. You were fighting so wildly that your friend Hul… Hal…"

"Haldor," I offered.

Here eyes were not too far apart, her mouth on the small side, and she had a quaint little nose. My gaze returned to her eyes, we locked again. She blushed slightly and glanced away. "That's right, Haldor—he knocked you out. The storm must have disoriented you."

Pretty, I thought. Not a classic beauty, but definitely prettier than average. But her eyes would make up for any imperfection in her being.

"Yes. I got lost when a spirit attacked me earlier on."

"That was no spirit, that was me."

"You!"

"Yes, me."

In her present posture it was hard to tell how large her bosom was. I would have to wait until she stood up before I could analyse that—and her hips. I caught her eyeing me up as well. She glanced away quickly.

"I didn't hurt you, I hope? Anyway, what were you doing out in the storm? You could have got lost and perhaps died out there."

"No, you didn't hurt me. I've been hit harder before. But we have saved others like this before, but not in so bad a samoom."

"But how do you not get lost as well?"

"Oh, that's quite simple. We tie a rope around our waist. That way we can find our way back. Otherwise it would be madness to venture out."

"Of course. It had to be something that simple. Silly of me not to think of it. How long have I been here?"

"Only a few turns of the glass."

"Turns of the what?"

"The glass. It's how we measure time."

"Ah."

"May I get up now?"

"If you feel up to it."

"I do," I said. With that I sat up, but had to pause when spots appeared before my eyes. Taking it slowly, I first put one leg off the bed, then the other. The dress she was wearing could have come straight out of Ancient Greece. It was ankle length, had short sleeves and was tied at the waist. She wore sandals. But I couldn't identify them as Roman or Grecian.

All the while she watched me. I wasn't sure if she was trying to make me out, or was waiting to catch me lest I fall. Then an idea struck me. On standing I faked a slight stumble and she reached out to steady me. I put my arm around her shoulders and put a little weight on her.

"Thank you," I said. "How far to the rest of the crew?"

"Oh, not far. They're all eating. But maybe you should get dressed first."

"Uh... oh yes. Maybe I should," I said, suddenly aware that I was leaning on a woman wearing nothing but my undergarments. Hiding my embarrassment, I sat back down on the bed. I then realised that I was clean. All the sand and mud had been washed away and a salve had been rubbed into my joints. I was too embarrassed to ask who had washed and cleaned me. But I think I already knew the answer. She fetched a garment from the back of a chair and said, "Here, wear this. It's not something you're used to, and is maybe a bit old fashioned, but wearable all the same."

I pulled the garment over my head, tied the waist cord and stood up again. Not sure if it would work a second time, I again faked the stumble. It did.

"By the way, I am Ulf Uspakson," and I leant on her a little more, forcing her to draw nearer to support my weight.

"I know," she said.

"Oh, you do, do you? ...And you are?"

"Oh, I'm sorry. I am Lydia."

She felt good and smelt even better.

We hobbled into the dining area and Haldor, as ever, was quick off the draw. "Well, look you here. Not an hour from death's door and he is already got a woman on his arm!" Laughter rang around the hall.

As Lydia went off to bring some food, an old grey-haired man, who had been sitting and talking with Kalas, stood and walked over to me. If he wasn't Kalas's brother, then he was a very close relative. His eyes, an intense blue, cut right through to the core of my being. This was a man who was used to commanding. The best commanders I knew had this same ability and had similar eyes. Harald was one of these, Yaroslav another.

"It is good to see you up and about. I am Iksander Ptolemeus, cousin to Kalas, who brought you here, and leader of the Hephthalite peoples, in this, our Hidden Kingdom."

"Another cousin?" Haldor asked. "Do you know he has them all over this place?" The humour brought a smile to his face.

"Ptolemeus, as in Alexander's Ptolemy?"

"I see you are a student of history. Yes, he was one of my ancestors. I am named after Alexander, as you call him."

Impressed, I said, "That is indeed a noble family line."

Suddenly feeling giddy, I said, "Excuse me, I must sit down."

Iksander's hand shot out to support me. For an old man he was incredibly strong. He guided me to the closest bench and I leaned on the table. Lydia came over and placed a plate of steaming hot food and mug of water in front of me. She sat down next to me on the bench.

"Is it warm in here or is it just me?"

"No, it is warm. Our, ah, residence, is underground and is heated by hot springs. We can't open the vents to let cool air in because of the storm. So I'm afraid we all have to be a bit uncomfortable for the meanwhile."

"Underground?" I asked. I had had enough of underground living for the rest of my life.

"Yes, not too far, but underground all the same. My apologies, I have been rude. When you have eaten and are feeling better I will give you a tour. Then we will have much to discuss. In the meantime I will leave you in Lydia's capable hands. When you are ready she will bring you to me."

"What a remarkable man," I said as he left.

"Yes," she said, "he is. He's kept this place going, since, oh, ever since I can remember."

The others joined us at the table.

"You have known him a long time, then?" I said.

"All my life," she replied. "He's my father."

The food was definitely filling the vacuum in my stomach. While the mug only contained water, it was the sweetest water I had ever tasted.

Ordinarily there would only be room for four at a bench. Rat had squeezed in next to me and Pesakh and Larz the other side of Lydia. Sitting room on the bench was now at a premium and Lydia was pressed tightly against me. I enjoyed her closeness again and concluded that if she wasn't enjoying mine, she would have already left, and she hadn't.

Feeling refreshed and strengthened after the meal, I was led to Iksander, who was instructing some men on repairs to a water channel.

"Ah, Lord Uspakson, you are feeling better?"

"Yes, I am, thank you. The food and the care I have received have been exemplary. And please call me Ulf. I find the title rather embarrassing."

"Well, Ulf, I am glad to hear you are felling refreshed. Come, we will walk and talk."

Ibn and Haldor joined us.

We walked through a number of relatively wide tunnels, wide enough so that at least two people could pass with ease, then up some stairs. Lydia walking close behind.

"This door is the entrance to the cave system." He opened it and I looked into a stable.

"Yes, the entrance is concealed. We have hidden it behind a caravanserai in a small village. How did we come to be here? Well you have to go back to the time of the great flood, as mentioned in the bible. Are you aware of the book and the story?"

"Yes, I am. Norway, the land of my birth, converted to Christianity about fifty years ago."

"Excellent. Tribal legend has it that we are descended from Japheth, one of Noah's sons, brother to Shem and Ham. After the great flood he was given the land of Asia by God. In Hebrew Japheth's name is "Yaphat Elohim le-Yephet" from which the name Hephthalite emerges. In Hebrew Yaphat also means beautiful people."

"Ah, hence the fair skin and blue and green eyes," I said, looking at Lydia. She smiled.

"Correct," Iksander said, not missing our momentary glance. He went on, "Come forward to about the year 100AD, to Henan Province in Tianxia, where we were the original inhabitants. There we were called the Pinyin Yada, the Yetai or Yeda. As you can see, all names derived from the name Japheth. Interestingly the Kushans called us the Huna, a name which later was shortened to Hun and was used by outsiders to label our race. But I digress; languages and their derivatives are a special hobby of mine. When you have little else to do than study, you have to have something to focus on."

He cleared his throat and continued, "Tribal legend also has it that our system of laws is directly descended from Noah and his relationship with God. While the likelihood is high, we have no proof of this, so it must be left as legend and not as fact."

He paused, letting the weight of what he said sink in. Seeing he had given me cause for thought, he started again, "Moving on. The Han multiplied faster than we did and we were soon forced out of government and then off our lands, even though we had brought government, laws and stability to the people. The exclusion of our tribe from Han society was made blatantly obvious in 221AD when emperor Shi Huang-ti had the Great Wall built. We were classed as barbarian and were refused the protection of the wall, nor were we allowed to pass through. We moved to the Ordos area, in the great bend of the Huang He River, which is a semi-arid area, with windy and sandy conditions. Access to more fertile lands to the south-east was cut off by the great wall. Despite this we prospered on the outside, raising sheep and goats, weaving and cloth making, as the soil was too poor to support any concerted agricultural effort. Our cloth and carpets became the most sought after in the region. All this to the chagrin of the emperor. He ordered the destruction of all that we owned and finally drove us out of the area. We gathered up what was left and became nomads and slowly migrated west, putting as much distance between the wall and us as possible. All the while we maintained our system of laws, freely passing them on to anyone who wanted a stable system of government. But a group of nomads with a sophisticated system of government is quickly seen as a threat to any tribal leader or structure, so we were always encouraged to move along.

Because of our nomadic lifestyle we had to train our people, men and woman, in the art of defence, as attacks on nomads were commonplace. It was not uncommon for Hephthalite women to lead men in battle. I think you will find Lydia to be an excellent sparring partner. She hasn't had anyone really test her yet."

"Lydia?" I said in astonishment. "You mean this Lydia?"

"Yes, the same. It's about time she had her comeuppance."

"Father!" she exclaimed, blushing. "How can you say that?"

"Because it's true. And it is about time. Where were we? Oh yes — the tribe eventually settled at Wulumqi, at the eastern end of the Taklamakan Desert. An area not too dissimilar to Ordos. But some still longed for the nomadic lifestyle and decided to migrate north up the Yenisei River. Others, my ancestors, migrated west up the Tarum River, around the northern edge of the Taklamakan Desert. But the core remained in Wulumqi. Eventually we crossed the Tien Shan Mountains and shortly before 400AD we settled in what is now Sogdiana.

"Those who went up the Yenisei later migrated westward through the steppe regions and at about the same time as we settled in Sogdiana, they settled in an area east of the Volga River.

"Because of our legal system, which sought to promote fairness and justice, we were turned to by the local tribes as independent arbiters in disputes. Within thirty years we had become the ruling class and had replaced the Scythians in Transoxiana, and as far west as Khorasan. Complete rule was achieved in 531AD under our king, Yedaiyilituo. Because of geography and the Oxus River, he moved his capital from Wulumqi to Bamiyan. Bactra became a centre of administration.

"Even though we had settled in Bactra and Sogdiana, we maintained contact with our brethren on the steppe and the Yenisei, and we still had influence down the length of the Tarum to Wulumqi.

"During the migratory years we had kept mainly to ourselves for reasons already given. When we saw that we were a natural physical match with the remnants of the Greek and Roman populations in Sogdiana, and saw that they had similar levels of sophistication, we intermarried with them, thereby adding new blood and increasing our population base. Hence my and Lydia's Greek names. We also integrated their alphabet and many of their customs and laws with ours, which resulted in a highly sophisticated society and a unique alphabet.

"Our society consisted of those who wandered the plains as nomads, who were also our eyes and ears. There were those who didn't want to be nomads but also did not want city life, and farmed the highly fertile valleys and provided food for the town dwellers. And in the towns we had merchants, physicians, academics, administrators, teachers, artists and lawmakers, who provided the infrastructure for the whole society.

"Getting round to your earlier question; soon after crossing the Tien Shan about seven hundred years ago, we were migrating through this area when we suffered an attack. After the attack was beaten off we searched out a remote place to bury our dead. We came across this valley and decided it was remote enough to prevent grave desecration. One of the men was enlarging a fissure in the rock, when he broke through and discovered the caverns, hollowed out by years of water activity. Initially it was thought of as just another cave and a place to bury the dead, and promptly forgotten. Well—almost.

"Over the next hundred years we invaded Persia and succeeded in making them vassals. But that didn't last long. The empire was also extended well into Kush, defeating the Guptan Empire. Bamiyan was ideally situated to rule the whole empire, south, north and east of the Hindu Kush. During this time we inherited and gathered a great deal of wealth, and with it came documents and books."

At the mention of books my interest was definitely raised. Iksander paused in front of a large door, drew an equally large key out of his pocket, unlocked the door and pushed it open. What faced me was simply amazing. A high vaulted chamber, carved out of the rock, which I later measured to be two hundred fot long and one hundred wide, crammed with row-upon-row of bookcases full of books, documents and maps. Iksander could see the wonder on my face. I stood in awe, wondering about what secrets the information in this library would reveal about the past. I was brought back into the present as Lydia slipped her hand into mine.

Iksander noted our contact and permitted himself a brief smile. He continued, "I must confess, I was hoping for someone like you to turn up one day. When your men appraised me of your military prowess and achievements and also of your learning in Kiev and Byzantium, I was convinced that you are the person to help this library survive."

Awestruck, I said, "Maybe. A library like this must not be allowed to disappear."

Lydia's closeness and the opportunities that such a library offered were a heady mix. Well, for me at least. I asked, "How did it come to be here?"

"Ah, now that is another story," Iksander said. "In about 530AD our steppe brethren, who have since begun to call themselves Turks, united with King Khosru I, and began a systematic campaign of driving us out of Persia. By about 540AD the results of the campaign were more than obvious; Toramana, our king, wanted to ensure that the great library survived. The Muslims were known to burn anything that did not give a positive reflection on them or their religion. No offence, Your Highness."

"None taken," said Ibn.

"Toramana ordered a place be found to hide the empire's wealth, history and library. Someone came across mention of these caves in an old document, and the race was on to expand the cave system and move the library and treasury here. We brought many of our Buddhist citizens here, mostly monks who were experts in building cave monasteries."

"Yes. I have experienced their handiwork first hand," I said.

"Ah, yes. Of course you have. The caves were extended and library was moved piecemeal between 544AD and 566AD. Moving it all at once would have raised suspicions, and our movements noted. So, every time an Hephthalite merchant went east along the Silk Road to trade, he was given books or documents to bring here. And just in time, too, for we lost Bactra and Sogdiana in 577AD. When Khosru arrived he found an empty treasury and an even emptier library. He was furious. By then just about all the Hephthalites had evacuated Bactra. Some went south to Bamiyan, others north to join our steppe cousins. But those he could get his hands on were cruelly tortured. Fortunately no one broke under interrogation. If they had we wouldn't be here today."

I stifled a yawn and said, "Excuse me."

"Quite understandable. I think that is more than enough for today. We will continue tomorrow. You must be tired, and perhaps have other things on your mind. We will continue tomorrow."

With that he left us alone in the library.

"I can't believe that this is happening to me," I said. "Just over a week ago I thought that I had had enough underground experiences to last a lifetime. And now here I am wanting to live underground."

"Oh, and why is that?" said Lydia, obviously fishing for information.

"Why? Well this library, for starters. Just think of the information and secrets to be revealed? How many years' worth of information does it hold?"

"More than one thousand years' worth. You said just for starters — what comes after starters?"

"Oh, exploring the area above ground. Finding out how your people have made this cave system work. How has it been kept secret for so long? You know, interesting things like that."

"Nothing else?"

My mother always told me that when courting there was nothing like a bit of teasing and playing hard to get to make sure the other party was really interested. I thought that I would put her advice into practice.

"Well, there could be. But I'm not sure yet," I said, frowning and being as vague as I could.

"Sure of what?" she said, putting on her best demure and coy look.

"As I said, I'm not sure yet. I'll let you know when I know for certain."

Sensing Haldor and Ibn were watching us, but trying to be discreet, I gave him a wink. He smiled.

"Oh, so you'll be wanting to get back to your men then?" she said.

"Yes, that'd be good. Could you show me the way?"

"Yes, follow me," she said, turning and walking towards the door. "We must close the door. It's a seal to stop moisture from the heating system getting in and ruining the documents," she said.

I helped her pull the large door closed. When she turned, she turned towards me and we found ourselves chest to chest, almost in an embrace. Her closeness and perfume made it hard not to sweep her up in my arms and kiss her. I stepped back and said with a smile, "After you."

A flash of confusion crossed her face, then she turned and flounced off. I was not sure how much longer I could keep the pretence going. Haldor and Ibn were almost beside themselves with laughter.

I had been so absorbed in Iksander's story that I hadn't noticed that we had walked through and bypassed storerooms, an armoury, and a wood store. All were more than adequately sized and stocked. I could see why it took over twenty years to scour out this underground town.

When we arrived back at the mess hall, we were told that the crew were in the gymnasium.

"The what?" I asked

"Gymnasium," Lydia said. "It's Greek. Gymnos means naked. There were schools in ancient Sparta where men and boys exercised naked. But they also taught academics and philosophy as well. It is a model the Hephthalites adopted after moving into Sogdiana and merging with the Greek societies."

"I know what Gymnos means. Does everyone still exercise naked?" I asked cautiously.

"Sometimes. Why do you ask? You're not embarrassed to exercise naked, are you?"

"And the women?"

"Oh look, here we are," she said, neatly avoiding answering the question. I was relieved to find that everyone still had their clothes on.

The men were watching the Hephthalites practising their swordsmanship, using wooden practice swords to reduce the risk of serious injury.

"Challenge you," said Lydia.

"Not today—tomorrow maybe, but today, no. I'm still a bit sore."

"Oh yes, I'd forgotten," she said, seeming a bit disappointed.

"But don't let me stop you. I'm sure you'll find a partner. How about that youth over there, he looks is in need of a sparring partner?"

"Alright," she said and walked on over to the boy, picking up and fastening a protective mask in place on the way over. At first reluctant, the youth joined her. Lydia started by slowly walking him through the basic moves. Standing next to her he began hesitantly, but copied her moves with increasing fluidity, their cadence gradually becoming faster and faster. Quick as a flash Lydia moved from his side to his front and engaged him. The move caused him to hesitate and Lydia moved in, flooring him. She pulled him up off the soft sand and facing him slowly started the moves again, gradually getting faster and faster. I was so wrapped up in watching her move that I did not notice Iksander join me.

"Oh dear, poor Kronos," he said, alerting me to his presence.

"She is very good," I said to him.

"She is. Even better than her mother."

"Her mother? So it runs in the family?"

"It does indeed," he said. "Why are you not partaking?"

"Oh, there is an old adage—know your enemy before you engage him. Not that Lydia's my enemy, of course. I am simply looking for a weakness that I can exploit tomorrow. Plus I want to be a bit less sore and feel a bit stronger before I stand in front of her."

"Of course," he said, smiling.

"She is slower on her left side, especially when her sword has been parried, but exceptionally quick when she cuts, a move she favours."

"I think that one day we are going to have an interesting match in the gymnasium," Iksander said before moving on.

Not long after Iksander had left, the youth, bathed in sweat and on his knees, raised his left arm in final submission. His right arm was so weak couldn't lift the wooden sword any more. Lydia, on the other hand, was positively glowing and looked around for another opponent. Not finding one she removed her mask and walked on over.

"Now I know why he was at first reluctant. Shame on you for picking on a boy," I said mockingly.

She shrugged and said, "He's younger than me."

"Even so. Double shame on you."

"Yes, I know. I was giving him a hard time."

"More like beating him into submission. Remind me never to get on your wrong side."

She laughed, "I have to go and wash now. I'll see you in the mess hall later for the evening meal."

"You don't need someone to wash your back, do you?"

"Ulf Uspakson, how dare you?" she said, her gorgeous eyes growing wide in mock shock. Then with a sweet smile she said matter-of-factly, "Not today, thank you. See you later," and walked off with a wave of her hand.

Dinner that evening was the traditional lamb stew. A fare we were going to become well acquainted with over the next few months. After dinner we broke into groups. Some just talking, others watching a new board game called Kass. It was a game that the Hephthalites had picked up when they ruled the northern half of Kush. It apparently involved a great deal of strategy and each piece had its own movement pattern. Too complicated for after dinner entertainment, I thought. I'd pick it up some other time.

Instead I sat with Lydia, Iksander, Ibn and Haldor. Iksander was very interested in our time spent in the Varangian guard. Haldor and I spent most of the evening regaling him with stories of our journeys and experiences. He was most interested to hear how we managed to outwit and capture the Dromon in the Kaspian, and even more interested in how we adopted the tactics we had learned in the Mediterranean to the Kaspian.

All through this Lydia sat silently, absentmindedly twisting a braid of her hair around her right index finger, listening with care, almost like a sponge absorbing water. Ibn, having heard most of the stories before, and having read most accounts in Kiev's library, was able to offer some insights as well.

Before we knew it, it was very late and I was yawning and having a hard time keeping my eyes open. I excused myself and then realised I didn't know where I was going to be sleeping that night. When I asked, Lydia offered to show me the way.

Haldor, quick as ever, said, "Mind that you make it to *your* room, Ulf," which led to other comments like "Don't get lost on the way, Ulf."

"Alright, alright, alright, you lot. You're embarrassing the lady," I shot back. And they were.

As soon as we turned a corner Lydia's hand sought mine and, taking my arm, she put it around her waist and threaded hers around mine. We walked in silence to our rooms, content with each other's company. We stopped outside a cell. Instead of a wooden door, it had a strip of heavy cloth covering the entrance.

"This is your cell. Wooden doors are a luxury we can't afford. If you, ah, need anything during the night, just call out. My cell is next door."

"Uh, thank you," I said. "Good night. Be sure to wake me in the morning." I bent, kissed her on the cheek and gave her a squeeze, which she reciprocated. She clung on a bit longer and I disengaged her hands and walked into my cell. My heart was thumping and my spirit soaring. I hadn't felt this way for over twenty years. I lay on my bed, not sure if I would ever get to sleep that night.

The following morning Ibn and I spent in the library with Iksander, who gave me more of the Hephthalites history. He started with the steppe branch of the Hephthalites, who had settled east of the Volga.

"In the late three hundreds a boy was born to one of the chiefs. His name was Attila, who later became famous as Attila the Hun."

Ibn audibly sucked his breath in.

"As you well know, by 430 AD Attila had united the Hunnic steppe tribes and conquered most of the Western lands."

"Europe," I said.

"Yes, Europe. He was assassinated by jealous factions in the alliance. After Attila's empire crumbled, a good number of his men migrated to Bactra and some to Bamiyan. Others liked what they had seen on their drive across Europe and migrated to an area west of the Pontus Euxinus. Of the men who came to us, their campaign experience boosted our armies and gave us the impetus to settle the Persian situation. It also gave us the means by which we conquered Kush.

"From about 480AD onwards we enjoyed what have become known as the golden years, until about 530AD when it all began to unravel. Coincidentally, this was at the hands of the same Hun families who betrayed Attila. It was those same jealous factions that struck up the alliance with Khosru.

"When the Hephthalite empire fell, most families followed the migration west around the Black Sea. The plan was that a few families would stay and care for the library. When the tribe was settled in their new lands and a new facility built, the library would be sent for and moved to its new location in the West. Obviously it never happened. For whatever reasons, contact was lost and we never heard from them again. So here we are now."

"Indeed a moving story," said Ibn. "But how have you survived?"

"When it became obvious that no one would be coming, families were sent out to live as farmers. To herd sheep, cows, goats and act as if they were normal citizens. We used what was left of our merchant base to keep trading, mostly east of here. This way we were kept in stock. Our merchants would always make a side-trip, ostensibly to the town of Sary-Tash, and would always stay overnight in the village above, stabling their animals in the stables you saw. Needless to say, in the mornings their loads were always considerably lighter."

"Weren't you ever found out?" Ibn asked.

"We have had some close shaves over time. But most of the people who have ventured up onto this plain have been lost. Usually we offered them hospitality in exchange for silence. Not always, though."

"But how have you kept you lineage going?" I asked.

"In the early days marriage was kept strictly within our society, and our numbers slowly grew. But it became obvious that we could not keep on doing this, so the laws were relaxed, gradually at first, then dropped altogether. However, when some of the remnants of Igor's host, who attacked Baku in the 900s, passed through this way, we eagerly matched with them. You see, it had become a sign of high birth if you had blue or green eyes, or red or blonde hair. When Ingvar Vittfarne came through…"

"Ingvar was here!" I broke in. Suddenly a lesson in history had come alive.

"Oh yes," Iksander said. "He stayed here almost two years and his men eagerly took wives. It had to be limited to two each, as there were not enough women to go around and our men were jealous of the blonde-haired, blue-eyed giants.

Ingvar studied here in this very library. He had journeyed to Baghdad, Bamiyan, Bactra, Bukhara and Maracanda, had easily achieved his goals and was in search of another more challenging adventure. He had heard of Shambhala, and was en route east to search it out when he became lost in a snowstorm. Purely by providence he found the caravanserai. He was brought to our attention and we invited him in. We took care of him and those men who survived the storm. He lost half his men in that storm, which greatly upset him. He married the younger sister of my wife, and two children resulted from the union."

"He was here and is related to you and Lydia!" I said incredulously. Never in my wildest dreams had I thought that I would get this close to Ingvar.

Iksander could see that this had had an effect on me.

"Why the interest in Ingvar? Was he a relation?"

"No, no. No relation," I said, and then spent the rest of the morning relating our story, ending with our arrival at the caves.

"My, my, my," said Iksander. "A story, if not more remarkable, then at least equal, to ours."

Just then Lydia came in and said that lunch was ready. On the way back to the mess hall she linked her arm through mine.

Over lunch Iksander continued to ask questions about Norway, Kiev and Byzantium, and the routes we used travel between the three. I also apprised him of the Novgorod – Volga – Kaspian route, now used almost as much as the Novgorod - Kyiv - Byzantium route.

After lunch some good news was delivered from above. The storm had lessened and the sun could be seen trying to break through the sand and dust.

"Should be done by tomorrow," Iksander said.

"How do you know?" asked Haldor.

"Oh, four hundred years of recorded observations. Not just sand storms but seasonal changes as well."

"Four hundred years," repeated Haldor in amazement. "That's an awful long time to be watching the weather. Makes one think how young we Vikings really are. We had only just started raiding Wessex, Mercia and Northumberland three hundred years ago, and here you were recording weather patterns for a hundred years before that. Makes you think a bit."

"Haldor!" I said. "I do declare you're mellowing. You must be getting older."

"Aren't we all?" he replied.

"Enough of this melancholy talk. Go and do something positive."

Armed with Iksander's new information, over the next few weeks my research into Ingvar's quest to find Shambhala was progressing quite well.

Ibn had engrossed himself in researching and evaluating Islamic documents never before seen in the Islamic world. He was amazed to find unheard-of documents and books by al-Nasawi, Ghiyath al-Khayyami and al-Jawhari of the House of Wisdom.

I found a note in the Hidden Kingdom's journal of the time that mentioned Ingvar's journey east. It also mentioned that he would be going in search of the fabled city of Shambhala. A notation referenced a manuscript in the library. Eagerly I searched out the manuscript and had a coughing fit when I dusted it down. Titled *The Chalice*, a section of it read thus:

"The Chalice of Amrita, the Chalice of Beauty and Attainment, the Holy Grail.

176

Legend: the chalice is a symbol of great spiritual achievement, as can be found in Shambhala. It is believed that the Stone, which is at present in the world, is in the Chalice, and accompanies historic events; later it is supposed to return to the "Heart" of Asia.

The Chalice itself does exist, and before the beginning of a new era, it is sent to where the Teaching of Kalachakra shall be affirmed (Shambhala). Many legends exist about this Chalice. One of these says that the Chalice always comes unexpectedly and through the air. Thus, at the proper time, it was brought to the Lord Buddha.

The origin of this Chalice is Egyptian, and its antiquity goes back to some twelve thousand years before the birth of the Christian Christ. After the death of Buddha, this Chalice was for some time in a temple in Qarashaher, from which it disappeared, and since then has been guarded in Shambhala."

While there were only two other documents on Ingvar himself, there were many that described the route and the conditions a traveller to Kaxgar and Qarashaher might experience. I made notes and discussed them with Iksander, Ibn and Haldor. Iksander was most informative.

"The route you would take is the reverse of the route on which my people migrated here. The Han before us and the Tang after used to control the area. Now most of the cities are garrison towns, but the eastern-most cities are controlled by the Qochoans. You see, after we lost power in the late five-hundreds, the Tang dynasty quickly took control of the areas we had previously settled along the Tarum River. Then in the late six-hundreds the Tang began to lose power, and when the cities realised that they could no longer rely on the Tang emperor for protection, they became city-states. From the early nine-hundreds the Sung has tried to reconsolidate but has not been able to rule the Tarum Basin, mainly due to the Qochoans."

"Have you ever been to any of the cities along the Tarum?"

"Unfortunately only one—Kaxgar, which will probably be the first stop on your journey."

Changing the subject, he said, "There is a private matter I wish to speak to you about."

Taking the hint, Haldor and Ibn left the library. Iksander waited until they had left, then continued, "Do you remember your first day here?"

"How could I forget?"

"Do you remember me saying I had hoped for someone like you to come along?"

"Vaguely."

"Well, what I meant was that we are probably going to be the last people who will live in this complex. Our numbers have been declining steadily over the past years. We must make a choice. We either go and leave the library and everything else in the Hidden Kingdom, or we take it with us."

Then the realisation struck home. Iksander had planted a seed and was watering it and tending it so very carefully. I said I would give it some thought. However an idea quickly formed and I decided to broach the subject here and now. "What you really want to hear is something along the lines of a move from here and for us to take the library along with us, hmm?"

"Yes, something like that."

"But you have a more definite plan in mind?"

Iksander wasn't surprised that I had quickly moved to the heart of what he had in mind. "I do," he said.

"Well, it's better shared than not. What is it?"

"To be short—that we transport the library to your friend Olaf, in Kyiv."

For an instant the boldness of the plan struck me numb.

I nodded and Iksander went on, "Our cousins, the Hun, moved to that part of the world, in the region south and slightly west of Kyiv. Why not follow their track? What I am unskilled at is planning and executing such a move. And I have no knowledge of terrain, while you, Ibn and Haldor do."

"Makes sense. I guess we'll have to call a planning session. I have always found it best to come up with a plan and present it, rather than asking people for input into a plan. That can take ages and then you spend more time pacifying people because they feel left out because their bit hasn't been included. No. I suggest that you, me, Ibn, Haldor and two of your seniors get together, plan it and then present it, laying out the whys and wherefores, the options selected and the options not selected."

"You have obviously done this before."

"Too many times, although mostly for battle. This I look forward to planning. At least it won't be setting out to destroy, but to save."

"Always a more enjoyable exercise."

"Always."

Before we could propose the move to the wider group, we had a problem to address — Ibn. As a member of the royal family, how would he react if he heard that we intended moving this library to Kyiv? Did he see the library as belonging to the Seljuks? Would he tell his brother and would he prevent the move? There was only one way to find out.

After our evening meal I invited Ibn to the library. Lydia was a bit put out that we weren't going to spend it together. Iksander started by reiterating what he had said to me earlier in the day. I then took up the baton,

"What we really want to know is, as a member of the ruling royal family, do you have any objections to such a move?"

"I see where you're coming from."

Iksander and I sat in silence as he thought. We glanced at each other as Ibn rose and paced back and forth for a while, deep in thought. Then he stopped and said, "No. I have no objections. So long as I can use the library at Kyiv, ad infinitum, or as close as a human can get to that state. No, I don't have any objections."

"Why not?" asked Iksander, curious.

"For the very reason you mentioned earlier. If the Imams or Ayatollahs found out about this library, they would burn it all. Islam has some great and magnificent teachings, but then so do the other cultures I have come across. I could never live with myself if all this — " he said, indicating with a sweep of his hand " — were lost."

"What about your brother?"

"What about him?"

"Will you tell him?"

179

"No. If he knew he would be obliged to tell the Imams. No, he need not know. Besides, he will have access to the knowledge through me."

"You are the most unusual Muslim I have come across," said Iksander.

"To tell you the truth, I feel more at home in the western countries than I do in the eastern."

"Why is that?" Iksander asked.

"Because it allows freedom of thought, and to an extent, expression. In the Islamic countries freedom of thought and expression is encouraged, so long as it gives glory to Allah. While I fervently believe in Allah and the Muslim way, I cannot condone the burning of books and the loss of knowledge simply because they are not of Islamic origin. In the western countries you are freer to debate the virtues of Christianity versus Islam or Judaism, the theories of the great philosophers and mathematicians and so on. In the East I could never have a free debate about religion. I would be branded a heretic and stoned to death.

"Anyway, if Islam, and not Christianity or Judaism, is the true religion, then the only way to prove it is to debate it and let it prove itself. Islam must stand up to the other religions on its own and be judged alongside Judaism and Christianity in the same free environment. The prevention of open debate and not allowing people to freely choose their religion is almost an admission that Islam is not strong enough to stand by itself and the only way it can stand by itself is by preventing, for want of a better word, competition from Judaism, Christianity, Buddhism and Hinduism. So there, these are my reasons."

"Most interesting," said Iksander. "You will never know what a relief it has been to hear you speak so."

We then called in Haldor and two of the senior members of the Hephthalite community. We reiterated the proposal and let Ibn explain his reasons for not standing in the way of the move. Needless to say that this raised a few eyebrows, especially among the Hephthalites, but there was a general acceptance that this was the status quo.

I then took over, "We have to plan this journey in utmost detail. It will have to be done with utmost secrecy. Although, it's going to be hard to keep secret once we're out of the complex and moving. I suggest Iksander, Ibn and I research the route and the options and then we reconvene to discuss them and decide which is best."

This was agreed to.

"In the meantime, this must be kept quiet. No member of the community is to know until we're ready to tell them."

Over the next few days Iksander, Haldor, Ibn and I worked together. My knowledge of the geography north, east and west of our location was almost nil, and while Iksander had travelled the immediate area and had a theoretical knowledge of areas beyond this, Ibn had travelled most of the area and above all had recorded his journeys. So he became our source of knowledge for at least the first part of the journey.

We decided up front that we would use Balgichi Simantov's warehouse in Hardzhy-Tarkhan as the mid-point staging post. The route from there to Kyiv was straightforward and well protected. What was going to be hard was getting out of central Asia with our secret and cargo intact. Once out, our major hurdle would be the Kyzlkum Desert. Transporting fifteen thousand books and a few hundred people was not going to be easy. But if the Hephthalites could do it a few hundred years ago, then we could do it now.

Throughout the planning exercise Lydia kept us well fed and watered. Much comment was made over the size and quality of my snacks compared to everyone else's.

In the end we decided on four separate routes. This would reduce the risk of losing everything should they be attacked or apprehended. All four routes would go north from the complex through the Taldyk Pass and follow the Buura River into the Ferghana Valley. There they would split and take four routes, coming together at Symkent before making their way down the Araxes River to the Kaspian Sea, along the Hardzhy-Tarkhan leg of the Silk Route.

The first group would head east towards Afrasiab, and skirting the eastern edge of the city would turn north towards Toshkent and north to Symkent.

The second group would take a slightly northern course through the Ferghana Valley via the salt mines of Namangan. It would then head north through the Kamcik Pass. Once over that it would turn west and pass through Angren. At the end of the Cotkol range it would swing north towards Toshkent, before joining the route at Symkent.

The third and fourth groups would take a more circuitous route out of the Ferghana Valley. They would initially follow the northern leg of the Silk Route to Zalalabad, and continue east through the Ferghana Range. Once through they would then turn north off the route and head towards Toktogul.

At Toktogul the third group would continue west and follow the Cotkol River to Circik. There it would turn north and travel to Symkent.

The fourth group would go north from Toktogul and pass through the Talass-Alatoo Range via the Ala-Bel and Otmol passes. They would then turn west and follow the Talass River to Taraz. Thereafter they would turn southwest towards Symkent and pick up the last leg of the Silk Route to Hardzhy-Tarkhan.

While all this was going on, Rat and Pesakh would ride on ahead to warn of our coming and help prepare the warehouse to hold the library before transhipment to Kyiv.

The varied distances meant it was unlikely that all four groups would be on any one stretch of the final leg to Hardzhy-Tarkhan at one time. Nor would the groups be instructed to wait at Symkent for the others. Their instructions would be to push on for Hardzhy Tarkhan.

Having the groups not only split, but travelling at different times, was also in our favour as it further reduced the risk of losing everything at once. Plus it was unlikely that a group of bandits would want a cargo of books. Instead they would be after more valuable cargoes of gold and silver. If only they knew the power that knowledge could give them.

With the details finalised and the exercise planned, I decided I needed a workout and I went down to the gym to find a sparring partner.

Chapter 19

THE CHALLENGE

We arrived in the gymnasium just as everyone was packing up after an afternoon's jousting. Haldor wasn't in the mood and declined my invitation. Disappointed, I was about to go when Lydia cornered me and said, "You promised me a challenge, remember?"

"So I did."

"Uh oh. What have we here, then?" said Haldor. "What sort of challenge?"

"Ulf and I are going spar," said Lydia.

"More like she challenged me."

"Alright, the bets are on," said Haldor. "I'll give two-to-one on Ulf winning and eight-to-three on the girl. Ah sorry, I meant woman. Lydia," he corrected almost immediately, weathering an icy stare from Lydia.

"So, I'm a girl, am I?" she taunted Haldor.

"I haven't seen you fight yet," retorted Haldor.

"Alright, then. Let's go, Ulf."

"Wooooooh! A woman of action. Beware all who cross her path," he teased.

And with that the betting started. Although, how they would pay I didn't know because we hadn't a copper coin to bet between us.

We donned our protective masks, took a practice sword, entered the arena and assumed our positions. I purposely took an amateurish, square-on stance, instead of the usual side on, which would have reduced my opponent's target area.

Lydia's eyes were bright with confidence and expectation. I stood with my sword tip slightly below the horizontal and waited for Lydia to make the first move; she did. She opened with a thrust, which I easily parried, having hardly moved my feet.

Resuming starting positions she again started with a thrust, followed by a lunge. I feinted a retreat and left my parry as late as I could, and let her close on me, straight into my arms. I gave her a hug. She violently shook herself free.

Haldor shouted, "Hey, Ulf, you're meant to fight her to death, not love her to death."

"I know which I'd rather do," I shouted back, keeping my eyes firmly fixed on Lydia.

When we resumed for the third time, I adopted the correct stance. Lydia said, "You didn't tell me you had been trained in sword use."

"You never asked," I replied. "Anyway, after recounting my adventures of the past twenty years or so, anyone with half a brain could have worked out that I would have had to use a sword at some time."

She started her move before I had finished my sentence, taking me by surprise. You old fool, I thought, you should have expected that. But I admired her tactics all the same. This time her opening was more subtle as she tried to get me to open my blade. I broke ground and took a step back. I counter-parried her move. As her tip moved past my body, I quickly moved forward, passing Lydia in a pirouette. The move caught her by surprise and she still had her back to me as I completed the move. To add to the insult, I slapped her behind with my blade at the end of the move.

"Ow!" she cried.

The move raised a cheer. Haldor shouted, "That's more like it!"

For the first time I noticed that the gymnasium was packed with just about every member of the Hephthalite clan.

"We have an audience," I said to Lydia. She stared back from her guard position, not saying anything. For the first time I could see doubt in her eyes. I knew then that she was taking this more seriously than I thought, or wanted her to.

She then came at me with a flurry of moves, which I fought hard to counter and block. We seesawed back and forth, probing and parrying, our cadence becoming an hypnotic rhythm. Thrust-block-retreat-cut-parry-thrust-lunge-stop-resume. I did not overuse my knowledge of her left-side weakness, as to do so would alert her, which would more than likely result in her adopting different tactics. As yet she hadn't used her favourite move, the cut, which I was expecting at any time. Then the finale began to develop. When it came from high on her right, I was prepared, but the force of the swing still jarred my arm as I parried it. I waited until her sword tip passed my body, bringing us in close together. I again used physical contact and I shoved her backwards. The move startled her. Not allowing her to assume her guard position, I quickly followed this with a thrust and a lunge. Sensing the move, she broke ground as fast as she could, but stumbled backwards slightly. I took advantage of her stumble and lunged again. My wooden blade made contact with her breast and knocked her off her feet. The crowd cheered and hooted.

It was rather sad, but strangely erotic, as I looked at the woman I wanted to be my future wife, lying sprawled spread-eagled upon the sand, resting on her elbows, her legs slightly apart, as she moved to a sitting position. Not wanting this to descend into a meaningless fight for honour, panting for breath, I removed my mask and offered her my hand, which she took. I pulled her to her feet, ripped off her mask and kissed her passionately.

Haldor shouted, "Hey, Ulf! You're supposed to kill your enemy, not kiss them!"

Ignoring Haldor's bawdy comments and the cheering crowd, I continued to give Lydia a long kiss. She responded with equal passion, wrapping her arms around my neck. They cheered even louder. Breathless, we broke apart and holding hands bowed to the assembled crowd.

Iksander walked across the arena and said to us, "A fine match indeed. And most sportsman-like, I must say." Turning to Lydia, he said, "I think you've met your match — in more ways than one."

She blushed, adding more colour to her cheeks, and looking down said nothing.

We retreated with the throng to the dining hall where some sweetened squeezed lemon drink was waiting. Standing, we thirstily downed our drinks, while watching each other over the rim of our tumblers, trying not to laugh. Her eyes were bright and alive again.

We sat down and Lydia snuggled up beside me, her head resting on my shoulder. Iksander, Haldor and the others joined us.

"Can I ask you a question?" I said to Lydia.

"Uh-huh," she nodded. "Go ahead," she said.

"Alright," I said, ordering my thoughts. "Here you are, a beautiful athletic woman, amazing eyes, glorious hair. You could have had the pick of any man. By now you should have had a tribe of children running around and hanging onto you. Yet you are not married — why not?"

"Well..." she began to answer.

Iksander cut in quickly, "I can answer that for you, Ulf," he said.

"Father!" cried Lydia.

Raising his hand to stop her, he went on, "It goes something like this: consider an exceptional young man. His swordsmanship outstanding, he can throw a javelin further than anyone else in the tribe, well almost. His wrestling skills are second to none. He is also a gifted student who can read, write and speak eight languages. And so the list of achievements goes on. Not only this, but he has looks and a physique to match his prowess.

"Now, consider a beautiful young woman, like all young unmarried women in the tribe, totally infatuated with this exceptional young warrior. A natural match, you might say. In a moment of play she challenges the young warrior to a sword fight."

"Sounds familiar," I said, squeezing Lydia's hand. She squeezed back.

Iksander smiled and went on, "Yes. Anyway she defeats him, and not by a simple margin. She soundly whips him. In an attempt to recover his honour he challenges her to a javelin-throwing contest, which he loses, as he does with knife throwing. The wrestling was a draw. His honour totally destroyed, he leaves the tribe. He must have thought, What would happen if she couldn't get her own way in a marital argument? Would she beat him up? Now, how many other young men, do you think, would ask for this woman's hand in marriage, knowing that she could outdo the best warrior at just about every physical sport?"

"Probably not many," I said.

"Actually none," said Iksander.

"Thank you for being so hypothetically obtuse, Father," said Lydia rather acerbically.

"My pleasure," he said, beaming.

The following day I spent in the library trying to develop a matrix that would allow for the re-categorisation of books into Olaf's library. Iksander had given his apologies and had arranged to have Lydia assist me. Sitting next to me she tried to explain the system. I couldn't resist putting my arm around her shoulders. She paused briefly, then pulled in a little closer. I slipped my hand under her arm and cupped her right breast. She paused again, looked at me and carried on. I then started playing with her nipple.

"Stop it!" she said half-heartedly, slapping my hand with a smile on her face. "We will have plenty of time for that later."

I let my hand fall to rest on her right buttock, which I squeezed. Trying to be serious, she said, "Ulf, we MUST concentrate to do this properly." But her eyes betrayed how serious she was. Not able to resist any further, I lifted her onto my lap, she squealing as I did it. I then kissed her passionately again. She responded in kind.

We were so wrapped up in each other we didn't hear Iksander enter, "Children, children, this is a library, not a harem."

Embarrassed, we broke apart and hastily rearranged ourselves. Iksander was smiling the broadest smile a father could give. He chuckled and said, "Maybe I should put a bell on the library door, eh? Lydia, why don't you give Ulf a proper and complete tour of our Hidden Kingdom?"

"I think that would be a good idea, Father. We're not getting much done here."

"Oh? It didn't look that way when I walked in."

"Father? Please! Don't be so embarrassing."

"Just remember, I was also young once."

The underground complex was spread over three levels. The top level had the entrance, stables, forge, armoury and some store rooms. The second level had the gymnasium, mess hall, living quarters, library, school rooms, a chapel and more store rooms. The lower levels were predominantly living quarters, but because numbers had dwindled, these were now used for stores.

The top two levels had their own water supply. A stream that came in at the top level was split into two channels, one for each level. The water was used for intake and also to wash away any waste or leftovers. This way any subsequent levels were not fed polluted water. It was one of these that Iksander had been directing repairs to on the day of our arrival. A strict rule was that any waste must be ground into a paste before being added to the stream. Individuals ground their own with the tools provided. This way it would dissolve more quickly. In the early days blockages had been caused by fruit rinds, pips and the like. Flooding had almost occurred and a strategy was quickly devised to ensure that it did not reoccur. As the stream emerged at a lower level on the mountainside, just above the Kyzylsu River, not ten mil hence, dissolution of waste was of high importance to prevent the discovery of the colony.

The top level housed the horses, not only because it was easiest to clean, but leading horses up and down ramps cut from stone was a slippery and dangerous task for the humans and animals alike. Plus it hid the entrance to the complex.

The forge and armoury, also located on the top level for pollution reasons, was what really interested me. I wondered how the smoke and fumes were exhausted from the complex. The Buddhists, ingenious as ever, had worked this one out a great deal of time ago, long before they had started building this complex. They built a chimney and directed one of the streams to fall through it, like a waterfall. This way most of the smoke passing into the chimney was collected by the water and washed away, reducing output considerably. Towards the top of the chimney, some one hundred fot above, there was a series of straw and stick filters, which ensured that by the time the top of the chimney was reached, the smoke was all but filtered out of the air. This way they ensured that they were not given away by pillars of smoke on the outside.

The complex was carved in exquisite detail. The floors were absolutely level and the stairs, originally square cut and roughened to give grip, had begun to take on a concave appearance as a result of centuries of wear. A banister with ornate carvings was cut from the rock to provide a handhold. Its surface was worn as smooth as the steps. The floors met the walls at right angles and I had yet to spot a join that looked anything other than square. The passage roofs were smooth and semi-circular. Most had patterns and designs carved into them. It didn't surprise me to hear that it was made by the same people who had created our cave-tomb.

On the second level, there were communal bathing areas fed by a mix of the hot spa water and cold stream water. The water supply for cooking and drinking was siphoned off before it entered the bathing areas. Four hundred years of use had meant that the rock had become as smooth as Sogdian glass in some places. As such, grooves were being cut into the steps all the time for better grip. The hot spa water bubbled out of a fissure in the rock and the cold stream fell from above into the bathing pool. The waterfall served as a shower. It was custom after spending time warming and heating oneself by the hot outlet, to quickly exit the pool and stand under the cold shower and then re-enter the hot water, not unlike the sauna houses and snow-rolling that was done in my native Norway in winter.

I found the chapel to be interesting. The floor had a chequered pattern of alternate matt and polished squares and the walls had amazing frescoes carved into them. One sculptor had used perspective so well that he made a three-inch-deep carving of the last supper seem to be in an adjoining room. The altar rail was also ornately carved rock. The altar was carved from solid rock as well and had Jewish, Islamic and Christian frescoes carved around it. The Christian cross, the Jewish Star of David and the Crescent and Stars of Islam all hung on the wall above the altar.

"This is surprising," I said to Lydia. "It must be the only place in the world where all three religions exist side by side—and in peace."

"Well, when you consider they all believe in the God of Abraham, Isaac and Jacob, why shouldn't they?"

"Have you ever tried getting an Imam, a Priest and a Rabbi together to tell them that? It would never happen."

"Oh, but it did—right here. When we settled this area the Hephthalites were all Zoroastrians. Then, at the height of our powers, the Nestorian monks passed this way in the five hundreds, most converted to Christianity. A few wanted to believe in the same God but in a more traditional way, and chose Judaism. Then over time the influence of Islam began to grow and some of our people converted, so we had to cater for them as well. With the exception of the

Zoroastrians, each group still worships here. There are strict rules about times allocated for worship. And even stricter rules about religious discussions, the main one being that we must agree to disagree and that tolerance is prime. Everyone has the right to choose their own belief system. When the Hephthalite Empire was falling, those who chose to stay agreed that we had to stick together for the sake of the Empire. Anyway, a very wise Hephthalite elder put it into context. He said that we will only know who was right on judgement day, and that there is no point in arguing about it until then."

I laughed at the simple logic of the statement, and we moved on.

It was at the end of our tour that Lydia and I found ourselves alone on the lower level. The lower level had had its water supply closed off a long time ago and was now only used for stores. She was busy nattering away explaining where the stores had come from, what they were for and how they would be used. I found my interest was not in the whats, wheres and whys of sacks of grain, wheat or barley, but in her. I slipped my left arm around her waist again and then drew my right hand up to her breast, which I began to massage. Her nipple responded immediately and she stopped talking. She pulled in closer to me, her head resting in the crook of my shoulder. She said, "Mmmmm. That feels so good."

She tipped her head back. I was quick not to waste this opportunity, and kissed her. She responded by kissing me back, holding me tight and pressing her body up against me. I undid the cord around her waist and the front of her apparel fell open. I slipped my arms around her back and ran my fingers down her spine, tracing a line to her buttocks. Through the kiss she gave a slight shiver and a moan. Squeezing her buttocks firmly, I pulled her hard towards me, her pelvis tight against mine. She moaned again. Hard as a rock, I was trying not to rush. She undid my top and pulled it over my head, then undid the tie on my undergarments and they fell to the floor. With the exception of my boots, I was as naked as the day I was born. She then wrapped her arms around my back, pulled me close, and kissed me hard again. I could feel her hard nipples against my chest. I slipped her garment off her shoulders and she let it fall to the floor. Her body was glorious and firm; her breasts ample and hips generous. I sat on the sacks and pulled her sideways onto my lap. I kissed her neck and followed a path to her nipples. She gasped as my tongue made contact, her body pressing hard into me. With my left hand I began stroking the back of her leg and she groaned again. I gently prised her legs apart and slowly moved my fingers up to the point of their meeting, gently pushing my way in. She gasped again as my finger found her clitoris. I began to gently rub it and she gave a deep moan.

Legend of the Last Vikings

"Oh, Ulf, is it always like this?"

"Always," I muttered back from her breast.

She responded with another moan. Her breathing began to quicken as she neared her climax. Suddenly she tensed, arched her back, squeezed her legs together and shuddered, gasping, "Oh yes, oh yes, OH YES!"

Taking this cue, I swung her around so that she straddled me. Sensing what was next, she helped make the move easy and guided me in and began a slow rhythmic movement on my lap.

Kissing passionately with our arms wrapped around each other, her slow and rhythmic movements gradually became faster and faster, our blissful moaning turning into panting as we built to orgasm. I wasn't sure how much longer I could hold out, when she arched her back again, squeezed her legs together and pushed down on me as hard as she could, letting out a scream as she came. Her last move driving me over the edge, I exploded within her, giving her a hard squeeze and letting out an equally loud groan of pleasure.

We slowly came back down from our high, regaining our breath in between kisses and stroking each other's bodies. We stayed in our coital position even after I had gone soft, enjoying the pleasure of our bare flesh-on-flesh contact.

Our lust sated for now, we dressed, and arm-in-arm we made our way back to the middle level.

The following day the news came down that the storm had finally abated and that it was now clear outside. There was a rush to get to the outside. Initially I thought it was just to see clear skies and sun again, but there was a more pressing reason. The vents that allowed fresh air in and warm air to escape had to be cleared. So the whole population was mobilised and we climbed our way to the outside.

The scene that met us was one of stark monotony. Nothing had been left untouched. The whole landscape was one of monotone dun. Not even the snow was white; it too was impregnated with dun-coloured sand. Iksander said, "Well in fifty or sixty years' time the water in the complex will not be fit to drink."

"Come again?" I said.

"Well, the stream that runs through the complex is glacier melt. In fact, from that one over there," he said, pointing out a glacier stretching into the distance.

"In order for the ice to form, snow first falls and is then compacted by further snow falls, turning it into ice. Eventually a layer of snow will reach the bottom of the glacier, where it grinds on the rock, melts and becomes our source of water."

"Most interesting," I said. I had lived in similar climes all my life, but had never considered the effect weather had on glaciers.

We were assigned tasks by Iksander and went about our business of clearing the vents and installing new filters. Nothing was wasted. The old straw filters would be burned in the kitchen fires tonight. I found myself working alone with Lydia.

"Strange, how you and I just seem to end up working together, and alone?"

"Yes, strange that. I can't ever imagine how it happened."

"I'm sure you can't," I said, slapping her backside as we knelt on the ground preparing the new filter. She squealed and punched me back. Even her playful punches packed a whack. Before she could retract her arm I grabbed it and pulled her towards me. She squealed again but didn't resist. Kneeling, we locked arms around each other and kissed passionately. It was hard resisting the desire to make love again. But we had a job to do. Not to mention that it in those conditions it would have been more than obvious that we had been making love. There was absolutely no way it could be done without getting covered in desert dust from head to toe and all spaces in between.

While we toiled away, I asked Lydia, "How often does this have to be done?"

"Twice a year at least. At the end of summer and winter, and after every sandstorm."

"Would I be right in saying that the warm air keeps them clear during winter?"

"Mostly. Sometimes one or two do get blocked. Then we have to venture out, usually in foul weather, to clear them. You do notice that by the end of winter they need replacing. The air starts to become quite stale."

Our task over, we made our way back inside to wash.

I spent the afternoon in the library scouring the catalogue, making a list of the books and documents I wanted to research before they were packed. They focussed on Ingvar and the route he took. I also made a second list of books and documents that contained the Hephthalite alphabet and the calligraphy they practised. There was a whole section on the house art of Afrasiab, which by the titles looked most intriguing.

I completed my two lists a few hours before our evening meal. With nothing much else to do, I went down to the gymnasium and sparred a bit with Haldor. He had been teaching some of the youths some of the finer moves of swordsmanship; moves we hadn't taught to the soldiers in Kyiv, only because they would never have had use for such finesse in battle. When we finished Lydia was waiting.

"Remind me never to take you on in a sword fight," she said.

"Oh, I thought you had learnt that lesson already."

"Yes, but you never used half the moves in your repertoire, did you?"

"No, I confess I didn't."

"Why not? You could have beaten me in a few quick moves."

"Lydia, my darling, one of the first lessons of leadership I learned was that just because you can beat someone, doesn't mean you have to. And to teach someone a, ah, lesson, doesn't mean you have to almost kill them to have taught the lesson."

"Oh, so you were teaching me a lesson, were you?"

"No. In the great library in Byzantium, there is a poem. A great poem, in fact, and I have adopted one of the lines as a life guide. Part of it says, 'All through life you will meet greater and lesser people than yourself'. I have taken this to mean that because I have been advisor to kings, have led hosts into battle and can read, write and speak a good number of languages, does not make me any better than a blacksmith, weaver or tentmaker."

193

"But you have accomplished so much more than these."

"Maybe. But do I have the skill of a blacksmith, a weaver or a tentmaker? Have I housed families or clothed people? No. Therefore in that respect they are greater than me. You see, it's all relative. We are all greater and lesser than every person we meet. It helps maintain a balanced approach to life. It has worked for me, maybe it could work for you?"

Walking to the bathing pools she was very quiet. Once or twice she started to say something, then stopped. When we reached the pools, turning to face me, she eventually spoke. "You know that offer you made me the other day? The one where you offered to wash my back? Well, would you like to wash my back now?"

"A thousand stallions couldn't stop me," I said. "But the pools are segregated. Which one would we use?"

"Neither of the communal pools." She then put on a mock-serious face. "Due to conduct unsuited for the communal pools, the elders had a few 'special' pools constructed. This was a long time ago, of course."

"Of course," I said, laughing. "It had to be. Lead on."

With that she took my hand and led me down a side passage. At the end three rooms ran off the passage. Each doorway was curtained off. Before entering she pulled a red scarf from her sleeve and tied it to an iron peg outside the entrance, then pulled aside a curtain and dragged me in. A pool big enough for two was carved out of the rock. We stripped in a frenzy, our craving for each other as hot and as urgent as it was yesterday. We sated our lust before entering the pool.

Immersing myself in steaming water after rampant sex was a uniquely satisfying experience. After relaxing for a while, Lydia rolled on top of me and we began the slow and meaningful lovemaking of couples wanting to make the most of each moment with each other.

That night I slept like a log.

Our daily activity slowly settled into a routine of library in the mornings, gymnasium in the afternoons, followed by lovemaking before dinner. I couldn't have been more content. On a few occasions we ventured into the outside. The landscape was now a pristine virginal white, after a few snowfalls.

Not venturing too far for fear of getting lost, we made love in the snow once or twice but abandoned it in favour of the hot pools.

Our activities were obviously no longer as clandestine as we thought, and our affection for each other, now totally unhidden, was growing every day. It brought smiles to the faces of the older women and even got us a few knowing looks. Iksander broached the subject one morning while we were alone in the library putting the final touches to our plans.

"Ulf, I know you and Lydia are more than fond of each other. You have not exactly hidden your affections, nor your actions for that matter. Do you intend to make your relationship more formal?"

"Ah, I hear a father talking. Yes, we have talked about this once or twice, but not in depth. You're asking if we plan to marry?"

"Exactly that," he said.

"Well, I'll have to ask Lydia first. But the idea is not at all foreign to me."

"Good, I'm glad to hear it," he said, and left it at that.

Over the next few days I decided a change in subject would do my head good and I spent time on my calligraphy, sketching out Nordic knot patterns and comparing them to some of the art from Afrasiab. Then an idea came to me. Careful not to let Lydia, or anyone else for that matter, discover what I was doing, I worked feverishly on a combined Nordic and Hephthalite knot design. When it was complete I took it up to the armoury and approached the blacksmith

"Have you ever worked with silver or gold?"

He paused over the piece of metal he was hammering, looked at me as if I were stupid and said, "Was Alexander a Greek?"

I laughed at my own foolishness and he chuckled too. I then laid out my request to him. He looked at my design, nodded and said to come back in two weeks.

A few days later Iksander asked me if I had thought any more about what he had said.

"All is in hand. All I ask is that you don't mention this to Lydia—yet."

He looked at me shrewdly and said, "I sense a game afoot."

"You sense correctly," I replied with a smile.

"Enough said."

"Good."

Our secret pact had been sealed.

Two weeks later I returned to the forge. Seeing me enter, the blacksmith retrieved a small package from behind a loose stone and beckoned me over. He opened an oily rag, I examined the contents and was amazed at the quality of the workmanship. Gleaming in the rag were two exquisitely worked gold rings inlaid with the silver knot pattern I had designed. How he had achieved such fine work with hands so large would always be a mystery to me. I asked him how much I owed him for the rings. He said, "If my wife ever found out that I had taken money for these rings, not only would I never have sex again, but she would probably kill me as well."

We laughed together.

"No, Ulf Uspakson, these are a gift from our family to you. A wedding present. Plus, anyone who could tame Lydia Ptolemeus the way you did deserves at least one free gift in his lifetime. Besides, you'll have to thank Iksander for the gold and silver."

"Iksander? Is there nothing he doesn't know about the activities in this place?"

"Almost."

"Many thanks again. We're most grateful."

Half bowing, he said, "My, or rather, *our* pleasure."

With that I left the forge and made my way back to the library thinking of how, where and when I was going to ask Lydia to marry me. You would think that after leading a host into battle against the Barbary Pirates, the Pechenegs, the English and the Moors I shouldn't be nervous. But I was.

An opportunity presented itself when one of the vents became blocked, probably by a small avalanche. I quickly volunteered Lydia and myself for the task. She looked at me rather surprised. I quickly covered by saying that I could do with some fresh air and needed to learn how to change a filter properly. The logic seemed to satisfy her.

We found that it was indeed a small avalanche that had blocked the vent. We shovelled the snow out of the way. Lydia scrambled down on all fours and stuck her head into the vent to examine the filter. Her garments were pulled tight over her buttocks and her figure was outlined in perfection. I knew then this was the woman I wanted for the rest of my life. It was now or never. I knelt next to her, rested an arm over her back and pinched one her buttocks.

"OW! Stop that."

"Only if you promise to marry me."

"Whassat? I can't hear you," came the muffled reply. This wasn't going the way I had intended. Then slowly she pulled herself out of the hole, "What did you say?" she said, looking at me with tears starting to form in her eyes, her face blackened by charcoal and dust.

"Oh, nothing much," I said nonchalantly. Her face went deadpan. "Only if you'll marry me."

One of the most memorable moments of my life, a moment I will always treasure, was seeing her eyes and her face light up. Only she could go from deadpan to radiance in a flash. And she was radiating joy and happiness now.

Throwing her arms around me, she cried, "Yes, yes, yes, you lovely man. Yes again, and again, and again." Tears were rolling down her cheeks, streaking the dust on her face, as we kissed in the snow on the roof of the world. I wasn't sure if we could get much higher.

We eventually pulled ourselves apart and hugged tightly. Arms wrapped around our backs, we stumbled back inside.

As we entered the mess hall one of the women was wiping down the tables and benches before lunch. She looked up and saw Lydia's face, and said, "He did, didn't he?"

Biting her lip, Lydia nodded.

She dropped her rags and ran off screaming at the top of her lungs, "He did! He did! He did! They're getting married! They're getting married!"
197

There were squeals of pleasure from the kitchen. Women and then men came streaming into the mess hall from all over the complex to kiss and hug Lydia and me.

I said to the cook, "Don't you think you should be in the kitchen seeing to lunch?"

She shot back, "Oh, you men. Always practical. Who cares if the food burns this one day? You don't realise how important today is. We never, ever thought she would ever get married."

With my arm about her shoulders, I said, "I think Iksander would mind if he had to smell burnt food for the next six weeks. Plus I'm rather finicky about eating burnt food as well. We'll have the whole afternoon to talk."

She said, "Oh, alright then," and waddled off to finish lunch.

The news had spread all over before lunch was started, and I had to endure round after round of back slapping and congratulations. All I wanted to do was eat my lunch, hungry after the morning's exertions.

Lunch now over, Lydia and I enjoyed a moment's peace together, not realising the storm of activity that was about to erupt upon us. We snuggled together, wrapped in furs, naked after making love. Holding her close, I squeezed her naked rear as she lay on top of me. Our lips touching, I said, "I love your bottom and I love playing with your breasts. It's just a pity your name doesn't begin with B, then I could love you, too."

"Oh, is that so?"

"Mmmmmm."

"Make love to me again and I'll change it to whatever you want."

Lying with her head on my shoulder tracing an imaginary line with her finger down my chest, she said, "I think your proposal was just in time."

"Uh huh. And why is that?"

"I think I'm pregnant."

I was dumbfounded. Not knowing what to say, she asked, "Well, aren't you happy for us?"

"Uh, uh, um, YES! Of course! I just hadn't expected it so soon."

"Well, what do you think happens when a man and woman have as much sex as we've been having?"

"I guess, I mean, I guess that is the ultimate result. When will it happen?"

"When will what happen?"

"The baby, of course."

"Well it's not an IT for starters! It's a baby. Your baby and my baby. The birth, not IT, the birth, will probably happen sometime near the end of summer."

"The end of summer. That is a long time away."

"Not when you have a wedding thrown in halfway through, it isn't."

"True," I said. "We'll have to start planning now, I guess. Just like a campaign."

"Ulf Uspakson, your baby and I ARE NOT a campaign to be won! Neither are we something to be planned! Not now, not ever!"

Standing stark naked and speaking as if she were addressing the senate, she said, "The damsel conquered, the campaign won, but can the great Ulf Uspakson, advisor to kings, manage the peace?" With that we both burst out laughing.

After our moment of mirth, she looked at me with an odd expression, as if she had something important to say. After a protracted silence she pursed her lips and said, "Ulf, I know about the move. There is no way you could keep it secret from me. After all, it was me bringing the meals and refreshments, and I've known that Father has had this on his mind for a long while now. So there, I know. And no, I haven't told anyone else.

"Now, if we're going to move to Kyiv, good. I will go with you to the ends of the earth. But what about your search for Ingvar Vittfarne? The last thing I want is in a year's time, or two years or five years, is for you to bring this up in an argument and blame me for stopping you from achieving a major goal in your life."

199

Humbled by her, I said, "I'm glad you brought that up, because it's been on my mind as well. Only, I've not known how to broach the subject. I mean, we're going to get married in a few weeks' time and I am torn between leaving you and going after Ingvar. I really am in a quandary about what to do."

"Then it's simple: I will go with Father and you will go after Ingvar and we'll meet up in Kyiv when you get back."

"But what about the baby?"

"Thousands of babies have been delivered, and are being delivered, en route to somewhere all the time. We Hephthalites did it for hundreds of years. One more won't be all that different. No, you must find the resting place of Ingvar and then return to me—quickly."

I was beginning to learn that my wife to be was just as strong in spirit as she was in body. Still, I wasn't complaining. I would rather have a wife who was proactive rather than demure and not always looking to me for answers. It brought a smile to my face.

"What are you smiling at?"

"I love you," I said, pulling her down and kissing her again.

That evening at mealtime, Iksander called for quiet and said, "For those of you who don't know, we are going to have a wedding. My daughter Lydia has finally met her match…"

"She met that the other day when Ulf whupped her in the arena," someone shouted.

He laughed and said, "She did that. But I, we, have some, ah, other news as well. As you know, our numbers have been dwindling for a long, long time now. And as you also know we have waited five hundred years for news to come that the new library is awaiting us. As you know it hasn't come. How much longer must we wait for the news we want to hear? You may even ask why we have waited so long to make this move. Well, there are a myriad of reasons for not having moved sooner.

"However, fortune, or rather, God has smiled upon us and has sent us two eminent scholars, Ulf Uspakson and Ibn Rashid al-Arslan, who have studied in the great libraries of Byzantium, Kyiv, Novgorod and Baghdad."

Sensing something important was about to be said, a dead quiet had descended upon the gathered Hephthalites.

"Ulf Uspakson and his comrades are not only scholars but experienced campaigners. Experienced at planning the movements of whole armies across half the world by land and by sea, fighting battles and winning.

Except on this occasion they have helped plan our move. Our move to Kyiv."

A murmur started and gradually grew to a hum. Iksander raised his hands and quiet descended again.

"Why Kyiv, you may ask? Well, our steppe cousins migrated to this area, albeit a long time ago. And also because over one hundred years ago a library was started that has gained a reputation as a place of learning. Both Ulf and Ibn have studied in this library. It is to this library that we will be moving ours.

"I cannot force any of you to move, but I would dearly love you all to come. Whatever you decide and whatever is left in the treasury will be split equally among us."

"Just how do you plan on getting there?" someone asked.

"As soon as the weather permits, I will send word to our widespread community. All but a minimum amount our flocks of goats and sheep are to be sold and camels and horses bought. Those who want to come must assemble here by the end of spring with their horses and camels. Whoever decides to come with us will be given responsibilities. They will be given two camels for personal belongings and two more to carry a portion of the library. In order to reduce the risk of loss we have decided that the move will be spread over four routes. This will reduce suspicion of anything untoward going on, as moving everything and everyone in one train would be too obvious.

"In the meantime you must decide amongst yourselves if you want to come. Before the end of this week you must inform me of your decision. There is no shame in not wanting to come and I do not want to hear any disparaging talk about those who decide to stay. Those who do decide to come must start preparing. You must take only what is absolutely essential. Remember, you will have money to start again at the other end.

"I have also drawn up a roster for packing the library. Everyone, irrespective of whether they move or not, will be expected to help. "

The rest of the evening was spent answering questions about the move. No, we hadn't decided who would be taking what route because we didn't know who would be coming. It would probably be done by drawing straws. What could we expect en route? And so on, and so on. Eventually Iksander closed the meeting, with more discussion promised on a day-by-day basis.

Thereafter, all hell broke loose. I hardly saw Lydia at all. It was as if she had been spirited away. It soon became apparent that the women were up to something. There was always someone on guard outside Lydia's room. Whenever I approached she would slip into Lydia's room and peek out through the curtain.

Her room was always shrouded in silence. Every now and again the silence was punctuated by a giggle or two, and I was sure I could hear whispers.

Chapter 20

the ceremony

Over lunch a day or so later Iksander raised the matter of what type of ceremony Lydia and I would like. Lydia said, "I would like a Christian ceremony."

"But you can't," said Haldor.

Shocked by Haldor's demand, Lydia said, "Why not?"

"Because if you do that you will offend Ibn. He's a Muslim and he can't go to a Christian church."

Pesakh piped up, "And you'll offend me too. I'm a Jew and I can't go into a Christian or Muslim church either."

Lydia looked from one to the other, quite confused. She looked at me and said, "What would my future husband and the advisor to kings suggest?"

"Oh, that's easy."

"It is?"

"Yes indeed. Do you remember saying that Christian, Jew and the Muslim all worship the same God, the God of Abraham, Isaac and Jacob?"

"Yes."

"Good, then it's simple. We have a wedding that combines all three traditions!"

Stunned, everyone looked at me, not sure if I were serious or not. But I knew I had called Haldor's bluff.

"Well, what's the problem?" I asked. "Besides, it will be quite fun to combine aspects of all three. Don't you think, Iksander?"

All Iksander could manage was to raise his eyebrows and say, "Uh, yes."

"Well that settles that, then."

Lydia objected, "What about my opinion? It's my wedding."

"What about your opinion? Anyway, it's our wedding," I teased.

Seeing the laughter in my eyes, she play-punched me, "Oh, you."

"This is going to be an, ah, interesting marriage, don't you think, Haldor?" said Iksander.

"Most interesting. I wouldn't mind being a fly on the wall in their house when they argue."

"Haldor!" objected Lydia.

A few days later Lydia and I managed to find an afternoon together. After making love I rubbed her tummy and said, "How is my little family coming along?"

"We're doing just fine," she said, wrapping her arms around me, hugging me tight and kissing me.

"Good," I said, nibbling on her ear.

"Mmmm, that's nice," she murmured back. "You know how you mentioned that we should have a combined wedding?"

"Y-e-s," I replied tentatively.

"Well, the women and I have been planning it. It will have the traditional aspects of all three. When it comes to wedding ceremonies, we have found a common thread running through three beliefs."

"No doubt with the help of Iksander."

"Of course, who else?"

"This is going to be a most interesting day."

"Are you scared?"

"Nervous, yes. Sacred, no."

"Good. Make love to me one more time."

In the run up to the big day, Iksander had the tailor cut me some new clothes in the Hephthalite style, which was a mix of just about every nationality they had been in contact with. However, the overriding style was Greek, followed closely by Roman. The only problem with the attire was that my legs would be bare, which I was not comfortable with. Well, not in public at any rate, and least of all in the middle of winter. The tailor suggested that this was the style. But my insistence paid off. So my garb for my wedding included a new pair of leather trousers as well.

The night before the wedding the women made me promise to stay in my room. I took some books to read and had my evening meal brought to me. Haldor and Ibn posted a guard outside my door to ensure that I did not try and escape to find out what was going on.

On the morning of my wedding day I was woken by a bleary-eyed Haldor bringing me my breakfast.

"What's up? Doesn't look like you've slept much."

"We haven't."

"We?"

"Slip of the tongue. You're not supposed to know. My lips are sealed from now on."

He smiled, turned and walked out.

A while later Iksander, Haldor and Ibn came and helped me dress. They then led me through the passages to the mess hall. Just before the hall they blindfolded me.

"What's this for?" I asked.

"Unfortunately there is no other way to the chapel except through the mess hall, and the mess hall is your surprise."

"My surprise?"

"Lydia's as well."

With one on each side, they led me through the hall, on what seemed a rather strange circuitous route. I had one of those eerie feelings; the mess hall was quiet, too quiet. But I sensed people standing silently watching me being led through. It sent a shiver down my spine.

Once safely through, my blindfold was removed. In the chapel I was led to a front pew. Garlands of dried flowers hung from the chapel wall. Ribbons of blue, red, silver and gold silk were strung between them. The cross, crescent and menorah had been burnished and buffed so that their original bronze gleamed in the candlelight as if gold.

"This is amazing," I said to Haldor.

"Wait until you see the mess hall."

"Is it better?"

"For people who live in such austerity, they sure do keep a lot of pretty things locked away."

"And that's it?"

"My lips are sealed."

"Yes, you said that before."

A rush of whispered "Here she comes" ran around the room. All heads turned and craned to see the bride enter. At a nod from someone standing at the door a small orchestra struck up a song that was trying to be formal, yet happy at the same time. The orchestra had a drum, some cymbals, a wooden flute and a lute.

When she appeared in the doorway I knew that I would love this woman to the ends of time. Her gown was floor-length cream silk, with silver and gold ribbons sewn into the hem and sleeves. A blue ribbon had been sewn in around the neck, which accentuated her magnificent blue eyes. Her hair was piled high in the Greek tradition, with ringlets framing her beautiful face. She was magnificent. I was so wrapped up in the moment that I did not feel Haldor nudge me. He gave me a sharp nudge with his elbow.

"Uh, what?"

"I said, I can see why you've fallen under her spell."

"Oh, yes. Who wouldn't want to?"

"Oh, Lord. Snap out of it, Ulf. You've got to have your wits about you today."

"Why?"

"Well you've got some questions to answer, for a start."

"Like what?"

"Like, do you take this woman for your wife?"

"Yes, I do."

"Give me strength. Do you have the rings?"

"The rings? Oh yes, in my pocket."

"It might be a good idea to give them to me now."

"Uh, oh. Yes, of course. Here you are."

Lydia arrived at the altar and Ibn nodded to his left. A few of the women started to wail hysterically. The screeching brought me back to reality with a start. Lydia was almost beside herself with laughter. She leaned across and said, "They're wailing my loss."

"Their loss, my gain."

I noticed the intricate henna patterns painted around her wrists. There would be time enough later to ask about them.

The wailing stopped. Ibn addressed Iksander and then Haldor, our sponsors, asking them if they wished to proceed with the ceremony. Both said yes. He then asked Lydia and me if we wished to proceed with the ceremony. Just to tease Lydia I almost said no. But then I thought better of it, as this was not the time and place for a joke.

He then asked us to come forward and stand under the chupah. Ibn then blessed us and said some prayers in Arabic, which I did not need to translate for

Lydia. When the prayers were over, Iksander came forward and placed identical garlands of silk flowers around our necks. I could see that he was battling to hold back the tears. What father wouldn't?

Haldor then threaded red and blue ribbons around my waist and around Lydia's, tying them in a bow between us. We then walked forward to the altar and lit two candles, bowed and returned to the chupah. Iksander then crowned us with wreaths of flowers made from silk and which matched those around our necks. He poured some red wine into a crystal chalice. Taking turns, we drank to signify that we would share the remainder of our lives together. In the Greek tradition Iksander dipped bread into the wine and fed it to us. He then led us around the altar three times, signifying that our lives were intertwined with God's as well. While we walked he reminded us that the word of God was to be our lead throughout our lives.

Haldor then returned and placed my right hand over Lydia's. He withdrew the rings and Lydia gasped.

"They're beautiful. Where did you get them?"

"That's for me to know and you to find out."

She gave me a mock mean look.

"Actually it was a joint effort," I said.

Haldor chipped in, "Children, can we move the ceremony along? I've been up all night and haven't eaten yet."

We laughed.

He exchanged the rings three times, signifying that our lives were intertwined forever. He then blessed the rings and gave them to Ibn, who led us through the next stage. I slipped the ring on the fourth finger of her right hand and as I did so said, "With this ring I bind my life to yours and take you for my wife."

The sniffs and sobs could be heard, and they weren't all coming from those gathered. Lydia was positively shedding tears.

With difficulty she took my ring and also placed it on the fourth finger of my right hand and, sniffing with tears streaming down her face, said, "With this ring I bind my life to yours and take you for my husband."

Pesakh, took the crystal chalice, wrapped it in velvet and placed it on the floor. I was invited to stamp on it, which I did, and everyone cried, "Mazel Tov!" With this final part of the official ceremony over, the congregation erupted in cheers. I swept Lydia into my arms and kissed her passionately. The congregation left and we were placed on chairs and carried to the mess hall, the chupah carried over us. As we neared the hall, someone trumpeted on a ram's horn and cried out, "Behold, the bride and groom cometh!"

The mess hall was a brilliant swash of colour. Once again the blue, red, gold and silver ribbons abounded. The tables arranged in the shape of a horseshoe were decorated in silk flowers like the ones we were wearing. We were placed on a raised platform covered in plush cushions at the open end of the tables. The chupah followed us to our platform making a mini-pavilion. Before us, an assortment of foods was neatly laid out on a carpet.

Iksander called for quiet and started the speeches. "Friends, old friends and new, today is an auspicious day. Two people, two unique people literally from opposite ends of the world have found each other. I do not believe by coincidence, but by divine providence. In a similar way that Ulf Uspakson's ancestral cousin, Ingvar Vittfarne, found his way to this very room, so did Ulf. In the same way that Ingvar took an Hephthalite wife, so has Ulf. Well, alright, almost the same way."

This raised a round of laughter.

"Though there is no record of how Ingvar won his wife, we do know how Ulf won his!"

The gathering clapped and cheered and Lydia blushed.

"Ulf, in the short while I have known you, and I'm sure I speak for all gathered here, you have shown yourself to be a leader, gracious in the extreme and above all, a man of honour."

"Hear, hear!" cried Haldor, which was followed by another round of clapping. It was my turn to show embarrassment. Lydia squeezed my hand.

Iksander continued. "If ever I were to place the life of my daughter, my only child, in the hands of someone, it would be yours. But I must say, you took your time in getting here. We were all beginning to get worried that you would never arrive and take Lydia off our hands."

"Father! How can you say that?" Lydia objected.

Then it was my turn to give a return speech.

"Uh, where do I start? To escape from the clutches of the Black Scorpions, travel halfway across Asia, at night, and become lost in probably the worst sandstorm for a hundred years, just short of my objective, only to think I was going to die. And then to wake up to see the face of an angel gazing at me, and speaking Ancient Greek—who wouldn't have thought they had gone to heaven?

"I, we, are most humbled at how you have opened the doors to your home and your hearts, so readily to us. You will never know how much it means to us. Oh, and don't let our rough exteriors fool you for a moment. Underneath these exteriors are men who live life to the full and love with passion."

"That's right—ask Lydia!" someone shouted, which caused my bride to blush.

"A wise man once told me, oh many, many years ago, that getting married is like learning to sleep on a bed of roses. From the outside it looks good and the fragrance smells even better than it looks. But when you lie down you're bound to feel the thorns."
"That's not the only type of thorn to be felt," bawled Haldor, which led to much laughter, causing Lydia to blush even more.

When order had been restored I continued, "At the beginning of the marriage you don't know where the thorns, both large and small, are."

"And I guess she'll soon learn where the big one is," quipped Haldor, which yet again raised more laughter. I could see he was going to make this hard for me.

"Alright, alright. You get the meaning. From the bottom of my, sorry, our hearts, we thank you. We thank you all. We are humbled to feel loved so unconditionally by so many. And thank you also for not besting Lydia before I managed to get here. The trip would have then been a waste of time. Thank you again."

Then it was cook's turn. She stood up and waddled into the horseshoe and said, "Before you start the feast of food, you must be made aware of the feast of life. You must know the meanings of what is laid before you.

On this tray, the Sini-ye Aatel-O-Baatel, are seven multi-coloured herbs and spices to ward off witchcraft, the evil eye and to drive away evil spirits. They are Kash-Khaash, Berenj, Sabzi Khoshk, Namak, Raziyaneh, Chaay and Kondor. Here we have Noon-e Sangak, with the blessing Mobaarak-Badd written on, to bless the feast and your married life. You can thank young Kronos for the calligraphy.

"And over here we have a basket of decorated eggs, another of decorated almonds and yet another of walnuts and hazelnuts to symbolise fertility. Although somehow I don't think you're going to need this blessing.

"A basket of pomegranates for joy.

"A cup of rose water to add sweet perfume to your life together.

"A bowl made from crystalised sugar to add further sweetness to your lives.

"A brazier holding burning coals sprinkled with wild rue to add incense and spice to your lives, and a bowl of gold coins, representing wealth and prosperity.

"A needle and seven strands of coloured thread to sew up your mother-in-law's lips. Although, thankfully neither of you will have this problem.

"A copy of the Bible to give spiritual guidance and a prayer carpet to remind you of the importance of prayer. The assortment of sweets and pastries are for later. But first we must break the sugar cones."

At this point a few of the women came forward and held a large silk scarf over our heads. Cook took two sugar cones and ground them together over the scarf. This done, the scarf was folded with the residue still inside and given to Lydia.

She then took a cup of honey and instructed us to dip the little finger of our right hand into the honey and feed each other. This symbolised that we would think first of the other before ourselves. We were instructed to dip our fingers again and to suck it off ourselves. An unspoken word passed between us and we fed each other again, to much applause.

The formalities over, the feasting could begin.

Thereafter the food flowed freely. There was raucous laughter and merriment all around. Nikokrates the blacksmith brought his wife over to see the rings he had so exquisitely fashioned. Lydia planted a huge kiss of thanks on his cheek, which embarrassed him. To see the giant of a man blush was a sight to behold. On seeing the rings, his wife puffed up with pride. I had an inkling of what would also be happening in their cell tonight.

Plates upon plates of food were delivered and devoured. Carafs of wine disappeared almost as fast as they appeared. Cook had done us proud. The orchestra played away and the people danced with seemingly endless energy. Every now and then a musician would be spelled so that all would be allowed some participation in the merriment. I danced with Lydia until she was snatched away by Haldor. She then spent the next half hour being passed from one partner to another. Likewise the same happened to me. I remember being firmly grasped by cook as we waddled our way around the floor to the great amusement of those who watched us. At the end of the half hour Lydia and I were absolutely exhausted.

As the afternoon wore on it didn't seem like the level of energy would diminish.

Late in the piece, Iksander clapped his hands and the orchestra stopped playing. A guard of uniformly clad Hephthalites ran out from one of the passages and formed a corridor. They all held lances, which were decorated with the blue, red, gold and silver ribbons, the colours of the Hephthalite nation. Lydia told me that the uniforms were those of the Empirical guard, not seen for almost three hundred years. We were being greatly honoured. Quiet descended upon the gathering and Iksander called us over. As we moved over, four of the soldiers lifted and carried the chupah over our heads.

"An ancient Jewish custom is that the groom is spared military service for one year, although I don't think that will be necessary here. Another custom is that the bride and groom are locked in a huppah for the first seven days of their marriage. We, your men and the Hephthalites, under my guidance, have prepared a huppah for you. I have looked forward to this moment with both happiness and sadness for a long time now." Lydia squeezed my hand.

On a signal from Iksander the guards snapped to attention and then lowered their lances so that their tips met, forming an archway. As we started walking the orchestra struck up a melancholy tune and my spine tingled as we walked down through the arch of lances on our way to the huppah.

Iksander led the way through the passages, followed by ourselves, the honour guard and then the Hephthalite throng. I noted that the huppah had a wooden door instead of the usual curtain. Iksander took a large key from his pocket and made a show of unlocking the door. Once it was open, he stepped forward and kissed Lydia on both cheeks and gave her a bear hug. He then took me by the hands and looked deep into my eyes, tears welling up inside his. He then stood aside and saying nothing he indicated with his hand that we should enter. I hefted Lydia into my arms and carried her across the threshold to much applause. Before Iksander closed the door, Lydia ran back and gave him a big hug and a kiss. He then closed the door and made an even bigger show of locking it. Well, it sounded that way.

The huppah was stocked with just about every requirement we could want; figs, sweetmeats, nuts, dried and spiced meat, rice, jars of honey and wine and more.

A sumptuous bed filled the middle of the room and was made up with a silk quilt and plush pillows. A canopy similar to the chupah had been constructed over the bed.

The day had been a fairytale come true for both Lydia and me; I had married a princess. We stood there just looking at each other, drinking in the visual spectacle. We stepped into each other's arms and hugged each other for what seemed like an age, not wanting the moment to end. Somehow we found each other's lips and before we knew it, we had stripped off our clothes and were passionately embracing.

Afterwards I wondered if I could I keep this up for the next seven days? I did not know the answer, but I was sure as hell going to try.

Chapter 21

EVACUATION

We were asleep, wrapped in each other's arms, when I heard the door being unlocked. We had briefly wondered when we would be let out, as the candles had almost burned out.

The door was slightly ajar, and Iksander called out, "Are you decently attired?"

"No. Give us a few minutes."

"Alright. I'll be back shortly."

Lydia stirred, "Was that Father?"

"Yes. Our incarceration is over."

Hugging me, she said, "Oh well. All good things must come to an end."

"I hope not for another thirty years, at least!"

When he knocked a few minutes later I bade him enter.

"Well children, your incarceration is over."

"I would hardly call it that. And, please, less of the children bit."

He laughed. "Come. We have prepared your new home, albeit a temporary one."

We were led down to the lower level. Passing through the mess hall, we were greeted as if we were an old married couple. There were few signs that a ceremony had taken place only a week previously.

Two of the storerooms had been cleared out and our new home had been prepared. A doorway had been knocked between the two. All the condiments of our marriage were there. Our chupah, minus its poles, hung over our bed decorated with our ribbons and flowers. The symbolic foods were all containerised, some in expensive Sogdian glass jars. Our garlands and crowns

214

had been neatly arranged upon our pillows. The gifts, and there were many, were neatly laid out, all labelled along one side of the room. If a gift wasn't made from silver or gold, then it had the precious metals inlaid or overlaid somewhere on it. The generosity was overwhelming. Lydia had to bite her lip to stop herself from crying.

The first signs of spring had shown themselves a few days into our internment. Iksander had sent the word out for the remainder of the clan to start buying horses and camels, with the instruction to do so in small numbers so as not to raise suspicion, and start shipping them to us.

The complex had started to resemble a goods warehouse. Most personal belongings had been packed, the library had been left until last.

Only five of the sixty-four families had decided not to come along, and they were mainly older couples who no longer had children. They would take over the caravanserai and continue to live in and around the village.

Then the packing of the library began in earnest. We estimated that we had about four to five weeks before the first camels and horses would begin to arrive. Iksander was most particular that all crates should be appropriately labelled so that when unpacking in Kyiv it would make re-categorisation to the Kyiv system easier. We were well under way when Ibn came over with a scroll. "Iksander, this piece by al-Nasawi—I don't recognise it."

"Let me see."

He handed over the scroll. Iksander unrolled it and said, "Ah, this is the rough copy of his first work, The Four Treatise of Number Classes. You will find the original document under the same reference number but with the character that looks like a W."

"You mean a copy of the original?"

"No, I mean the original, off which the copies were made. The original is in Sogdian. When al-Nasawi went to Baghdad, your great uncle, the first Sultan, persuaded him to re-write it in Arabic. However, before going to Baghdad, he donated his workings and the original book to the library. It was most generous of him."

"Why is the work so important?" I asked.

"Well, up and until he wrote this work the Arabs used a sexigesimal system of counting. He was the first Arab to use the decimal place-value system, originally used by the Kushans. He combined the Kushan system with the Casting Out Nines checking procedures, from the *Chinese Mathematics in Nine Books* series, and has revolutionised mathematics in the Arab world. Now, lecture over, enough of this idle chitter-chatter — we have packing to do."

With that admonishment we recommenced our task.

While we were working in shifts and resting in between, Iksander was not. He spent all day in the library, from dawn until dusk, supervising the packing. He was beginning to look tired. Lydia tried to get him to rest but he would not, claiming that the packing was too important. If anything wasn't packed correctly it would be ruined and he wasn't about to allow that to happen. So until the final document was packed, he would remain on duty. I reminded Lydia that it was only for a few more weeks and wouldn't be forever. Still, she wasn't happy.

At the end of week three the first camels and horses started arriving. Each family would be allotted two camels for personal belongings and each family member over sixteen would be allotted the responsibility of two further beasts, which would be carrying part of the library.

At the beginning of the fourth week it became obvious that we would have to despatch the caravans as soon as they became ready. A hundred or so camels and horses would soon strip the countryside bare of any fodder. That evening we drew the first straws.

Haldor would lead the first group. Following Pesakh and Rat's arrival in Hardzhy-Tarkhan, his presence would verify the endeavour we were about to undertake. Iksander and Lydia would also be first to go, as it would be necessary for Iksander to be in Hardzy-Tarkhan when the library began to arrive. Lydia would also be going first, so her journey would hopefully be over before it was time to give birth.

On the day of the first departure, Lydia's departure, everyone was busy scurrying about checking and double-checking their loads.

Lydia and I had started the day by making love. The knowledge that we were going to part today for what could possibly be a whole year was unspoken, yet acutely felt. To say the atmosphere was charged would have been an understatement. It was just as well that we had tasks to do, otherwise I am not sure that either of us would have handled the day at all well. After breakfast, for the first time in a long time, we went our separate ways, each with our own list of tasks to be carried out.

By midday the camels were loaded and there was nothing much more to be done, except depart. Iksander's last act was to go to the back of the library, where he removed a loose stone and withdrew what looked like a wooden tablet.

"What is it?" I asked, having already concluded that it was something valuable.

"It is called the Diamond Sutra. It is regarded as the first book ever published. As opposed to a scroll, it has seven pages and is dated 868AD. It came into our possession just over one hundred years ago and is a much sought-after piece. This travels with me."

As we walked up to the surface I said to him, "If you are attacked, and heaven forbid you are, don't you think it would be obvious that this was more precious than the cargo on the camels?" I asked.

"I see what you mean."

"It is sometimes better hidden if it is in plain view, rather than locked away."

"Have you been reading Confucius?"

"Tsun Tzu."

"Ah." He stopped, gripped my arm and intensely looked at me, and said, "I will look after your Lydia, our Lydia. But you know that already."

"I know you will. And I know she will look after you."

"This can't be easy for you."

"No, it isn't. I now know how all those married men felt each time we went a-Viking. Not knowing if they would ever see their families again."

Iksander looked at me without saying anything.

"Still," I said, "I've survived this long. At least I'm not going into battle."

"Yes, that is a blessing. Come, let's not hold up the caravan."

On the surface the caravan was waiting, and so was my Lydia. Her bottom lip was trembling as she stood by her camel. It seemed so unfair that on such a glorious, clear and bright spring day, we should be parting. A feeling of déjà vu came over me. Ingvar had left but with her aunt, probably in similar circumstances, not forty years before and they had never been seen again. I'm sure it had crossed her mind as well. I hugged her tightly and said, "You are so strong. Your father and our child will need your strength—until we are together again. I promise you I will not dally. I will ride swiftly and when I have found Ingvar's resting place I shall return as fast as I can."

"I know, my love. I know you will."

Iksander placed a hand on her shoulder and said, "It is time."

This served as the catalyst and Lydia burst into tears and clung to me sobbing. Through the salt of her tears I kissed again and hugged her tightly. Then with great difficulty I unwrapped her arms and helped her onto her camel. With a snort and a bray her beast stood, its reins taken up by a youth in her party. The look she gave me wrenched my heart and I had to turn away. Thank goodness Haldor was standing there waiting for us to finish our farewells. We hugged in true Viking style before wishing each other good and safe journeys.

"I promise you that I will see no harm comes to your Lydia. With my life, if need be."

"I know you will, good friend. I know you will. Anyway I plan to be in Hardzhy-Tarkan by the end of summer."

"Until then."

"Until then."

Then with ponderous slowness the caravan started moving away. Lydia craning around to savour that last look, as if she was etching me into her memory. I stood and waved, watching the caravan slowly make its way north across the plain until they were dots on the landscape. I swear I could see Lydia looking back and waving.

I was brought back to reality as Pesakh and Rat came over to bid their farewells. I said to Rat, "You will soon be back with your Serakh. Ride carefully and don't take any risks. Remember, it's better to stop and consider the alternatives to a situation than it is to rush in without considering them. Remember the Jewish saying, fools rush in where angels fear to tread."

"I know, I know," said Rat impatiently, although I knew he really didn't know at all. At least he would have the level-headed Pesakh to add caution to his impetuousness.

"Look out for him," I said to Pesakh.

"I will, I promise."

"Thank you," I said.

They mounted, gave a wave and trotted off after the caravan on their faithful Bactrian steeds.

Over the next three weeks we despatched the remaining three caravans , although none with so heartfelt a tug as the first.

Then it was our turn to prepare for departure. With the exception of the remaining five couples, there were only seven of us left. Because we were travelling light, preparation did not take long. I was going to miss Haldor; his acerbic wit, his advice and his usefulness in dangerous situations. Who would now stand at my back in a time of battle?

Chapter 22
Kaxgar

So here we were, Ibn, Sven, Larz, Knut, Kalas, his son Marsias and me. I reread my notes on the paper:

"Shambhala – legend says that its name "Sham" was derived from "Shem" the eldest son of Noah because he chose to live there after the flood.........Shem - Hebrew: Sun.

....the land of Shambhala lies north of the Tarum River, beyond the Araxes / Kur River. ...The remains of the mighty castle, a 'mother of castles', the ancient fortress of Kabalah / Kalapa, is situated on a hill on the great Tarum River that flowed from the mountains of Tarum in northern Persia.

Legendary home of the Chalice of Amrita, also known as the Holy Grail.

The imperial rulers of Shambhala, who are called the Rigden Kings (Persian/Pars: Rig = King + Den = Wisdom), *are inhabitants of the 'cosmic mirror' – also known as the "ultimate drala". When you make contact with the wisdom of the cosmic mirror, you are connecting with the ultimate dralas, the Rigden Kings of Shambhala. Through their vast vision they watch over and protect human affairs* (not too dissimilar to the mythical gods of Greece).

The heart of the compound is slightly elevated over the surrounding buildings. The whole structure has been built in the shape of the lotus flower. Its palaces are made of gold, silver, turquoise, coral, pearl, emerald, moon crystal, and other precious stones (how much opium had this person smoked when they said this?).
In front of the thrones are crystal looking glasses that allow one to see far into the distance (I had one of these). *It has beautiful gardens.*

North of Kalapa are wooded and rugged mountains. (possibly the Tien Shan?) *The faces of the peaks have been engraved with images of the Buddha and the gods.*

South of Kalapa is a sandalwood grove. In the centre of the grove is the mandala circle of Kalachakra.

East of the grove is a small lake. To the west is another white (or silver?) *lake made in the shape of a lotus flower.*

Legend of the Last Vikings

....The King, or Kalki, and his queens possess the four aims of life: sensual pleasure, wealth, ethics, and liberation (sounds too good to be true)

....The houses in the villages of Shambhala are two-storey houses. The people have fine bodies and appearances and they are very wealthy (Hephthalites?). *The men of Shambhala wear caps, and white or red cotton clothes. Women wear white or blue garments pleated and patterned with beautiful designs* (ties in with the Hephthalite cloth-making/weaving capabilities)."

I thought to myself, What had been Ingvar's true goal? Riches, the mythical powers that the holder of the Holy Grail would inherit or the alleged wisdom and insights that Shambhala offered?

I folded the paper and tucked it into an inside pocket, pointed into the distance and said, "That way—I think."

Kalas, Ibn and the others laughed and we spurred our horses and rode away from the Hidden Kingdom shortly after breakfast on the second day after the last caravan had left, we rode south out of the Taldyk area. The day was grey and dismal, not at all like the day my Lydia had left going in the opposite direction. I couldn't help but wonder what she would be doing now. Haldor would have had the whole caravan up, fed, watered and on the road by now. The fatter members would be cursing having to do so much exercise. Give them a month and they would be as fit and as trim as anyone else in the caravan.

On reaching the main artery of the Silk Road we turned east and made for Kaxgar, Ingvar's first point of call after departing the Hidden Kingdom. We were flanked by the Tien Shan on our left and the Pamirs on our right. Both ranges stretched majestically away as far as the eye could see.

If the sheep and goats hadn't devoured the vegetation during summer, then the extreme cold over winter killed off any above-ground growth. Hence there was nary a tree nor shrub to be seen. The whole scene was of white, snow-covered ground merging with sheets of blinding white glaciers that stretched as far as the eye could see. These in turn mingled with the clouds. The grey and brown rock faces also merged with the snow-capped peaks and the grey and leaden sky. This monochrome vista had a unique beauty of its own.

And it was cold. Freezing cold. But if we wanted to make it to Hardzhy-Tarkhan by the end of summer we had to start our journey now and put up with a little discomfort.

The only people we encountered were shepherds moving their flocks early, trying to get to the most succulent pastures before anyone else did. Kalas asked one if anyone had come through from Kaxgar yet? We were told that the pass was still closed and probably would be for a week or so yet. This was not news I wanted to hear. Still, we pressed on, our Bactrian mounts as sure footed as ever in the icy and slippery underfoot conditions.

By the end of our first day we had made it to the village of Ulugqat, at the head of the pass. We set up camp in a few disused shepherds' huts rather than pay the exorbitant caravanserai fees. Kalas did some investigating and a while later came back to say the pass, while mostly covered with snow, could be traversed with horses but not yet with camels.

The following day we started our ride early. The snow had drifted in places and we had to dismount and plough our way through. Each time Kalas took the lead, as he knew the route. After a while I wondered if this had been a good idea, but we pressed on. Thank goodness it was mostly downhill. Fortunately as we descended, the amount of snow lessened until the lower reaches were totally clear. However, it was with sodden boots and frozen feet that we made the village of Wuqia at the base of the pass in late afternoon and made for the nearest caravanserai to warm up and dry out. Starved after hours of exertion and a quick cold lunch, we were surprised to find a welcoming committee awaiting us. Being the first travellers through the pass this season, we were regaled with questions. Was the pass open? What were the conditions like? How much snow remained? When did we think it would be open? Would camels be able to pass through now?

In the end to gain some peace and quiet I paid the caravanserai owner a little extra for a private dining room and a little extra again to ensure that we would not be disturbed that night. He had instructions to wake us in the morning earlier than the other guests.

The following morning we were up before it was light, had breakfast and were departing as the caravanserai guests were waking. Kalas said that Kaxgar was but a day's ride from here so we did not push our steeds, not after the hard work of yesterday. It would also do us good not to push ourselves too much now, for we still had a whole spring, summer and probably autumn of travel ahead of us.

On exiting the mountains we crossed a flat featureless plain and cantered into Kaxgar in mid afternoon, after another cold and light lunch. I thought deserts were supposed to be hot and dry places; I was wrong. This one was cold and dry. The sun was without warmth. It was more of a bright disk obscured by clouds and the fine loam dust blown into the atmosphere off the Taklamakan Desert and it tended to disappear behind the mighty wall of the Tien Shan by mid afternoon. Had I known at lunch-time that we were so close to Kaxgar, I would have pushed on, just for the warmth and a hot meal that a caravanserai offered.

And then there it was—Kaxgar, pearl of the Silk Road and the place where empires meet, situated at the foot of the Pamirs where the Tien Shan and the Qara Qorum ranges intersected. It was a fertile oasis town on a strategic cross-roads through which everyone had to travel to get to and from the commercial capitals of the east and west; producer of wheat, corn, barley, rice, beans, cotton, melons, grapes, peaches, apricots and cherries; manufacturer of rugs, carpets felts, cloth, leatherwear, pottery, wool, hides, furs and some copper goods. Many merchants had stopped travelling the Silk Road and simply set up shop here instead. But never had I seen a marketplace like it before. I had seen the markets from Byzantium to Alexandria, but none compared to this. I tried to spot anyone standing still but concluded that I must be the only one who wasn't moving in the entire place. Some merchants had stalls while others simply placed a blanket on the ground, arranged their wares, and sitting, legs splayed, and hawking away.

After the calm and silence of the Hidden Kingdom and the tranquillity of the mountains the place was an assault on my senses. Looking around I could see that Ibn, Kalas and the others were feeling a little queasy as well. I stopped for a moment and the motion was like a blur, except for... For a moment I was sure that someone else had, like me, stopped, and was watching us. But by the time I tracked back to where that person had been standing, he had gone. I couldn't help but think of the Black Scorpions. Or was I being paranoid?

The smell of spices pervaded the senses. Areas of the marketplace had been created using rough-hewn wood, branches or saplings. Food stalls had been set up all over the place selling cooked meat, stews, kebabs, soups, satays, pilaf rice and fruit. People were gathered together in twos and threes negotiating, buying and selling anything from pigeons, wheat, chickens, sheep, cloth, spices, oils and carpets. While alongside them barbers were shaving heads and trimming beards and alongside them again merchants were displaying the latest designs in copper ware. Bolts of brightly coloured silk and cotton were draped over bales of wool and delivery boys drove donkey-drawn carts while others pushed theirs, crying POSH! POSH!—get out of my way!

223

As Kalas led us away from the market I saw the man again, coming towards us. Well dressed in a deep blue silk shirt and black cotton trousers, he wore a matching blue and black headpiece with gold beading. An ornate scabbard hung from his belt, almost touching his calf-length leather black boots. He was carrying a small wooden chest under his arm. As he neared us he seemed to stumble and drop the chest. Big Sven, as courteous as ever, bent down and retrieved it for him. The man thanked Big Sven and went on his way. Big Sven sucked his index finger.

"Are you hurt?" I asked.

"No, it's nothing. I just nicked my finger on a corner of the box."

We passed through the city's winding roads past single-storey limewashed houses with royal blue doorways. Some had simple awnings constructed of heavy cotton, supported by dressed tree limbs to keep the doorways clear of snow. Our destination was a hotel owned by a man with Hephthalite roots and sympathies. He went on to say that most of the people of the Tarum Basin have Hephthalite roots anyway. After centuries of conquest and rule by the Tibetans, the Han and now the Turks, they were afraid that any display or claim to Hephthalite nationhood would be dealt with severely. So in the main any ideas of an Hephthalite resurgence were buried so deep that they had been forgotten about, except by a few.

After stabling our horses we had an early meal and Kalas brought the hotel owner up to speed on the latest developments. He was saddened by the move out of the Hidden Kingdom as this severed their last connection to the empire of old. Kalas told him he would be welcome to follow suit and migrate to the new lands.

We then told him we were searching for men of European looks who passed through Kaxgar about one hundred years ago. We asked if he knew anyone who had knowledge of Ingvar Vittfarne. He looked at us with a pained expression and said, "We are forbidden to talk of him. To do so will get me killed."

"Why? What happened?"

Looks of doubt crossed his face, then he said, "Alright. I will tell you because you are Hephthalites or related to Hephthalites. But a warning—do not speak his name or ask about him outside this room, for it will surely get you killed."

"But why?" Ibn asked.

"I will have to start at the beginning."

Chapter 23

TASHKURGAN

"In our language Tashkurgan means 'stone tower' or 'stone fortress', and that's all that Tashkurgan has to offer, or rather had to offer. A long time ago, legend has it that a great king of Persia had taken a Han princess as a wife. He had sent an escort to accompany her back to Persia. When the party reached Tashkurgan they were prevented from passing through the valley by brigands. The princess was placed on an isolated mountain peak and guarded day and night. When order was finally restored it was discovered that the princess was with child. Fearing the wrath of their king, the officials of the escort party panicked, even though they were told by the princess's servant that she had been visited by a god of the sun everyday at noon and that he was the father of the child she carried.

Afraid to return to Persia, the party had a fortress palace built from which the princess ruled the area, which became known as Sarikol. In time she bore a son 'of extraordinary beauty and perfect parts. He was able to fly through the air and control the wind and snow'. He came to rule the entire region. He died at a great age and was interred in a great mountain cave. Even after his death he continued to perform miraculous deeds. About four hundred years ago his remains were seen by the monk Hsuan-Taung, hundreds of years after his death, and they had not decomposed. The words of Hsuan-Taung were that it was as if he were asleep.

Not long after Hsuan-Tang passed this way, the Han lost control of the Tarum Basin and the Tibetans overran this area. They introduced Buddhism and more particularly the Path of Vajrayana, which was a dangerous mix of Buddhism and Manicheanism.

"Then the Qarakhanid Dynasty was established about one hundred years ago with its capital here at Kaxgar. They rejected Buddhism and were the first to embraced Islam in the Taklamakan. Hence two kingdoms existed side by side—the Islamic Qarakhanids here and the Buddhist Karakhojas at Khotan. More recently our Khan, Satuq Bughra, an Islamic extremist, conducted many bloody jihads against the Buddhist kingdom. Tashkurgan was sufficiently isolated to serve as his place of imprisonment and torture for those he captured. Like the Taklamakan Desert, those who went in never came out.

"During this time trade was severely disrupted and when Satuq Bughra Khan realised his treasury was running dry because of the lack of trade, common sense prevailed once more and peace was restored and trade resumed, but that didn't stop him enforcing Islam on everyone. The fortress of Tashkurgan continued to be used as before, until the time of Ingvar Vittfarne, about forty years ago.

"Ingvar and his men had been in Kaxgar for about a week seeking out information on Shambhala. No one would speak to him about Shambhala due to its Buddhist leanings and for fear of being arrested and imprisoned in Tashkurgan. One day the group was lunching in the marketplace when suddenly the usual rhythm of the marketplace was interrupted. A group of soldiers started clearing a space in the square, ordering merchants and hawkers to pack up their goods and move out.

"A large crowd began to gather around the cleared space.

"A tripod was carried into the square and a crossbeam fixed in place just above head height. A young man and woman, Hephthalite in looks, with hands tied behind their backs, were dragged forward. Their hands were retied to the crossbeam shoulder width apart, and they were bound to the uprights at the ankles.

"A soldier then began to read out a declaration, "This man and woman have been found guilty of breaking the laws of the great Satuq Bughra Khan and the laws of the holy Quran. The accused have been living together as man and wife and in the eyes of Allah have not been married in the holy and sacred way. They have therefore been living an adulterous life. The Great Khan, Satuq Bughra, has decreed that these two are to be flogged to death as an example to those who would break his laws and the laws of the holy Quran. Begin the flogging."

"Due to his time spent with the Hephthalites in the Hidden Kingdom, and his Hephthalite wife, this act incensed Ingvar. Because of this and his wide travels, he had come to respect the different religions of the world and an individual's right to worship whomever he or she chose. He strode forward with one hand and grabbed the flogger by the wrist just as he was about to deliver the first blow. A cry rose up from the crowd and the flogger tried to break free, but Ingvar's superior strength held him easily. With his free hand he removed the whip from the flogger's hand and cast the man to the ground, challenging him to take him on. A deathly silence descended on the market place. Never before in the history of Kaxgar had there been such a silence. The dogs did not bark, the

227

cocks did not crow and the pigeons did not coo. Something great was about to happen.

"The head soldier ordered his men forward, and as they came forward so did Ingvar's men, swords drawn. Satuq's men did not want to take on these fine-boned and muscled white men. One of Ingvar's men stepped forward and freed the captives. The soldiers withdrew from the marketplace and the crowd rejoiced, for Satuq Bughra Khan was a cruel and vicious man, even to his own people. That night in the market place a great party was held and much rejoicing took place. Ingvar was hailed as a saviour of the people, the restored Hephthalite king, for he spoke our, at least their, language. Before the rejoicing was over that night, he had been told how to find the fabled Shambhala.

"Overnight Satuq rushed reinforcements from Tashkurgan and surrounded the market square. In the morning he arrested Ingvar and some of his men, who were taken in chains to Tashkurgan. A few of his men managed to hide amongst the bales of wool and cotton and weren't captured. One even rolled himself in a carpet.

"With the euphoria of the previous day gone, no one wanted to help free Ingvar. They all said that the fort was impregnable and that to try and free him would be suicide. After all, it had been standing there for almost a thousand years.

"That day another decree was read out, that if anyone spoke of Ingvar and his act of bravado or the Hephthalites ever again, they would be beheaded on the spot without a trial. The people had good reason to believe that the Khan meant what he said.

"That night Ingvar's remaining men crept out of the city and made for Tashkurgan. They crept up to the fort and hid themselves on the hill, observing the comings and goings at the fort, watching for that weakness that would allow them to break in and free Ingvar.

"Word of their plan somehow filtered back and slowly in ones and twos and threes, people, mainly young men, made their way to Tashkurgan. If you had been to the fort, you would know that with any more than fifty people you begin to run out of places to hide.

"Instead of storming the fort, they sat there on the hillside. This unnerved the soldiers and initially they tried to drag the people off and away, but they were fighting a losing battle, for more came everyday. And they sat silently in their thousands on the hills, watching and waiting. Everyday the soldiers shouted at them to go away.

"But still they sat. Then the soldiers tried killing a few people. They beheaded six where they sat and no one moved nor resisted. They just sat and watched and waited and the soldiers went back to the fort.

"By the seventh day there were thousands on the hill and on the plain and they began to sing in a foreign tongue:

> *Ingvar is still a youth*
> *And he seeks the truth*
> *He is ready to take the pain*
> *But truly it would be in vain*
> *For in death he be set free*
> *And Allah he will see*

"Over and over, louder and louder until the soldiers fled the fort with their hands over their ears. Only then did Ingvar's men go forward through the open gates of the fort. Inside they found Ingvar unharmed, for the soldiers were afraid to harm him lest the people held them accountable and attacked them. They also found Satuq sitting on his throne staring blankly into space. There they left him.

"As he exited the fort, the people's singing rose to a cheer when they saw Ingvar emerge unharmed. He raised his hands and called for silence, and addressed them. "People of Kaxgar, you have shown a wisdom beyond that of ordinary men, in that you have overcome force with peace and evil with love. Remember forever those who died these past few days, for they are true martyrs. It is easy to hate, but harder to show love and caring. If you want to be a truly great people you must love and forgive. Forgive the soldiers and forgive the Khan for his indiscretions, for I have already done so. This fort has become the symbol of the evil that Shaytan would spread on this earth. Destroy this fort today, make it unusable for ever more."

"The people then surged forward en masse and most of the fort was torn down by hand and has remained so ever since.

"Satuq, suitably humbled, was restored to his throne and never again called a jihad against anyone, although his successors did.

229

"Ingvar and his men left Kaxgar and continued their travels east towards Agsu and Kuga.

"The following summer we heard that he was in Lou Lan and then all trace of him seemed to disappear."

"That was quite a story."

"It is no story, it is the truth."

"Even the bit about the sun god and his son?"

"I believe it to be so. The remains of the palace are still there to be seen."

"Well then, we won't linger here any longer than necessary. It's Lou Lan we're heading for."

Chapter 24

SITA DARYA

The next morning we made an early departure from Kaxgar. We joined the "Pei-lu", as the northern arm of the Silk Road was colloquially called. On our ride to Lou Lan and Lake Lop Nor we would be following a course that ran parallel to the Sita Darya, along the southern base of the Tien Shan. Our host in Kaxgar said it should take eighteen to twenty-five days, dependent on the weather, bandits and the horses.

While the wind off the Tien Shan was still decidedly cool, it was definitely warmer here that it had been at the Hidden Kingdom. What did surprise me was the amount of cultivated land, greenery and forest along the route. Ibn pointed out that there were many ice-melt streams that fed the Sita, off which the vegetation fed. He likened it to the Nile in Egypt. And like the Nile, outside the immediate vicinity of the Sita, the desert reached away to the horizons, with dunes like frozen golden waves stretching out across an ocean of sand. All the while we kept watch for any telltale signs that we were being followed.

The Tien Shan amazed us with a rich variety of colours and hues of greens, reds, oranges, ochres and maroons, which changed during the morning as the sun rose and changed back again as the sun set. The route wove its way into and out of the yellow sands of the Taklamakan and the desert never let you forget that you were its guest. Skeletons and grinning skulls of camels, horses, goats, sheep and humans lay scattered along the trail; some in piles, others strewn about the place. Although we all saw this, no one mentioned it.

On our second day out we passed through the small town of Artush. Kalas informed us, "Satuq Bugrah Khan, he of Tashkorgan fame, is buried here. He had a grand tomb constructed, but within a year of his death the tomb was destroyed by an earthquake. The locals believe it was God's way of letting everyone know that Satuq did not find favour with Him."

"An interesting theory," said Ibn. "But we'll only know if it is true when we get to heaven ourselves."

"Maybe. But what God would condone the slaughter of tens of thousands in His name?"

On the sixth day of travel Kalas led us off the main route to a complex of abandoned Buddhist caves at a place called Tumshuq. They had been abandoned since the Tang Dynasty pogroms over a hundred and fifty years ago. The more recent rise of Islam, which did not permit the worship of idols and statues, had kept it this way.

As we approached the caves the terrain changed and became hillier and rockier; an ideal place for an ambush. I asked Kalas, "Aren't you afraid that bandits might be in the area waiting to ambush us?"

"No. It is too early in the season. It is more convenient, safer and warmer to stay in or near the towns than out in the countryside during winter. Not only is it bitterly cold, but there is no one travelling and therefore no traffic for business."

Touching his nose, he said, "Besides, I have contacts," and he would not be drawn into elaborating further.

If Kalas was confident then it was good enough for us and we let him lead us to the grottos without any further argument. The caves themselves were works of art. It was disappointing to note that fires had been lit at random and many of the once beautiful frescoes were now coated with soot and fine desert dust and were hardly visible. Most of those that could be seen had accompanying Brahmi inscriptions, on which I commented.

"This is to be expected," said Ibn. "Buddhism was imported from Kush over eight hundred years ago, hence the Indian facial figures on the characters and the Brahmi script."

In one cave we found an eight-fot-high defaced stone statue of Buddha. Behind the Buddha I found some thin planks of discarded wood, which I gathered to use for firewood. Before I lit the fire I noticed what seemed to be some inscriptions on the wood. I took them outside and in the fading light the inscriptions became more legible. I raced back inside and stopped Kalas from setting fire to the remaining pieces. Taking them all outside, I sorted through the pieces and those that were too badly damaged or too faint to read I gave to Kalas for the fire. The remainder I wrapped and put on my packhorse. Some I noticed were written in Sogdian and others in a script that Kalas said was old Tocharian. These would be a good surprise gift for Iksander and Olaf.

The following morning we were up early. After a lifetime of shepherding and living in the open, waking up before dawn had broken was as natural to Kalas as breathing.

It was Big Sven's turn on fire duty, and I noticed that he was favouring the finger he had nicked. I asked to look at it. The fingertip was red and inflamed. I called Ibn over. He examined it and suggested that there may have been some dirt on the box that had infected the finger. He told Sven to keep it clean and wash it at every chance he had.

We were on the road just as day was breaking.

Our daily activity soon became routine. Rise, eat, ride, eat, ride, eat, sleep. And so it continued day after day. Within a few more days we were approaching Aksu. On the approach we saw many sand mounds that Kalas said had once been buildings of the Han dynasty and had long since been abandoned to the elements. The landscape was also dotted with the Han dynasty watchtowers, also long abandoned, now made eerie by the early morning fog clinging to the ground and the base of these buildings.

It was easy to see why Aksu had been built at this location and so named. Three tributaries from the Tien Shan and Qara Qorum met here to formerly form the Sita, the primary river in the region. Being spring, all three were in spate and the now milky river rushed and roared its way eastwards. Ibn's comparison to the Nile came to mind again.

Kalas informed us that Aksu meant "clear waters" and there was much free-flowing water. We had experienced a short dust storm the day before and were now covered in a fine layer of loam dust. We sought out a secluded spot and stripped with great relish and bathed in the river, washing off the fine dust. It seemed that Ibn took even greater pleasure in the activity now that he had learned to swim. After our bathe I noticed Sven examining his hand. I too examined it and saw that his whole finger was now inflamed and the infection had reached his palm, thumb and third finger as well. I realised then that this was no mere cut and that the man I had seen in Kaxgar had indeed been watching us. Too many for him to take on at once, he had obviously decided that picking us off one at a time was his best strategy and had started by using the coward's weapon—poison.

Obviously the order for our demise had made it as far as Kaxgar, and the Black Scorpion, seeing us after our winter in hiding, had decided to act on his own initiative. After all, why not? If he could claim to be the agent that killed us, it could only earn him praise and would improve his standing with his superiors. It was exactly the kind of action I would have expected from one of my men and it would have been rewarded.

I informed the others of Sven's condition and of my conclusions, and that we needed to be ever vigilant of attack from the Black Scorpions. Kalas informed us that he knew of a place but a few days' ride from here where there was a doctor who could treat Sven's hand. With no other viable options open to us, we agreed to go along with Kalas's suggestion.

Over the ages Aksu had been a capital to a number of kingdoms; Han, Hephthalite, Tibetan and Tang, to name a few, and had hosted all the major religions; the Buddhists, Zoroastrians, Manicheans, Christians and now Islam, and the effect of each civilisation's architecture was clearly visible. Although neither part of the Kaxgar kingdom, nor the newer Sung dynasty, the city was still garrisoned by about two thousand soldiers. We spent a night in Aksu and wandered around the large bazaars before turning in. On a few occasions I stood still, as I had done in Kaxgar, in a vain attempt to see if I could spot anyone as still as I was. But I was unsuccessful and wondered if I were becoming paranoid. With nothing to be gained by lingering, and with Sven's poisoned hand in mind, the next day we pushed on hard for Qiuchi, leaving the green poplar groves behind and riding out into the golden, yellow gebi.

As we neared Qiuchi I was beginning to doubt that we would make it as we intended. However Kalas said the place he was thinking of was very near. He led us off the main track, onto one that passed north of the town. The track ran through low scrub and flowering shrubbery, punctuated here and there by tall grass wherever surface water was present. He said he was taking us to another complex of abandoned Buddhist caves called Qizil, which lay on the northern bank of the Muzart He. But this time he warned us, "Because it is so close to Qiuchi, the grottos are inhabited by those unable to afford accommodation in Qiuchi and those who would be given, ah, 'other' accommodation by the local Mandarin. The grottos are an old temple and monastery cave complex and have plenty of room. But we will be safe — I know the leader. Let us say that I have done him a few favours in the past."

"Oh, how so?" asked Ibn.

"In particular, when they have been evading pursuers intent on capturing them for, ah, activities not in keeping with modern society."

We chuckled at Kalas's diplomatic description of banditry.

He went on, "A few Black Scorpions have attempted to infiltrate this society, with the view of taking it over. Their deception discovered, they have never left this place."

"Honour among thieves?" I asked.

"Something like that. There is thieving and there are the Black Scorpions. These men openly admit they are robbers and bandits. But one thing they are not is evil. To suggest it would get you killed without a moment's hesitation. No, their fall into banditry is mostly as a result of the lack of desire in society to help the downtrodden and poor. However, there is no need to fear. These men will hold you in high regard because the Black Scorpions have tried to kill you, and are still trying. When I tell them how you survived the mine attack, they will most likely toast you as heroes."

Unlike Tumshuq, the telltale signs of occupation were visible well before we arrived at the former Buddhist cave monastery. Rising smoke, well-trodden paths, goats and sheep and small crops indicated the presence of people. On approaching we were challenged by a sentry. Kalas said to wait while he rode forward. Men, women and children moved freely about the place and paid us no mind. After speaking to the guard for a short while Kalas waved us forward.

The caves were carved out of the cliff face, in much the same fashion as the temple caves at Aybāk and Tumshuq. Impressed at the level and complexity of construction, Marsias commented, "These Buddhists were certainly intent on leaving their mark, weren't they?"

"So it would seem," I said in agreement.

As we approached, two guards rode forward and formed an escort. One at the head, the other at the rear of our small column. At the cliff face we were asked to dismount and with the guards still at the front and the rear, we were led up steps cut out of the rock. Not only were the caves cut out of the cliff, they were cut into the cliff. It reminded me of a place near Jerusalem called Petra, which Haldor, Harald and I had visited after being ordered back from the siege.

Thinking of Haldor brought Lydia to mind and a feeling of emptiness suddenly washed over me. What was she doing now? Was she alright? Approaching the top of the steps I realised I would have to overcome such feelings, especially at a time like this.

At the top of the steps we were led through an ornate entranceway into a large cave. My examination of the interior was cut short by a greeting called out from the far side of the room.

"Kalas, my old friend. It is good to see you, welcome. Help yourself to some refreshments, I will be with you shortly."

The man was short and rotund. While his dress was most certainly that of a Mandarin, from this side of the room I couldn't make out his features so did not know if he was Hephthalite, Arab, Kushan, Tibetan or Tianxian. Kalas stepped up to a table and poured eight drinks into what turned out to be golden goblets. The bandit trade certainly did have its benefits.

The small man came over and Kalas greeted him, "Cheng, it is good to see you too. Business planning, I assume?"

"You assume correctly. Please introduce me to your companions."

"These are friends from the Hidden Kingdom, and as you can see these four are not from around here."

"Yes, I saw. We don't get too many Europeans through here. One or two a year, maybe."

"First, this is Lord Ulf Uspakson, marshal and advisor to the King of Norway, a northern country where there are more trees than sand. And he is son-in-law to Iksander."

"Ho, ho, ho — married to the beautiful Lydia. You will most certainly have an interesting life. But what is the advisor the throne of Norway doing here?"

Here was a man with a finely honed mind, able to weigh and process information faster than it took a beam of light to cross a room.

"Looking for the resting place of a fellow Viking who passed this way about forty years ago."

Raising a finger and nodding, he said, "Ah, I think I know who you mean."

"You do?"

"But of course. Lou Lan is where you want to go. You may find something but don't hold your breath. Lou Lan is now all but dead. It has, in the

main, run out of water. There was a small colony of brethren, but I haven't heard from them for a long while now. Most trade now goes through Jiaohe."

This confirmation was music to my ears.

Kalas then went on to introduce the others. Eyebrows were raised when Ibn was introduced. I noted that Cheng did not bow or use Ibn's formal title. We all chuckled when Cheng almost broke his neck looking up when he was introduced to Big Sven. Kalas said, "This is not the half of it. Wait until you hear their story and how the Black Scorpions tried to murder them."

Cheng looked at us with a look of incredulity. "You managed to survive a Black Scorpion assassination attempt?"

"They surely did. But I think that it should be told at length over a good meal. But first, an attack in Kaxgar has poisoned the hand of Sven—the large one. We would like to avail ourselves of your medical services."

"Of course, of course. Let me see."

Cheng sucked in his breath when Sven produced his poisoned hand for inspection. After a cursory glance, he called over a guard and gave instructions for him to take Sven to see the doctor.

"Now, Kalas, you say that these men have escaped the clutches of the Black Scorpions?"

"Indeed they have. But the story is long and eventful and would best be told after a good meal."

"Ah, Kalas—ever the diplomat. It would seem that I have been talked into putting on a feast tonight."

With that he clapped his hands and started issuing orders, after which he excused himself, as he had other matters to attend to.

Following our short audience with Cheng, Kalas led us to the doctor's quarters. They were situated in a large cave. Cai Hui's quarters were a sight to

237

behold. One half of the cave was covered in shelves holding labelled jars, books and manuscripts. Paper banners decorated with fairies, deities, the sun and the moon, insects, horses and other animals hung from the ceiling. Against the third wall was a raised bed on which Sven lay with coloured threads tied around his wrists. The bed was covered in a blanket, which had many colourful depictions of centipedes, lizards, scorpions, snakes and toads. The fourth wall had an inbuilt altar, which had a few lit candles and a container burning incense. A circle was painted on the wall above the altar. Within the circle was divided so that it looked as if there were two tadpoles trying to swim around each other. One was painted blue the other red. Cai Hui was leaning over Sven examining his wound and hand, muttering to himself.

"Is he…"

"Asleep. I find it easier to work and concentrate without the patient, *or concerned relatives,* asking foolish questions," said Cai Hui assertively without turning from his patient. Ibn, Kalas and I glanced at each other and I raised an eyebrow. Taking the hint, Kalas led the others out while Ibn and I stayed behind. This seemed to somewhat satisfy Cai's temper. Turning to us, he said, "That is better. As I proceed I will explain what I am doing and why I am doing it. It will be easier than having you two ask me hundreds of meaningless and foolish questions, which will divert my concentration. Understood?"

"Yes," we chorused with a nod of our heads. I'm not sure when last a prince of Persia had been spoken to like this, but the last time I had been spoken to thus was when I joined my father's ship as a mere lad and was put under the instruction of old Johan Hallarsson, the ship's master. Ibn and I smirked.

"Alright. Your friend has been poisoned. How do I know? Come here and I will show you."

He placed three glass goblets on his workbench.

"Before we start, I invite you to inspect these goblets."

We picked them up and examined them. Clean and almost identical, we couldn't see anything untoward in or on any of them.

"I will place an equivalent amount of water from this jar in all three," and with that he quarter-filled each beaker from a single jar.

"I will now add some of my blood to one." He picked up a porcupine quill and pricked the tip of his finger. A droplet of blood formed. He then squeezed his finger over the goblet until three drops had fallen.

"I will now add the blood of your companion to the second," and he repeated the process from Sven's inflamed hand.

"Now I need the blood from one of you to go in the third."

Both Ibn and I stepped forward, but he chose Ibn and repeated the process a third time.

"Now, come look. I will add a pinch of Rhinoceros horn to each. The one that produces a white foam is the one that has poison." Ibn and Cai's concoctions remained still and unchanged while Sven's produced a pink and white froth.

"See the froth? It is an indication that poison is present. But in modern medicine, one indication is insufficient. We must have at least two to prove our case." He picked up a pair of silver chopsticks and, handing them to us, said, "Please polish these until they shine."

Mystified, we rubbed away while he continued, "Now, it has been long known that silver will tarnish when it comes into contact with poison, which is why you hardly hear of an emperor of Tianxia being poisoned." Touching his nose, he continued, "They all eat with silver chopsticks. Not gold, but silver. That should be enough polishing let me see." We handed over the eating utensils and Cai examined them.

"Yes, that will do. Now watch as I place them in the first." He dipped the chopsticks in, removed them and examined them. After a short examination he showed them to us and said, "See, no tarnishing." He wiped them off and did likewise with the second, with the same result. After dipping them in Sven's beaker the tips of the chopsticks turned a dull grey. There was a menacing hint of black where the liquid was more concentrated along the edges and at the tip of the chopsticks.

"Now we have definite proof that your friend has been poisoned."

Ibn and I were now more than convinced; convinced that Sven had been poisoned and convinced that this was no shaman.

"Now for the hard part. We have to find out what poison it is, so that we can treat it."

"Aren't you concerned for his life?"

"No, not really. At least not yet. The poison is spreading slowly. If it were stronger, he would already be dead. So no, no significant concerns—for the moment. We have some time yet. In the meantime, LIU!"

His shout made us jump.

"Yes, master?" a youth called as he came bounding into the cave, jerking to a stop and bowing to Cai. The time it had taken him to respond indicated that he must have been waiting in close proximity.

"Hang the tiger zhi ma and when you have done that, dispose of the contents of the beakers. But be careful, one has poison."

"Yes, master," said Liu, bowing again before going about his tasks.

Turning to us, Cai said, "Here we do not treat just the physical, we treat the whole being: body, mind and spirit. The tiger paper joss will suppress the spirits of the five poisons, as will the five coloured threads tied to his wrists and the symbols on the blanket he is lying on."

Ibn involuntarily raised an eyebrow.

"You don't believe me?" said Cai, on seeing Ibn's eyebrow rise, his eyes narrowing.

"I...I..." Ibn stuttered.

"Ah, you Arabs! You think you know it all. When your Ibn Zakariya Razi wrote his book on medicine about a hundred years ago, we Tianxians had already been using a similar, but more expansive text, for almost seven hundred years."

"Seven hundred years?" repeated Ibn, incredulous at the statement.

"Correct. Our first recorded emperor, Huang Di, wrote our first medical interlocutor about three thousand, six hundred years ago. Needless to say, being the first it had limited information and was of limited use, but it did standardise the naming and treatment of diseases as well as the naming of the plants and medicines needed to treat the diseases. So from that viewpoint it was invaluable. Over time our medicine progressed so that by, oh, about one thousand, two hundred years ago, the Shen Nong Ben Cao Hing had been published, which identified three hundred and sixty five medicinal plants divided into Yao. The Yao are divided into superior, average or inferior Yao. I prefer the regal categories of Emperor, Minister and Messenger Yao.

"Over time more were added. During the time of Emperor Tang, which ended about a hundred and fifty years ago, a further one hundred and fourteen Yao were officially added, bringing the total to eight hundred and forty four. After these additions the Tang Ben Cao was published. So you see we Tianxians, despite our seemingly backwards ways, are infinitely further ahead of you Arabs and Europeans — in the field of medicine at least.

"Now, enough of the history lesson, let's see what we can do to heal your friend."

As we turned our attention to Sven, Cai continued, "Because the poison has taken so long to work, I must conclude that it is a messenger Yao of inferior quality. I must also conclude that it was made by an amateur and not by someone skilled in poison making. Therefore it would most likely be made from a commonly found plant out of which the poison can easily be extracted. Probably from the tuba family, something like the wu'tou or the ch'uan wu."

Taking a large leather-bound book from a shelf, he ran a long nail down the pages, then inserted it between the pages and flipped the tome open. He tut-tutted and flipped a few more pages before emitting an "Ah, yes. I think I have found it."

Stroking his white beard, he continued tut-tutting and read further, running his finger down the columns of Tianxian ciphers.

"Ah, well I never. As simple as that? Oh well, no great challenge today."

"You sound disappointed," I said.

"Yes and no. I do enjoy a mystery and a challenge, but when there is a life at stake I will always take the simplest and most effective route. The Tang Ben Cao says that Yunnan Baiyao should be tried in the first instance. All Tianxian soldiers carry a pouch of Yunnan Baiyao as part of their personal first aid kit. Yunnan Baiyao has been in use for well over five hundred years and has amazing properties for healing wounds, expelling pus and counteracting poisons."

He again called to Liu, who came running as before.

"Is it ready?" he asked.

"Yes, master," said Liu, bowing.

"Good. When I call bring it quickly." Crooking his finger, he called us to follow. "Come, it is time to carry out the treatment."

Cai shuffled over to his wall of medicines and stood for a while examining the contents. He then selected a jar, which contained a light-tan coloured powder, and placed it in my hands. Turning, he selected a large silver knife from a tray of utensils and gave it to Ibn.

"Unfortunately the area where the poison entered the body has sustained significant damage. So he will lose the tip of his finger, which is a lot less than losing his life."

He pulled a low wooden table over to where Sven lay and placed his hand on the table, palm up, arranging it so that the infected finger lay in its centre. He spread the fingers and asked for the knife, which Ibn produced. He placed the blade over the knuckle and gripping the haft with his right hand and, placing the palm of his left on the blade, pushed down firmly. Blood and puss erupted from the severed digit.

"Liu — NOW!" he bellowed. Liu came rushing forward with a red-hot poker in his hands and applied it skilfully to the raw wound. The blood and skin sizzled and an aroma not unlike roast pig permeated throughout the room.

"Alright, enough!" barked Cai. Liu picked up Sven's severed fingertip and returned to where he had come from, with the red-hot poker in hand. The whole action had taken less than a minute.

"Now we have to counteract the poison."

He washed the knife in a solution and then proceeded to cut a slit down the fleshy part of each finger and across the top of Sven's palm. Giving the knife back to Ibn, he then asked for the jar of powder. He removed the stopper and took a pinch, which he spread down the incision in Sven's now shorter finger. He did this to each incision that he had made.

"Liu, the bandages," he called.

Liu came forward with strips of fine cotton cloth, which Cai wrapped around Sven's limp hand.

"When he wakes, I will give him a herbal tea, which should expunge the poison that has managed to get into the rest of his body. Come back tomorrow in the afternoon and the patient should be up and about. He should be well enough to ride the day after."

Before departing Cai's quarters, Ibn asked, "Cai Hui, I am a student of life. I have travelled to many towns and places in the East and the West and observed the way people live and work. I would like to document what we have witnessed today. May I spend some time with you tomorrow doing this?"

His ego obviously flattered, Cai replied, "Yes you may. Come by after breakfast. I will use it as an instruction session for Liu as well."

I then said, "Cai Hui, never in my life have I witnessed anything like you have done today. I must admit that at first I was sceptical, but I have been humbled. I thank you for saving my friend's life. He and I have been brothers in arms for a long time now and it would not have pleased him, nor me, to know that it was a poison, and not a sword, that was his undoing. Once again, I thank you."

"The pleasure is mine, but it is not over yet. We will see tomorrow how successful we have been," said Cai Hiu, smiling and bowing. "Now if you will excuse me...?"

That night Cheng laid on a princely feast accompanied by music and dancing. As leader of our group, I was given the place of honour alongside him. He was remarkably well educated and well read. He told me that as the son of a wealthy merchant and advisor to the Emperor, he was in training for a senior role in the civil service and had had hopes one day to become a Mandarin. He and a colleague were vying for an important position in Changan, which would have meant certain promotion. Being honest, open and naïve, he had been set up by the colleague and had been accused of theft. Not seeing any alternative, he had fled Changan and made his way west, eventually ending up here. Starving, the bandits took him in, and in repayment for shelter and food, he soon found his brains being used to plan the raids and manage the coffers. He later set up an intelligence network in the city-states along the Silk Road so that they could target the more valuable and easily re-saleable cargoes. Eventually he became

243

leader of the brethren and ran the settlement in the same manner as he would have a town.

The brethren became so well organised that merchants ceased trying to disguise their cargoes and started to arrange protection in exchange for being robbed. As a result more merchants took this option and there was now almost no banditry and the road was safer than ever before. By unspoken mutual agreement, Cheng resided in the old monastery and stayed out of the city's way and the city stayed out of his.

Then Kalas stood up and clapped his hands and raised his arms. Silence fell upon the gathering.

"The story I am about to tell you is true. It started a long time ago in a land far, far from here, where there are forests as large as the Taklamakan. It is a story that has adventure, death and, above all — love."

As if by unseen signal the women and girls sighed in unison and the children sat with looks of great expectation on their faces. Kalas launched into our story, not leaving out a detail. We were amazed at his ability to remember the story so well, having only heard it twice before. He covered our flight to Miklagaard and the journey back. When our engagement with the Pechenegs and the Black Scorpion Dromon was narrated, the more inebriated were calling out cries of "kill them" and "slay them" and a cheer rose up when they were told of the burning and sinking of that dreadful slave ship. When he came to our escape from the cave and emergence from the pond, he described us in detail, and those gathered began to nudge each other, whisper and point.

Cheng picked up on this and rose with a cry, interrupting Kalas's narration, "You — it is you! Is this true?"

"It is," I said, bowing my head, uncomfortable with the attention now being showered upon us.

Cheng shook his head in wonder. "Remarkable, truly remarkable. This is indeed cause for a celebration. If I'd known, tonight would have been better than this," he said, indicating the assembly.

"Fill up the tankards. Let us toast these brave men. Men who have escaped the murderous plans and machinations of the Black Scorpions."

With that we had a round of toasting. It would have gone on for longer but Kalas again intervened, calling for silence, and continued his narration through our night ride across the roof of the world, the samoom, my marriage to Lydia and our journey here to Qizil. Many of the young girls had wishful looks on their faces as they dreamed of a marriage ceremony like ours had been. It immediately brought Lydia to mind and a pang of longing struck my breast.

At the end of the story, Cheng stood and said, "Tonight we have heard an amazing story of bravery, adventure, escape, death and love. This story will be told for many years to come, not only because we have had the real adventurers in our presence, but also because of the wonder and truth of the story. I toast you and pray and ask that the gods keep you safe and bring a swift end to your journey and a happy reunion with your families."

After our celebratory feast Cheng took us on a tour of the monastery.

"Qizil is also known as the Thousand Buddha Grottos. While there may have been a thousand statues of Buddha, there are only two hundred and thirty six caves."

He pointed out a cave, which sat about two thirds of the way up the cliff. There were no steps up and a rope ladder hung down.

"A hermit lives up there. We send him a bucket of water and a bucket of food every week, though why one would want to live in such isolation is beyond me."

"If there are no steps up, how did they build it?"

"That is beyond me as well."

We chuckled and walked on. Walking through caves there were many wonderful murals depicting past life in and around the monastery. At least these had been kept in better condition. I mentioned this to Cheng, who said, "It is an unspoken rule and a matter of pride that families who are allocated a cave maintain the murals to the best of their ability. Whether or not the individual approves of Buddhism is irrelevant. It is a part of their history and culture and a people who ignore their history and culture will damn the future of their children."

"Oh, how so?"

"Approximately eight or nine hundred years ago Buddhist missionaries came to Tianxia from Kush. The people readily adopted Buddhism and lived peacefully for over eight hundred years. Even the Xiongnu, Kalas's ancestors, who converted to Buddhism, became more peaceable. By the year 3542, about your year 845, the Tang Empire was in decline. The emperor, seeing that the power of the Buddhist church was greater than his, in a vain attempt tried to assert himself by suppressing Buddhism. In the ensuing violence that followed over four thousand, six hundred monasteries were destroyed and over three hundred thousand monks put to death. While it killed Buddhism, it opened the door to Islam — no offence, Your Highness. But over the past one hundred and fifty years the Muslims, who abhor idol worship, have destroyed many temples and statues and with them a lot of our cultural history. Those they could not destroy, they defaced. The moral of my story is not to slur Islam, no; the Tang Emperor took his eye off his history and off his culture and destroyed the future of his people."

It was obvious that despite his fall from grace, Cheng still believed in his people, their culture and their way of life.

I noted two distinct styles of art in the murals, the earliest showing the Kushan influences, undoubtedly helped by the Hephthalite Empire, which extended from northern Kush into this area and west to Afrasiab, including Bamiyan. The next period showed Sassanian influences. There was no depiction of the Tianxian culture, which I found odd. The two periods depicted were obvious by the changes in the ethnical features and dress of the figures depicted. I commented on this to Cheng.

"Very observant. Are you a scholar?"

"Of cave art? No, I'm afraid not. It's very new to me. Ibn here is the scholar of people and customs, although I have made good use of the libraries at Novgorod, Kyiv, Byzantium and more lately the Hidden Kingdom."

"A soldier and a scholar. I am impressed."

"Only because the opportunity presented itself."

"Ah, but how many of those who went with you didn't avail themselves of the opportunity?"

"True."

"There, you see? What happened was that this part of the empire was very Kushan in its Buddhist discipline. Most of the monks were Kushan and hence the only figures depicted were Kushan and Sassanian. Now, this cave you may be interested in."

In saying this, we swept into a cave. On the opposite wall was a depiction of Buddha dressed in multi-coloured, shimmering robes and floating over a surreal landscape surrounded by flying Apsaras.

"This one we call the Cosmological Buddha. We believe that the artist had visited Shambhala not long before he painted this mural."

"I can see why."

"It is almost certain that your Ingvar Vittfarne saw this mural as well."

"Well, if he did, then I'm sure it would have made him all the more determined to seek out his goal."

"And you? Do you seek the fabled Shambhala or Ingvar Vittfarne?"

"The latter."

"Ah, but is it not the same thing?"

"No. I am not pursuing the spiritual enlightenment that Shambhala promises. I am seeking the resting place of one who may have. Although, I think that his search for Shambhala would have been to seek earthly enrichment rather than spiritual enrichment."

"And you, do you seek earthly enrichment?"

"No, I already have that."

"Then you are very fortunate."

"Yes. But, like all gains in life, it came at a cost."

"Ah. If you have already learnt that lesson, then you will have little need for any enlightenment that Shambhala could offer; either spiritually or physically."

"You speak as if it were a real place."

Cheng cocked his head, gave a knowing smile and suggested we get back before we were missed.

The next morning I woke early, only to remember that we had a day's rest, and I drifted back to sleep. Sometime later I was woken when Kalas and Ibn removed my blankets and shook me awake.

"Come on, sleepy head. If you don't hurry up you'll miss breakfast," said Ibn.

"How late is it?"

"Very late. The sun is halfway to its zenith," said Kalas.

"Uh huh. What about your audience with the great Cai Hui?" I asked Ibn, pulling on my clothes, which had been washed and were neatly laid out at the bottom of the bed.

"Been there, done that"

"Already?"

"Already. It was most instructive."

"Any news on Sven?"

"Yes. He had some pain, but Cai Hui stuck some needles in his hand, twiddled them about and his pain disappeared as soon as it had come. Cai Hui has also made him some tea with Emperor, Minister and Messenger Yaos and it too has had the most amazing effect on Sven. If you thought him healthy before, you should see him now."

"Needles and Emperor whats?"

Ibn consulted his notes, "About one thousand, four hundred years ago, a chap called Huang Ti Nei Ching Su Wen wrote a book called the Yellow Emperor's Classic of Internal Medicine. In this book he discussed the balance of the body, or chi as it is called. He traced meridians through the body, which when stimulated by the insertion of needles, relieve pain and discomfort and put the body back into balance. The Emperor Messenger…"

"Alright, alright. I believe you. And his hand?"

"Almost healed. Some of the incisions have a little way to go, but as Cai said, he'll be well enough to travel tomorrow."

"Amazing."

"You're telling me. I wonder what our magnificent Arabic doctors would make of my observations?"

"Probably wouldn't believe you."

"You're probably right. Ah—here we are."

Breakfast consisted of fruits of the melon family, grapes, juiced oranges, cheeses, bread, nuts, goat's milk and steaming hot tea.

Watered and fed, we dropped in on Sven. Cai Hui greeted us, "Ah, Lord Uspasson." Like most Tianxians he had difficulty pronouncing the K in my surname. "You have come to check up on my handiwork?"

"No, Cai Hui, just making sure the big oaf is not shamming."

Cai Hui gave a long high-pitched laugh. Liu looked up, startled. Kalas informed us later that it was the first time that Liu had heard Cai Hui laugh. Sven sat perched on the end of the bed looking slightly off colour, but healthy all the same.

"Ah, Ulf. I'm sorry about your finger, but it was that or your life. How are you feeling?"

"A lot better than yesterday. We need a few hundred like him back in Norway," said Sven, nodding towards Cai Hui. "Could've done with him and his kind at Miklagaard and Stamford Bridge."

"We most certainly could have. Cai Hui, what is his prognosis?"

"As I said yesterday, he can travel tomorrow. For the rest of this morning he must remain here and rest. I have one or two more treatments to perform. Later this afternoon he can walk about some. But nothing until then."

"Alright then, we'll leave him in your good and capable hands."

Sven shrugged and with that we left the surgery.

With a day free to do as we pleased, Kalas suggested we visit the Spring of Salt Tears. Ibn, forever wanting new information for his travelogue, was all for the idea. With nothing better to do, we collected the others and started our short hike to the spring.

The route wound through a steep-sided gorge that became steeper as we progressed. Clambering over the rocks was difficult, as direct sunlight hardly ever reached the bottom of the gorge, hence the rocks were covered in slime and moss, making what should have been a straightforward journey long and somewhat hazardous.

Eventually as we neared the head of the valley, we came upon the spring. It wasn't a spring in the true sense but rather a cliff wall covered in moss down which water seeped and converged at the base in a pool. What was odd was that the water was salty and not fresh.

"How odd," I remarked.

Ibn agreed. "Salt water in the middle of a desert. How is this so?" he asked rhetorically.

"That is easy," said Kalas. "I will tell you the legend. It is said that in ancient times in the country of Kuqa, a beautiful princess..."

"Ah, ever the beautiful princess," said Ibn sarcastically.

Kalas gave him a withering stare, which shut him up. "As I was saying, a beautiful princess fell in love with a common youth."

"Had to be," interrupted Ibn again. "Why can't legends be about normal people?"

"Because if they were normal there would be nothing out of the ordinary to say. Now if you really don't mind, please let me continue!"

"Alright, alright. I do apologise. It's just that..."

"Ibn!" I said. "Let the man finish."

"I promise. No more interruptions."

"Thank you, Ulf. Now the king, upon finding out, made things difficult for the youth. He said, dig one thousand caves and you can marry the princess.

The youth dug and dug and after many, many years and after he had completed the nine hundred and ninety ninth cave, he died of exhaustion."

We all looked at Ibn. Raising his hands, he said, "I'm not saying anything. Although..."

"Ibn!" I corrected him. "Kalas..."

"In her grief the princess embraced the corpse of the young man and cried and cried. Using up all her tears she too died. The cliff was moved by her grief and tears, and has cried salt tears to this day."

"Well it is a bit different. I'll make a note of this one," said Ibn, somewhat condescendingly.

Our tour over, we had a light lunch and then made our way back to Qizil.

The following day Sven was up and about, looking as if nothing had happened. We were just about to mount our horses when Cai Hui, with Liu in tow, pushed his way forward and said, "Don't forget your Yunnan Baiyao," and gave out a small leather pouch to each of us.

"Cai Hui, we thank you from the bottom of our hearts."

"Just so long as it's not from the heart of your bottom," he joked, and those who caught the joke laughed out loud. Cai Hui was certainly in a good mood.

"Cheng, we thank you for your hospitality and opening this, your city, and your arms, to us."

"Yes, yes, yes," said Cheng dismissively. "If there's ever any way you can repay me, I'll be sure to let you know. Now may the gods keep you safe and speed you on your journey."

I was glad he had lightened the situation; there's nothing more boring and hypocritical than an overdone farewell. We mounted our horses, bade our farewells and rode out of Qizil.

Qiuchi was one of the larger city-state power bases in the western regions. It was a centre of politics, economy and culture. Despite the purges that Cheng had spoken of, it was still a centre of Buddhism.

En route to the town the terrain became more dramatic and beautiful. Kalas informed me that the landforms were called yardang, formed by years of wind erosion. In some places the sand had been blown completely away, leaving fields of rock. In others the yardangs were at least two hundred fot high and stretched away into the desert, almost to the horizon. Other yardang looked like a giant sculptor had used the desert as the material for his artform, and had left his wild and surreal sculptures dotted about the landscape at random. An inebriated traveller passing through this area at night might well think that it was haunted and that the rocks were reaching out to him with hooked and clawed fingers.

Apart from the natural beauty of the area, like before, we also passed a large number of temples and ancient fortresses, in the main in ruins and derelict, but a few were still being used, although probably not in the way they were originally intended.

As we neared the town the evidence of agriculture began to show. By the time we reached the city walls we had noted the cultivation of grapes, pomegranates, plums, pears, peaches, and almonds.

We were surprised when we came upon the city walls. They stretched as far as the eye could see. The gate guard eyed us suspiciously. Foreigners who travelled the Peilu without any goods for trade could only be officials or spies. As we were not officials we had to be spies. However with no proof he eventually let us through. We made our way to the marketplace through broad tree-lined streets. The shade was cool and refreshing in comparison to the hot and dry desert. The marketplace was almost totally different from Kaxgar. Set in an ancient dried-up riverbed, it was far more orderly and the pace a great deal slower. Merchants displayed goods of cloth, wool, silk, copper, iron, lead and tin. Most had signs written in the Kushan-Brahmi script we saw at Tumshuq and in the pictographic script of Tianxia. The women were smartly dressed in ornamental garments of shimmering silk covered in exquisite embroidery. But then this was the Silk Route and we were in the land of the Tianxians, the land of the silkworm.

Buskers filled the air with the soft and pleasant sounds of the lute, pan and reed pipes, stringed instruments and jie drums. Impressed by the quality and sound of their music, we stopped for our midday meal opposite one of the troupes.

Ibn, as ever ready with his knowledge of foreign customs, filled us in over lunch. "Musicians from Qiuchi are famous throughout the east. They have even played at the court of my uncle and father in Baghdad. They have also played at the court of Pharaoh in Egypt and one of them even claimed to have played at the court of... now let me see," he said, flipping through his book. "Ah, here we are. Yes, at a land east of Tianxia, called Nippon."

"Strange name for a country. How far east?" I asked.

"No stranger than Norway or Svithjod. But I'm not too sure how far east, I didn't get to ask that. Never in my wildest dreams did I ever think I'd come *this* far east. Had I known I would have asked in more detail."

Kalas added, "It is also reported that the court of Tormarana II, in the land of Kush, had resident Qiuchian musicians as long as five hundred years ago."

"That is indeed a long time to be producing good musicians," I said.

"It runs in our blood."

With lunch over and with no need to stop any longer, nor any need to replenish our supplies, we crossed a two-arched bridge that was inscribed with the words "The Ancient Barrier of Qiuchi". Ibn made a quick sketch and noted this in his book and we carried on through the city. At the eastern end of the city a mosque was being built. Ibn stopped and talked at leisure to the foreman. He then made further entries into his book and we headed for the eastern gate.

On exiting the city, Kalas said, "Did you see the man following us?"

Ibn replied, "Yes. He wasn't too good at concealing his motives, was he?"

Twisting in my saddle, I turned to see if our pursuer was still there.

"He disappeared as soon as we left the city," Ibn said.

"Is that why you stopped at the mosque?" I asked.

"One reason. But I'm always interested in buildings that will gather the believers of the faith."

"Sorry, I missed that all together. I was too busy taking it all in."

"Yes. We noticed that as well," said Ibn, smiling.

"Did he fit the description of the man I saw in Kaxgar?"

"No. This one was a local. Probably sent by that suspicious gate guard."

At the end of that afternoon's ride we came into the ancient temple-city of Zhaohuli. The city, divided by the Kucha He, was now in lesser use after the purges. In the centre stood the grand temple surrounded by towers, halls, monasteries, pagodas and houses. Kalas said, "This was the major Buddhist Temple of the Qiuchi Kingdom. Originally it was called the Queli Temple but is now more commonly known as the Subashi Temple. One of the region's most famous sons was Kumarajiva. He lived here about six hundred and fifty years ago. He was an accomplished translator of Buddhist scriptures. He and his monks translated the Buddhist texts from Kushan into Tianxian. It was through his translations that Buddhism was revealed en masse to the people of Tianxia."

"How come you know so much about this place?" Ibn asked.

"After my early studies at the Hidden Kingdom, I was sent out to study Buddhism and was sent here. In its heyday there had been about one hundred convents, with over five thousand disciples. But when I was here there were little more than five hundred disciples and even less today, by the looks of it."

"It is the same, yet it is different from the others," observed Ibn as we rode down the main thoroughfare.

"That's because of all the Buddhist centres, this one was more Kushan than Tianxian in its discipline and architecture. All other Buddhist centres in Tianxia have been styled on this one, usually with a bit of local interpretation as well."

He led us off the main street and through the winding back streets of the former city to a house with stables attached.

"Don't tell me," I said. "Another cousin or more brethren?"

He grinned and said, "Right on both counts."

After seeing to the horses, we washed and had a hearty meal. Our host would not accept payment, saying that the son-in-law of Iksander and his companions would always find an open door and a seat at his table. I thanked him with as much grace as I could muster.

The following day after winding our way out of Zhaohuli we rejoined the Peilu on our eastwards trek. Up and until now we had been travelling slightly north of due east. Our direction now swung to a point between south and east. Kalas said that Zhaohuli was closer to halfway between Kaxgar and Lou Lan than anywhere else. If that were the case then it looked like we would beat our twenty-day estimate. I took comfort in the fact that on horses we were covering almost twice as much ground that the merchants with their plodding camel trains. As we travelled the towns of Simsim, Kirish, Acigh-Llak and Shorchuk, all merged into a haze of rise, eat, ride, eat, sleep, in this strange, dusty and amazing foreign land. With nothing to keep us at these ancient and magnificent towns we kept our stops as short as possible, preferring to spend our time travelling. I noticed that the slight bulge around my waist, which had started to develop at the Hidden Kingdom, was now all but gone.

I was struck by the same pang I had felt at Tumshuq. It felt as real as if someone had thrust a spear through my chest. A picture of Lydia sprang to mind. I wondered if it was a sign or if it was the pang of loving so intensely and then not having held or felt her for almost a month. A month! Had we really been separated that long? I wondered what she was doing now. How far had they travelled? Had any ills befallen them?

Chapter 25

QARASHAHER

Qarashaher—the Black City, also known as Yen-ke or Cialis, depending on which nation you had been born into and which empire of the past you pined for the most.

It was currently the western border of the Uygur Kingdom of Qocho, situated on the on Kaigdu He. It had also been the capital of the ancient Tibetan Kingdom of Agnidesha. Then from the late 480s to at least 560 AD it had been the eastern-most town of the Hephthalite Empire. My research at the Hidden Kingdom told me that the Hephthalite King Yedaiyilituo had sent at least thirteen emissaries to the Northern Wei Emperor during this period in the area's fluid history. Qarashaher was not the biggest town I had been to, but nevertheless as the westernmost entry point into the Uygur Kingdom it was strongly fortified. The security here was a great deal more intense and thorough than at Aksu or Qiuchi. This would be our last major stopover before our push on to Lou Lan and hopefully the resting place of Ingvar.

The Sita Darya had, over the years, changed course and as a result it was now some distance from the town. The Kaigdu He, now the only source of water, was tapped in many places and qanats criss-crossed the countryside, connecting reservoirs in what would otherwise have been barren desert. In many places the qanats and reservoirs had been covered, even sent deep underground, to prevent evaporation and keep it cooler.

As with all the other city-states along the Peilu, Manichaeanism had been the religion, which was supplanted by Buddhism, which in turn was supplanted by Islam, with Christianity arising briefly in between the latter two. This last transfer occurred in 751AD when the Kaxgar, Khotan and Qiuchi garrisons were defeated by the Arabs. Despite this there were still more than four thousand Buddhist monks in residence at Qarashaher, as well as Manicheans and Nestorian Christians. Indeed, a true cosmopolitan society of the East. It was here that the Western and Eastern worlds truly met with more diversity than Byzantium, albeit on a much smaller scale. Walking through the market place you could hear Sanskrit, Uyghurian, Tianxian, Syriac, Sogdian, Turkish, Tokharian and Khotanese spoken. Like Aksu and Qiuchi, the major influence in the area had been from the Kushan-Kashmiri culture of Gandhara and Bamiyan, so much so that you couldn't ignore the Buddhist architecture, which was in evidence in and on the many vihāras, chaityas and stûpas.

Qarashaher is at the very mouth of the big valley leading down from Tien Shan uplands. As such it was the gateway to Qocho and like all similar gateways it had to be closely guarded against invasion. We joined the queue for entry into the town and were eventually questioned by the gate guard. Kalas and Marsias, the only ones who could speak Tianxian, answered for us. The guard was not happy at probably his first sighting of tall blonde-haired, blonde-bearded, well-built men, and sent another to fetch their commander. The commander, obviously a cut above his troops, arrived and, immediately assessing the situation, asked, "Why have I been called out here?"

"The white skins, sir. They could be spies."

"They could also be emissaries. Have you thought of that?"

"N-n-n-no, sir," stammered the guard.

We allowed ourselves a small smile. Addressing us, he said, "Your throats must be dry after riding the Peilu. Would you like to come in for a drink?"

"We would like nothing better," I replied. To refuse would have raised suspicions and if anyone knew what was going on in this vicinity, this was the man.

"Chan, take their horses and make sure they are watered, fed and rubbed down." He then said to us, "Please follow me."

We dismounted and followed the guard commander inside. This man wasn't that stupid. He knew the best way to find out if we were spies would be to get us to lower our guards over a glass or two of beer. Separating us from our horses and getting them fed and watered would engender trust and also reduce any attempt to escape. And while we sipped our refreshments his men would search our saddle bags at their leisure.

He led us into what I took for being his private chambers, furnished to a much higher standard than the quarters we had just walked through.

"Allow me to introduce myself. I am Lin Ya, commander of His Imperial Majesty's Qarashaher garrison."

I introduced myself first, leaving out any official titles. While we were going through the introductions a servant girl appeared, laid out the goblets and left. Another arrived and poured the drinks. It was all too smooth. Lin Ya had obviously done this before. The introductions over, we were invited to sit.

"So, Ulf Uspakson, what does bring you and your companions to Qarashaher?"

Unlike most locals he had managed to pronounce the K in Uspakson, which surprised me.

"We are in search of an ancestor who passed this way, oh, about forty years ago, we believe he made it to Lou Lan. Nothing was heard from him again."

"That was a long time ago."

"Yes. But we have been gathering evidence since Bactra. Investigations I have carried out in Afrasiab, Kaxgar and Qiuchi, all indicate that he made it to Lou Lan."

I produced my now well-worn notes, which unsurprisingly he read. His eyebrows rose and he mouthed the words "the Chalice of Amrita" when he passed over the section on the Holy Grail. When he had finished he handed them back.

"You have come a long way. Unfortunately you will find Lou Lan all but deserted. The Sita Darya and Konqi He change course as many times as we have earthquakes and dust storms. Over the last seventy years the course of the river has totally changed and Lou Lan has all but been cut off. However if you insist on going, you must stop at Tikanlik to rent donkeys and buy ice from the local merchants. They will wrap it in wool and cotton and the ice should last you about two weeks. This should be sufficient time to get to Lou Lan, conduct a short investigation and get back. You will not, however, find Shambhala at Lou Lan."

"Nor are we expecting to. Lin Ya, you have been most helpful, and you have also been a most excellent host. We thank you for your hospitality."

"It has been my pleasure, Ulf Uspakson. But I also feel I must warn you — there have been reports of some odd goings on in the Lou Lan vicinity. Merchants who make the crossing from Tikanlik to Miran have reported hearing large packs of wolves. Some people have even disappeared from their camps during the night."

"I see. I didn't know that Qocho had desert wolves?"

"We don't. The wolves are usually found in the mountains on either side of the Taklamakan, but never recorded in the desert."

"Have these packs been seen?"

"Not directly. But travellers have reportedly heard them and some claim to have seen shapes flitting in and out of the dunes while they travel during the day. Then at night the packs start howling, and in the morning one of the party is usually missing."

"Only one?"

"Yes."

"Most interesting. You would think that one human would hardly be enough meat for a large pack of wolves. I take it you have sent soldiers to investigate?"

He looked at me with troubled eyes. After a short pause he looked down and said, "Yes."

"and...?"

He looked up at the ceiling and said, "They never returned."

"I somehow think that you are not dealing with wolves."

"I have come to that conclusion myself."

"Well then. If we find anything of significance, we'll be sure to let you know."

"You are still going?"

"Oh yes. There is one more favour I would like to ask, if I may?"

"But of course. You have only but to ask."

"Thank you. Could you recommend a good inn in Qarashaher?"

"Is that all? Of course I can. Try the Inn of Perpetual Happiness. It is very popular. Say I have sent you and they will treat you well and give you favourable rates. My man Chan will give you directions."

"Lin Ya, we thank you again for your hospitality and for the valuable information."

When we exited, our horses were tethered to the rail outside the quarters. They had been watered, fed and brushed. With instructions to the Inn of Perpetual Happiness we mounted and rode out of the compound.

Waiting until we were out of earshot, I asked Kalas, "Kalas, what about this inn?"

"I believe it is alright. But not one I would recommend."

"Oh, and why not?"

"It is not run by one of us."

"And you know of one run by *one of us*?"

"I know of one that's comes highly recommended. But then I have never been to Qarashaher before."

"To the market, then?"

"To the market."

The wolves of Lou Lan were not mentioned.

Unlike most of the towns we had been through, the market was situated on the north side of the town, with one side open to the plains. A great crowd was gathered, some standing and watching in silence, as if deep in thought. Others cheered and others jeered. A mini city of nomad yurks covered the immediate landscape except for a corridor down the centre leading out onto the plains.

"I wonder what's going on?"

We rode a little closer. Over the heads we could see horses and riders lined up. Out on the plain we could see riders galloping their horses; some on their way out, some on their way back.

"It's a horse fair," said Ibn. "They're showing what their mounts are capable of."

A rider galloping back towards us suddenly dropped sideways out of his saddle, and leaning down, scooped an object off the ground and pulled himself back into his saddle in a movement that seemed almost seamless.

"Oh for a thousand who can ride like him!" said Sven. "Just imagine how much easier and quicker Sicily would have been."

"It would indeed. But it's not that simple. You need the horse and the rider."

A stranger, overhearing us, said in Greek, "Ah, Westerners. Are you from Greece?"

"No. But we have been there."

"Well then, where are you from?"

Indicating the Norsemen, I said, "We are from Norway, Ibn here is from Baghdad, and Kalas and Marsias, Afrasiab."

"Even the closest is a long way from home."

"Yes, we are."

"Well then, to answer your question, you are looking on the finest horses in the world."

"And just how big do you consider the world to be?" asked Ibn.

"As far west as Rome, and as far east as Nippon."

"That's a fairly large world, friend. But not all of it."

"So I have been told."

"Where did you learn to speak Greek?" I asked.

"In Greece," he said nonchalantly.

"Then you have travelled as far as we have."

"Almost."

"How do you come to be in Qarashaher?"

"It is my job to select horses for the Tianxian cavalry. I come twice a year to select horses. Like now in the spring, and then again in the autumn. The Khoshut and Torgut tribes, who you see camped out here, breed these horses in large herds on the Bayanbulak grasslands north of here, up into the Yulduz uplands in the Tien Shan. The horses are descendents of the Bactrian "Heavenly Horses" which you ride, but with some improved breeding."

"Oh, how so?"

"As you can see they are ugly as hell with those large hook-nosed heads, but have powerful chests and necks, well-built legs and an incredibly fast gait. They have been known to cover almost one hundred and eighty of your mil in a day! Because of this, they are exclusively used by the Tianxian cavalry. The horses from this region are sent as regular tribute payment to the court of the Sung Emperor. They are very strong animals. We only select those over eleven hands high."

"One hundred and eighty in a day! I can see why the Tianxian cavalry would want them. But how did they get to be so damned ugly?"

"I don't really know. Probably the extra breeding. The last Tang emperor believed in them so much, he had a whole army of clay horses, riders and soldiers buried with him."

"Just how big was this army of clay?" asked Ibn.

"It is said to be more than a thousand."

"More than a thousand!" exclaimed the others.

"Enough to conquer the world he was entering."

"Indeed."

"Well, we're not buying, so we will be on our way. Good day to you, sir. And thank you for being so informative."

"My pleasure. Good day to you too."

With that we turned away from the crowd, the dust and the cheering. Back in the market we sought directions to the caravanserai.

On our way we discussed the strategy of whether we should buy our donkeys now or rent them later at Tikanlik.

Kalas argued, "If we leave it to Tikanlik we are likely to have less choice and we may be held to ransom by the merchants for animals that are inferior. Here we will at least have more choice and will be able to negotiate a lower price."

"True," agreed Ibn. "But our next leg to Lou Lan will be slowed by having to lead a train of donkeys. All we need is one or two stubborn ones to slow us up, and we will have to find fodder and water along the way as well."

Sven put his penny's worth in as well. "Will any time gained by riding fast and light to Tikanlik outweigh cost savings in buying them here?"

By the time we reached the caravanserai we still hadn't resolved our conundrum. We stabled, fed and watered the horses and walked back to the market. With more time to notice my surroundings, I saw this as a city that was as dirty as it was grubby. It suited the name given to it—Black Town. Flea-infested hovels hung off dark and dirty alleyways, littered with all kinds of waste and the dregs of society. The sooner we were out of here, the better.

In the market I decided to trial my theory of observation and purposely walked to a central point and stood still to see if I could pick out anyone with an overt interest in us and not in the market.

On completion of my experiment, Kalas said, "You are going about it all wrong."

"I am?"

"Yes. To observe and not be observed you have to place yourself on the periphery and not in the centre. It is even better to hide oneself on the periphery. Being on the outside you have a far wider field of vision than you do at the centre, for at the centre you can't see what's happening behind you. But when you are at the edge you have no need to see what's behind you, for what you want to observe is all in front of you."

"I think the master has just given the student a lesson," said Ibn.

"He most certainly has."

It was comforting to know that there was at least two in our intrepid group that were infinitely better at observation than I was.

"You don't mind being the student?" asked Marsias.

"Not at all. There will always be aspects of my life that need improving. And where I am clearly deficient then I am prepared to learn how to overcome them. In this way I am student in some and master in others."

"A good philosophy. I can see why you became an advisor to a king."

"Well that's all over now. Let's enjoy the sights, sounds and aromas of the market, shall we?"

After an hour we had seen all we needed to see and Kalas brought up the question of when to buy the donkeys. All looked to me to make the final decision.

"In the interest of saving time, I think we will buy the donkeys at Tikanlik. I know this is a risk, but then we can always persuade the merchant to come along with us as the donkey carer, can't we? The tip of a blade and the clink of gold coins will always persuade the most reluctant merchant."

With no further business in the market we made our way back to the caravanserai.

On the following day we departed the city by the western gate as soon as it opened. We skirted along the north shore of Baghrash Kol, which was surrounded by soda-whitened marshes and beds of tall grasses of monotonous steppe reed dotted with the occasional tamarisk cone. The only sizeable lake in the vicinity, although shallow, contained an abundance of fish, mainly of the Barble variety. Fishermen had already constructed their reed shelters along the shore as a base for their summer fishing. Small boats dotted the lake and fishermen could be seen casting and drawing nets. We counted an additional sixteen smaller lakes, one of which was a breathtaking mass of pink and white water lilies. Here we paused a while to take in the beauty and allow Ibn to update his notes.

"Did you see him?" Ibn asked Kalas.

"Yes, but he is a good few mil back, keeping out of view.

"We are being followed?" I asked.

"We think so," said Ibn.

"Well then. We'll give it a few more mil to make sure. Then we'll come up with a plan of action."

Our tail confirmed and the lakes behind us, we travelled along the northern edge of the Quruktagh Mountains, aptly named the Thirsty Mountains, for not much water flowed out of them. On the second day we turned south, off the Peilu, and onto the north-south trail that crossed the Quruktagh Mountains and Lop Desert to the old fort at Miran. This was the original silk route to Dun Huang via Lou Lan before it changed route through Jiahoe. With our plan agreed upon, just after passing through a neck in the land we sped up and Sven and Kalas peeled off to hide. After passing through the next narrowing, Ibn and I reined in and placed ourselves in the middle of the track facing the way we had just come. The others spread out and hid on either side of the track. Now we waited.

Further back on the track a solitary figure cantered along unaware of the trap about to be sprung. Kalas and Sven let him pass and, when he was out of earshot, broke their cover and rode out onto the track behind him.

"How much longer do you think this will take?" asked Ibn.

"Patience, my friend, patience. Shouldn't be long now."

No sooner had I said the words than the lone figure came cantering around the corner. When he saw us he reined in and sat looking at us, unsure whether to proceed or retreat. Too far away yet to make him out, Ibn and I looked at each other and shrugged. Still he sat and looked at us, unsure whether to go back or approach, quite understandably. If it were a stranger, he must be thinking that he was about to be robbed. How could he know that all we would do would be to offer him company for as far as we were going? But he would be totally unaware of this.

Then he turned in his saddle and Kalas and Sven came into view with swords drawn. His shoulders and head slumped in resignation and he gee-ed his horse forward, followed closely by Kalas and Sven, who had now mysteriously sheathed their swords.

As they drew closer I recognised the man. "Alright, break cover," I called, and the men rose from their hideouts. Marsias brought the horses out from their hiding place.

"Thank goodness," said Marsias. "Knut was more intent on breaking wind than on breaking cover. I don't know what he ate last night, but it was having a definite effect on him — and me."

We all laughed and the three cantered up. Still smiling, I greeted the rider, "Lin Ya, I am surprised, but then I am not."

"Ulf Uspakson, you should have been a Uygur."

"Why were you trailing us?"

"When that whole troop of men disappeared, I lost face and honour. I have been passed over for promotion time and again and stuck in that festering pit of a town for years.

After your visit I began thinking and decided that if I could find out what happened to them, then maybe I could regain some honour."

"Why didn't you ask about joining us? We would have been only too happy to have you along."

"You had already left. Anyway, what I am doing is strictly illegal."

"Ah, well, welcome anyway."

"I also think you should know that shortly after you left, a few men came through asking questions about you. Who were you, where you were going, and so on. I think they were Black Scorpions. I discreetly had them directed to Qocho city. You see by then I had already made up my mind to join you and I didn't want them interfering with my plans."

"Excellent! They were probably Black Scorpions. They have been trying to kill us since before Bactra. They have had three main attempts and have failed on all occasions, I am pleased to say."

"Except for the tip of my finger," said Sven, examining his shortened digit.

"You must have greatly annoyed them."

"Oh yes. I, or rather we, sunk one of their pirate ships and have killed a few hundred of their members in the process. We have also been instrumental in closing down one of their torture chambers and destroying, or almost destroying their network in and around Afrasiab. You see, we weren't quite truthful when we introduced ourselves. Ibn here is a prince of the Seljuk Empire, the fourth son of Sultan Alp Arslan, and brother to the current Sultan."

"Ah, I thought he was better educated and more cultured than most Arabs I have met." Then, bowing in the saddle, he acknowledged Ibn, "Your Highness."

"We do not have any need for formality in our group," said Ibn.

"Thank you."

"I have relinquished my claim on the throne of Baghdad. My mission in life is to observe and record the habits and customs of the peoples of the world."

"Ah, most interesting. Maybe I can give you some insights into the people of Tianxia."

"I would appreciate that."

"Well then, you can talk while we ride," I said.

We were eight again and with the addition of Lin Ya to our group the level of expectation amongst us had risen. We were now at the most a week away from Lou Lan. Doubt crossed my mind; would we find what we were looking for? What if we didn't, what next? We had no leads. Would it be a wasted journey?

Consciously dismissing the negative thoughts, I convinced myself that we would find the resting place of Ingvar within the week, bar being eaten by the wolves of Lou Lan — now there was a mystery worth resolving, almost as mysterious as the disappearance of Ingvar himself.

We broke out of the Quruktagh just as quickly as it had enveloped us. The golden gebi stretched out in front of us to the horizon in row upon row of yardangs, all lined up like ranked soldiers waiting to march into battle. We reined in, taking in the panorama. A warm breeze was blowing off the desert.

"Now you can see why so few make it out," said Kalas.

To the west was the Taklamakan Desert and to the east the Qurutagh Desert, and somewhere in the middle was Lou Lan. Each desert was held apart by the two thin bands of blue; the Sita Darya, and the Konqi He glistened aquamarine, silver and cobalt blue amongst the white, gold, and brown hues of the dunes. Here the Konqi He rightfully earned its name as the Peacock River.

The rivers meandered their way eastwards ending in the Lop Nor Delta, barely visible as a green dot in a mosaic of golds, reds, yellows and browns. It was most unusual to think that a vibrant and flourishing delta could exist in the middle of a desert.

"And that must be Tikanlik," said Ibn, pointing out a small settlement nestled up against the Konqi He.

"Must be," said Kalas.

Sven commented, "There's nothing to be seen but sand."

"Hah!" snorted Ibn. "You have never lived in a desert, have you? Stay here long enough and you will soon see just how alive this desert is."

"You must be kidding. You can't see anything but sand."

"Ah, but that's where you're wrong. Follow the Sita Darya. You see where the large loop almost meets the Konqi?"

Sven gave a tentative "Yes".

"Alright. See that small patch of grey — yes?" Sven nodded. "Well that small patch just happens to be wild camels grazing."

"You're kidding?"

"No, I'm not. They're feeding on the grass in the fertile patch between the rivers and they have plenty of fresh water."

I half listened to the exchange and with my eyes followed the well-worn track from Tikanlik across the Sita Darya to the Astin Tagh, and then on to the far horizon. In the crystal-clear air I could just make out the snow caps on a darker grey of a mountain range, before it merged with the sky.

"What are those?" I asked no one in particular.

"Must be the Himalayan range on the southern Peilu," answered Kalas, who had obviously been conducting the same exercise as me. "That we can see them is a miracle. They are at least two weeks' ride away."

"Either that or they're very high."

"Or both," said Marsias.

Focusing again on the two rivers, I followed them until they disappeared into a mirage on the horizon. But was it a mirage or was it the fabled Lop Nor? Whichever it was, it was where we were going.

We gee-ed our horses into motion and started down the slope into the desert.

Immediately after starting, Kalas reined us in.

"What now?" I asked impatiently.

"You see that dust cloud on the western horizon? Well, it's going to be here by tonight. Either we ride hard for Tikanlik and shelter, or camp out here and sit it out. It will not be as bad as the samoom you experienced at the Hidden Kingdom and will only last a day at the most."

"How bad would it be if it were to catch us before we made Tikanlik?"

"We would have to bed down or we could lose our way and end up somewhere out there."

Thinking back to my one and only experience with a samoom, I said, "Then I would rather wait here and see it out from the periphery rather than the centre."

Lin Ya suggested, "We can do better than that. There's the ruins of Shanguo, the capital of the ancient Mountain Kingdom, a few mil that way," he said, pointing west towards the pending storm.

"Had to be," said Sven, rolling his eyes.

Having local knowledge was already paying dividends.

"Alright, we'll make for that."

With that we turned our horses and headed back into the Quruktagh mountains.

The following morning we dusted ourselves off and gave the horses a rub down; there would be nothing worse for the horses than having the fine sand chaffing their backs under the saddles. We headed back down to the old route. Although the storm had blown through, there was still a fairly stiff breeze coming from the northwest.

The previous evening we had galloped into the ancient and decaying city, all but reclaimed by the desert. More concerned with finding shelter, we hadn't had time to take in the finer details of the old town. Besides, we wouldn't have seen much in the decaying light.

Now in the full light of morning we could see the old town. It wasn't hard to imagine the city in its glory days. Most of the adobe houses had stood the test of time. In the dry climate, the larger and more substantial timbers had survived, and in what had been the main square a stone building, ostensibly a palace, stood proud. We didn't go in. We needed water, so we divided into teams and went off in search. Ibn and I followed an old, sand-filled aqueduct and about three mil later came upon a crevasse in the rock out of which a stream gushed. Unlike the immediate surrounds, the area was green with grass, plants, shrubs and small trees. There was even moss in the places where the sun never reached. Evidence of wild camels and sheep abounded. The stream flowed for about two or three hundred fot before it disappeared into the sand. We dug a small pool and when it had settled, filled our skins and returned to the camp. On our return we found that Kalas and Marsias had killed a wild sheep and had already skinned it. Not in any hurry to leave our small oasis, we lingered another day, feasting on the sheep and exploring the area.

We left early the next morning and as we neared Tikanlik, Kalas said, "My informant has told me that Lou Lan is on the southern side of Lop Nor, so it would be better to follow the southern bank of the Sita Darya, which runs further out into the desert."

"My intelligence tells me the same," Lin Ya offered.

"Alright. After Tikanlik we will follow that advice."

We arrived at Tikanlik not long after midday. A warm breeze was blowing off the desert. There were four merchant premises that sold water and ice to travellers about to cross the desert. Sven was about to ride into the first when Kalas said, "No, not the first. Try the second. You're more likely to get a better deal from him, as most travellers will usually go to the first."

With that suggestion we bypassed the first ice merchant and entered the second. Lin Ya conducted our negotiations. "He says that he does not have any water barrels left. The last travellers left with them only yesterday. He says they will be back in fifteen or twenty days. He does however have ice and donkeys and shotas to carry the ice."

"Sho-what?" asked Sven.

"Shotas. Two ladder-like frames tied at the top, which fit over the backs of donkeys and camels, off which the ice is hung."

"Well, I'm glad that's cleared up. Alright, we'll go for ice then. Ask him if he will be prepared to act as our donkey master. Tell him we are prepared to pay. Don't tell him we are prepared to pay in gold, though."

Lin Ya spoke again to the ice merchant. After much gesticulating and babbling conversation he turned and said, "He says he will not and cannot go to Lou Lan with us. His first reason is that he is the only one here to run this end of the business and he must be here when a train arrives from Miran. Secondly, he flatly refuses to go to Lou Lan as he says there are only spirits and ghosts there. He does however know of someone who will be prepared to go, but at a high price."

"Alright, let's see him."

Lin Ya turned and spoke again to the merchant, who nodded, turned and walked into the back of his premises. He returned with a young man and beckoned Lin Ya. They spoke for a while, then Lin Ya turned to us.

"He says the young man has twice been to Lou Lan—and returned. Although, he won't say exactly why he has been to Lou Lan or how he has managed to escape the spirits and ghosts."

"Probably treasure hunting. Alright, we'll take him. I don't see that we have any other options. Warn him that if he tries anything foolish I'll skin him alive over a fire."

Lin Ya chuckled. "It seems that the language of threat is the same the world over. Alright, I'll tell him."

"Also tell him he doesn't get paid until we get back—alive!"

With negotiations over the ice merchant and his stooge went about preparing the ice for the journey.

271

Lin Ya and Marsias went with them to ensure the ice we were getting was from a fresh water source and not from the closer salt marshes. They placed the ice in huge bags of wool, which would insulate them from the heat. The bags were then hooked onto the shotas, which in turn were placed on the backs of the donkeys. All in all we had twenty-four blocks of ice loaded onto four donkeys. This would give us enough for fifteen days plus a few extra blocks for contingency. Dry rations were loaded onto another four mules.

After the preparations had been made, with nothing much more to do we walked around the town. In the small market place a number of hawkers had set up stalls and were plying their trade. I was amazed to see necklaces of seashells on display. I walked over to a stall and fingered the products. A few young girls were seated next to the stall making the necklaces. One nipped off the top of the shell and the other threaded the twine through.

I asked Lin Ya to translate for me. "Where do you get the shells?" I asked.

"The children dig them out of the loose shale and gravel on the river's flood plain," the hawker told me.

"Sea shells this far from the sea?"

"I have heard of this sea but never seen it," she said. "It must be a truly amazing sight. Is it larger than the Baghrash Kol?"

"Indeed it is. It is more than twice as large as the Taklamakan."

"Never! I have never seen more water in one place that's larger than Baghrash Kol."

"It is so large that you can travel from one land to another to another."

"Have you done this?"

"I have. I have sailed upon it in boats as big as houses."

"Never!"

She said something to Lin Ya, who laughed out aloud.

"What did she say?" I asked Lin Ya.

"She said the words of a foreigner can't be trusted."

"If I bought one of her necklaces would she believe me?"

Lin Ya interpreted and laughed heartily at her answer.

"Well?"

"She says if you buy one of her necklaces she'll believe anything you say."

I too laughed and shelled out a few coppers, which she studied closely, bit, then nodded and gave me a necklace of blue and grey shells. I added this to my collection of gifts for Lydia.

We left Tikanlik early the next morning with our donkey train in tow. The going was so much slower than before. We crossed the Sita Darya on a rickety rope bridge and then turned east, following the river on its south bank. That night we camped in the ruins of the ancient and abandoned city of Kroran. Unlike Shanguo, we were too tired to investigate the ruins. We made our campfire from the splintered and shattered beams of nearby houses.

Around the fire talk turned to speculation on what had happened to cause this once vibrant, ancient city, right on the Silk Route, to be abandoned. The only visible signs were the remains of some of the outer walls, broken waterways, collapsed two-storey houses and the remains of pagodas, one of which we were camped in.

Relaxing further, our conversation then somehow drifted into what we had done in our pasts. On hearing about our time spent in the libraries of Kyiv, Byzantium and the Hidden Kingdom, Lin Ya said, "You would enjoy the library established by Emperor Song Tai Zu, which is reported to have over one hundred thousand volumes, not counting parchments and scrolls."

"One hundred thousand!" exclaimed Ibn.

"And growing all the time," said Lin Ya.

"If only I had the time," wailed Ibn.

Suddenly Sven, sitting opposite me, tensed. Looking over my shoulder into the night, he exclaimed, "What was that?" His hand was on the pommel of his sword.

"What was what? I didn't hear anything."

"No, neither did I. But I'm sure I saw something flit across the way."

"Probably a bird."

"You forget, there aren't any birds out here."

He rose, and taking a burning stake with him, went outside to investigate. Kalas joined him. They returned a few minutes later.

"Must have been my imagination. We couldn't find any trail."

"There, you see? Nevertheless, we'll post a guard tonight. An hour each should do the trick."

We turned in after Kalas had divided us into watches.

Like the sun and the heat, we started early and followed the river east. At around mid morning our guide led us away from the river. He explained to Lin Ya that from here on the river started turning into delta and salt marsh, and that underfoot conditions would start to deteriorate.

Initially we travelled south between the dawans on the firm floor of the desert, with our backs to the river. Every now and then we would cross a patch of ground and water would squeeze out from under our feet. I stopped and tasted the water. It was brackish and wouldn't be any good to man or beast. Our guide watched me do this and laughed when I pulled a face at the sour taste of the water.

Not long after my water-tasting exercise we came across the remains of a canal, half filled with sand, with water puddled in the hollows. Our guide indicated that it was time to dismount and start walking.

He turned east again and started walking straight up the side of the dawan. We shrugged, some groaned, we all followed. At the top he walked straight down the other side. We found evidence of the canal on the other side of the dawan. And so it continued for the remainder of the day. Up and down, up and down.

Along the way we came across ruins of a watchtower. On climbing to the top of the next dawan, we could see a line of them stretching away to the east. Lin Ya informed us that they stretched all way to Tun Huang. He went on, "It is thought that the Han constructed a fortified road from Tun Huang across the desert of Lop Nor to Qarashaher, which had a two-fold purpose; first to guard against the marauding Hsiung-nu and also to give a window on the west, to prevent Tianxia's isolation. And they succeeded."

"Almost an extension of the Great Wall itself."

"Without a doubt it served that purpose. You have to remember that hundreds of years ago the first major powers on the Silk Road were Tianxia and Rome. It is believed that a Roman garrison was stationed in Tianxia to help protect the Road. But there is no conclusive evidence to confirm the rumour."

We squeezed ice-cold water from the now-leaking woollen insulation into our drinking cups and drank thirstily in the heat. Our guide informed us that we were now nearing Lou Lan.

Not long before dark we came into what seemed to be an old lake bed, with dunes rising to about thirty fot on either side, and we decided to make camp here. Sven dug down into the soil and found more brackish, salty water.

That night, without any wood for a fire, we ate a cold dinner, posted a guard and retired early.

It seemed that I had just dozed off when it started. At first there was a blood-curdling single howl, at what seemed like a fair distance away. A short while later the first was answered by a second. Then a third and a fourth joined in, closer than the first two. Then more joined in, all the while coming closer and increasing in numbers and intensity. It sounded as if the demons of hell had been let loose. Still the howling went on.

We were now all awake and with swords drawn, we drew ourselves into a defensive circle in the middle of the lake bed awaiting the arrival of the wolves.

With no moon there was little natural light, which made it hard to see them, but by their howling we knew they were closing in. Slowly the sounds grew closer and slowly, very slowly they began to become one sound. Then the darkness began to shimmer and we could just make out, not wolves but upright figures dressed in dark, hooded robes, standing in a circle around us, heads thrown back, howling like wolves. The howling grew louder and louder. A figure detached itself from the shimmering wall of darkness, walked a few paces forward, lit a torch and raised it high. The howling ceased so suddenly that the silence itself was deafening.

The figure stood there looking at us, not moving, the torch held high.

Slowly the hooded figure walked around us, the torch held away from its person, illuminating only us. We held our swords at the ready. Still the figure circled, taking longer than normal strides as it circled us. On the third circuit I lowered my sword, placed the tip into the ground and rested my hands on the pommel, watching as intently as we were watched. The others, seeing what I did, followed suit.

He slowly, painstakingly, completed a fourth circuit around us. Then slowly the figure walked up to me and said, "Welcome to Lou Lan. We are the Lang Ren. We have been waiting a long time for you. Come, you have not eaten well. A hot meal awaits."

In no position to argue, we quickly broke camp and followed.

Chapter 26

LOU LAN

As before, we followed the old canal and not long after daybreak we ran into the ruins of ancient Lou Lan. In the early light of morning we were led through the remains of the main gate and past old, crumbling houses. Some were so dilapidated that they were totally uninhabitable. Dishevelled figures came out of some of the long-abandoned houses. Some stopped what they were doing and silently watched us walk through their city. They all stood staring in silence as we were led past. They were dirty and unkempt. Their faces, arms and legs were streaked black and brown with dirt. All had long stringy hair, some down to their waists. Equally unkempt children stopped their early-morning games of tag and catch to watch us pass. Like their elders, they too were mainly barefoot.

Some of the buildings had faded paintings of Buddhist deities on the walls. There were fine-turned wooden support columns sticking out of the ground at all angles. Most had been bleached white with age and some were weathered grey, others showed signs of faded paint. Wood was strewn about and here and there carved figurines lay amongst the low mud-brick ruins.

We were led into the main square of the old city, past the central well, at which a few women were drawing water, and on across into a large building, which was probably the former city prefect's palace and administration centre. Not turning into any of the many side passages, we were led straight into a large hall.

Our host clapped his hands and steaming hot dishes of pilaf rice and lamb stew were brought out. Never in my life had hot food looked so good and appetising. Our host went to the head of a long table and sat. We were all beckoned to sit and I was asked to join him at the head of the table. I took Lin Ya with me as my interpreter.

"Eat," our host instructed. We didn't need this command to be interpreted. Soon after, mugs of frothing beer were brought out and plonked in front of us. It was so bitter as to be sour. I glanced at Sven, who raised his eyebrows. Nevertheless we drank thirstily.

Then our host introduced himself in a voice as mellow and seductive as I have ever heard. "My name is Lou Pyi, and this is my mate Can Sui," he said, indicating the hooded figure sitting on his left. For the first time I took a hard look at the figure opposite. Her face still hidden within her hood, I was able vaguely to discern the contours of a woman's figure beneath the unflattering robes. On being introduced she removed her hood. Her face was misshapen and I tried hard not to stare. Her left cheek was slightly bulbous and lower than the right and her nose was misshapen. A scar ran across her brow from her hairline on the right to just above her left eye. Her left cheek was also scarred. Around her neck hung a large, beautiful moonstone in a silver setting. Her hair was jet black and long. In a voice as soft and gentle as a mountain stream, she said, "Please, it is alright, I don't mind you looking. I am not offended. I am quite used to the stares and would rather talk openly about it than have people stare and make assumptions. I no longer experience any discomfort."

"You are very gracious," I replied through Lin Ya.

It was clear that had her face not been so misshapen, she would have been most beautiful.

"Now you're wondering how she came to be so?" said Lou Pyi through a mouthful of food and waving his fork about as he spoke.

"You are most perceptive," I said.

"And you know how to use words. Not so?"

I nodded. Lin Ya chipped in, "He has studied at some of the finest libraries in the Western World."

"Ah, well then." Then addressing his mate, he asked, "May I tell it or do you want to?"

"Go ahead. You're much better at telling it than me."

"Thank you. Can Sui was borne in a village in the Kunlun mountains. By the age of ten her beauty was well known. At age twelve she was betrothed to a rich merchant from Yarkant." He spat out, "A fruitful match for her father's coffers. At fourteen she was married and left home to join her husband's harem. Oh, he lived in a large house, more like a small palace, and was advisor to the ruler of Yarkant. His merchant staff acted as spies and couriers and brought information back from places as far afield as Bactra, Tibet, Wulumqi and Dunhuang."

As he spoke I wondered why he hadn't removed his hood. But I guessed that what it hid would be revealed by the end of the morning. He continued. "Can Sui had everything she could want. A husband, wealth, servants, a large house, the best clothes, relative freedom and anything money could buy. What she didn't have was her husband's love, nor his trust. He bedded her two, three, four times a week. He saw how men looked at his luscious young fifteen-year-old wife as she walked through the market place. He could see the lust in their eyes. At first his chest swelled with pride.

"Despite bedding her three times a week, much to the displeasure of the other wives, she did not fall pregnant. The other wives, jealous of her status, were quick to capitalise on her husband's mistrust. They began to sow seeds of doubt, and fed his suspicions with false rumour. His distrust grew and he had her watched day and night. The pride he had formerly felt when other men watched her turned to jealousy and for no reason other than rumour her husband's mistrust deepened and his jealousy increased.

"He became so jealous that Can Sui was refused permission to leave the house. But it didn't stop there. Eventually, driven insane with jealousy by the other wives' malicious whisperings, he had her locked in a bare room all day and night.

"Still the wives whispered and on returning from a trip, in a jealous rage he beat her unconscious. When she eventually recovered from her beating, her husband saw what he had done and how, by his own hand, he had destroyed his most beautiful and prized possession. He couldn't bear to look upon what he had destroyed, and plagued with guilt had her sent away to a house of ill repute near Jiaohe. But on the way her escort stripped and raped her. Now naked, they abandoned her in the desert near Miran, where I found her almost dead from sunburn, hunger and thirst. I brought her here, fed and clothed her and over time we fell in love. You see, I could see past the surface and could see the beauty within."

"Not unlike the tale of Prince Huo's daughter," commented Lin Ya.

"I don't know the story, but I can guess its gist," I said. "And you, why are you here? What is your story?" I asked.

"I was banished for this…" he said, removing his hood. He was a handsome man, probably not long past his thirtieth year. And then it struck me—he had yellow eyes. At least, the whites of his eyes were yellow. This feature, offset against his black pupils and black hair, gave him a decidedly malevolent appearance. I frowned when I saw them, not sure if what I was seeing was real, or if it was a trick of the light. "Yes, that's right, yellow eyes. How many people have you seen with yellow eyes?"

"You're most certainly the first."

I noticed that he too wore a moonstone on a silver chain, which matched Can Sui's.

"As a child the fever that turns people yellow swept through my village. I contracted the disease and when I recovered the whites of my eyes had turned yellow. The local sage said that in time they would return to their natural colour. Only they didn't.

"Fearful of the local superstitions about yellow eyes being the harbingers of death and evil, like tigers and wolves, my parents protected me as long as they could. But when the officials found out they were hiding me, I was banished from the village as a bringer and harbourer of evil. All the ills of the village were blamed on me and I was stoned out of my home. I ran into the hills and mountains and hid.

"For a while my parents and family brought me food but then this stopped and I found out that the local magistrate had confiscated and sold all their possessions, including our home, and had had them imprisoned for feeding me. Me—a six-year-old child!

"And when I was starving the wolves did not attack and devour me, but fed me instead. They kept me alive. I followed them to their kills and they always left a morsel or two for me after they had eaten their fill. In time they came to trust me and I went to live with them in their lairs. I learnt how to hunt and live like a wolf, how to move in, and with, the forests—carefully and quietly. They taught me about respect and sharing, and cooperating while hunting. About looking after the young, caring for others and about having pride.

"When it became obvious that I was self-sufficient and there was nothing more to be learned, they told me it was time to return to my people, but not the people who had banished me.

"They brought me to a place not far from here, a high ridge from where this portion of the Taklamakan can be viewed for many li in all directions. One night, while honouring the moon, I was shown the city of Lou Lan, standing proud and tall, lit silver, purple and black in the bright moonlight, and I knew that this was where I was meant to go. Travelling only at night I made my way here and found others here who had been banished or exiled for one reason or another.

"Despite my appearance, I was accepted as an equal and was soon teaching them the skills I had learned when I was with the wolves. I taught them how to feed themselves and that hunting in packs was more profitable than hunting alone. Above all, I taught them the wolf creed, the creed by which we live here in Lou Lan."

"Which is?"

"Respect the elders, work with the pack, hunt when you must, share your affections, leave your mark, teach the young, play when you can, rest in between, and voice your feelings."

"A noble creed indeed. You called yourselves the Lang Ren?"

"Yes. It means People of the Legendary Wolf."

"Ah. But your being cared for by the wolves is not unique — Romulus and Remus, the twins who founded the great city of Rome, were raised by Lupa, a she-wolf."

Ibn added, "And Tu Kueh, who founded the Turkish nation, married the she-wolf who reared him."

"There is more," Kalas said. "In Greek mythology, a king named Lycaon began to neglect his people's worship to their patron god Zeus. Zeus disguised himself as a peasant and visited the city to see what was going on. His sons suspected who the newcomer was and convinced their father to serve him a meal with human entrails. In a rage, Zeus turned them all into wolves."

"Ha! I knew it. You will have to tell me more of this Rome and of this Turkish and Greece. Now you must rest. Sleep. After the sun passes its zenith I will show you what you seek."

With that he rose and held out his hand. Can Sui took it and they walked out. One of the serving women led us to our quarters, which had at one time been sumptuous, but were now shabby and badly in need of renovation. Not realising how tired I really was, I was asleep as soon as my head hit the straw-filled pillow.

As promised, we were awoken not long after midday. After freshening up, Lou Pyi led us north and slightly west out of the ruined city. Setting a brisk pace that was more a half-trot, we crossed a number of dawans and by the mid afternoon came upon some temple ruins, where we took a short rest in the shade and re-hydrated ourselves.

Soon after we took off again at an equally brisk pace and soon came across more ruins set in a small natural amphitheatre in the side of a hill. As I looked at the site, I realised that these were not ruins of an area that had been inhabited. It took a while before I realised that this was a cemetery. As this realisation dawned, my hopes for finding the resting place of Ingvar suddenly soared.

In the main the ruins were now barely visible above ground level. Unlike the others, one building seemed remarkably intact. Lou Pyi led us straight towards it.

Although evidence of hinges was present, the building had no door. There were two mock pillars on either side of the doorway and a triangular lintel lay across the top of the two, in the Greco-Roman style of architecture. A gargoyle had been fixed in the centre of the lintel, a round portal window above the gargoyle.

As we entered it took a while for my eyes to adjust to the dimly lit interior from the bright sunshine. I first saw that the room was lit by six large candles. Above each candle was a gargoyle. Their contorted faces fixed forever in stone looked down from each of the six corners of the hexagonal tomb.

Then I saw the Lang Ren elders formed up in a semi-circle around three coffins, each on raised plinths facing the door. They stood silently in black silk robes, each with a gold and silver wolf's head embroidered on the left breast. Eight tall candelabra, each holding eight candles, were evenly spaced around the perimeter of the room. The walls were covered with carved icons and faded frescoes. Various faded deities from different religions, from Christ to Buddha, gazed benevolently upon us. This must have been the mausoleum of a wealthy official or merchant. Then I looked up. The roof was covered in an identical fresco to the Celestial Buddha we had seen at the Thousand Buddha caves. Unlike the walls it was as if the fresco had been painted yesterday. And then the realisation struck: slowly we turned to the three wooden coffins, which lay alongside each other on the sandstone plinths. Judging by their sizes, I guessed them to belong to a man, a woman and a child. I wasn't wrong. Ibn offered a short prayer to Allah and the others muttered prayers to Christ or intoned sayings to ward off the curse of the dead.

Lou Pyi walked over to the largest box and placed his hand on it and looked at me. It took a moment to realise he was waiting for me to give him the go-ahead to open it. Silently I nodded my approval and he raised the lid. Inside were the perfectly preserved remains of a man. His skin was so well preserved that he looked as if he were sleeping. He had long fair hair and a matching full beard and moustache, which had tinges of grey. His eyes were closed and his head was covered by a fitted Norse-style helmet. A long broad sword had been centrally placed on his body, the haft on his chest and his hands wrapped around the hilt. He wore a sleeveless leather jerkin and a pleated leather roman-style kilt. His legs were bare except for a pair of leather boots, which ended not far above his ankles. I stood there lost in contemplation, gazing at his body. There was no doubt in my mind. This was Ingvar Vittfarne. I glanced across at Sven, who in a mannerism so typical of Sven, raised his eyebrows and nodded his head. Here lay Ingvar Vittfarne. This was no Shambhala and his hand did not hold the Holy Grail. I thought of taking his helmet as proof that we had found him. But I somehow knew that I would never be going back to Svithjod nor would I see my beloved Norway again. Our journey was over—or so I thought.

I looked up and nodded to Lou Pyi, who moved to the second coffin and opened it as well.

An elder moved forward and resealed Ingvar's coffin. On seeing the remains of a woman my knees went weak, my heart began to pound and my head began to spin as I battled for breath. After all I had been through in my life, I never thought this would ever happen to me. I clutched my heart and reached out with my other hand. A firm grip steadied me, Ibn on one side and Kalas on the other. She was the identical twin of my Lydia.

"How...?"

"Iksander told you. Ingvar married the younger sister of Lydia's mother."

Recovering enough to stand on my own, I said, "But the likeness... She's identical."

"Yes. And it's always the strong features that get passed down the generations."

"You're right, of course."

Lou Pyi asked, "Is everything all right?"

"Yes," Kalas replied. "The woman is his wife's aunt, and they are almost identical. At first he thought he was seeing his wife when you lifted the lid. I did at first, as well."

He nodded and said, "Ah."

She had shoulder-length dark hair and her skin and nails were in perfect condition. On her head she wore a felt cap onto which two goose feathers had been fixed. She too looked as if she were asleep. Like Lydia she had a fairly prominent nose, probably a result of her Greek heritage. Her upper body was wrapped in a wooden blanket of the style the Hephthalites wove from their days on the plain of Ordos. Her lower legs were wrapped in sheepskin and she wore leather shoes.

Speaking to the body, I said, "Hello, Aunty. Be sure to know that if it wasn't for your sister, I wouldn't be one of the happiest men in the world. Your niece is absolutely beautiful. I guess much like you used to be."

The others stood in silence, expressionless while I spoke to the body. Finished, I nodded to Lou Pyi, who replaced the coffin lid.

He then lifted the lid on the third coffin. It contained the bodies of two children, no more than three or four years old. Clearly they were the children of the two. Making light of what had become a sombre moment, I said, "Well, we can tell Iksander that we have seen his brother-in-law, his sister-in-law and his niece and nephew."

At the back of the room an hexagonal plinth stood. A shaft of light from the portal above the doorway shone directly onto it. It was obvious that an ornament of some sort had had pride of place on this plinth. I walked over and examined it. A faint circular mark had been left by whatever had stood there.

Ibn commented, "Whatever stood here was considered to be important."

"I agree."

"The Holy Grail, maybe?"

"Could be. Maybe that's the reason for the tombs and graves. The hope that proximity to the Chalice may give them a better start in their next life. I've seen enough, let's go."

We closed the remaining coffins and exited the tomb. Outside we sat in the shade and drank our fills from our water skins. Replenished, there was nothing left to do but head back to Lou Lan.

On the return trip as we crested a large dawan we could see the remnants of a watchtower in the near distance. It was obvious that we were returning on a different route. We were well on our way back when I asked Lou Pyi, "How did you find the tombs and the towers out here in the middle of nowhere? I mean, there's no reason to come out here?"

"One of the lessons I had been taught when living with the wolves was to know your territory, and know it well. You never know when you might have need of it."

"Yes, of course. Always a good strategy."

"Anyway, we need to cross this area when travelling to and from the delta for fishing and trapping wild camels and horses."

That night a huge bonfire was built in the city square. Two deer and a boar, caught in the hills only the day before, were roasted on a spit. Beer was served with the meal. I noticed that even children drank beer. No one seemed to drink water. When our meal of venison and pork was over, stories of wolves were told as if they were their own ancestors being talked about. The wolves were individually named and children and adults alike were wrapped in an aura of awe and wonder. Needless to say, wolves featured strongly as the heroes and saviours of the day in most stories. In between each story a song of the hills and mountains was sung.

The following morning Lin Ya sought me out.

"Last night I found a good number of my missing troop living here. They're still alive!"

"Did you speak to any of them?"

"I tried to. But they wouldn't speak to me."

"Wouldn't?"

"Correct — wouldn't. I tried speaking to them and they said they were sworn to secrecy."

"I see. Well, don't rush off and try and do anything, understood?"

"Understood, Ulf Uspakson."

"Let's give it a bit more time. These things have a way of unravelling and explaining themselves without being forced along. So — patience, my friend. Patience."

Later that morning I addressed the matter of leaving with Lou Pyi.

"But I can't allow that."

"But why not?" I asked.

"Because if you return, you can inform that we are here, and then Lin Ya will send his armies in and will capture and imprison us."

"But you have done the same to Lin Ya's men."

"In order to preserve our society. Besides, it's not as if we captured them on purpose."

"Oh, how so?"

"We found them in the desert dying of thirst. We had watched them for days and kept our distance. It would have been better for all if they had simply turned around and gone home, saying they found nothing. But they made mistake after mistake. In the end they all would have died, so we took pity on them — my first mistake — and brought them here to recover — my second mistake. I thought of swearing them to secrecy, but then I realised just how vain that was. So I kept them here under threat of death if they tried to escape. One did try, and fortunately I have only had to kill one to maintain my oath."

"Well, your secret is out. As you know, Lin Ya is commander of the Qarashaher garrison. They know where he has gone and with whom. If none of us returns, they are bound to send a scouting party. When the party gets to

Tikanlik they are guaranteed to come across the ice merchant and he will tell them that he has provided a guide who has made it to and from Lou Lan on a number of occasions. So it is therefore reasonable to conclude that we are alive and in Lou Lan. The rest you can work out for yourself."

He looked crestfallen and at the same time as if a weight had been lifted from his shoulders. "You are right. I have known that this has been coming for a long time now. But what to do?"

Lin Ya, who had been relatively quiet up and until now, said, "I have a suggestion. Continuing to live here is just not a long-term viable option, from the points of view of natural resources, military and governance. I mean, the water is so tainted you have to filter it and then turn it into beer in order to make it palatable, and even then the quality is debatable. Not to mention a growing population and dwindling food supply.

"However, there are the ruins of Shanguo, an abandoned city in the Quruktagh Mountains not far from here. It used to be capital of the Mountain State, which was one of the thirty-six states of Qin. Take your people there. There is plenty fresh, clean water and good hunting in the mountains. Plus you will be out of this unbearable heat."

"But Quruktagh means the dry or thirsty mountains."

"The meaning is true. But that's because not much water comes out. What water that does leave the mountains is quickly swallowed by the dry sands of the desert. But in the mountains there is water aplenty. In the meantime, Ulf Uspakson and I will put a case to the governor in Wulumqi. If I am correct the only action he would require from you is to agree to come under his authority."

Can Sui had joined us, and stood behind Lou Pyi. When Lou Pyi started to argue against the logic, she squeezed his shoulder firmly and Lou Pyi held his counsel.

Lin Ya continued, "However, this may not be a bad thing. You will get schools and doctors, be in charge of law and order and you will give your people a second chance. But above all you will get recognition! After all, you have proved yourself a worthy and capable leader. You have cared for your people under the harshest of conditions and have overcome seemingly impossible odds, both personally and from a governance point of view. And you have risen to rule your own kingdom with fairness and justice."

"You flatter me overly, and give much to think about. How do I know you will not betray me?" he said, looking from me to Can Sui, who nodded.

"You don't. Besides, whether you stay here or go is irrelevant. Either way, you can be found. However what I can do is leave one of my men as a security hostage. If you are betrayed his life is in your hands."

"Two men, and I decide which two!"

"Then two it shall be."

"Before you petition the governor at Wulumqi, you must first lead us from Lou Lan to this mountain Nirvana."

"Lead, yes. As for Nirvana, well that will be what you make it to be."

"Then leave me," he said, dismissing us with a wave of his hand. His brow furrowed and he said, "I have a lot of thinking to do."

I thought it was going to be a lot harder to persuade Lou Pyi than it was. But I always find that logic prevails over emotion and I was sure that he had already made his mind up.

Leaving Lou Pyi to consider his options, Lin Ya and I sought out Ibn. We found him in the company of the Lou Lan shaman, scribbling furiously in his book. Both looked up and nodded as we entered the house, but carried on their conversation. The shaman was speaking, "Wolf energy and wolf spirituality have five elements. Water, which represents the emotional, air—the mental, fire—the dynamic nature of our lives, earth—the physical and, last but not least, the spirit."

He said this while placing his hands over his heart. "Overlay on this the wolf creed, which is to respect the elders, work with the pack, hunt when you must, share your affections, leave your mark, teach the young, play when you can, rest in between and voice your feelings. Do this and you have a complete credo that addresses all the aspects by which you should live your life."

"Thank you very much. I do appreciate you taking the time to speak to me."

"It's a pleasure speaking to someone who wants to listen. The young people nowadays have little respect for the old and proper way of life."

"This is not a problem particular to Lou Lan. I encounter it everywhere I go."

We left the shaman's house and made our way back to the great hall for lunch, which not surprisingly again consisted of pilaf rice and lamb stew.

Over our meal, Ibn gave a précis of his meeting with the shaman.

"As the Lang Ren, they believe they hold the powers of the east and possess the power of night. They believe they have the healing powers of the spirits, and the wisdom to instil courage. They also believe they can predict the weather far in advance and are alert to other humans and animals, which enter their domain. And they will never kill a wolf."

Lou Pyi, who had sat down alongside us, said, "You doubt we hold those powers?"

Ibn gave Lou Pyi a hard look, nodded and said, "Yes I do."

Lou Pyi bowed his head and made a gesture with his hands that implied that Ibn was entitled to his doubts. I couldn't help but wonder if he planned a demonstration for us that would remove the doubts.

Conversation continued, discussing the many different aspects of the Lang Ren's unique beliefs and culture, until Sven just happened to mention, "Where we come from, some ancient warrior societies believed that wearing wolf skins into battle would give them stealth and strength when they attacked enemy camps. Even the Romans had a Wolf Legion…"

A deathly silence had descended over our table. Everyone had stopped eating and was staring at Sven. Realising that he was the only one speaking and was the focus of many stares, he said, "What? What did I say?"

I broke the silence. "Sven, the Lang Ren, our hosts, believe that it is wrong to kill a wolf, and even worse to wear its skin."

Sven looked at me with a frown on his face as I spoke.

"They believe the spirit of the slain wolf would revenge its death on the one who committed the act."

He shot back his answer as quick as lightning. "Well then, I guess that's why there are so few wolf warrior societies left. The wolves must have taken
289

their revenge," he said, shrugging, and picked up morsel of meat with his chopsticks and stuffed it in his mouth.

After a momentary pause Lou Pyi let out a loud and hearty laugh and his people joined in, even though a little nervously at first. Although some were not exactly sure what the joke was.

After lunch Kalas and I explored the remains of the once great city. It was clear that it had stood empty for a long time before the Lang Ren reoccupied it. In the eastern quarter few houses were occupied. Those that were still in a usable state had sand-filled doorways and interiors. These houses were in an altogether worse state than any of the others we had seen, which led us to speculate as to why this quarter was worse off than any of the others. The only plausible answer we could come up with was that the eastern quarter was the victim of an earthquake. This reasoning could also explain why the city was evacuated. The earthquake would also more than likely have shifted the water flows; a certain death knell for the city.

The remains of a water well stood in the middle of a square. I picked up a stone and dropped it in. After a few seconds I was rewarded with a dull thud.

The remaining houses in the southern and western quarters were of an altogether lower quality. Because of this they were more easily repairable and as a result had higher occupancy.

While we walked, we discussed the possible reasons for the demise of the city.

"I assume the canal in the dunes was an attempt to channel more water in."

"It would seem so. But it would have been an almost impossible task, trying to keep the canal clear of sand and the dawans in check."

"Yes. And have nature playing by her own rules, dealing out earthquakes whenever she chose, changing the course of the water supply. That the city existed for so long is a wonder."

"Not only that, but with the high evaporation I guess the salt levels increased, which in turn seeped into the underground supply, which is why the current water supply is so sour."

We came across a large wooden octagonal Buddhist pagoda standing some thirty to forty fot high. It stood on a square base and had a circular roof. We walked and looked around. It was completely bare. We gingerly made our way up the stairs onto a small first-floor landing. From a central vantage point I could see the well in the main square and the road we had just walked along. I could also see the well I had dropped my stone in. The street was incredibly straight. On the fringes of the southern quarter I could just make out the green of the vegetable gardens. We made our way back outside and walked around the pagoda. Another well stood nearby. I concluded that there must have been an underground water channel cut through the rock under the city. This way evaporation would be kept to a minimum and the water would always be cool. I dropped a stone into this well and was once again awarded with a dull thud. It was clear that the water supply to the rest of the city had been cut off, slowly strangling Lou Lan to death. If the population grew any larger, history would repeat itself. An earthquake would certainly seal her fate once and for all.

On returning to the great hall, we found Ibn in the kitchens speaking to some cooks. One rather plump woman was speaking while the others nodded in agreement, "We follow the Nyida."

"The Nyida? What is that?"

"It is an ancient vegetarian diet that originated in Shambhala."

Shambhala, there was that name again.

"Nyi represents the yellow and green foods, primarily vegetables and fruits, and da the white foods, such as milk, yogurt, cheese and tofu. Although, here we only get tofu every once in a while.

"We eat as much yogurt, milk, white butter, cheese, fresh vegetables, raw fish and white rice as possible. You should refrain from garlic, onions, fat and other meats. Although, we supplement our meat intake with lamb and mutton. No beef."

"Is there any particular reason for using this diet?"

Can Sui had come in to check on the menu for the evening meal and was listening silently on the periphery.

"No, I'm not too sure where it came from. Ask Can Sui, she may know."

And with that the cook ended the discussion and turned to her work.

Can Sui took up the discussion. "The Nyida diet was widely used by the Manicheans in Tibet. It consisted mainly of green and yellow foods. It is believed that light is concentrated in these foods and our bodies serve as filters for the particles of light contained in the plants. The belief, our belief, is that spiritual enlightenment comes not just from the mind, but from within the body as well. Now you will have to excuse us, as we have a meal to prepare."

"One more question, please? Why lamb and mutton?"

"What else would a wolf eat? Now you really must excuse us, please?"

"Of course. I should have known."

I quickly asked, "Has Lou Pyi made his mind up yet?"

"I cannot answer for Lou Pyi. You will have to ask him."

The lady should have been a diplomat.

Lou Pyi kept us waiting a full two weeks. All he would say was, "Patience, patience. I am considering all the options."

And all Can Sui would do was shrug and say to ask Lou Pyi.

All I wanted to be was away on my way home to my Lydia. Her belly would be swollen and would probably swell some more before she gave birth. I had not considered that I would possibly be helping a whole city of people migrate to a new location. To be involved in the migration of one people to a new home was remarkable in itself. But two migrations in one season? Winter would be upon us before I could get back to Kyiv. The thought of this saddened me.

We passed time by trying to fish in Lop Nur. We accompanied the fishermen from Lou Lan on their daily pilgrimage to the lake, which at this time of year was not far. We tried fishing Norwegian style, with a long stick, line, hook and bait, without much success. Our attempts to fish without nets earned us many smiles and just as many laughs.

Ibn learned that during winter, when the lake was smaller due to diminished river flows, the fishermen would walk out onto the ice-covered lake and look for the fish through the transparent ice. They then cut holes in the ice and inserted their nets. This done, they would form a wide ring and move slowly closer together stamping on the ice, driving fish into the nets. Once again the wolf pack worked together.

I knew something was afoot when three runners came straight out of the desert and into the palace without stopping to drink or wash. That they went straight into closed council, with Lou Pyi and Can Sui, told me all I wanted to know. Lou Pyi, being the astute leader he was, had sent scouts out to find the proposed location and check the water supply and look for any traps that we might have been setting for him.

Anticipating what might be coming, I called Kalas, Ibn and Lin Ya into a council of our own and briefed them on what I had concluded. I also prepared them for disappointment, which included the possibility that our stay may be longer than we planned; not that our stay at Lou Lan was at all planned.

Through the rest of the morning many came and fewer went. Lou Pyi was obviously holding council with his most trusted advisors.

After our midday meal we were called into council with Lou Pyi. Also present were Can Sui, the three runners, now freshened up, and a dozen or so of Lou Pyi's senior advisors.

"No doubt you're wondering why I have taken so long with my decision?"

"I had wondered, yes. That is, until I saw the three runners come in this morning."

"Ah, you are very perceptive."

"You sent them to Shanguo in the Quruktagh to verify that what we say is true."

"Yes I did."

"A wise and precautionary move. I would have done the same."

He nodded in acknowledgement, "I know."

"And… is it to your liking?"

"It is indeed."

"Good. And your decision is?"

"You, Lin Ya and Kalas may proceed to Wulumqi to petition the Governor."

I nodded. "A change to our original agreement?" His face clouded over, and I quickly continued, "…but nevertheless acceptable."

His frown changed into a smile. "Good. While you're in Wulumqi we will move to the new location. You leave at first light, as do we," he said, making a sweeping gesture including all in the room.

On exiting the chamber, Kalas said, "Well he doesn't waste time once he's made his mind up, does he?"

"He who hesitates is lost," said Ibn. "The art of being a good ruler is to make your mind up and then stick with that course of action. Otherwise you'll lose everything."

That night a special gathering was called in the main square. The people must have guessed an announcement of import was about to be issued, as there was no meat on a spit, nor were the tables laid out. Without any fanfare, Lou Pyi stood on the steps of the palace, flanked by his elders. He raised his hands and silence descended. He addressed the gathering.

"My people, my fellow Lang Ren. When I first arrived here eleven, or was it twelve, years ago, you welcomed me with open arms when so many others had scorned and rejected me, even stoned me. You gave me the opportunity to become one of you and you allowed me to teach you the way of the wolf. Then you elected me as your leader, an honour I truly cherish and one that still humbles me today.

"It was foretold that the round eyes would come to us, and they did. They came in search of a forefather who disappeared many years ago. And as you now know, the round eyes buried in the desert tomb are indeed their forefathers. You also know that over the past few years our water supply has become less and less and has also become more and more bitter. We have learned to survive on little water. But we cannot survive without water. The round eyes have told us of a place not far from here, called Shanguo, where there is another city, much like this one, but which has much more water."

A murmur had started in the crowd.

Lou Pyi paused for effect, making eye contact with the odd individual and holding it for a second or two.

"After they told me of this place, I thought that they were leading me into a trap. I sent Wu, Li and Huang, our most able scouts, to scout this location and seek out traps and look for signs of deceit, but it was not so. They couldn't find any and neither could I in the man Ulf, their leader."

The murmur was fast becoming an excited babble.

Uncharacteristically, Lou Pyi raised his voice and called for quiet. The hubbub quickly subsided.

"Wu tells me that there is enough water and good land to plant more and larger crops. The mountains also contain many wild sheep and goats. Today the elders and I have been discussing the merits of such a move. Without dissent we have all decided that a move would be of benefit to the Lang Ren. So tomorrow we leave for Shanguo. Be good wolves — take only what is necessary. Possessions can be easily replaced. Go now and pack your things. Make ready for the journey."

Unlike the move from the hidden kingdom, the option of staying or going was not offered. It was expected that all would go.

The following morning we were awoken early and had breakfast with Lou Pyi, Can Sui and the elders. On exiting the building our horses were waiting, as was our guide. The rest of our team was there to bid us farewell. I addressed them. "I have one simple instruction — give Lou Pyi and his people as much assistance as you can."

I then spoke to each of the remaining five and gave them words of encouragement. We mounted and rode out of Lou Lan without looking back. I wondered if I would ever see them again. A lot was riding on a single positive response from the Governor of Wulumqi.

Chapter 27

Baku

While we were journeying around the eastern fringes of the Taklamakan, we were totally unaware of the effect we had had at the Maiden Tower in Baku......

"What do you mean they've disappeared?" hissed the man menacingly. Ahmed al-Marhani was seated on the throne. He was dressed entirely in black silk. His keffiyeh was also made from black silk. A gold eight-legged scorpion brooch adorned the front of his headpiece.

A slack-jawed plump man, clearly nervous, stood trembling before him. "Well, Your Highness, reports are that they escaped from the sealed mine by other tunnels."

"It couldn't have been sealed then, could it?"

"No, Your Highness."

"And where are they now?"

"We don't know, Your Highness. They've simply disappeared."

"Seven men can't simply disappear. They have to be somewhere."

"Yes, Your Highness. We are..."

The seated man rose and began pacing back and forth, animatedly moving his hands while he mimicked,

"Yes, Your Highness. No, Your Highness. Can't you say anything else?"

"Yes, Your..."

"SHUT UP, YOU IMBECILE!" he screamed, turning and raising his hand as if to strike the man cowering in front of him. al-Marhani's position was fast becoming more perilous. Since he had engineered the takeover of the Black Scorpions he had lost their prized Greek Dromon in the Sea of Aral, and the centre of their central slave and illicit trade hub, not to mention a few hundred good men as well. Just then a messenger jogged into the room, out of breath from running up the eight flights of stairs in the Maiden Tower. al-Mahrani stared malevolently at the man,

"Your Highness," he panted, bowing his head and falling to his knees,

"YES. What is it?"

"The Varangians... have been... seen..."

The black-clad man's head snapped up and before the messenger could finish the sentence he demanded,

"Ah! WHERE?"

"In Kaxgar... sire."

"Ha—you see? At least someone has their eyes open. Kaxgar, you say?"

"Yes, sire."

"Well? What are they doing in Kaxgar?"

"They are on their way to Qarashaher."

"I thought you said they were in Kaxgar?"

"They were spotted there, sire," said the messenger, who now had his breath back.

"Your servant Khatir poisoned one of them with a prick on the finger. He believes that the poisoned one should be dead by now."

"Good, good," said the black-clad man, rubbing his hands together.

"Send extra men to the region. They must never be allowed to return. What is Khatir doing now?"

"He has been following them, sire. He instructed me to inform you that he is waiting for reinforcements and the opportune time and place to deal the death blow."

The black-clad man threw his hands into the air and cried out, "Revenge at last, for my brother and our drowned and slain brethren!"

The leader of the Black Scorpions knew the loss of the Dromon and the mine had been a severe blow to his credibility. He knew that just now he couldn't afford to show weakness. "You, Mänär. You could do with some exercise. For failing so badly at Bactra, you will go to Qarashaher and personally lead the final assault on these cursed Varangains. This time if you fail, don't bother coming back."

That should satisfy his opponents in the Tower — for the time being.

Chapter 28

wuLumqi

Our return journey was the reciprocal of that by which we had travelled to Lou Lan. Not long after we made camp in the depression where we first met the Lang Ren, a caravan of thirty-or-so donkeys arrived and decamped shotas of ice and barrels of water in preparation for the migrating Lang Ren.

Over a light evening meal we discussed Lou Pyi's tactics and strategy.

"He certainly has all the makings of a great leader," said Lin Ya.

"He does at that," I said. "He must have given the scouts the authority to order the ice and water depending on whether or not they thought Shanguo was an acceptable location."

"He must have a lot of trust in the judgement of his scouts," said Kalas.

"More importantly, he had already made his decision prior to sending the scouts to Shanguo. He was two steps ahead of us all the time."

"….and just needed confirmation," said Kalas.

"Correct. However, his actions also say that he has trust in us, which is a good thing."

"How so?" asked Kalas.

"Well, if the Governor of Wulumqi decides to attack Lou Pyi and the Lang Ren, he is unlikely to kill our five comrades."

"Ah."

"Now, let's get some sleep. I'd like to get to Tikanlik tomorrow and over the top of the Quruktagh the day after."

As per usual Kalas was up at daybreak, which being summer, was early. We were breakfasted and packed before the sun had gained its strength. Taking advantage of the ice caravan, we refilled our water skins and departed the campsite.

We made quick time and were soon scrambling our way over the rope bridge on the way into Tikanlik. There our guide left us.

The following day we pushed on through the small town past the girls selling the shell necklaces and started up the long climb into the Quruktagh Mountains. Late in the afternoon we passed the turnoff to Shanguo, soon to be the new home of the Lang Ren.

Once through the Quruktagh mountains we rejoined the Peilu and turned west. It felt odd to be going west after going east for so long. Travelling fast, we skirted around the perimeter of Baghrash kol and turned north towards Qarashaher.

We stopped at Lin Ya's headquarters, where he was bombarded with thousands of questions. We established that the Governor was at Wulumqi and swapped horses and rode north out of the town on the road to the Qoltagh gap and Wulumqi.

Unlike the Peilu, this road passed through a fertile and well-watered land. We saw fields of wheat and corn, groves of peach trees and vineyards on the hillsides. Roadside merchants offered gold and copper trinkets and jewellery inlaid with jade, from stalls that looked as permanent as the dawans and yardangs we had crossed.

We stopped at a makeshift market in a village and feasted on Chü-shih grapes and Hami melons. Lin Ya assured us that these were the foods of kings and gods, and after our limited rations of the past few months I certainly believed him.

A few days later we rode up to the town gates of Wulumqi. We bypassed the queue and rode directly up to the guards. "I am Lin Ya, commander of the garrison at Qarashaher. I must speak to the garrison commander at once!" ordered Lin Ya in a voice we hadn't heard for a while.

The slouching sergeant was snapped back into reality by the hard edge in Lin Ya's voice. He straightened up and replied with a smart "Yessir!" and disappeared inside.

A few minutes later a smartly dressed commander exited the guardhouse. "Lin Ya!" he beamed. "It is good to see you."

"You too, Zhang Wen."

"Unfortunately I am under orders to place you under arrest for dealing with at the Governor's leisure and displeasure."

"Oh and why?"

"Because you deserted your post at Qarashaher."

"Well then, consider this — if I were a fugitive, would I be travelling in such obvious company? Also, how many fugitives do you know that would ride up to a guardhouse and demand to see the garrison commander? No. I bring news that the Governor would like to hear — must hear, and as soon as possible. You and your men may 'escort' me and my companions to the governor — after a cup of your best tea, of course."

"If the news is so important, surely we should go straight to the Governor now?"

"Zhang Wen, you never really could prioritise work, could you? If it were that important would I have stopped here at your guardhouse or ridden straight through?"

"Ah, I see. Tea it is."

We dismounted, and the sergeant, none too pleased to be acting as a stable boy, led our horses away. Over tea we filled in Zhang Wen with the details. His questions helped us get our story straight before we were taken before the Governor. After tea, we freshened up and, looking more presentable, were escorted by Zhang Wen and his men to the Governor's palace. Our arrival there caused quite a furore.

"What is he doing here?" shouted the commander of the palace guard as he hurried out of the palace onto the steps. Gesticulating, he continued, "He should be in prison, in chains! Guards!"

While the tirade went on, Zhang Wen sat on his horse and pointedly looked bored. He examined his right boot and flicked an imaginary fleck of dirt off the boot with his whip. When the tirade was over we found ourselves surrounded by palace guards.

Then Zhang Wen looked at our accuser and said with a patronising tone, "Wu Chi, you were always one for overstating the situation, weren't you? Lin Ya has been on a mission of estimable value to the Governor — and the Idiqut. He brings important news. Would you like to be the one who tells the Governor that this news is rotting in his cells?"

The last few words of Zhang Wen's delivery were as sharp and hard as a man could make them. The effect was that Wu Chi visibly took a step backwards, and his face showed all the rage and emotion of a man bested, and also that of a man not used to humility.

"Well?" asked Zhang, "What is it to be? Prison or the Governor?"

"I'll—I'll see if the Governor will see him," he said with confusion written over his face. He turned and scurried into the palace.

"That's what you get when family is given rank over the able," said Zhang Wen with unhidden contempt. "Come on, let's go see the Governor."

Unchallenged, we dismounted and made our way up the palace steps.

As we passed through corridor after corridor the decoration of the palace became more eloquent and elaborate. After what seemed like an age we arrived at two large, ceiling-height, carved wooden doors. Each had three equally ornamental brass hinges. The centre of each door had a large circular brass relief depicting scenes from the Idiqut's coronation.

On seeing Zhang Wen, the door guards snapped to attention and unbidden opened the doors. I was suddenly taken back to similar scenes in Byzantium. Wu Chi was inside standing before the Governor, still gesticulating and pointing. Officials stood around. Some were in discussion, some impatiently waiting for their turn to petition the Governor, others were bemused by the spectacle that Wu Chi was making of himself. The Governor, seated on the large carved wooden seat lined with velvet cushions, looked bored. On seeing us enter he stood and greeted us with a smile, "Ah, Zhang Wen. Just in time."

Wu Chi stood silent, with rage colouring his face at being so deliberately slighted. His malevolence and hate were openly displayed on his face.

Zhang Wen and Lin Ya walked up and bowed to the Governor. "Your Excellency…"

"Lin Ya, how good to see you. I trust you have something worthwhile for me?"

The emphasis on the word worthwhile made the threat all too obvious.

"I do, Your Excellency. But first may I introduce Lord Ulf Uspakson, a lord from the land of Norway, on the other side of the world."

I bowed and greeted the man "Your Excellency."

"And Kalas Ptolomeus from the Kaxgar region."

"You certainly have strange and varied travelling companions."

"Picked by fate, sire. Picked by fate itself."

"Ah. Come, let us retire to more comfortable quarters. This hall is too busy, draughty and noisy."

When it became obvious that he was not invited, Wu Chi's face grew even darker with rage and jealousy. A hum of protest arose at the Governor's sudden exit. We retired to a smaller room furnished with cushions and drapes in the Arabic style.

"Most impressive, Your Excellency. You have excellent taste."

"Thank you, Lin Ya. Now..."

"Sire, you remember that I sent a troop of men in the vicinity of Lou Lan when trying to discover the reason for travellers going missing? I have been bothered by this ever since they disappeared and did not have the spare manpower to dispatch another search. Well I, or rather we, found them – and more."

The Governor's eyebrows rose. "I see. Continue."

"When Lord Uspakson and his men passed through Qarashaher, I questioned them as to their reasons for their travel."

"Which were?"

"They were in search of a long-lost forefather who travelled through our land a long time ago."

"Ah." Despite having voiced his expression of interest, the Governor's face was passive and showed no emotion whatsoever. But his eyes were bright and shining. Lin Ya had his attention.

"The intelligence they had gathered all pointed to Lou Lan, to which they were en route. I decided that it was about time that I discovered what had happened to my men."

"Yes. It has taken you a rather long time to get around to doing something about it."

"Ah. Yes, sire," said Lin Ya uncomfortably.

I couldn't hide my smile.

"I decided to trail Lord Uspakson and his group. To cut a long story short, they discovered my tactics and invited me to joint them."

Lin Ya looked at me and I nodded. The Governor grunted.

"We picked up a guide and water supplies at Tikanlik, on the road to Miran. After crossing the Konqi He we departed from the road and headed across the desert towards Lou Lan. On the second night out from Tikanlik, we were camped in a depression and found ourselves surrounded by howling wolves."

The Governor's eyebrows rose.

"It turns out that they were not wolves but men, and women, who call themselves the Lang Ren. We were taken from the depression to the ancient city of Lou Lan.

"Lou Lan!"

"Yes, sire. Lou Lan. Their leader, Lou Pyi, was cast out of his village aged six and was brought up by the wolves. They have their own code based on how the wolf lives its life."

"Why was this six-year-old boy cast out of his village?"

"Sire, the whites of his eyes are yellow."

"Yellow?"

"Yes, sire. He had the yellow fever as a boy and the whites of his eyes turned yellow. The villagers believed that his eyes were a bad omen and would attract wolves and tigers and so banished him."

"Ah. Sometimes I wonder how we can consider ourselves to be civilised. Go on."

"At some stage he came to Lou Lan. He claims the wolves showed him the way. At Lou Lan he was accepted into their society. He taught them how to hunt in packs and work together and eventually he was elected leader."

"Ah."

"The Lang Ren would watch the caravans as they passed and would steal necessary supplies and kidnap people they thought would be of benefit to them. Hence the capture of my soldiers."

"They are still alive?"

"All but one. There are now approximately three hundred to four hundred people in Lou Lan, but the town has started running out of water. Lou Pyi is now moving his people to the ancient site of Shanguo, where there is more clean water and space for agriculture. He has pledged fealty to the Kingdom and has agreed to fall under your benevolent governorship—if you would so have him and his people."

"And if I don't?" Immediately upon putting the question, he raised his hand and said, "Don't answer, it was a rhetorical question. It seems I have no choice. How many of his people are criminals?"

"None, sire. It is not tolerated. Plus all who go to live with the Lang Ren have to pledge that they will live by the wolf code or else face the consequences."

"Which are?"

"Death or being cast out. Usually the former."

"Ah, so simple. How I hate all the laws we have. Make one law for this and create a hundred legal loopholes for the devious and sly to use. Close one loophole and create another. When will they arrive at Shanguo?"

"Within a week, sire."

"So soon?"

"Yes, sire. They started the migration the day we left."

"Ah." He paused for thought and after a while said, "Come back and see me in the mid afternoon. We will discuss it further then."

After our audience Zhang Wen led us out to an inner courtyard where our horses were waiting. On the way out we happened to pass a ceiling-height polished brass mirror. I was taken aback by my reflection. My face was now a deep brown, as if I had been treated in a leather tannery. I looked down and so were my forearms. My usually yellow-blonde hair was now bleached white.

"Now I know why I am seen as a stranger. I am almost opposite in complexion to the Qochoans."

"Indeed you are," said Lin Ya.

"I never got to look like this even when I was in Byzantium."

"Come, gentlemen," said Zhang Wen. "Our horses and midday meal await."

Later that afternoon we were ushered back into the Governor's private chambers.

"I have given what you have told me much thought. Here is what I have decided," said the Governor with all the authority that went with his rank.

"Zhang Wen, you will accompany Lin Ya and the northern gentlemen back to Shanguo and oversee the garrisoning of the town under Lin Ya's command. If you recognise any criminals you are not to apprehend them, but to bring this to the attention of Lou Pyi. Heaven only knows our courts and jails are full to overflowing as it is.

Lin Ya, your second in command will deputise for you at Qarashaher. He's been doing it for over a month now and hasn't lost any troops—yet."

The barb was delivered with humour and was accepted with a bow and a smile.

"Zhang Wen, Wu Chi will deputise for you here."

Zhang Wen made to speak but only got as far as opening his mouth before the Governor raised his hand.

"I know, Zhang Wen. I fully remember what happened last time. Please credit an old man like me with some intelligence. I will visit Shanguo a month from today. By then you will have suitable accommodation for the Idiqut's representative. Understood?"

"Yes, sire," chorused the two.

"Now here are your orders." And with that his aide stepped forward with four scrolls. He handed over three scrolls and said, "On your way out send Wu Chi in, will you?"

"Yes, sire," said Lin Ya. Both left the chambers with smiles as broad as the Taklamakan on their faces.

It was easy to see that the Governor was offering both Lin Ya and Zhang Wen the opportunity to prove themselves. After all, it wasn't every day that a new city was founded. If they were successful, promotion beckoned. The Governor had dangled the carrot and Lin Ya and Zhang Wen were willingly pulling the cart.

Chapter 29

Konqi he

On exiting Wulumqi the first thing Lin Ya said was, "I think we have trouble."

"Oh? How so?"

"You remember I told you that I redirected three men, possibly Black Scorpions, to Wulumqi after you had passed through Qarashaher?"

"Yes."

"Well, we passed them just before we came through the gate and all three recognised me, and I think you."

"Curses. I had hoped to be rid of them by now. Well, at least forewarned is forearmed. We'll have to keep a sharp watch while we're on the road."

"If we push it we should be able to make Qarashaher in three days."

"That could be one day too long, for I think we'll be attacked before then."

As sure as spring follows winter three men followed us out of Wulumqi and rode behind us, keeping a respectable distance. We proved that they were indeed following us by intermittently speeding up and slowing down. Our pursuers always maintained the same distance between us.

That night we made camp and as soon as we had finished our meal doused the fire so that there was no light to impair our vision. Being summer this would not be seen as unusual. Had it been winter it would have been suspicious and confirmation that we were expecting an attack. In the dark we quickly stuffed our blankets with our spare clothing and retired to the rocks surrounding the camp to await our attackers. We divided the night into watches and settled down as best we could.

As tired as we were from a night spent waking to every unusual sound, we were on the road before sunrise, as were our pursuers. At least our horses had had some rest. They had adopted wear-down tactics and it was precisely these tactics I was afraid of; I had used them on others to good effect. Wear the opposition down, tire them out and sooner or later they would make a mistake. That was the time to pounce.

I addressed this with the others, "I fear our enemy is trying to wear us down and hope we make a mistake—before we get to Qarashaher."

"What suggestions do you have, Ulf?"

"Today we conserve our horses. Tonight we have a quick meal and then ride through the night to Qarashaher."

"Ah. That way we avoid an attack and make safety in one swoop."

"Correct."

"Have you read Tsun Zu?"

"I have read a little of his writings."

"A great Tianxian general. One of his articles was "Be where your enemy doesn't expect you to be."

"Ah, a wise man."

So as not to arouse suspicion, that night we adopted the same tactics and after our meal doused the fire and created our dummies. Only this time we crept away into the darkness and with our horses in tow we slowly and quietly slipped into the dark night.

When we were about half a mil from our campsite we mounted and at a walk started our all night ride. The plan was to walk the horses until dawn, rest, have a meal and then ride on to Qarashaher as fast as our mounts would be able to carry us. Eighteen hours of continuous travel would surely test our stamina and that of our mounts. We walked on in the dark silence, stopping every now and then to check for signs, or rather the sounds, of being followed. If we were being followed, our pursuers were an extremely quiet lot.

Just before first light we ate a cold breakfast and fed and watered the horses. Wanting to make the most of every minute of available light, we mounted and rode for Qarashaher, now but a morning's ride away.

We rode straight through the town to Lin Ya's headquarters, not stopping despite many calls to do so. There he called his second in command into his office. Not wasting words, he started, "This is the situation. We went to Lou Lan and found our lost men."

The captain's eyes grew wide. He started to question Lin Ya but was cut short.

"Not now, another time. A group of people are now migrating from Lou Lan to the ancient city of Shanguo, where they intend to settle. I am to take thirty men to garrison the new town. You are to remain here and take over command of the garrison. Here are your orders from the Governor," he said, handing over the sealed envelope to a beaming captain. Lin Ya continued, "However, three men will come riding into town in the next few hours. They have been following us since Wulumqi, but we gave them the slip last night. They will probably ask after us. Let them know that we are here and are resting. Also let slip that we intend to travel to Shanguo tomorrow via the Konqi He. Let it also be known that only we three will be travelling, light and fast. Then put a tail on them. When I arise I want a full report on where they are, what they have been doing and who they have seen. Understood?"

"Yes, sir," said the newly appointed, still smiling captain.

"One last thing. Select thirty men to accompany me to Shanguo. They are to pack as if they are about to move barracks. Their baggage can follow later. That is all."

The captain left us, with a noticeable spring in his step.

Too tired to eat, warily we washed quickly and fell into soft comfortable beds.

Later that evening we awoke famished and devoured a table full of food.

Lin Ya's captain then delivered his report. The three had arrived not long after us and as predicted had asked questions, which had been answered as dictated by Lin Ya. The men had stayed in town. They had visited a few suspected Black Scorpion contacts. Two of them laid up in a hotel while one had taken up a position alongside a merchant just down the street. He had been relieved in the mid afternoon and the second watcher relieved not half an hour ago.

"Good," said Lin Ya.

"Now here's what we will do tomorrow: we will leave after breakfast. When the three leave, following us, you are to hold back the thirty men for an hour then instruct them to follow discreetly and not be seen. We will set our trap in the gravel beds south of the Korla Bazaar, the area where we camp on our patrols. Who have you selected as sergeant?"

"Hwong Ming."

"Hmm, he'll do. He's been around long enough. What I require Hwong Ming to do is, once the Black Scorpions have entered the beds, is to surround the encampment area with his men. He is to have them evenly spaced and then to advance into the beds, closing the trap. Is this understood?"

"Yes, sir."

"Good. Thank you, Captain. That is all for now."

With our bodies temporarily thrown out of harmony with the natural world, we stayed awake until the late hours before retiring again.

Kalas woke me with a now familiar shake on the shoulder. I rolled upright and swung my legs out of the bed. The grey of the false dawn silhouetted the town's buildings.

We rode due south out of Qarashaher, following the road to the Korla Bazaar. The low light of early morning cast long shadows and accentuated the features and colours of the rocks and hills as the world around us slowly awoke. How I loved being out and about at this time of day.

We rode steadily without looking back. We used our stop for our midday meal to check that our pursuers were in tow.

We stopped briefly at the Korla Bazaar to refill our water skins, and browsed the merchandise on display as we pushed our way through the crowds. Then suddenly we were clear of the clinging masses and back into open countryside. It never ceased to amaze me how fertile the land around the river was, with its light forestation and plenty of bird and animal life. Yet not another three mil beyond this was a land that was as dead and deserted as any other I had ever seen before.

We realised that if we carried on at our current pace we would arrive at the gravel beds too early. To fill the time we made a side trip to an abandoned Buddhist temple, where we lingered for a while, showing false interest in the building and its art before resuming our journey.

We entered the gravel beds, which consisted mainly of fine stone deposited by the river over the ages. There was no vegetation over knee high. The beds themselves were an area of various-sized gravel dunes, an ideal place to ambush wary travellers. I could see why the Peilu had avoided this area and taken its current route.

We set up camp just as the sun was beginning to sink towards the Tien Shan. We chose a site in the middle of a large flat area. Lin Ya informed me that it was the only large flat area in the beds. Anyone wanting to attack would have to do so over open ground. Suddenly a feeling of déjà vu overcame me.

"I don't know about you two, but doesn't this seem a bit familiar?"

"How do you mean?" asked Kalas, and then realising what I meant laughed and said, "Yes it does. It does indeed."

I took solace in the fact that any approach would have to be made over the gravel and the sound of boots crunching on gravel would definitely not make it easy for a would-be assassin.

Driftwood abounded and we soon had a roaring campfire going. While the fire would have a detrimental effect on our night vision, it would most certainly assist Hwong Ming and his men to see the silhouettes of our foes.

Then we settled down to wait, all the while maintaining the fire. Kalas had the first watch. Even though Lin Ya and I lay rolled in our blankets, sleep did not come easy.

A few hours later Kalas gave my shoulder a now familiar shake. Not being deeply asleep I was immediately awake. Kneeling beside me with a mug of cha, Kalas whispered, "They are out there. They have moved around to the west, which is to my back. They have been there quite a while. I think they will wait for the moon to dip below the Tien Shan. It will then be darker than it is now. That is when they will attack."

Standing and stretching, I asked Kalas, "How long until the moon sets?"

"About four hours."

"You hear that, Lin Ya?"

My question was answered with a grunt.

I wandered around the site, kicking the odd stone and gathering more wood. I feigned cold and rubbed my arms and stamped my feet. I then built the fire and stood warming my hands, all the while watching the moon slowly sink towards its horizon out of the corner of my eye.

As it grew close to the jagged horizon that was the Tien Shan, I pulled a heavy log up to the fire and sat on it, warming my hands and hugging myself. Just as the moon dipped below the peaks of the Tien Shan, I slowly let my head droop, guiltily jerking it up and looking around, just as soldiers do when they are doing their damnedest to stay awake while on guard duty. I did this a few more times, each time letting the interval become longer, eventually letting my head sag down against my chest, emitting a loud buzzing snore.

Lying in front of a fire I was fighting a real battle with sleep. I was instantly brought alert when I heard the clink of stones. Despite the temptation to roll and face my attacker, I lay still. The silence seemed to last forever. Then it came again. Not able to control their excitement and disbelief that they had managed to creep up upon their quarry, the three Black Scorpions started their final assault a little too early. Their charge gave them away and gave the three of us time to roll up out of our pretend slumber to standing positions with swords drawn.

With the sudden realisation that they had been trapped and the element of surprise gone, the three Black Scorpions checked their headlong charge. The leader spoke, his voice low and filled with hate and menace,

"You, Varangian — I am going to enjoy killing you."

"Oh? And pray tell me why?" I asked in mock seriousness.

"Because there is a heavy price on your head."

Playing for time, which would allow Lin Ya's men to creep up, I said, "And why is that?"

"Because you sunk our Dromon, you uncovered and stopped our smuggling operation at the mine, but most of all because you have killed so many of my brothers."

"No, sorry. You have the wrong man. It couldn't have been me. I have been in Qocho since last summer working with the King's men here in the Lop Nor area."

Doubt and consternation showed on his face. I continued, "If you don't believe me, ask General Lin Ya," I said, indicating Lin Ya standing on my left.

His frown deepened. In the background I could see Lin Ya's men creeping nearer.

"General Lin Ya?"

"Yes, General. Why do you think we were at Wulumqi?" When I received no answer, I continued. "We have been on a mission for the His Holy Majesty, the Idiqut at Lou Lan. The mission was a success and we returned to report to the Governor. On hearing of the mission's success, Captain Lin Ya has been promoted to General, his second in command to Captain, and is now in charge of the Qarashaher garrison."

"Hah. You are just playing for time!"

"Not really. Why don't you ask Lin Ya's bodyguard? They're behind you right now."

"You won't fool me that easily. Now you will die!"

And before the Scorpion could charge Lin Ya's men stepped into the circle of light, swords drawn. One Scorpion dropped his sword, hurdled the fire and disappeared into the darkness and the other dropped his sword and raised his hands in surrender. The realisation that all was indeed lost showed on the lead Scorpion's face. He screamed and charged straight at me, sword raised.

I met the charge, parried the lunge and sidestepped the now off-balance Scorpion. Two of Lin Ya's men pounced but he wriggled out of their grasp, losing his sword in the process. So focused was he on his task that he did not even consider escape, but instead immediately came back at me, with a dagger in his hand. This was going to be harder than just another swordfight. I dropped my own sword and drew my dagger.

Wearily we circled each other, the Scorpion making a few feints. Then he lunged. His dagger was not aimed at my body as I expected, but at my hand. A bit slow to respond to the danger, his dagger cut into the flesh between my thumb and forefinger. Pain seared up my arm. So severe was the shock that I almost dropped my weapon and grasped my right hand with my left. He smiled at the visible pleasure of having drawn first blood and at having caused pain. His eyes were wide and wild, his grin evil and transfixed.

The blood was pouring out of the wound and into my hand, making my grip tenuous. I knew then that I would have to finish this quickly or submit and the latter was not a consideration.

He lunged again. This time I was prepared and stepped to his left. I gripped his free arm with my left and leaning back I threw him as hard as I could. He cart-wheeled across the gravel. Before he could rise I fell upon him and pinned his knife hand above his head with my good left hand. I thrust the dagger deep into his midriff. Again and again I thrust it. Then hands were dragging me off and slowly the mist and fog cleared and I realised that I was covered in blood, with the Scorpion lying on the stones, his sting removed forever.

"Where did he get you?" asked Lin Ya.

"Here, in my hand," I said, indicating the wound. "Do you think it was poisoned?"

Hwong Ming was quick to reply, "No I don't think so. The dagger was well used. See, it has been sharpened quite a lot," he said, presenting the weapon, blade forward.

"He probably used it for eating, so it is unlikely that he would risk poisoning himself."

While this discussion was going on, a guard had taken charge of my hand and was cleaning it with water, which stung like fire. As men have done countless times over the generations, I sucked a breath in. With the wound now cleaned of all dirt, he fished into his bag and brought out a needle and thread.

"If you thought that was sore, this next bit will hurt even more. Sit down and rest your hand on the log."

Not being in a position to disagree, I did as I was instructed.

"Here, bite on this," he said, offering a thick green twig. Having placed the twig in my mouth he sprinkled some Yunnan Baiyao into the wound and began sewing it together. I screamed through, around and over the twig clenched firmly between my teeth.

Just as the medic finished stitching my wound together the sky started to lighten. He bound the wound in a light bandage and instructed me to air the wound for up to three hours per day.

I wiped the sweat from my forehead and accepted a cup of hot cha, thrust into my hand by a soldier. Not hungry, I rinsed the pieces of bitter green wood out of my mouth then sipped my cha while the others ate breakfast.

After breakfast the dead Scorpion was buried in a shallow grave. No-one offered to say a few words for him.

Chapter 30

Shanguo

On mounting my horse the exertion and loss of blood had its effect, and I had to grip my pommel while a dizzy spell passed.

The ride to Shanguo was one of the most uncomfortable I have ever had. I had to hold my right hand in an upright position. When held low the blood rushed into it and caused a lot of pain. Seeing my discomfort, one of the guards fashioned a neck sling in which I could rest my arm without effort.

Kalas reined in next to me. "Ulf, what happened in the fight? I have never seen you so possessed. Do you know what caused it?"

"After he cut my hand I knew I had to end it soon, as I was fast losing blood and finding it hard to grip my dagger. Then a picture of Lydia, all beautiful and pregnant flashed before me, and I thought, 'Who is this man to deny my unborn child the right to see its father?' and in that instant something snapped and just killing him wasn't enough."

"I have had other men tell me similar, of similar experiences."

"It is not uncommon to us Vikings. Many Vikings have reported similar experiences in battle, time and again. They tell that the whole battlefield slows down and they see everything in amazing detail. They have told that they can sense when someone is about to attack from behind, and have also told that they feel absolutely invincible."

"And is that how you felt?"

"Yes."

"Have you felt his way before?"

"No. And I hope never to feel it again."

Riding down the north bank of the Konqi He, we found were not short of food, as game abounded in the lush vegetation and woodlands. These were interspersed with gravel beds, which showed where the river had once flowed.

Every day the medic dressed my wound and sprinkled a little more Yunnan Baiyao on the surface of the wound, which, like Sven's, was healing faster than I had expected it to.

On the fourth day, with our captive in tow, we entered Shanguo, which was now a beehive of activity. A thousand years of sand was being cleared from the streets by chains of bucket-passing Lang Ren. Up on the hill gangs of Lang Ren were clearing and repairing the old aqua duct. The houses clinging to the sides of the narrow valley suddenly seemed more alive than the last time we were here.

As we rode in a tall, long-haired figure in a long coat detached itself from a work party and strode purposefully towards us. Lou Pyi raised his hands and called out, "Ulf, Lin Ya, Kalas! Welcome to Shanguo in the ancient Mountain Kingdom of Mo-shan. I see you bring a garrison."

Here was a man with a purpose. The happiness and enjoyment was written all over Lou Pyi. Then he saw my sling, and the smile vanished. "You had trouble?"

"We did. And we handled it. We have brought you someone to reform."

"Ah."

He stepped up to the Black Scorpion, who was shaking with terror at the thought that he would be dealt with by this man with yellow eyes. We sat in silence and watched the spectacle. Like our first meeting, Lou Pyi silently walked around the man once, twice and then a third time. He stopped in front of him and looked him straight in the eye. This seemed to go on interminably, then came that voice. The voice was so low and authoritative that it still sent shivers up my spine. The Scorpion had never experienced anything like this. He was being spoken to by a real live wolf. The experience was so terrifying that he soiled himself. Lin Ya's soldiers looked nervously at each other.

Lou Pyi sniffed and said, "Take him away. I will deal with him later."

"You have most certainly been busy."

"Yes indeed. We have your man Ibn to thank. He has taken charge and has planned the activity for the whole city."

"Yes, a man of many talents, and he is good, isn't he? And the others?"

"Ibn has assigned them to teams and has them dispersed all over the city. He even has plans to build a canal to bring in more water. He plans to build a dam down there with an outflow towards the south," he said, pointing to the low point of the city.

"Why am I not surprised?"

"On the subject of water," said Lin Ya, "did you know that there is a stream directly on the opposite side of that hill?"

"No. I haven't explored that far yet."

"I was thinking of a system I saw some years ago, where engineers had been faced with a similar situation and they tunnelled into the mountain from one side and redirected the water through the mountain to the other side. You may want to consider something similar here."

"Yes. It would be good to increase the availability of water, but unfortunately we don't have the engineers to undertake such a task."

"Oh, don't worry about that. Ask the Governor when he arrives next month."

"The Governor is coming here?!"

"Oh yes. Sorry, did I not mention that?"

Lou Pyi let out a long breath and said, "No, you did not!"

"Ah well. There, now you know."

"Indeed. These things are sent to try us. Now come, let's get your horses stabled and your hand seen to."

Not able, or wanting, to start our return journey until my hand properly healed, we all settled in to work to do as much as we could before the Governor arrived. I did what I could with my left hand. Can Sui had been fussing over me like a mother hen since the day we arrived. Under the guide of their sage, she had taken charge of my health. As she changed my dressing I told her, "If you continue to fuss over me like this Lou Pyi is bound to get jealous. Besides, I'm already married, and what will the men think?"

"Oh, shush! You have a long ride ahead of you. The sooner we get your hand healed, the sooner we can get you back to your wife. And I know she wants you back as soon as possible. I'm a woman — trust me, I know."

"Yes, Mother."

And with that she tied the knot that held the bandages together and gave me a playful slap on my shoulder.

"Well, it's feeling almost as good as new. A bit stiff, but nothing like a bit of exercise to get over that."

"You are very lucky that the guards' medic was in fact a doctor before he became one of the Captured Battalion. He knew what he was doing. I hate to think what damage an untrained medic would have done. Just think, you may have ended up like me…"

"Ah, Can Sui. What was done to you was unforgivable."

"That's where you're wrong. I've forgiven them."

"How long did it take before you forgave them?"

"A long time. Lou Pyi was instrumental in helping me get to the point where I could forgive."

"…and forget?"

"No, I could never forget. How could I? Every time I see my reflection I am reminded. But I have come to terms with it."

"Well, it's good that you have. I have seen men torture themselves to death for being too proud to forgive."

"You must have seen many things in your life. Oh, how I would love to travel and see the many wondrous things the world has to show."

"Well, when you and Lou Pyi have settled Shanguo, then you will have to come and visit Lydia and me in Kyiv. Oh, and bring Lin Ya and Missus Lin Ya as well."

She laughed, and her laughter ran all around the room like a brook bubbling its way to the sea.

"What's this I hear?" said Lou Pyi, walking into the room. "Laughter when you should be working? Tut, tut. I will have to do something about this," he said, scooping Can Sui into his arms and kissing her.

"Ulf has just invited us to visit him and Lee-dee-ya in Kee-ef. He said to bring Lin Ya and his wife as well."

He looked thoughtful and said, "Well maybe, just maybe we'll take you up on that. But what was the joke?"

"Just the thought of Lin Ya with a wife. Ulf called her Missus Lin Ya." And with that she broke into peels of laughter again.

We looked at each other and shrugged.

Later that day I was directing a few gangs of men and women when Lou Pyi came up to me.

"I have never seen Can Sui so happy. She has laughed more in the past few weeks than in the past few years. Thank you for giving her, us, so much hope."

"Maybe it has less to do with me and more to do with you."

"What do you mean?"

"The change in you is very visible. You walk with a purpose and talk with authority and your eyes can see the future. You are now truly leading your people, probably because you no longer have to live from day to day. You now have a vision, and with that comes objectives and from objectives, plans. However I have to warn you — when this is all up and going, and the objectives and plans become fewer and fewer and there doesn't seem anything to left to achieve, what then? Prepare yourself for the monotony of ruling, for the drudgery of deciding if the chicken really belongs to Mrs Chen and not Mr Chan."

"I hadn't thought that far out. It is a long way off."

"It will be here sooner than you think."

"And is that why you invited us to Kee-ef?"

"Partly. But also because I would like to have you as a guest in my house, as I have been one in yours. You also have great potential, and I would like that potential to be realised and not go to waste. I think Shanguo is the next step towards something greater. Think about it. And when you think you are bored, then will be the time to start preparing your visit."

"I now see why you were an advisor to a king. You too have vision."

"Gifts can be a curse as well as a blessing. Changing the subject, how does our Black Scorpion friend fare?"

"Oh, him. He wets himself every time I walk into the room."

"Maybe you should have him brought to you and conduct the interrogation in a larger room with your face hidden or your back turned to him, or maybe in the dark?"

"Yes, maybe I should."

"Glad to be of assistance. Now I had better check up on how we are progressing."

The following morning I stood on the balcony of my ancient apartment overlooking the sleepy city, now slowly awakening. Smoke and mists had settled across the valley floor and the morning air was definitely cooler than it had been a week ago. The early morning sun reflected off the low mists and smoke, bathing the city in a warm, yet surreal, golden glow. I flexed my right hand open and shut. This was the exercise that had been recommended to bring the hand back to its former state. It was still a little stiff and I couldn't open it as wide as I had used to. Still, I could now hold a sword again, but only for a limited time before it became tired and sore. After two hundred flexes I picked up a fist-sized ball of wax and started squeezing it. Kalas joined me briefly and we stood in silence taking in the vista.

Two hundred squeezes later, my forehead beaded with sweat, I rolled the now soft wax into a ball again. I poured a pitcher of water into a basin and washed my face and hands. Dried off and now fully awake, we went in for breakfast. Slowly, in ones and twos, the others joined us at the table. When all were seated and eating I said, "It's time we started back."

Seven heads rose in unison and faced me, with grins fixed on their faces.

Legend of the Last Vikings

"We will go the day after tomorrow. After the Governor's visit. I will tell Lou Pyi."

"Rather you than me," said Sven.

"Oh, it won't be that bad. He's been expecting it."

Fed and dressed, we departed for our day's assignments.

The day was spent decorating the city in preparation for the Governor's visit. There was still a lot of work to be done, but enough had been accomplished to make the city presentable. Ribbons had been strung across the now sand-free main street leading up to the palace. Rows of beacon fires had been set in preparation for the evening's festivities and row upon row of tables and benches had been set out in the main square. Parties of hunters had sought and killed a number of the wild mountain sheep. These had been skinned and prepared in the kitchens.

Cauldrons had been brought out and placed on stands, fires lit under them and water boiled. The Lang Ren had washed and scrubbed, probably for the first time in years. Clothes had also been washed and some had simply disintegrated. The excess water at Shanguo was an indulgence for people more used to drinking sour beer. The cauldrons had been washed out and more firewood had since been stacked in preparation for the next day's cooking marathon. Work continued throughout the day and well into the night.

The city was awake earlier than usual the next day. I stood on my balcony, wax ball in hand, watching people scurry about inspecting and correcting miniscule details on displays that would at the least be ignored, and at worst destroyed, by the end of the day.

I turned and went inside to breakfast. After the meal Tsai Ming, a Lang Ren girl assigned by Can Sui to dress me for the ceremony, asked, "Does My Lord want to get dressed?"

"Not yet, thank you, Tsai Ming. A little later. The Governor is not due for some time yet."

"Does My Lord wish his hair and beard to be cut?"

"You can do this well?"

"Yes, My Lord. I cut my father's beard and sometimes his hair."

"Is Lord Lou Pyi's hair being cut?"

"Yes, My Lord. But why do you ask?"

"Well, Tsai Ming, it's all to do with me not being the most important man today. Today is Lou Pyi's day and it wouldn't be good if I looked better than him."

"Ah. You don't want him to lose face."

"Precisely."

"My Lord is very wise. Now sit here and I will cut your hair."

After my haircut, I dusted the cut hairs off as best I could.

"Now it is time for you to get dressed, My Lord. Otherwise you will miss the ceremony altogether."

"Very well, Tsai Ming."

I heard sniggering from the adjoining room.

"I can hear that! I've had men whipped for less."

The sniggering turned into raucous laughter. Tsai Ming laid out a hooded jet black silk robe onto which a gold and silver wolf's head had been embroidered. Just last week Kalas, Ibn and I had been made honorary members of the Lang Ren Council and had been presented with these robes as a mark of our standing. My shirt already off, I removed my boots and leather trousers. Tsai Ming blushed as she brought the garment over. I slipped it on and it felt cool and light yet at the same time warm. I pulled my boots back on.

"Now I think you must cut the hair and beards of all my men."

Her eyes widened, "Must I cut the hair and beard of the Big Yellow One?"

"Him first. Don't worry, I'll be in the room when you do it. I won't let him harm you. Sven! Come here now."

A voice called out from the next room, "Must I?"

"Yes, now. It's time to stop terrorising the Lang Ren and show how decent you can be."

"Oh, alright."

Tsai Ming was visibly shaking with fear. I whispered in her ear, "He's just like a giant bear. All soft and cuddly. Believe me, I know. I've lived with him for at least the past twenty years."

As Sven came into the room, Tsai Ming moved behind me and peeked out from behind my back as Sven seated himself. I spoke to him in Norwegian and told him he had better put the girl at ease. I promptly stepped out of the way and left Tsai Ming standing, eyes wide, in front of Sven. He laughed when he saw how wide her eyes were with fear. He took her hand, knelt before her, kissed it and with overplayed mock seriousness said,

"May the hand of the woman that cuts my hair truly be blessed amongst all women."

Tsai Ming's hand shot to cover her mouth as she fought to contain a fit of giggles.

"You can sit now," I told him.

With the fear factor removed, Sven's hair was cut with extra care and attention. I did notice the two making a lot of eye contact during the exercise.

Ibn, Kalas and I made our way to the town square and took our places in the second row behind Lou Pyi, Can Sui and the Lang Ren elders. Lou Pyi looked across at us and nodded his head in approval. He and the elders had not had haircuts, but instead had their hair tied back in ponytails.

The main street from the ruined city gate to the square was lined with a Lang Ren Guard of Honour in their traditional hooded black robes, the hoods worn off their heads in a mark of honour to the Governor. Each held a staff in his right hand and each also had his hair tied back. Many of the waiting crowd had done the same but others chose to wear their hair as they always had done.

In the distance a trumpet sounded and we knew that the Governor had entered the city walls. As the Governor's retinue passed down the main street the Lang Ren Guard of Honour fell into place and marched behind. Soon the procession slowly came into view. When they entered the square we stood and, with Lou Pyi and Can Sui in the lead, walked down the steps so as not to be higher than the Governor when he arrived at the podium.

Eight horsemen in dress uniform preceded the Governor and he had a further eight behind. In a practised move the Lang Ren Guard of Honour fanned out and took up positions around the square.

The Governor was not riding. He was carried on the shoulders of a further sixteen guards on an elaborately carved open sedan chair. He was dressed in a brilliant blue robe on which gold and silver fire-breathing dragons had been embroidered. A traditional cap in matching colours sat upon his head.

Lin Ya stepped forward and in a loud voice introduced Lou Pyi and Can Sui, "Your Excellency, may I present Mayor Lou Pyi and Mayoress Can Sui?"

The crowd cheered and the Governor sat on his chair, nodded, and took in the scene before him. He then nodded at Lin Ya, who gave the order to set the chair down. The Governor descended and Lou Pyi, Can Sui and the elders knelt before him.

Opening his arms, he said, "Arise, my friends, please."

We all stood and Lou Pyi bowed his head and said, "Your Excellency, we are honoured…"

"No, Lou Pyi, it is I who am honoured."

Taking Lou Pyi's arm, he led him up the steps. "In time you will find just how boring governing can be. An event like this is to be savoured. Now turn and face the crowd. Raise your arms and wave. Always remember to smile."

The crowd went wild. Through his smile, he said, "Milk it for all it's worth. That's right, wave a bit more. A bit longer. Now turn and face the other side. Alright, that's enough."

Both dropped their arms and Lin Ya stepped forward and motioned for silence. The volume dropped almost instantly. The Governor stepped forward and addressed the gathering.

"Lang Ren. My new friends…." The Governor's opening was interrupted by applause. He raised his hands for quiet and a hush descended upon the crowd. "I have here a message from the Idiqut, from his summer palace at Beshbaliq."

Legend of the Last Vikings

An audible intake of air was hard from the assembled crowd. He unrolled a scroll and began to read. "It reads: I hereby recognise the existence of the Lang Ren and their leader Lou Pyi as loyal subjects of the Kingdom of Qocho. Let their contribution be long and fruitful. I therefore take great pleasure in proclaiming the city of Shanguo to be the newest, and oldest, city in the Kingdom. As a gift for your new-found status, I proclaim an amnesty for all past misdeeds and I bestow upon the citizens of Shanguo citizenship of the Kingdom of Qocho. From henceforth let Shanguo be included in all future census counts."

The crowd erupted with cheering and applause. The Governor turned and gave the scroll to Lou Pyi. Lou Pyi bowed with clasped hands and then took the scroll and stepped forward to make his acceptance speech. Holding the scroll high, he said, "Friends, comrades, my fellow Lang Ren. Through your hard work over the past month you can be sure the name of the Lang Ren and Shanguo will be held high throughout Qocho. Be proud of what you have achieved. No longer will we have to wait in the dunes to ambush travellers for our supplies. No longer will we have to confine ourselves to a single dwelling place for fear of discovery. We are now citizens of a kingdom and free to go where we please. Let it also be known that Shanguo will be a refuge for the weary, the outcasts and the unwanted. Let it be known that here, at Shanguo, through the Wolf Creed, they will find companionship, friendship and acceptance; and if they are lucky, they will also find love."

The crowd erupted into applause again. Lou Pyi raised his arms for quiet. When the applause had died down, he said, "Let the ceremonies begin."

Almost immediately drums started beating and instruments playing. The crowd fell back and opened an area in front of the rostrum. Dancers appeared as if from nowhere and began acting out the legends of the Lang Ren. Lou Pyi, sitting on the Governor's right, and Can Sui on his left, took turns to explain the meaning of the moves for each dance. While all this was going on a low table laden with snacks was placed in front of the dignitaries and cha poured into cups for us to sip while we watched the formal ceremonies.

After the formal session a carnival was quickly set up in the marketplace, which went on for the rest of the day. The Governor was given a tour of the city and was impressed by the restoration work that had been undertaken. In addition to the Governor's official retinue, a small crowd followed us everywhere.

When the tour was over, we retired to the official residence for lunch and refreshments.

Once we were all seated, the Governor said, "Well, Lou Pyi, if you carry on like this I may have to consider moving my official residence from Wulumqi."

"Your Excellency is too kind. I alone have not achieved this."

"Well then, maybe I should promote you and bring you to Wulumqi instead, where you can whip my artisans into shape. When I think of how much you have achieved here in only a month and how much my artisans have achieved in a year, I am saddened by their lack of progress."

"Necessity has driven the Lang Ren to achieve much in so short a timeframe. The lack of a roof over their heads and a lack of water have given them a lot of incentive."

"Indeed they have. And you, Lord Uspakson, what of you? How long will you stay?"

I had expected the question to be asked at some stage. "We leave for Kyiv tomorrow."

"Tomorrow!" the surprise showed on the Governor's face. "Why so soon?"

"We have a long way to travel. Leaving it until now means we may not be back before the first snows of winter."

"What route will you be taking?"

"We intend going north to Wulumqi and then west along the northern side of the Tien Shan until we intersect with the Araxes River, which we will follow to the Kaspian Sea. Then it's either around the northern end of the sea by land or across by boat to Hardzy Tarkan. From there we travel to the fortress at Sarkhan and then onto Kyiv. But I fear it may be a winter in Hardzy Tarkhan before we reach Kyiv."

The Governor nodded his head.

By now the sun had set and we donned our coats and went back outside to the podium for the final part of the day's celebrations.

While we had been inside, the Lang Ren had placed hollowed out bamboo halves on either side of the aqueduct and filled them with oil. At the city end the bamboo guttering ran right into the main square. At the opposite end, it ran for almost half a mil along the aqueduct's walls and then at a point where the canal disappeared into the hills, the guttering ran up the ridge of the hill. Here it was filled with oil-soaked wool. At the apex of the ridge, unseen to the observer in the city, a fireworks display had been set up. In all, the Lang Ren had created an extra long fuse.

Walking out into the square the carnival had all but ended and most were enjoying an evening meal with family and friends. Torches were lit and placed at either side of the podium.

Lou Pyi addressed the crowd, "My friends, today you have done the Lang Ren proud. It has been a long day, but like all good things it can't go on forever. Now as the day ends I ask our Governor to light the fuse to mark the end of celebration and to mark the start to our new life here at Shanguo."

He lifted one of the burning torches and turning to the Governor he proffered it with an extended arm. The Governor rose. "What do I have to do?" he asked.

"Can Sui and I will walk with you."

Taking the burning torch the three descended the steps and walked over to the oil-filled bamboo gutter. The governor dipped the torch in and the oil immediately caught. The crowd gave a gasp and a few young children ran and hid behind their parents. They returned to the podium in time to see the fire work its way along the aqueduct and then up the ridge. Many pointed and gestured but they didn't have to; the spectacle had drawn everyone's attention. When the fire reached the pinnacle and nothing immediately happened, the cries and comments of "Is that all?" and "I would have expected more than that!" were cut short as the fireworks erupted in the night sky. Babies squealed at the sound and children clung to their parents and with necks craned skywards; all stood transfixed, mesmerised by the exploding and thundering exhibition of light and colour.

When the exhibition was over, we returned indoors, feeling the evening chill for the first time. Lou Pyi turned to the Governor, "Thank you for supplying the fireworks, they were the ideal finish to a remarkable day."

"Lou Pyi, it was a pleasure. Now if you will excuse me, I am going to retire. It's not often that I get a chance for a full night's sleep."

"Then a very good night, Your Excellency. May you sleep well and wake refreshed in the morning."

"Oh, I shall, Lou Pyi. I shall."

And with that Can Sui led the Governor off to his quarters, accompanied by his guard.

"Lou Pyi, I think I'm going to do the same. It has been a most splendid and remarkable day and I have a long way to go tomorrow."

"You do indeed. We are going to miss you."

"And I you. But you know where Kyiv is — more or less, that is."

"Yes. Ibn has drawn me the maps. I had no idea the world was that big."

"Oh believe me, it is bigger than that. I know of Vikings who have sailed west from Norway and Svithjod and returned to tell of a great land with tall trees, green pastures, large rivers and all the space a man could want, at least a month's sail west."

Can Sui arrived in the silent manner which only she could do and slipped her arm through Lou Pyi's.

"Oh stop, Ulf. If I let you carry on, you'll have Lou Pyi travelling off around the world with you by tomorrow morning."

"You're right. Good night, then."

"Good night, Ulf."

Chapter 31

Farewell

The following morning I awoke early and did my exercises in the usual way. The canal and aqueduct were now outlined by the black soot left over from last night's fires. Here and there the odd chard of bamboo that wasn't consumed by the fire could be seen.

Just as I was finishing Tsai Ming bustled in and laid out my travelling clothes. As she was doing this, Sven knocked on the door and came in. I caught the look between them.

"What's this, now?" I asked.

"Ulf, ah, Tsai Ming wants to come back with me — us."

"Oh. That was quick, wasn't it?"

"What was?"

"Your courtship."

"Oh yes. No, not really. It's been developing for some time. Slowly, that is."

"Oh? And now at the eleventh hour you've decided you can't live without each other. Hmmm?"

"Yes," they chorused.

"Tsai Ming, what do you parents say about this?"

"I have not yet told them, Lord Ulf."

"Well then, I can't sanction you accompanying us until you have their permission."

"I have only a mother, Lord Ulf."

"Even more reason, then. I can't have you abandoning your mother."

"I have a brother as well, Lord Ulf. He will look after my mother."

"Even so. You must get her permission."

Looking a bit deflated, she said, "Yes, Lord Ulf. I will do so right away," and she turned to go.

"No, you won't." They both checked and looked at me in surprise. "Both of you will do so right away." Giving Sven a pointed look, I said, "Agreed?"

"Agreed," said Sven.

"One more thing before you go—Tsai Ming, can you ride?"

Tsai Ming glanced at Sven and then back at me and said, "Not very well, Lord Ulf. But I will learn. Really, I will."

This did not bode well if we were to make Kyiv before the full onset of winter. I stood cross-armed and chewed my bottom lip as I pondered the pros and cons of taking an unblooded rider with us. But she was young and having grown up in Lou Lan amongst the Lang Ren she would be hardy.

"Alright. But Sven, she is your responsibility. I can't have any hold ups. Understood?"

"Yes, sir," said Sven and they left to get her mother's permission.

The dining room looked more like a baggage room than an eating hall. All were packed and ready to go. Instead of the normal leisurely eating and discussion time, breakfast was wolfed down in a short time. We slung our mediocre packs over our shoulders and started downstairs. On the way we met Lou Pyi, who said, "I have had your horses brought out front for you."

"Oh good. Thank you," was all I could manage and we walked the rest of the way in silence. On exiting the building a surprise was in store for us; the Governor, his Guard of Honour and all the Lang Ren were gathered. The main street down to the city gate was once again lined with a Lang Ren Guard of Honour, dressed in black and standing to attention, staffs in hand.

Lou Pyi stood aside and the Governor came forward and addressed us. "Ulf Uspakson and the men from the North and the West. In a very short time you have made a great impact in this part of the world. For this the Idiqut and I will always be grateful. In appreciation for your work on behalf of the kingdom I take great pleasure in bestowing on each of you the gift of one of our heavenly horses."

The gathered crowd applauded.

"Your Excellency, if I may be permitted to request one thing from you?"

Without a word, the old man raised both eyebrows.

"Your Excellency, please try and make contact with a man named Cheng."

"I know of this man."

"He lives at the Qizil caves. A long time ago he was wronged. But he has arranged the people of Qizil in the fashion he was taught. He has much to offer. As much as the Lang Ren."

Unpredictably, he reached out and held my left forearm with his two old hands. "It often takes fresh eyes to show us what has all the while been obvious. I will see what can be done."

"Thank you, sire."

"No, thank you, Ulf Uspakson," he said, bowing. I was taken aback and returned the bow.

Then it was Lou Pyi's turn. "Throughout our lives we will meet people. Some will stay long and have a lasting influence on how we see the world and how we behave and are remembered with fondness. Some stay only a short and have little impact and are soon forgotten. But those who stay a short time, and have great impact and who act with nothing but honesty and integrity will be remembered in the Lang Ren folklore for ever more."

Turning to me, he clasped my arms and looked into my eyes and said, "You and your men are such people."

This time the crowd applauded louder and longer. Keeping my tears at bay was getting harder.

"Forever you will have my friendship and forever you all will be welcome around the Lang Ren campfire. In appreciation of your friendship, your assistance, your honesty and your guidance I too give you each a heavenly horse. This way you will be able to cycle the horses and cover greater distances and hopefully get home before winter sets in."

The crowd applauded and cheered at length.

Lin Ya stepped up next. "Ulf, Ibn, Kalas, all of you," he said with a sweeping gesture. "As a fellow military man I'm sure you know that more can be said in silence than with words. There is not much more I can add to what has already been said. In appreciation of your friendship I give you bridles and saddles made by the finest craftsmen in Qocho. This way whenever you ride off on a new adventure, know that the Kingdom of Qocho will be supporting you all the way."

We all broke out in laughter at Lin Ya's joke. At least the solemnity of the situation had been lifted. Lin Ya's men took the bridles and saddles and fitted them to our horses.

All now looked to me to say a few words. I gulped then started. "I have been a military man for a long time, as were most of my travelling companions. In battle you take, and seldom give. You take lives, and if you win, you take bounty. But you leave the battlefield hardly ever having made a new friend.

It is not often that I have been given the chance to give hope and opportunity, not just to one individual, but to a whole people. When the opportunity arose to help the Lang Ren move to another and better location, I realised that this was such an opportunity and I — we — have relished the time we have spent working with you, building a new city out of the ruins of an old.

When we came to the Lang Ren we had only our horses, saddles and clothes we stood in. We now leave wealthier, a lot wealthier. Not for the horses and equipment you have kindly given to us, but we leave richer, so much richer, for the friendship you have shown us and for the friends we have made. No amount of gold, silver or silk will ever be able to replace the memories we have of Qarashaher, Lou Lan, Wulumqi and Qocho."

I had opened my mouth and was about to start my final sentence when a commotion broke out in the crowd. An old woman was remonstrating and crying and clinging onto a young girl. I recognised Tsai Ming. Can Sui made her way over to find out what was going on. Can Sui spoke briefly and then glanced up at me. Realising what the fuss was about, I indicated that they should come up. Can Sui looked bewildered and I again gestured, at which she led Tsai Ming and her mother on up to us.

I looked around for Sven, called him forward, and asked him, "Did she give permission?"

"Yes, but it seems that she has changed her mind."

I turned to Lou Pyi and briefly explained what was going on. He nodded and spoke to Mother Tsai.

"Mother Tsai, you know that at some stage a cub ceases to be a cub, chooses a mate and goes to live with that mate."

Through her tears Mother Tsai nodded. Silence had descended upon the crowd and they now strained to hear what was being said.

"This is such a time."

"But she is going so far away," she wailed. "I will never see her again."

"Sometimes a wolf mother never sees her cubs again. Sometimes the cub goes and lives with another pack in another area."

"But he's so big. He will crush her!" she wailed.

Those who could hear the exchange broke out in laughter. I stepped forward. "Mother Tsai, may your rest be assured, I will make sure he loves her and doesn't crush her."

This brought some sobriety to the situation and Mother Tsai looked somewhat eased, but the pain of losing her daughter still showed on her face.

"Alright, let's get on with it, then," said Lou Pyi. He called out in a loud voice, "Who gives this woman to this man?"

A young man stepped forward and said, "I do."

"Thank you, Tsai Li," said Lou Pyi. "And who gives this man to this woman?"

"We all do!" chorused our troop, which brought laughter all round.

"Governor, will you pronounce the blessing, please?"

The Governor beamed at being included in the short ceremony. "Of course. I would love to." He shuffled over and indicated to Sven and Tsai Ming to kneel. He then placed a hand on each head, and looked comically out of balance with one hand raised quite high for Sven's head, the other low for Tsai Ming.

"May the gods bless you and your marriage. May they bless you with bounty, with many children and a long and prosperous life. I now pronounce you man and wife."

The two stood up and Sven scooped little Tsai Ming up and kissed her. The crowd cheered and Mother Tsai could be heard wailing over the cheers

"You see, he will crush her. I told you so."

At which point Sven put Tsai Ming down and gathered up Mother Tsai in his arms and gave her a great bear-hug and kissed her on the cheek. She tried returning the hug but her arms only just made it past Sven's wide shoulders. She kissed him back and rattled off a string of instructions in Qochonese so fast that Lou Pyi had trouble in interpreting for me.

When the impromptu wedding ceremony was over, it was time to once again become serious, say our farewells and be on our way. There was much back-slapping and hugging. Eventually, with great difficulty we managed to break away and with Lou Pyi and Lin Ya accompanying us we rode down the street towards the main gate. As we passed each guard they snapped to attention. As a result I held a salute for the entire length of the street. On exiting the city we reined in and said our final farewells. Lou Pyi reached into his tunic, removed a package and pushed it into my hands.

"This should answer all your questions. It is your ancestor's journal, written in a language we cannot read, so is of no use to us."

All I could say was, "Thank you."

Without looking back we reined our horses around and rode north through the Quruktagh towards Qarashaher and Wulumqi.

Chapter 32

RETURN

That day, the first day of our journey back, we exited the northern Quruktagh Mountains and made camp at the traveller's caravanserai. Keen to be on our way, we were up early and joined the now familiar Peilu, riding westwards around the southern shore of Baghrash Kol towards Qarashaher, where we stopped for the night and took advantage of the garrison's comfortable sleeping quarters.

In the morning we turned north and rode for the Qoltagh gap towards Wulumqi. Just over a day's ride from Wulumqi we turned west and rode for the Ili He and the town of Kulja. Instead of returning via the Peilu, Kaxgar and Bactra, we would return via the less frequently used northern route. I had chosen this route primarily to reduce our exposure to the Black Scorpions but also because it had more water and I had been reliably informed that it would be shorter and hence quicker. It would also be a welcome change in scenery.

By the end of the fifth day I estimated that we had covered more than two hundred and fifty mil. We had worked out a riding pattern. Each morning we rode one horse and swapped to the other for the afternoon. This enabled us to use the horses' ability to cover long distances to great effect. Travelling light, the second horse did not have much load, which gave it a degree of rest. Depending on the weather we usually did not stop for a morning break and tended to make camp a little earlier in lieu of an afternoon break. I made sure that the horses were well watered during the long hot days and rubbed down at the end of each day.

All through these days Tsai Ming never complained. I knew that, not having ridden before, she must have been feeling the effects of our hard riding. I was also aware that Sven and Tsai Ming had not really had any amount of time together, not as Lydia and I had done. No one minded eating a little later than normal when on occasion she and Sven took longer than usual to gather wild herbs and firewood. Although, the furtive glances between the men told me they knew what was going on. We all took it in turns to cook and by the end of the first week Tsai Ming had adopted a supervisory role and was showing us how to use wild herbs to improve the flavour and quality of our food.

The Ili River Valley was at least ten mil wide and getting wider as we followed the river down its course. The valley floor was covered in agriculture and the valley sides were well forested. A system of qanats criss-crossed the valley and most streams that would have fed the river never made it thus far, being diverted into the qanat system well before they reached the river itself. Despite this diversion of the water, the river was full and wide as it meandered down the valley.

We came across the remains of stone-built Buddhist monasteries. This was a sight we were not used to, as the majority of monasteries we had seen had been carved out of rock faces and were not freestanding.

In order to be near water, at first we camped near the river but were attacked by swarms of mosquitoes. We added green grass to the fire to create smoke, which kept them at bay for a while. Thereafter we topped our skins and watered the horses in the late afternoon then camped a fair distance from the river, which helped a great deal.

As we progressed down the river, we rode through a most amazing valley. The rocks were fantastic shades of striated red, white, brown and pink. Every here and there we could see the ruins of former settlements. Low shrubs hugged the rocky slopes, brilliant green against the red background.

A day or so later we turned up a valley and it wasn't hard to believe that we had entered an imaginary place of castles and monsters. Fantastic shapes could be seen in the rock. We took great pleasure in identifying them, calling out names and pretending to name the rocks as we passed. Sven teased Tsai Ming with vivid descriptions of the beasts and she feigned horror and fear and cuddled in closer to him. Coming to the valley head, we realised we had taken a wrong turn and retraced our steps, seeing different shapes and figures on the reciprocal route.

All down the remainder of the valley we came across burial mounds made from piles of stones. Alongside most were lifelike statues of the buried person. We also came across petroglyphs carved into the rock. Some were ancient depictions of stick-men and beasts with elongated horns. Others were more modern and depicted scenes of Buddhas with Sanskrit writings and other ancient and unknown alphabets. We stopped at one of the larger towns to replenish supplies, and we used Tsai Ming as our interpreter. After purchasing the food she had been instructed by Ibn to ask about the significance of the burial mounds and about the people. Before long she became excited and turned to us and, almost breathless, said, "This valley is the home to the legendary Wusun. Wusun in their language means wolf."

"This is amazing," said Ibn. "Have you told him of the existence of the Lang Ren?"

"I did."

"And... what did he say?"

"He has sent his brother to tell the town elder of our arrival. He said they would be very interested in learning of other wolf people."

Word quickly spread throughout the market place. No longer were we merely getting the strange-people-in-town stares, but people were now gathering in groups and pointing and whispering as well.

In a scene reminiscent of the arrival of Kalas after our emergence from the stream, there were shouts as the town's mayor was borne through the crowd in a sedan chair, the crowd parting as he was rushed forward. He arrived with a flurry of activity, his bearers panting and puffing as they lowered the chair from their shoulders. People crowded around, keen to see and hear what was going on. A short, rather rotund little man popped out of the vehicle. Despite his size, his presence caused a lull in the hubbub. Ignoring the crowd, he began to speak. Tsai Ming translated for us.

"He is Fu-Li, an elder of the Wusun people. He is speaking Tianxian, not the language of the Wusun. He has been told we are from the Lang Ren, whom he calls the Southern Wusun. He wants to know what we are doing here."

"Tell him we are indeed from the Lang Ren, on an ambassadorial visit to the Court at Kyiv far to the west," I said, indicating with a sweep of my arm. "Also tell him that the Lang Ren would more than welcome contact with their northern cousins."

Tsai Ming translated and the little man's well-tended eyebrows rose, then he smiled and spoke again.

"He wants proof that we are Lang Ren. May I suggest your Lang Ren elders' robes?"

"Good idea."

Before I could turn to retrieve the robe Sven handed it over. "Just how much of what was being said could you understand?"

"Most if it."

"So it would seem."

I took off my leather jacket and put on my black silk elder's robe. There were audible gasps from the crowd as the gold and silver wolf's head was revealed. The little man spoke again. Before translating, Tsai Ming rapped back a reply in Tianxian and the little man looked shocked. He muttered something else and bowed. Sven was battling to suppress his laughter. She turned to us and said, "He has requested you dine with him and the elders tonight." After a moment's thought she added so sweetly, in a way only a woman can do, "Oh, he thought I was your servant. I let him know that I am Sven's wife, and now I am also invited to dine as well."

Stifling my laughter, I nodded a short bow to the short man, and said, "Tell him we accept."

That evening we dined like Kings and gave the Wusun elders information on how to contact Lui Pyi, the Lang Ren at Shanguo. If Lou Pyi could secure an official embassy between the Wusun and the Lang Ren his standing with the Iliyut would increase dramatically.

Ibn recorded the legend of the Wusun, which went something like: the first Wusun king, Kun-Mo, lost his father and was left in the wild, then miraculously was saved from hunger by suckling from a she-wolf. The Xiongnu Shan-yu, that is the ruler, was impressed and adopted the child. When the child grew up the Shan-yu gave him command of his tribe and ordered the Wusun to attack the Yue-zhi, the enemy of the Xiongnu, who had taken refuge in the Ili Valley. The Yue-zhi were completely crushed and fled further west to Ferghana and the Fergana Valley, and finally settled in Bactra between the range of the Hindu Kush and the Oxus.

The Wusun then settled the Ili Valley and since expanded to occupy a large area. During the time of the Han emperors they had close ties with Qichi and became a respected force in the area.

At the mention of the Yue-zhi being crushed and fleeing west to settle in Bactra, I glanced at Kalas, who gave a slight nod of his head. In the Wusun tongue, Yue-zhi translated to Hepthalite.

The following morning we were given finely crafted gifts of gold and silver, mined from ancient Han mines in the hills. I apologised for not having any gifts to return. Fu-Li very diplomatically replied by saying that the he was sure that had we known of the Wusun we would have come prepared. I knew that he knew that the information we had brought the Wusun was of greater value than any man-made gift. The wily elder knew that any treaty with Qocho could bring peace, and with peace came stability and prosperity, and even possibly a military alliance, which would bring greater and hopefully more enduring peace.

We departed, not knowing if the wolf people would ever make contact or if anything fruitful would ever eventuate from that contact.

As the valley widened further, we found ourselves riding through apple orchards, full of great big juicy red apples hanging from the trees. They had been growing all summer and were almost ready for harvesting. Ibn reached up and plucked one as we rode on by. He wiped it down and was just about to bite into it when a shout erupted from within the trees. We turned to see an angry farmer running towards us shaking a wooden implement. We stopped and waited for him to get to us. He remonstrated for a while in a language we didn't understand and at the end stood staring at Ibn with his hands on his hips. Ibn withdrew some coins and threw them to the farmer, who retrieved them, bit on them, smiled, nodded and walked away. After that we helped ourselves to an apple each and rode slowly and quietly through the orchard, crunching our way through the apples, juice running down our faces.

At the end of the day we found ourselves in the bustling town of Almaty, named for the apples and apple orchards. We stabled the horses and bedded down for the night.

From here on we travelled further west, keeping the Tien Shan on our left flank. The small steppe streams and rivers kept our skins full and the many small hamlets and villages meant our supplies didn't run low. It was almost two years since I had seen steppe country and after the desert it looked and smelt good. The air was cooler and the rolling plains meant that you could see where you were going. You could also see anyone approaching as soon as they crested the horizon.

After Almaty, the villages, towns and cities came and went in fast succession. At Shu we left the land of the Wusun behind and entered the land of the Kipchaks and the Kirgiz.

When we intersected the link route through the Tien Shan we decided to make camp early. A small settlement had grown up straddling these crossroads, ideally situated on the northern foot of the Tien Shan. In time it would probably become another Qasgar. Ibn recorded its name as Pishkek, which I thought to be an odd-sounding name.

We met merchants who had taken the northern route through the Tien Shan from the Peilu to trade at Taraz. Some were pedalling goods and trinkets. Others were intent on trading slaves at the renowned slave markets on the Jaxartes River. Their live, wretched merchandise, chained at the neck, were corralled and guarded at all times. Whenever one moaned or asked for water, he or she was more likely to get the butt of a spear thrust into the gut or face than any form of relief.

At Pishkek Ibn uncovered an interesting legend about the Kirghiz, which he recounted around the campfire. "Legend has it that the Kirghiz are the descendants of Forty Maidens. The story is that a long, long time ago there lived a Padusha, a kind of Sultan, who had an only daughter. To stop his daughter from feeling lonely, the Padusha gave her forty personal girl-servants and built a palace just for them, a long way from the city. One day, as the maidens were walking near a lake, they saw some foam in the water and decided to go swimming. Some time later it was discovered that all were pregnant. The indignant father ordered them to be taken to the distant mountains and left there. The Kyrgyz claim to be the descendants of these maidens."

This caused much mirth and comments like, "…and we know what kind of foam that was, don't we?"

"Serves the Padusha right for leaving so many girls unsupervised to their own devices."

Sven chipped in, "Please mind your language and insinuations in front of my wife," at which Tsai Ming blushed and play-punched the gentle giant.

Ibn had also been told about the great Ozero Balkash, which when interpreted meant 'the warm lake', so named because it never froze, even during the harshest winters. Unfortunately it was too far north of our route to make a deviation.

At Taraz we encountered a city much like Bactra. It was populous and the city had shady gardens and noisy markets where we heard Persian, Sogdian, Turkic, Tianxian and a smattering of unknown European languages. Ibn informed us that it was much as Al Maksidi had reported it almost one hundred years earlier. The area was now predominantly Islamic and we found hardly any signs of Manicheanism and even less of the Nestorian Christians, whom Al Maksidi said had had a flourishing community not three hundred years before.

Legend of the Last Vikings

As we passed through the city I counted five defensive walls surrounding it in concentric rings; these people were serious about their health and welfare.

After Taraz we passed through Zhanatas and then Sastobe. From Shu the scenery had begun to change. From open steppe it gradually changed to low scrub and then almost desert.

Not long after leaving Taraz we crested a ridge and surveyed a scene that was reminiscent of the one we had viewed before we had descended into Tikanlik. It was much like the desert of Lop from the top of the Quruktagh Mountains. A desert stretched out before us with a thin blue ribbon winding and meandering its way across a palette of yellows and browns. Like the Qonchi He, the river banks were treeless.

Barely a day later we arrived at the oasis city of Otrar, on the confluence of the Jaxartes and Arys rivers. It was the sixteenth day of our journey back. This was a significant point in our journey, for it was from here that we began to cross from Asia back into Europe.

Otrar was a well-organised city. It was also widely known as a centre of science and knowledge. The locals called it the Great City of Otrar. But I guess I had been spoilt and any city paled into insignificance when compared to Byzantium. It had a large wall surrounding the city and a large garrison. We entered through the eastern gate and found ourselves in the potters' quarter. At the market we replenished our supplies and bought large waterskins in preparation for the trek across the Kyzylkum.

Just as al-Maksidi had described in his travel journal, there was a mosque off the market square. Because we were almost in Seljuk territory, it was here that Ibn went to the Imam at the mosque and arranged for a letter to be sent to his brother. Even though he kept the narration of our wanderings and adventures brief, it took the better part of a day to compose.

After the letter had been written and given to the Imam for safe keeping, we bedded down for the night at a caravanserai in the western quarter. We bought hot, freshly baked bread for breakfast, which we combined with chicken leftovers from last night's meal, and washed down with a mug of hot cha.

We exited the western gate as soon as it opened and started on the road to Shavgar and Yengi Kent on the Sea of Aral. This would be an even less interesting section of the journey, as it would take us through the Kyzylkum; the red desert, the very same desert which had given the sand for the samoom that led us to the Hidden Kingdom, and me to Lydia. I couldn't help but wonder where she was and what she was doing now.

Unlike the steppe, streams from the Karatau mountains were few and far between. Most water was absorbed by the dry and parched land or simply evaporated by the blazing sun long before it could make the Jaxartes. For the most part the route stayed close to the Jaxartes, despite its many meanderings to and fro across the desert. The Jaxartes had some waterborne trade, but of significantly lower volume than the Oxus.

Despite the scorchingly hot days, the nights were becoming cooler, much cooler than they had been a few weeks ago. It was obvious that summer was slowly slipping into autumn. This gave me more incentive to push harder. The horses had performed amazingly well and had just seemed to eat up the distance between towns. However I was aware that we had covered a lot of distance and the last thing I needed while crossing the Karakum was for a horse to go lame.

Shavgar, considered to be the Second Mecca of the East, was a focal point of the trade routes and for nomadic tribespeople of the steppe. It was a vibrant town full of industry and trade. Ibn, who had visited the town as a boy, now recited from his book the words of al-Maksidi, "'Shavgar is a large town with an extended rustrak, or stronghold. There is a wall around the town. On the edge of the market there is a mosque.'"

We replenished our supplies and moved on.

Late one afternoon we made Yengi Kent, on the eastern shore of the Sea of Aral, and were tired, dusty and hot after a longer than usual ride. We all slurped down ladles of cool water at the caravanserai. The horses too drank deeply. This was the end of the well-watered section of the ride. From here we would bear further north, away from the Sea of Aral.

We had been riding hard for twenty-two days. I decided to rest the horses for a day before we tackled the long desert ride to Saraichik. Intelligence gleaned from travellers had told us that there was only one river of note on the long ride, the Zhem. While there were a few oases with wells, the amount of water at these oases depended on how much rain had fallen in the north and how much had been diverted for agriculture.

Well-rested animals were a necessity for a desert crossing. We would not be able to ride as hard as we had been doing, despite my desire to do so. There is nothing worse or more debilitating than trekking across a desert through the heat of the day. I decided that we would do our riding in the cool of the morning, rest during the middle of the day and ride again in the cool of the late afternoon and early evening.

After a good night's rest we spent the following day wandering around the town, which while still Islamic, definitely had a more European feel to it.

We left Yengi Kent before sun-up and put the oasis and cultivated fields behind us. The road abruptly opened into the desert. At sunrise all we could see was a parched plain stretching out before us, covered in hardy shrubs, gnarled trees and the occasional sand dune. A wind blew across the road, bending the shrubs and trees as it blustered its way eastwards, swirling dust into our eyes and suspending a thin veil of sand in the air. The wind was so consistent that it had blown most of the topsoil away, gouging hollows in the landscape. Despite the wind, it was still hot. The temptation to sneak back to Yengi Kent crossed my mind. Oh to enjoy another day of rest, a hot meal and begin again tomorrow! But the longing to see my Lydia, now so much closer, drove me on. So with faces wrapped against the stinging sand, we hunkered down in our saddles and plodded on. More than once I thanked God that our horses were used to similar conditions. Any beast, other than a camel, would simply not survive this sort of weather.

I had purposely chosen this less popular, more northerly route along the Jaxartes that would take us around the northern tip of the Sea of Aral, rather than the more popular southern route, which originated in Kokand and Samarkand and passed the southern end of the sea before crossing the Kyzylkum Desert. I hoped that this way would reduce our exposure to the Black Scorpions and we would hopefully avoid contact with them altogether. However, in these conditions I doubted if anyone could find us.

In the late morning we stopped at a well to refill our skins and replenish our horses. A man slightly younger than me arrived at the well, and stood waiting patiently, leaning on his staff, while we cycled through. He was thin and scrawny and looked like he hadn't eaten for over a month.

Having finished first, I waved him to the front of the queue. If we were thirsty from a morning's ride, he must have been parched from walking. Thirstily, he drank his fill, water spilling down his front. He splashed his last ladle of water on his face then turned and thanked me, while the refilling process recommenced.

"Thank you very much for letting me drink."

"Not at all. It was my pleasure."

"You are not a Muslim?"

"In the main we are not. But Ibn, just finishing, is."

"Ah. You are merchants?"

"No. Just travellers and explorers on our way home."

"You have travelled far?"

"Yes. Last year we started at Kyiv and have travelled to Hardzy-Tarkhan, Bactra, Kaxgar, Kucha, Qarashaher, Lou Lan, Wulumqi, Taraz, Otrar and are now on our way back to Kyiv via Hardzy-Tarkhan."

"You have travelled to places I have only dreamt of. The farthest east I have gone is Kaxgar. I was there at the beginning of summer."

"As were we. It is likely that we were there at the same time. We wintered over in the Tien Shan and were the first travellers into Kaxgar from the West."

"Then yes, we were in Kaxgar at the same time. I had studied in Kaxgar last year and through the winter. I am now on my way to found an Islamic monastery in the Mangistau region. Oh! Please, forgive my manners—I am Beket-Ata. At your service," he said, bowing.

"I am Ulf Uspakson," I replied. "This is Ibn Alp-Arslan, the big blonde giant over there is Sven and the little lady is his wife, Tsai-Ming. Then there is Larz, Knut, Kalas and his son Marsias."

Ibn asked, "What sort of monastery are you intent on founding?"

"One where we can be secluded so that we can study the Koran, meditate and pray without interference and temptation from the outside world."

"A noble aspiration. I am interested, how do you intend building this monastery?"

"Oh, out of the rock, just like the Buddhists. If they can do it so can we Muslims. I have studied the architecture in their cave monasteries in detail, and I believe I can build one as good as theirs, if not better."

"Hah! I like this man. I like the way he thinks." Ibn took out his book and started writing. As he wrote, he spoke, "If...you have...any problems...or need...any assistance. Go to my brother...Malik Shah...Governor of ...he will provide whatever you require." As he finished he neatly tore the page out of his book and gave it to a wide-eyed Beket-Ata.

"Your brother is the Governor Malik Shah? Sire, forgive me..."

"There is nothing to forgive. I have renounced my claim on the throne of Baghdad. I am now a student of peoples and cultures, just like al-Maksidi, Ibn Khordo Adbeh and Ibn Fadlan before me."

"Aah." Relief and understanding registered on the face of Beket-Ata.

Apart from his staff I noted that like the Buddhist monks we had come across in Qocho, he travelled without any means to support himself. I asked, "Will you join us for lunch? We will not be resuming our journey until later in the day, when it is cooler."

"I would be honoured and delighted."

Over lunch, in the shade of a building, Beket-Ata informed us he was heading for the area where locals had carved a necropolis out of the limestone. There the stone was its softest and easiest to work.

After lunch Beket-Ata thanked us profusely for the food. Before departing I pressed a few gold coins into his hand and told him it was to be used to buy tools for his project. Again he thanked me profusely and then departed as he had arrived, on foot.

We encountered many more natural wonders on our trek across the Usturt. It was another of the most desolate areas I had encountered on my many travels. Never before had I come across a desert made almost exclusively of limestone. The wind had eroded the white, green and pink rocks into an abundance of fascinating shapes. Here water formed lakes in depressions, but was unfit for human consumption.

We saw wild boars and steppe antelope, desert lizards and a few instances of hedgehog, gazelle and wild cat. Kalas and some of the men did us proud by catching a wild boar, on which we feasted. During the day we saw the vultures circling over prey that was dead or about to die and knew that it wouldn't be long before the remains of our boar would be put to good use. We also saw eagles and falcons, wings fully extended, drifting overhead, held aloft by invisible forces.

It was here that I saw my first flamingos. Pink and white, they sifted the brackish water with their beaks before taking a step forward. When they moved en masse it was as if a giant pink carpet had been shaken. Kalas and Sven wanted to catch one and try the meat, but I forbade the killing of such a beautiful bird. Sven and Kalas were like little children, begging their parents to let them out to play.

"No, you may not kill such a creature of beauty."

"But, Ulf, there are literally hundreds, if not thousands down there."

"My mind is made up. But I will tell you what I do want." Disappointment quickly disappeared from their eyes and hope returned. "I do want four of the brightest pink feathers to hang over my baby's cot. You may choose whatever method of entrapment you like, but you may not kill or maim a bird. Understood?"

"Understood."

And so the competition was on. Ibn, Kalas, Tsai Ming and I spent the better part of a day splitting our sides with laughter in trying to judge who was the most skilful. Sven was hopelessly outdone. To try and hide such a big frame in so open an area was all but impossible. Not to mention that the birds were in effect waders and were some distance from the shore. It was after an hour or so of solo vain and valiant efforts that they began working together to shepherd the birds. At first they tried in pairs, but found that one man couldn't hold a bird. Its long neck curled around and pecked him at will. Eventually a four-man squad managed to isolate a single bird. Two shepherded the bird into the trap, one pounced and held the body, the second the neck just behind the head to stop it from pecking. One of the shepherds grabbed the scrambling feet while the fourth plucked the bright pink feathers from under the wings. This done and tried, the others soon started using the same method and by the end of the day we had an abundance of bright pink feathers.

That night we camped at the foot of a limestone bluff. Kalas and Marsias hunted and caught another wild boar, which Sven and Tsai Ming roasted, and laid on a feast. Where they kept the herbs and spices was a mystery to us, but a veritable feast it was, even if the meat was tough from spending years surviving in an almost waterless environment.

It was while we were eating that Knut and Lars noticed what they thought were sharks' teeth in the rock. They both got up and chipped away at the rock with their daggers. After about half an hour they both had a handful of teeth. Knut brought them over to show me. "Here, Ulf. What do you think these are?"

I examined them. "Now that is interesting. Sharks' teeth in the middle of a desert."

"You're telling me. Not just the middle of the desert but at least thirty fot from the surface. Hey, Ibn, there's something for your book!"

"It surely is. But are you absolutely sure they are sharks' teeth?"

"As sure as I've spent most of my life sailing the high seas. Except for the past year, that is."

"Well then, it must surely be proof that the great flood was anything but a story."

"What are you going to do with them?" asked Kalas.

"I think… I'll make a necklace."

"For who?" said Lars.

"Some poor unsuspecting maiden, no doubt," said Ibn.

By now the discussion held everyone's interest, and Sven's last statement led to a flurry of activity at the rock face.

"See what you've done? I've been leading a bunch of miners around the world!"

The northern route around the Sea of Aral was definitely less frequently used, and we had to use the sea as our primary navigational aide, keeping it on our left at all times. We travelled around the north of the sea and then down the west coast, passing through endless expanses of soda marshes and limestone formations. We stopped at Ancient Karakolja on the west coast, before striking west across the desert towards Shirkala and Hardzy Tarkhan.

When we made Shirkala Ibn informed us that we were almost across the desert. He said that Saraichik, which interpreted means Little Sarai, on the northern tip of Kaspian Sea, would be the end of our desert travels.

"If Saraichik is known as Little Sarai, where then is Big Sarai?" asked Sven in his usual nonchalant manner.

"Who knows?" responded Ibn. "For it to be called Little Sarai there must have been at least a town or city, maybe someone had the idea of building a Big Sarai and never got around to it."

We were all sitting on our horses grinning from ear to ear as Ibn waffled on. "Yes, yes I know. However, for all we know it may be buried right beneath us as we travel. Take Chorasmia as an example—a great city-state all but buried by the desert."

As we approached Saraichik we came across tents dotted about the landscape with teams of men digging.

"Must be mining," said Ibn.

"Now, why does that seem familiar?" I asked.

"No, not mining. Not that close to the surface, they're not," said Kalas.

We stopped by one of the teams nearest to the road.

"Good morning," Ibn called. "May we enquire what you are, ah, mining for?"

A fairly large, mean-looking man raised his head from the diggers. "And just why would you be interested?"

"Well, we're passing through on our way to Hardzy Tarkhan and were wondering why there are all these tents with people digging in the earth?"

He eyed us carefully before answering. "Well, the answer to your question is easy. Legend has it that the Hun of Saraichik had twenty-seven children; thirteen daughters and fourteen sons. His favourite daughter would ride the Ural River, which is just yonder, in a golden boat, waving to those on shore. A painting of such a scene adorns the walls of his now unused palace. Beloved by many, the girl had treasures of gold and jewels bestowed upon her. But she died at the tender age of fifteen.

"Heartsick, the Hun buried all the girl's treasures with her. Hundreds of friends attended her funeral at a secret location in order to preserve the sanctity of her grave and leave the gold in its place. However, attending that funeral would have its price. As you know the best kept secrets are those with no witnesses. The Hun had all the friends in attendance executed after the funeral, their heads chopped off. The treasure has been searched for ever since."

We all laughed. "Well good luck, my friend. We wish you success."

"Thank you," he said as we rode off towards Saraichik.

We clattered across an old wooden bridge over the Ural River into the town itself and headed for the nearest caravanserai.

Once the horses were stabled, rubbed down and watered, we splashed water over our faces and washed evidence of the desert off our bodies. We then headed inside for a well-deserved hot meal, after which we handed our clothes over to a servant girl for washing. When they were brought back it was obvious by the look on the girl's face that some were in urgent need of repair, if not replacement. When she showed them to me I agreed. I gave the girl a few gold coins with instructions to go to the market and purchase replacements or to have the necessary repairs made to those items which were salvageable.

That evening we all had too much to eat and drink and most of us woke in the morning with sore heads.

From Saraichik we turned south for Hardzy Tarkhan. Who and what would we find there? In my heart I somehow hoped that my Lydia would be there, waiting for me. But I knew that by now, barring a mishap, she should be in Kyiv.

And so we left Saraichik behind and headed out across the area called the Karagie. Once again we came across flamingos wading in small lakes formed in hollows, and once again the water was unfit for human consumption.

It never ceased to amaze me that the horses could smell water long before we humans did. Their gait picked up and a walk turned into a trot before breaking into an all-out gallop. This occurred a number of times at the rivers that criss-crossed the Karagie. Each time we took advantage of the fresh water and bathed and swam before filling our skins and moving on.

Seeing the city walls of Baku, the horseman let his horse go. He had been in the saddle for weeks, only stopping for overnight rests. He was sure that the personal delivery of this important news would bring him a promotion. The city walls drew slowly nearer.

As soon as he had made his escape from what was so obviously a trap, he had remained in the desert for three days. His backside was still sore after being burnt by the fire as he had hurdled it. Remaining undiscovered, he carefully made his way by night to the Konqi He to drink. On the third night he was sure that he was considered dead and instead of returning to the desert he followed the river north towards Qarashaher.

Once he had safely made Qarashaher, the Chapter Master had recommended he personally deliver the news to headquarters in Baku. The Master had given him a letter of recommendation to be used at the Brotherhood's chapter houses for refreshment and fresh horses on his return journey.

It was on his way out of Qarashaher that he saw a group of horsemen ride out of the town. He followed them towards Wulumqi and when they turned off the road and started up the Ili Valley track he recognised the giant blonde one and followed at a discreet distance until they camped for the night. That night he snuck up on the group and confirmed his worst suspicions. The group were primarily the Varangians that Manar had been sent to kill. They had obviously chosen to return home via a different route, probably to avoid detection and capture. He returned to his horse as quickly as he could and immediately resumed his journey, only now with added urgency.

Along the way chapter masters had been only too eager to help speed him along with his important news.

It was every Black Scorpion's dream to stand atop the Maiden Tower in Baku. To stand on the very platform off which traitors and enemies were thrown to their deaths and left for the vultures and crows to feed on. Some served their whole lives without ever seeing Gorgan or even Bactra. And here he was, galloping towards the place he had only ever dared dream of.

As he approached the gates, a black-clad guard ran out of the gates and deployed themselves. At first he thought it was a guard of honour for him, but as he drew even nearer he realised that they had deployed across the road, blocking his way. He slowed his steed, bringing it to a canter and then to a walk, and stopped a few feet in front of the guard. The troop leader, who had been leaning against a pillar, watching him approach, straightened up and walked over to him with his hand extended. He produced the now dog-eared letter. The troop leader pulled a face on seeing the dirty and worn letter. Nevertheless he read it and glanced at the troops, who continued to block the way.

"You have never been here before, have you?"

"No. I…"

"Through the gates and follow the road to the market square. Turn left and go up the hill. Keep going up until you get to the tower. Present yourself and this letter to the guard."

"Thank you."

The troop leader nodded to the guards, who fanned out into two lines down either side of the road. He rode through. He had his Guard of Honour after all.

Following the troop leader's instructions he rode through the town, turned left and rode up the hill, which rose steeply, quickly giving a panoramic view of the Kaspian and all the lands to the horizons. It didn't take much intelligence to work out why the tower had been built upon this spot and had been later chosen by the Black Scorpions as their headquarters.

At the tower entrance the gate guard stopped him and read his letter. He ordered him to dismount. He then instructed him to take the letter through the main doorway. Another guard led his sweat-caked horse away.

Inside the tower the air was cool, much cooler than outside, and his cooling sweat caused him to give an involuntary shiver. As his eyes adjusted to the dim interior, a measured voice seemed to emanate from nowhere.

"Yes? Can I help?"

"Oh, yes. I have come all the way from Wulumqi with news…"

"About the Varangians? They are dead?"

"Yes, no. Everyone but me was killed. We were led into a trap by Manar."

"That idiot! And Khatir?"

"Dead."

"That is not good news. He was one of our best."

"Yes, I worked with him for a long time."

The official stood and read the letter. He then silently considered his options. He snapped out of his contemplation, smiled and said, "Alright, follow me."

The official then turned on his heel and proceeded through an arched doorway. The messenger followed him through and started up a spiral staircase. On each landing they passed closed doorways, which were stencilled with Black Scorpion numerals.

At number six the official knocked and waited. After a long wait someone called them to enter. As he opened the door, three scantily clad girls came out giggling, their breasts and other bits jiggling as they went down the steps. The messenger's eyes grew wide in astonishment as he stared after the girls. The official snapped at him, "This way. You'd think he'd never seen women before!"

Inside the curved room, a man lay on a couch. He wore a loose-fitting black caftan. The symbol of the Black Scorpions was embroidered in silver on the left breast.

"What is it Qatn?"

"A messenger from Wulumqi, Your Excellency, with news that I thought you should hear first."

"Indeed. Proceed."

Qatn al-Usmi nudged the messenger, who started his report. All through the verbal report Bolon Ermias's face remained passive. However, his blue Macedonian eyes burned bright as his mind received, stored and processed the information. When the messenger finished he said, "Thank you. Please wait outside."

The messenger nodded and retired to the stairwell. As soon as he had exited, Bolon said, "Qatn, my old friend, you have done well. If we play our cards right we could be in control of the Scorpions by sunset. It is time to put our plan into action."

The day's business over, Ahmed al-Marhani and his senior council retired to the seventh level for their daily feast on grapes, cheeses and fruits brought in from the lands surrounding Baku. Lying on couches they were fed by slave girls wearing nothing but expensive jewellery stolen from royal palaces from Rome to Chang'an. The senior council of Scorpions discussed plans in progress, strategy, tactics and whatever subject was raised. The tone of the talk was relaxed and easy. Every now and then a girl squealed as a hand found its way between her legs, or when she had a breast squeezed.

After about an hour Qatn al-Usmi knocked and entered with the messenger. "Sire, forgive the intrusion. A messenger from Wulumqi with news," he said, bowing low.

"Enter, enter," said an unsuspecting al-Marhani. The messenger came forward and bowed.

"Report," ordered al-Marhani.

The messenger reported as he had been coached by Qatn al-Usmi. Ahmed al-Marhani's face grew pallid as the messenger proceeded.

"Lies! All lies!" he screamed.

"I assure you, sire, it is the truth," said the messenger, sinking to his knees and bowing his head, offering his neck as proof that he was speaking the truth.

al-Marhani's hands clawed as he turned and paced in confusion, frustration and anger. Bolon Ermias nodded at Qatn and he gave a single clap of his hands. From behind the heavy curtains, out of ornamental clay jars and through the door, came six black-clad men, their faces masked by ornamental lacquered black scorpions.

"No! No!" screamed al-Marhani.

But the men advanced across the room. Rather than experience death under the swords of assassins, al-Marhani turned and fled through the only remaining escape route, onto the platform of death. He stopped at the edge and turned. The senior council followed to the doorway and stood in silence watching al-Marhani.

"Damn you all. I'll see you all in hell!" al-Marhani screamed before jumping to his death, screaming until he hit the platform six stories below with a dull thud.

"Strange?" muttered Bolon Ermias.

"What is?" asked Qatn.

"That he used a Christian curse. He was obviously NOT a good Black Scorpion. Ah well. I am so glad he jumped. I hate the bloody mess an assassination leaves. Now let us retire indoors for the next order of business."

Inside there was no sign of the black-clad assassins. The council returned to their couches and resumed their former reclined positions. There was no objection when Bolon Ermias took up a position on the leader's couch.

"Qatn, be so good as to have the golden brooch retrieved before the vultures shred it."

"Of course, Your Highness," said Qatn, bowing and exiting the room. Waiting until Qatn had exited the room, Bolon, through a mouthful of succulent grapes that had just been fed to him by a naked nubile maiden, said, "I propose that Qatn be promoted to be our Arabic representative."

"He has the instinct. But does he have the intellect?" asked the Kyvian representative.

"Oh, I think he will grow into the role," said Bolon. "In the meantime he will be a most willing puppet, to be moulded, shaped and directed at our will."

"Very well, I concur," said Romanus Argyrus, the Roman representative.

"Any other dissentions?" asked Bolon, not really expecting any. "Good. I also propose that the messenger be given a chance to redeem his honour and that he ride immediately and join Captain Elpidio at Batumi from where they will sail north to intercept the Varangians when they cross the Tuoni River. Agreed?"

A chorus of ayes were forced out through mouthfuls of food.

"Good. I love it when everyone agrees with me," he said gleefully.

He clapped his hands and the naked maidens cleared away the food, only to appear a few minutes later to start undressing the council members.

Chapter 34

OLD FRIENDS

The masses of reed beds gave away the fact that we were approaching fresh water. That they stretched out for mil upon mil indicated it was a large river. Islands of reeds could be seen out in the river. Slowly but surely the smell of fresh water intermingled with the smell of human habitation until the latter superseded the former.

Just as the smell of human habitation increased, so did the occurrence of fishermen's shacks, then houses, until at last we were well and truly back in this eastern city of canals and bridges.

We meandered our way through the city, overwhelmed at its size, business, noise and bustle. It was at total odds with the quiet, open expanses of the desert and steppe. Not even Otrar and Tengi Kent were comparable in size or activity.

Finally, after a few wrong turns, we found ourselves in the silversmiths' row. It felt as if I were being reacquainted with a long-lost friend. Eventually we came to Balgichi's shop, although it could never be called a shop. I rapped on the door and a female voice from the inside called out, "Ver iz dort?"

"I don't profess to understand what you're saying, young lady, but I believe you have a young man of mine…"

The door flew open and Serakh, Rat and Pesakh burst out. Rat flung his arms around me and thumped me on the back and shouted, "ULF! At last! We have been waiting and waiting and had almost given up. We have ridden the approaches day after day and scoured the port looking for you…"

Then he realised his predicament and withdrew all embarrassed. Not one of the crew laughed, but the grins on their faces told me that they understood.

"Come in, come in," said Pesakh.

We entered the shop and it struck me that what had before been choked with books, maps and manuscripts, was now totally bare. Only a light layer of dust covered the floor.

"What…? Where is everything?"

Balgichi Simatov came out from the back, "It is all gone to Kyiv."

"Kyiv? But why? You said that it was your books that kept you here."

"And so it was. Well, I want to be near my grandchildren. When they arrive, that is." He gave Rat and Serakh a soulful look.

"Am I missing something?" I asked.

"No," replied Rat with a grin plastered over his face. "Only that Serakh and I were married two months ago."

"So now we have a Missus Rat, eh? Ah, I know what it was, you couldn't wait to dip your wick, eh?"

"No, it's not like that…" he started.

Blushing, Serakh tugged his shirt.

"Oh, you're teasing again," said Rat.

"I surely am. Do you mean to say that I missed your wedding? And a feast?"

"Yes, sorry," he said, looking like a scolded child. He then added quickly, "But Lydia and Iksander were here."

"Ah. Well then, we'll just have to have another celebration. We have a long and interesting story to tell.

Sven, are you going to introduce Tsai Ming or what?"

"I think 'or what' should about do it."

"Who is Tsai Ming?" asked Rat.

"Sven's wife, of course."

"Sven's wife! Sven has a wife? Where is she?"

Little Tsai Ming was brought forward and Sven placed a protective arm about her as best he could.

"She is Sven's wife!" exclaimed Rat and Pesakh together, staring at the diminutive but beautiful Tsai Ming.

"But she is so small," said Rat.

Serakh elbowed Rat in the ribs and he winced. Serakh and Tsai Ming had made eye contact and both smiled broadly. Now they could look forward to the journey to Kyiv in company other than that of ten boorish men.

"Rat, when did they leave for Kyiv?"
"Seven weeks ago, tomorrow."

"Well they should be there by now," said Sven.

"Yes, they should. Well, why are we standing here? We have just crossed the world and are thirsty and hungry."

Teasing Serakh, I said, "Well then, are you going to just stand there or are you going to cook for us… or… are we going out?"

"I think we'll go to a tavern," she said. "There's too many to cook for at this late hour."

"Just as well," said Sven. "I don't think there's enough beer here for a double celebration. Or is it a triple celebration?"

"Who cares?" said someone. "It's a celebration whichever way you look at it."

Tsai Ming whispered something in Sven's ear.

"Tsai Ming would like to change into something more comfortable before we go out."

"Alright. Make it quick, though—we're all hungry."

Tsai Ming and Serakh disappeared into the back of the shop and emerged a short while later in splendid female attire. A few whistles emanated from the crew.

"That's enough of that," chorused Sven and Rat, which brought on a reply of "Woo-hoos".

As we walked into the tavern the sight of a diminutive but beautiful oriental woman clad in shimmering green silk turned just about every man and woman's head in the place. She instinctively moved close to Sven, who draped an arm across her shoulder.

While we ate Ibn led the recounting of our travels in, around and across the Taklamakan and the Kingdom of Qocho, with the help of his diary. Like most young men their age, Pesakh and Rat were visibly upset on having missed out on so much high adventure. I had to remind him that he had caught a wife instead of desert sand in his nostrils, which pacified him a little.

The recounting of the story led to others in the tavern taking an unusually high interest in what was being said. As the night wore on, eavesdropping turned to blatant interest in proportion with the amount of beer being consumed. Eventually we found ourselves the centre of a fairly large crowd. The beer flowed as quickly as the story, and commentary on what was being told was not withheld. As with any story, there were those who didn't believe a word of what was said. Unsurprisingly it was discovered that most of the doubters had never been beyond the boundaries of Hardzy-Tarkhan. Nevertheless they stayed for the duration of the tale.

Now that we were in closer proximity to the Black Scorpion headquarters I had tried to scan the crowd that night for anyone who may give the slightest indication of being a Scorpion. I noticed that Kalas was also doing the same. Despite my efforts I did not identify anyone who showed signs of being one.

When we left the tavern that night, we left with many looks of admiration and the tavern keeper did not charge us for our meal, saying that never before had he had such good business and could we come again tomorrow. I told him that tomorrow we would be gone, on our way to Kyiv.

Once outside, I called Kalas over. "Did you pick up anyone who had the telltale signs of being a Scorpion?"

"No. But news of our storytelling will undoubtedly spread. If a smart Black Scorpion should hear of it he would not take long to come to the obvious conclusions."

"Unfortunately true. Oh well, we'll just have to keep our wits about us."

A few of the more inebriated crew had linked arms and were marching down the centre of the street singing an old Viking song.

He smiled and said, "With this lot?"

I smiled and said, "I know, I know."

After staggering back to the shop, I insisted that we pack in preparation for the following morning's departure, which brought on howls of drunken protest. However, having half packed would save some time in the morning.

As per usual I was woken by Kalas giving me a light touch on the shoulder. It always amazed me that while I woke almost instantaneously at his touch, I never woke on his approach.

The grey half light of dawn silhouetted the buildings as we went around waking the others. Tsai Ming and Serakh heated some unleavened bread, which we washed down with some cha from Tsai Ming's seemingly endless supply.

When breakfast was over, we packed our supplies onto the horses. Our spare mounts were now taking the last of Balgichi's stock and the extra supplies needed for the overland trek to Kyiv. Before packing I checked just what Serakh was loading and had to call Rat over and have her remove some of the unnecessary luxuries she was intending to carry.

We clattered out of the courtyard into the silversmiths' row just as dawn was breaking.

Pesakh and Rat led the way out of the courtyard, through the city and out into the country. Travelling with Balgichi meant we would be travelling more slowly than I would have liked. If all went well, it meant we would probably make Kyiv just as the first snows were falling.

We reined in a few mil outside Hardzy-Tarkhan and I gave Balgichi and Serakh the chance to have one last look at the city that had been their family's home for generations.

Both stared and said nothing, flicking through a lifetime's memories. Without saying a word, Balgichi touched his daughter's arm and both wheeled their horses and turned their backs on their beloved city.

I had thought of returning via Sarkel and visiting my old friend Barjik Chernetsov, but Ibn quite rightly pointed out that this route would be a dog-leg to the north and would lengthen our trip unnecessarily. So Barjik and Sarkel would have to wait. Instead we struck out on a more direct course that would take us slightly north of due west, away from the Volga River, across the almost flat plain of Kalmykia. Our route would take us almost to the northern tip of the Surozke More, through which we had passed just a year ago, albeit using water-based transport. It seemed like an age and a lifetime of activity had occurred in that one year. Thereafter we would head north of west for Kyiv. With Ibn's help I reckoned it would take us at least a month to complete our travels. Then Lydia. Oh how I missed her! And what of our child? Was it born yet? If it was, was it a boy or a girl? I mentioned this to Ibn.

"Would it matter if it were a boy and not a girl?" asked Ibn.

"No, not at all. If it's a boy I'll have my heir, something I had almost given up on. If it's a girl then she's bound to be like her mother, and I'll love her just as much as Lydia."

"I agree. Allah forbid that a girl should look like you. But there is no need to worry about your child. As we in the Islamic world know, the human gestation period is forty weeks, so by my reckoning Lydia has a few weeks to go. Also, as this is her first child, she may be anything up to two weeks late..."

"Late? What do you mean late?"

"Well, our doctors have calculated that conception can occur up to two weeks after the women has her, um, period of bleeding. Therefore there is a two-week window of variance on the calculation."

"I see."

"So if we get a move on, we may just be able to make Kyiv in time for the birth."

"Well then, we'll have to get moving, won't we?"

"Yes, but I'm not sure how Balgichi is going to handle the extra few mil we will have to do each day."

"Why don't you ask him?"

We reined in and waited until Balgichi caught up. Pesakh, Rat and Serakh were riding with him.

"Balgichi, how are you managing?"

"Well, I only wish I were twenty years younger."

"I know what you mean. This is probably going to me my last such journey. I don't think I could handle another like it."

"Don't be so sure, Ulf. Don't be so sure."

"Oh? Do you know something I don't?"

"Only that I see it in your eyes, Ulf. There is still life there and where there is life there will always be a yearning to live. And for you that means travel. But you didn't wait for me to have me tell you what you already know, hmmm?"

"No. The seasons are changing and we need to get a move on if we are to make Kyiv before the winter sets in."

"Not to mention if we are to get to Kyiv in time for your firstborn's birth?"

"That as well."

"So how many extra mil do we have to ride each day?"

"You should have been a general. Do you know that?"

"Had the Kahzars not been beaten and pushed back by Svaitoslav, Yaroslav's father, I may have been."

I looked hard at him and wondered how much he had had to give up because of that defeat. How much expectation, promise and potential had been shelved, never to be used, because of another man's ambition to extend his empire? This then was the campaign he had never been on; his one and only opportunity to realise his dream of riding on a campaign before he died. Therefore I knew that he would do it, even if it killed him.

"A minimum of ten, a maximum of twenty."

Legend of the Last Vikings

"So fifteen should suffice?"

"More than suffice."

"Then fifteen it is."

"Thank you, Balgichi. Pesakh, Rat, it is your responsibility to see that Balgichi and Serakh are as comfortable as possible."

"Ulf, if we are going to slow you down then you must push on ahead without us."

"That is not an option. We started this together, we'll finish it together."

"That is an admirable..."

I rudely interrupted and said firmly, "There will be no further discussion on splitting up. Is that understood?"

I received a varied mixture of nodding heads and mumbled "yessirs" from the group.

We continued our westward trek. It still felt extremely good to be going west instead of east. Each footfall was another closer to my Lydia.

The plain of Kalmykia was like all steppe — open, vast and boring, dotted here and there with small lakes. But it was not as boring as the desert. At least here there was grass, water and a more varied wildlife.

The end of the plain was marked by a low ridge of hills where we met the headwaters of the Sarpa River. Balgichi informed us that he had ridden out here a few times as a boy to hunt wild sheep with his friends. Thereafter we descended into the Manitch River Valley, which we would follow until the Surozke More. On the way we forded a few tributaries and crossed others by ferry. Had I not had the supplies and the women I would have saved time and made all the crossings without the aid of ferries. But as it was I had more than just the men to consider.

On arriving at Cherkask on the Tuoni River we restocked our supplies. The town had a pall of smoke hanging over it from all the kiln fires. Great pits had been dug into the almost treeless landscape, where clay had been removed for the pottery works. Not wanting to linger in the smelly town, we headed for the docks and took the first available ferry across the Tuoni. The crossing was not a short, swift affair. Here the Tuoni was wide and there was a large island between us and the opposite bank, with the main channel on the far side of the island. On the approach to the harbour I could see ships' masts protruding above the island's tree line. A single familiar mast stood higher and prouder than the rest. The ferry proceeded up the Tuoni and then swung out across the main channel. The ferryman allowed it to drift downstream with the current as he pulled for the opposite shore. Coming around the top end of the island, the anchored ships came into view, and it was just as I thought.

"Sven, do you see what I see?"

"I surely do," he replied.

Moored in the main channel was a Greek Dromon.

A few sailors on the Dromon idly watched us drift past as the ferryman rowed for the shore. None looked like regular Byzantine navy and with the sail furled I couldn't tell if it was a Byzantine navy vessel. A sailor wearing a black, knotted headscarf around his head and black sleeveless vest stood with his foot resting on the gunwales, chewing on a piece of grass. He took more interest in us than the rest and before we had fully passed by he turned and called a crew member and began speaking to him in an animated fashion. It was when he turned his back to us that we saw the telltale signs of an all too familiar tattoo protruding from under his vest on his left shoulder.

"Oh hell," said Sven.

"Right now the devil may be the least of our worries. I have the feeling that we may just be standing at Hell's door."

"God help us," said Sven.

"He may be the only force standing between us and the evil of this organisation."

Chapter 35

FLIGHT

Now only too aware of what we might be up against, I turned to tell the others what we had discovered. Shock and horror registered on their faces and we made all haste to disembark and be on our way. Once ashore we rode as quickly and as hard as we could to put as much distance between us and the Black Scorpion vessel as possible. As soon as we were a fair distance from the ferry landing, we found a secluded clearing off the main track where we reined in to discuss our next moves.

Ibn started, "There are two possible reasons for the Dromon. It may have transported a small land force to here to get ahead of us, or it may be just a coincidence."

"I don't believe in coincidences. But would they send a small force just to kill us?"

"Undoubtedly. We have sunk one of their ships, closed down a lucrative mining operation and killed a good number of their men. Not to mention closing down an entire network of evil."

"Now that you put it like that, I would probably have sent a small force as well. At least we now know what we're up against. But I'm not convinced they have sent it just for us. Why would they send a ship? Why not send the force overland? They would have had a better chance of intercepting us."

"A ship is faster and as we know the sailors double as seamen and soldiers."

"Well, they were probably expecting us to travel to Kyiv by the shortest and fastest route. Let's outwit them, shall we?"

Sven chipped in, "Have you forgotten the Pechenegs?"

"No. But they're going to be the least of our worries. If the Scorpions get to us first there won't be much left for the Pechenegs to pick over."

"Allah help us."

"I pray He does."

We had to quickly develop a strategy for what seemed like an imminent attack. Not knowing the strength of the enemy, supposed or not, meant our best option would be one of avoidance, not engagement.

"Ibn, you have a better knowledge of the geography of this area, can you provide some insight on the lay of the land?"

"I can do better than that. I have a map somewhere in my book. Let me see....". He leafed through the book and then paused at a page, "Ah, here we are."

We crowded around the book and studied the map.

A long way to the north and slightly west lay Kyiv. To the west was the Dniepr, and the south was limited by the Surozke More and Sea of Euxinus. To the east and slightly north was the Fortress at Sarkel, and safety.

"It would seem that had we taken your suggestion of travelling via Sarkel we would now be safe," said Ibn.

"Not really. We would still have ridden into the Scorpions later rather than sooner and we would then have found ourselves in a similar situation, and probably in unfamiliar territory. No. Kyiv is still our best bet."

Thinking out aloud I said, "I suggest we travel south and west along the coast of the Surozke More and then strike due west until we reach the Dniepr, crossing somewhere below the rapids. Thereafter we ride up the west bank of the river to Kyiv. If there is a land-based force of Black Scorpions, they would be expecting us to come from the east and would more than likely also be on the east bank of the river. If they found us and we were on the west bank they would then find it more difficult to engage us as the gorge would be between us for protection. But note that I said *more* difficult, not impossible. It will take us longer to reach Kyiv, but this way I believe we have a better chance of arriving alive."

The gravity of the situation now fully realised, the group nodded in silence.

We remained hidden until dark and then rode back towards the landing and then took the coast road west. It was then that I remembered the night ride we had done to the Hidden Kingdom. I suggested to the group that we start riding at night to give ourselves an even better chance of evading our enemy. By doing so we could avoid contact with people, which would make it harder for the Scorpions to pinpoint our whereabouts. This received a favourable response and so our mode of travel was set.

So in the dead of night we bypassed Rostov and later Taganrog. A few nights later we came across a village overlooking a familiar, large bay at the mouth of a river. The bay glistened silver in the moonlight against a black landscape.

"If I remember correctly the village is called Adamakha and the river is the Kalmius. We anchored here a few times when we were in Miklagaard's employ. Ibn, can we look at the map, please?"

Ibn retrieved his map and it looked as good a place as any to start heading inland.

I asked Kalas, "Do you think you and a few of your men could find some food at the village?"

"Surely we can," he replied. And without another word they slipped into the night.

During the next week or so we made good time, even though we spent a lot of time taking wide berths around villages so as not to be seen or heard. The last thing we wanted was a barking dog and a cautious or curious villager investigating the disturbance.

We intercepted the Dniepr just above the delta area where the river was already quite wide. This posed a problem as I did not want to hire a fisherman to ferry us. Not only did it have the potential of giving our position away, if there were a fisherman and boat to hand it would take all night and some of the day to ferry us across. Our only option was to ride up river to the nearest safe crossing. If I were a good Scorpion commander I would have someone watching the crossings. Nevertheless this was our only option, so we turned north and continued our travels by moonlight. Navigation was easier now, as all we had to do was keep the silver ribbon of river on our left, and there was a well-worn path alongside the river.

However we took care not travel along the valley floors, nor along the ridgelines. Movement was more easily spotted in either of these places. Instead we travelled half way up the hill sides where it was more difficult to spot us, but was easier for us to see movement on the ridges and the valley floors.

Soon the river began to narrow and the valley sides grew steeper. Although I had never travelled this area by land, I recognised some of the land features from my river travels, as did Rat, who had done the river trip more times than any of us.

From this we knew that there was a large mid-stream island not far ahead. Here the river

flowed in the shape of an extended Latin letter S. At the top bend the river split into two channels for the body of the S and then came together at the base of the letter. The island, lightly inhabited, lay between both channels, the eastern channel being wider and slower moving than its western counterpart.

We found a good spot where we could hide during daylight. I sent Sven and two others out as scouts with instructions to find a crossing downstream of the village, preferably via the island. Crossing upstream would mean having to pass by the village and risk discovery. If something should break free of one of the horses on the crossing it would drift downstream and could be found by a villager. If such an incident did happen it would tell that person that someone, or something, foreign had been in the river. So downstream it had to be.

Just before dawn the scouts returned dripping wet. They said that they had found a few places to cross but recommended one, not far away at the southern tip of the island, which was the most sparsely populated with lagoons and marshes. There was also more tree cover at the southern end due to the lagoons and marshes, which would suit us well. Sven reckoned that we could all cross to the island before sunup. But I chose to stay put, as I did not know what cover existed on the island or the other side of the river. Neither did I want to spend a day in a mosquito-infested marsh.

Camping this close to a village meant a fire and a hot meal would without a doubt mean someone coming to investigate. Today there would be no cup of Tsai Ming's hot cha before I slept. I set the guards and settled down.

As soon as darkness fell, I sent the scouts forward to check that the path was clear. When the all-clear signal was received we started out from our hiding place, walking the horses quietly down to the river. We swam across to the island without any problem and regrouped away from the shore. Sven and his scouts led the way across the island to the second crossing point. We had one or two scares along the way with birds taking to flight in the dark, scared by our progress through their forest. In turn almost scaring the life out of us and setting our hearts racing so that we could hear our blood pounding through our heads. Tsai Ming or Serakh gave a squeal, only to cut it short when they realised it was only a bird, and anything louder or longer would definitely have given us away. The tension now broken, all other animal movement in the forest was handled with aplomb.

Our senses were already heightened by the threat of the Black Scorpions and more so tonight by creeping around in the dark. So it was no surprise that the hairs on the back of my neck suddenly stood on end and a shiver ran down my spine. I froze, slowly turning my head and squinting into the darkness, trying to pick up the telltale signs of an unusual shape or movement. I saw that Kalas, too, had become very still and like me also stared into the darkness. Like him I did not manage to identify that something, or someone, that had caused our senses to kick in. I had expected to experience this sensation a lot sooner, and the fact that I had not I took as a sign that our efforts to evade our enemy had been successful. But now here it was. Because Kalas had also experienced a similar sensation, I passed the word to be extra observant and to mention anything unusual. And so with peering eyes and straining ears we crossed the fast-flowing smaller channel to the west bank of the Dniepr. We quickly found the main trail and crept out of the valley.

The sense of relief at making the crossing unchallenged and undetected was immense. Silence quickly gave way to nervous laughter and chatter. I had to remind the group that it wasn't over yet. This brought some order and a sense of calm returned to the group.

By night we continued our travels north. Now and then the trail took us close to the gorge and we could hear the water roaring over the rapids. From the security of the forest we scanned the dark, opposite bank of the river for signs of life, but couldn't see any. When we arrived at the top of the rapids I knew we were now oh so close to Kyiv, and to Lydia. The longing to see her and hold her in my arms again was now stronger than ever. Like a whirlpool, the pull was strongest the closer you got to the centre, and here we were so much closer to Kyiv. All I wanted to do was break from creeping around at night and ride hard and fast to her.

I decided that once we had passed Cherkassy, a wild frontier-like town, we would be well within reach of the protection of Kyiv and we could start riding by day again. There would be nothing worse than to arrive at Kyiv in the middle of the night and to have to sit outside the walls waiting for the dawn opening of the gates, knowing that my Lydia was just on the other side.

Early on a late-September morning we rode into Cherkassy. The air was now much cooler. Haldor would have said that it was fresh. Haldor; I hadn't thought of him in ages. How was he? Had he managed the journey well? I know that he too would have dearly loved to have come with us, but both he and I knew that I could, and would, only trust him to get Lydia and the others through to Kyiv. It was his loyalty and friendship that I was counting on.

So here we were back in Iziaslav's domain good and proper. We found a public house that was willing to serve us breakfast and give us a bed for a well-earned rest. A proper cooked meal after so many days of dry, often stolen, bread, with meagre meat or any other flavour or garnishing would make a welcome change. Even double helpings of inventiveness by Tsai Ming and Serakh couldn't disguise the blandness. And so a piping hot meal of poached eggs and hot bacon was served up. After eating bland meals for so long, the flavours burst upon our senses and the appreciation could be seen on everyone's faces as they savoured the tastes running over their tongues and through their mouths.

When we asked for mugs of hot water the innkeeper thought we were mad. But when he saw us adding Tsai Ming's chai he came over to find out what it was and was taken with the fragrance and flavour and asked where he could get this herb. Sven promised to secure a supply for him.

After a most fulfilling meal, bloated and satiated, we retired to our inviting, soft beds.

Chapter 36

Cherkassy

The glade was beautiful and peaceful. The sun was shining and clouds drifted by while a stream gurgled through an apple orchard, much like the orchards of Almaty. The apples were large, red and juicy and a few apple cores lay around me. Filled, I dozed under one such apple tree. Lydia, her belly swollen to the point of bursting was dressed in the white Grecian frock she had worn the first time we met. Her head nestled in my lap, while she absentmindedly twirled a lock of her raven-black hair around her forefinger.

Suddenly, unexpectedly, with the roar of a thousand lions, the brook rose vertically and in liquid motion, metamorphosed into a cobra with its hood fully flared. Up on its tail at full height, it hissed a cloud of vile-smelling black-brown fumes across the stream, which covered us and the tree. It then turned and slithered away. It was then that I saw the Black Scorpion tattoo on the back of its head.

Then Lydia was screaming and pointing up into the tree. The ripe apples had withered and turned rotten and were falling to the ground, bursting as they hit the ground and spraying us with foul-smelling liquefied pulp. A force greater than any I had ever experienced took hold of me and started crushing my chest, forcing the air from my lungs. A serpent's head appeared from behind me over my right shoulder, grinning and hissing while it took obvious pleasure in causing me pain and discomfort. Its breath was foul. All the while Lydia helplessly screamed. I thought to myself, *It's not like my Lydia to be helpless.*

I managed to bring my right arm up and pull the serpent's head back from my face and away to my right. My breathing eased and I sucked in a lung full of air. All the while Lydia screamed. I knew I couldn't withstand this attack for much longer. With the extra air in my lungs I puffed myself up as big as I could and flexed my shoulders. The serpent's coils reluctantly eased their death grip. Forcing the coils over my head, I freed myself and threw the serpent into the stream. Still Lydia screamed.

Suddenly the bright and beautiful day changed to dark and cold night. There was no moon. I was about to shout at Lydia to shut up when I was awoken by an extremely cold wind. Wildly I looked about and realised I was standing in the middle of my room panting for breath. There was a gaping hole where the window had been, the late autumn evening wind blowing in off the steppe. Tsai Ming's screaming penetrated my daze. Realising that I had been attacked, I unsheathed my sword and still in my underwear made my way out of my room and down the passage towards the screaming.

I burst into Sven's rooms and saw him backed up against the wall, holding a large man from behind in a headlock. Tsai Ming was backed into the opposite corner, her shaking hands raised to her face, screaming and wailing. Sven held his attacker more than firmly. His large belly protruded towards me as he struggled to break free. Recognition of what was about to happen registered in his eyes. Without hesitating I thrust my sword into his enormous belly in an upwards motion and immediately withdrew it. His eyes opened wide and he sagged to the floor. Blood appeared almost instantly on his lips, spurting from the gaping wound, pooling on the floor.

Sven grabbed his sword and we left the screaming Tsai Ming and ran out the door and down the hall. We were just about to open a door, behind which we could hear fighting, when it crashed outwards, broken off its hinges. It landed on the landing with a thud, an unsavoury character on top of it. Not recognising him as one of our own, Sven promptly sent him to Valhalla. Knut was inside, his left hand and shoulder bleeding.

"TSAI MING!" I bawled. "Stop that damned infernal screaming and get in here now. Knut needs help."

We left the room and re-entered the hall. Rat came out of his room and looked up and down the hall. Seeing us, he raised his throwing arm and shouted, "DUCK!" Instinctively we both ducked and his knife hummed overhead and with a sickening slurp lodged in someone behind us. A gurgling and sighing followed. We turned and saw a man sinking to his knees clutching at his throat with his left hand, trying to dislodge Rat's knife. Rat pushed past and withdrew the knife, slicing the jugular on the way out. I pulled the man forward onto his face and ripped his shirt at the left shoulder. An all too familiar tattoo was revealed.

"THEY'RE SCORPIONS!" I yelled. "WE'RE UNDER ATTACK BY THE BLACK SCORPIONS!"

The whole inn was now shuddering with the fighting going on within its walls.

We three made for the last upstairs room. We burst in and found a Scorpion in a death frenzy, repeatedly stabbing a bloody and lifeless Larz. As he was unaware of our presence, Rat stepped up and, wrapping his left arm around the Scorpion's forehead, pulled his head back. Exposing the throat, he slashed it with the knife in his right hand. Bright crimson blood spurted forth like a geyser, leaving a trail across the wall as the Scorpion lost consciousness.

After he dropped the nearly dead scorpion to the floor we listened for fighting but could only hear action coming from downstairs. We raced on down to find a group of Scorpions engaged with a group of unknown men in the main dining area. The fact that they were assisting Ibn and Kalas was enough of an introduction for me. A few bloody, lifeless men lay here and there on the floor. The furniture that hadn't been smashed had been pushed back towards the walls. The fighting was waxing and waning across the room. The Scorpions were using curved Arabic Scimitars and our unknown allies were using Roman short swords and using them well.

The weeks and months of sword training in Kyiv were paying dividends. Ibn stood in the classical fencing pose, his left hand placed on his left hip while he took his opponent apart piece by piece. The Scorpion had neat symmetrical slices on each cheek, from which he bled profusely. If the situation hadn't been so serious it would have been comical. Each shoulder was also cut and bleeding. A tirade of Arabic abuse emanated from Ibn and was hurled at the bleeding Scorpion, who now had cuts on each forearm. If the sword didn't kill him then Ibn's curses were bound to. It was only a matter of time.

The arrival of three extra swords swung the odds in our favour and with an unspoken agreement we fanned out along the back wall and in a pincer movement encircled the Scorpions. Not wanting to take the satisfaction of the kill from our new-found allies, every time one was backed towards us he received the sharp end of our broad swords in his back, forcing him back toward our unknown allies.

Looking around the room I recognised the black-clothed sailor from the Dromon, his knotted, black headscarf immediately giving him away. We made eye contact and, immediately forsaking his opponent, he made a beeline for me. Screaming, he raised his sword in a fashion that made his arm and sword look like the cocked tail of a scorpion about to sting.

The whole world seemed to slow down. Sven and Rat screamed a warning, which sounded like the spirits of the dead shouting at me from beyond the grave. I brought my sword to the ready and turned side-on as the screaming,

375

wild-eyed Scorpion came across the room at me in slow motion with his mouth and eyes wide open. I glanced around and it seemed as if the whole room had stopped to watch. Waiting until the last moment, I stepped to his left, which neutralised his attack, and simultaneously slashed upwards, catching him below and behind his jaw, and cut him to his ear. The Scorpion carried on straight past me, his head flopping disjointedly. He crashed into and through a wooden wall, collapsing into a heap in the adjoining room. He rolled onto his back and raised a hand pointing at me. He tried to mouth an insult but found he couldn't move his jaw to speak. I stood and watched the life drain out of him.

The world, sound and movement returned to normal and all I could hear was my blood pounding through my head and my breath being sucked into my lungs as I panted. The remaining Scorpions, now totally surrounded, outnumbered and suddenly leaderless, threw down their swords and raised their hands in surrender. I looked around for the innkeeper but he was nowhere to be found.

With the sound of fighting over Tsai Ming and Serakh came downstairs, half-carrying our wounded. They quickly moved into action tending the other wounded and were soon assisted by locals, who had gathered outside during the fighting. I was infuriated that we had lost Larz in such a manner. I wasn't sure if it was because we had been through so much together or if it was because we were so close to home. Probably both.

We searched the building for any survivors and found the innkeeper, his wife and family, bound and dead in their storeroom. There was no external sign of killing so we concluded it must have been poison. I had a few locals remove them for burial.

I returned to the dining area, which now resembled a small battle site rather than a place of fellowship and food. The remaining Black Scorpions sat in a guarded huddle in the centre of the room, their hands on their heads.

Our unknown allies waited patiently, their blonde-haired leader in front of his small host.

I walked over to him. "Who do I have the honour of addressing?"

"My name is Bohdan Hetman, but it is irrelevant. Know this, we are the Kozak."

"The Kozak?"

"Yes, Ulf. Kozak," chipped in Ibn. "A Turkish word meaning free men. Men freed from bondage and slavery."

Pointing to Ibn, Bodhan said, "He knows." Bowing, he said, "Whom do I have the honour of addressing?"

Before I could answer, Ibn bowed and said, "You have the honour of addressing Lord Ulf Uspakson. Formerly captain in the army of Grand Duke Yaroslav the Wise, Captain of the Byzantine Varangian Guard and Counsellor to King Harald Hadraada of Norway."

"That is indeed a pedigree I aspire to. Now I understand why you bested me that day on the rapids."

Not fully realising what he said, I continued, "What made you come to our aid today?"

"Once you spared my life when you were within your rights to take it. Now we are even."

The realisation of who he was suddenly dawned on me. "Now I know. You're the Pecheneg who attacked us on our trip down the rapids almost two years ago."

"That is correct. We have been watching you since the isle of Khortytsia at Zaporozhe, where you crossed the river."

"You were on the island?"

"Yes. We have made it our base. You passed right by our camp."

"But you didn't attack us?"

"People who travel by night have something to hide or are running from something. We decided to wait and see which it was.

"You are learning the art of leadership and strategy."

Someone called out that soldiers were approaching.

"It is time for us to go. We are not well liked by the soldiers."

"I hope that some day, if and when we meet again, it will be as allies, like today."

377

"Myself as well. If ever you have need, you know where to find us."

"I surely do. If ever you are in Kyiv, you will be welcome at my fireside. Safe journey, Bohdan Hetman. I wish you and your Kozak success and prosperity."

"Thank you, Ulf Uspakson. Fare well."

And with a wave the Kozak filed out of the building, mounted their horses and rode off into the night.

Kalas touched my arm and said, "Ah, Ulf, I think you should get dressed now."

Looking down, I too, realised that I was half-naked. I suddenly felt cold. "Yes, you're quite right of course," and I turned and went upstairs.

I returned downstairs to find a soldier standing in the middle of the room with his hands on his hips. He had my crew and the Scorpions shepherded into a corner of the room under guard.

"And just who do you think you are?" he demanded of me.

"That is beside the point. Why have you arrested my crew?"

"For killing these men, that's why. You still haven't told me your name."

"If I told you, you wouldn't believe me."

"Try me?"

"My name is Ulf Uspakson."

"That's Lord Uspakson to you, soldier boy," quipped Sven.

"Oh, ho ho. Do you expect me to believe…"

"Told you," I said to him, shrugging.

The soldier stood for a moment in thought. Then he turned to me. "If you really are Lord Ulf Uspakson, and I have heard tales of him, prove it."

"Bring your men inside."

"Why?"

"You want proof? Then do it!"

"Alright. Sergeant, bring the men in."

"There is no need, Captain," said the sergeant.

"Why?"

"Because I served with Ulf Uspakson, Harald Hardraada and Haldor Snorreson, when as part of Grand Duke Yaroslav's army we subdued the Pechenegs in the north. This is indeed Lord Uspakson. A bit older, but nevertheless it is Lord Uspakson." Turning to me and bowing slightly, the sergeant said, "My Lord, it's been a long time. It's good to see you are well."

"And you, Sergeant, and you." I smiled back.

"Well, My Lord, may we escort you back to Kyiv? It is fortunate that we were on patrol in this area, camped outside the town, when we heard the fighting."

"Yes it is, isn't it?"

"My Lord?"

"Never mind, Captain, never mind. You may understand one day."

"Do you have any instructions?"

"Yes I do. Retrieve my dead crew and we will bury them at first light. The Black Scorpions here are to be given the poison that they gave to the innkeeper and his family. Then burn this whole place to the ground."

"Kill them? You can't do that! They're entitled to a trial."

"They didn't give the innkeeper and my men a fair chance at a fight, never mind a trial. No, they die here. This is where it ends."

"But burn the building? It's perfectly salvageable. You can't burn it — it's private property."

"Not anymore, it isn't. The owner and all his family are dead, killed by those scum with the tattoos of scorpions on their left shoulders. They will die and it will burn, either by my hand or yours."

"So be it. Sergeant, you heard the man. Deal with the criminals and then burn the place to the ground."

"Yessir!"

Our dead retrieved and buried, we sat on our horses outside the inn, ready for the final leg of our trip to Kyiv. The sergeant lit a few torches and gave one to me. I rode forward and tossed it in. Immediately the oil caught and black smoke filled the room. Soon flames could be seen licking at the windows through the thick black smoke that was now billowing from just about every window.

We waited until the whole building was ablaze and then turned our backs on Cherkassy, not long after the sun had crested the horizon.

Oh, how I looked forward to holding my Lydia again. Holding her, kissing her and caressing her. Even now I could smell her hair. It wasn't hard to imagine holding her, and she holding and hugging me back. Nor was it hard to imagine the hug turning into a long and lingering kiss. A jolt from my horse brought me back into reality.

Chapter 37

New Life

After three days of hard riding we made the outskirts of Kyiv. A light snow had begun to fall, dusting the landscape as if God had opened a sack of flour in heaven and sprinkled it about. The pure white snow contrasted with the dry, brown earth.

"Captain, would you perchance know where my wife and her father live?"

"No, My Lord. But it shouldn't be hard to find out. But I think you had better present yourself to the Grand Duke first."

"The Grand Duke can wait. I have travelled halfway across the world and have not seen my wife for almost a whole year. No, it's my wife first, the Grand Duke tomorrow."

"On your head be it, then."

"It always is, Captain. It always is."

At the southern gate the captain asked and found out that the Grand Duke had been generous and given Lydia and Iksander residence in the Upper City.

"Would you like an escort?"

"No. We know our way. Did you ask if Haldor Snorreson was quartered there as well?"

"No, I..."

"Never mind. You were not to know. I didn't ask you to."

"My Lord," the sergeant broke in.

"Yes, Sergeant?"

"Lord Haldor is quartered in the Upper City as well. He has been training new recruits over the summer. And a fine job he is doing, too."

"Thank you, Sergeant."

The captain asked, "My Lord, will your crew be requiring accommodation?"

"Thank you, no. They will be coming with me. Also, if you could find out where the arrivals from the east have been billeted as well. Some have family with them."

"Of course. Sergeant, find out where the others are billeted and then report back to Lord Uspakson."

"Yessir."

And so it was that we rode up to the gate of the Upper City. A soldier sauntered out of the guard house and stood in the road, his hands on his hips while he eyed up Tsai-Ming and Serakh. An undisguised look of pure lust was written all over his face. We sat patiently waiting. Eventually he said in a not-too-friendly tone,

"And just what do you want?"

I agreed that after six month of travel, our clothes were not in the best condition and we probably did not look like the most likely residents of the Upper City.

"I would like you to open the gate so that I may go to my wife and family," I replied as civilly as I could.

"And just who the hell are you?"

I opened my mouth to reply, but a voice boomed from behind us, "He is Lord Ulf Uspakson, you oaf! Newly arrived from travels and adventures in farthest East. He is the man who, just two winters ago, made sure that the people of Kyiv were fed. Also the man who trained the army of Kyiv that winter. The man who fought with Harald Hadraada and Lord Haldor Snorreson for Grand Duke Yaroslav the Wise in subduing the Pechenegs."

The guard's eyes opened wider and wider as the speaker went on.

"Do I have to carry on or are you going to open the gate?"

The guard, shocked at having been so rude, scrambled to open the gate.

During the interlude the speaker came forward, but he didn't need any introduction. We proceeded through the gate.

"*Boris,* how are you?"

"My Lord, you remember?"

"How could I forget?"

He laughed and said, "No, of course not."

"You have been studying up on your history."

"Better than that. I surprised myself, and Olaf, and proved such an able student that I am now assistant to Olaf. When he retires I am to run the library."

"Every dark cloud has a silver lining."

"Indeed they do," he said, beaming.

"Although, I had never thought of Olaf as the retiring type."

"Indeed not. He will go on until he dies."

"And that does not worry you?"

"No. Now that I've had a somewhat decent education, I realise just how much he knows and how much I don't. No, Olaf has a lot to teach me before I take over the reins. Not to mention the cataloguing of all the books and documents that you have sent from the Hidden Kingdom. There's a lifetime's work in that as well. "

"And Iksander?"

"Oh, he and Olaf are as thick as thieves. They spend more time discussing and debating the merits of documents and books than they do cataloguing them. I don't mind. I am learning all the time. Ah, here we are — this is your house."

"Thank you, Boris. We are most grateful. Ah, Boris, just one more thing."

"What is that, My Lord?"

"Even when you are in charge, don't forget you will always have something more to learn."

"That I have already learnt—on a dock almost two years ago," said Boris, paying me a very high compliment. I inclined my head as Boris bade us good night and disappeared up the street. We dismounted and walked the horses around to the stables. Sven took over their care and I rapped on the door. Iksander opened it and uncharacteristically shouted back over his shoulder

"He is here! He is here!" which took us by surprise. Then he said, "Welcome, Ulf. Welcome, all! Quickly, quickly. Come in, come in."

"Where is she?" I asked.

"In the bedroom lying down," said Iksander, pointing inside. He led the way down a passage and opened a door. I walked in expecting to have Lydia rush into my arms. Instead my Lydia was lying on a bed, her hair plastered to her head with sweat, her nightdress pulled up around her waist and her naked legs splayed open. She screamed at me, "Ulf Uspakson, where on this damned earth have you been! I have been holding this birth back as long as I could just for you! Ye gods this is painful! It's like pushing out pumpkins. If I had known that all that pleasure was going to give me this much pain, I wouldn't have let you lay a hand on me! OW! By the gods, that's sore."

An Arab physician, assisted by a plump Kyivian midwife, shrugged. The expression on his face said, *I've seen this all before and there's nothing I, nor you, can do.* I smiled back, unsure of what I had walked into. The midwife bustled about wiping the sweat off Lydia's face with a cool cloth. She rinsed it in a bowl of water and placed it next to a panting Lydia.

"Not long now," said the physician, examining Lydia's lower abdomen. "The head is engaged. A couple more pushes and we'll be there."

"WE won't," spat back Lydia. "I will!"

"Now, now, Lord Uspakson," said the midwife. "This is not the time for men. Could you wait next door ple…"

"Like hell he will!" bawled Lydia. "He was there when it was made. He will be here when it's born," she forced out through her panting. "He can see first hand what he's putting me through. I only wish he could experience it."

Even the midwife was taken aback by her outburst. Wide eyed, she said meekly, "Yes, My Lady."

"Oh, God help me. I just want this to be over."

Less than a third of an hour later Lydia, my Lydia, gave birth to a small, perfect, pink and blue boy.

While the midwife held the child, the physician took a knife off a carefully laid out white towel and cut the child's umbilical cord, which he tied off in a knot. This done, the midwife washed him in a basin of warm water and wrapped him up in a soft cotton blanket. She handed the bawling boy to me.

While I had more than roughly played with children in Nidaros, Novgorod and Holmgard, I had always avoided the smelly and usually screaming infants. As such I had never learnt to hold one. I was all fingers and thumbs.

The midwife clucked and scolded me, "You can wield a sword like it was a matchstick, travel to the ends of the world, defeat all kinds of evil and command armies, yet you don't know how to hold a baby?"

"No. I don't know how. I've never been a father before."

"Never?"

"No, never."

Her demeanour changed immediately and she became soft and caring. "Here, let me show you." Organising my arms and hands, she said, "See, you support his head with your hand and then rest him in the crook of your arm, just like this," and she placed the infant in my arms.

"I see. That simple?"

Looking down at this helpless little life I had helped create, I was fighting to hold back the tears.

"Yes. That simple. Isn't he beautiful?"

"Um, yes." This may have been my child but all I could see was a pudgy, pink face with squinty eyes and a head covered in black hair. I couldn't see any beauty in this. Well at least, not yet.

No sooner had she handed him over to me, when a second bawling sound filled the room. Lydia had given birth to an equally small, perfect, pink and blue girl.

"Two? Two? I thought there was only one."

Iksander slipped out to pass on the news.

As Lydia regained her breath, she said, "You weren't here to tell. Doctor al-Dabili was the only one to pick up two heartbeats when he examined me, which is why I kept him on and fired the others. It is over. Thank you, God."

I laughed. This was more like the Lydia I knew. I walked over to the bed and sat next to her on the bed while the physician and midwife repeated the cord, washing and wrapping procedure. I kissed her forehead and said, "I love you."

"After this you had better," she said with a wry and weary smile on her face.

The physician called for a bowl and towels. The midwife hastily gave our baby girl to Lydia, and upon smelling Lydia's milk, the baby turned her head towards Lydia's breast and began making suckling sounds with her mouth.

"Not yet," said the physician. "First we must deliver the sack."

"The what?" I asked.

"The sack. The sack from the womb. It is what your babies have been living in for the past eight months or so."

"Oh."

"Ah, here it comes."

The physician pulled a large, bloody, purple, blue and red mass from between my Lydia's legs and dropped it in the bowl with a slurp. She winced slightly as it was removed. The physician and midwife then proceeded to wash the blood from Lydia's lower abdomen and legs, while the babies hooked on and began suckling greedily.

"Ow!"

"That's just the milk coming down," said the midwife. "The next time 'round it won't be as sore, until eventually you'll be so used to it, it'll be like breathing."

"It had better be!" said Lydia, closing her eyes, relaxing and lying back for the first time in hours.

Iksander put his head through the door and motioned for us to go outside. We left the physician and midwife to clear up the mess and settle Lydia in. Outside he said, "Not quite the homecoming you were expecting?"

"Not at all. Was it that obvious?"

"It was written all over your face," he said, laughing.

We walked into the main living area and were met by Haldor, Tsai-Ming and Sven, Ibn, Rat, Balgichi and Serakh. Without a word Haldor and I hugged and slapped each other on the back, held each other at arms' length and then slapped each other on the back again.

"How are my babies?" asked Haldor.

"Your babies?"

"Yes, mine. You only made them and then handed their care over to me. Remember?"

"Yes I do. It all seems so long ago."

"Does it ever? It has been the longest delivery in the world. All the way from the Hidden Kingdom on the Roof of the World, across the deserts of Asia to the steppe of Europe," he said with a sweep of his hand. We all laughed.

"Well congratulations — Father. I never thought I'd hear myself say those words to you."

"And I never thought I'd hear you say them."

"Does it feel good?"

"It does. Although all the planning in the world couldn't prepare me for this."

The physician came through. "She's all settled now. You're lucky she had twins. There has been a small amount of ripping when they were born, but it is considerably less than with a single baby, and should heal quite quickly. You see, twins don't grow as large as a single child."

"Oh, of course." I wasn't sure that this was the sort of information I needed to hear.

"However, no sex for six to eight weeks — at least."

"After nine months apart, that was definitely not what he wanted to hear," said Haldor bawdily, elbowing me in the ribs. After so long out of his company I was going to have to get used to Haldor again. I then went through a round of congratulations and back slapping from all in the room. Sven lifted Tsai-Ming, who gave me a peck on the cheek.

The midwife came out. "My Lord, she's calling for you."

"Excuse me. I am summoned by my Goddess."

I walked back into the room and Lydia was lying on clean sheets with her eyes closed. A babe suckled on each breast.

"It's not fair," I said.

Opening her eyes, she said, "What's not fair?"

"I mean, here I am wanting you so badly after being apart for so long, and they get the first go at all your parts. And now I'm told I have to wait eight weeks before I get my chance!"

"Ha-ha-ha. Very funny. Anyway, you'll have the rest of your life to ravish my body."

"Yes, but I have to wait eight weeks before I get my next chance."

Sitting next to her on the bed, I put my arm around her shoulders and said, "I do love you, you know."

"I know," she said, snuggling in.

"Pooh! Ulf Uspkason, you smell."

"Yes, I do need a wash. As do the rest of us. Can I bring Tsai-Ming in to see the baby?"

"Tsai-Ming? Who is Tsai-Ming?"

"Oh, she's a concubine I was given as a gift by the Idiqut of Qocho."

Her eyes opened wide as she exclaimed, "A concubine? What Idiot? Where's Qocho?"

"Idiqut not idiot. Shush, you'll wake the babies. Yes, a concubine. I wouldn't be at all surprised if she were pregnant by now."

"Pregnant? Wake the babies! Ulf Uspakson, tell me you're lying to me?"

"I am. She's really Sven's wife."

Lydia broke out her gorgeous smile. "Sven's wife! Big Sven has a wife!"

"He surely does."

"Yes, yes. I want to see her. Send her in."

"Don't act surprised when you see her. Rat, Serakh and Balgichi are here as well."

"Why? Oh, good. Send them all in. We might as well get it over with."

I returned to the living area and told all that they were welcome to go through and see the newest additions to the Uspakson family. Family, that was a new word to me. The only family I had known for the past twenty or so years was the army and my friends. My closest and most trusted relation had been my sword. Sven, Tsai-Ming, Rat and Serakh went through first.

Not long afterwards, a messenger arrived saying that I was required immediately for an audience with Grand Duke Valdimir.

"Tell His Majesty that I humbly beg his pardon. Tell him I have just ridden half way around the known world, and have been attacked a good number of times, almost losing my hand in the process. Tell him I have just witnessed the birth of my firstborns, a boy and a girl. Tell him I am tired, weary and absolutely famished. Tell him I smell like the sewers of Cairo and that I will be in attendance first thing in the morning—after I have eaten, washed and seen to my wife and children."

Colour drained from the messenger's face as I spoke. "I can't tell him that."

"You can and you will. If you don't I will separate your head from your body. Come to think of it, if you do he probably will as well. Now be gone with you!"

Not having eaten since midday, I suddenly realised just how famished I really was.

"Where's the food?" I asked. "I'm starving."

Iksander clapped his hands and a servant girl came out.

"Bring His Lordship some ham, cheese and bread. And bring some ale as well."

"Make that as much as you can muster. The others will be hungry too."

She nodded and left. A while later the food was delivered and we sat down to eat. Iksander sat watching us and said, "I guess some information on where you went and what you got up to will have to wait?"

I laughed. "Stop fishing, Iksander. Yes it will. Anyway, it will take more than one evening to recount our story. And I dare not start without Olaf and Balgichi."

"No, I guess you had better not."

I walked up to the Grand Duke's palace before breakfast and was immediately shown into a morning room to breakfast with the Grand Duke. He invited me to sit, with a smile on his face.

"I believe congratulations are in order."

"Thank you, sire."

"I trust that you are now clean and refreshed, Ulf?"

The use of my first name took me by surprise.

"Indeed I am, sire."

Taking a bread role, he broke it and said, "Your response aged my messenger by years. I must ask you not to do that again. Good staff are hard to find."

I laughed and promised not to. Following suit, I took some bread and chicken and we ate in silence while we supped strong Arabic coffee. Finishing before I did, he sat back and studied me, before saying, "Tell me about the Black Scorpions."

He had cut straight to the one issue that could have the greatest effect on Kyiv. Over the next half hour I filled him in on the limited knowledge of the Scorpions and of our run-ins with them. I concluded, "I fear that my interaction with them has led them to Kyiv. I am not sure what that will mean for Kyiv, yourself, me and my family."

"Come, come, Ulf. You know exactly what it will mean. What do you propose?"

I outlined a basic strategy for dealing with the threat from the Black Scorpions.

"Good, I was counting on you having something prepared. Do you intend returning to Norway?"

"With your majesty's permission I would like to settle here in Kyiv."

"Why?"

"Well none of us is getting any younger and Kyiv definitely offers a more comfortable retirement than does Nidaros. Also, I now have a family and Kyiv is fast overtaking Byzantium as a centre of learning and what with the library from the Hidden Kingdom..." I shrugged and raised my hands, leaving him to finish the sentence for himself.

"Good. I was hoping you would say that. Although, don't think you will ever retire in Kyiv. There is too much to be done. Now tell me about the Kozak."

He was well informed. I filled him in on the details I knew, recounting our initial contact with them on the Dniepr and again at Cherkassy.

"Your first order of business will be to try and set up an alliance with the Kozak. A mobile force on our southern frontier will be of great benefit. Heaven only knows that Kyiv needs every ally it can get at the moment. The second order of business will be to recount your travels to the court, one month from today."

"Of course, sire. It will be our pleasure."

"Good. Now excuse me I have matters to attend to."

I rose as he got up to go.

"No, stay. Finish breakfast at your leisure," he said, before leaving the room.

I finished a hearty meal at leisure, attended by the Grand Duke's servants. To not take advantage of such luxurious setting and attendance would have been a shame. I asked one of the attendants to call the chief cook through. A flustered middle-aged woman came through, clearly anxious at being summoned.

"Cook, thank you for an excellent morning meal."

She broke her frown and her face lit up like a single candle in the dark of night.

"However, I must insist that next season you try and get your hands on some cha."

"Cha, My Lord?" she said with a puzzled look on her face.

"Yes, cha. I'll send a young lady with a sample. She is from Qocho and is very small and very beautiful. She will make you a cup. It is most refreshing and I'm sure the Grand Duke will be most grateful for this addition to the royal pantry."

"Uh, yes, My Lord. Will that be all?"

"It will. Thank you, cook."

"Thank you, sir," she said, curtsying before exiting.

I arrived back at the house in time to see Lydia and the midwife settling the babies down after their morning feed.

"Well, my husband, how did it go?"

"Extraordinarily well. I have been given two tasks. One is to set up an alliance with the Kozak and the other is to present a tale of our journey to the court a month from today."

"The Kozak? Who or what are the Kozak?"

"Now, now. You'll have to wait a month to find that out."

She playfully threw a heavily embroidered cushion at me, wincing as she made the effort.

"Well then, you'll have to wait even longer for what you want."

"You wouldn't do that, would you?"

"You'll have to wait and see, won't you?"

"Alright, I give in. You are most persuasive. I'll arrange for a retelling with Olaf and Iksander. But it will have to be here."

"Why here?"

"Well, until your condition has improved, you're unlikely to be travelling very far."

"But..."

"No buts. That's final. I saw you wince when you threw that cushion."

She pouted and said, "You see too much."

"I see what I need to. Now lie back and enjoy the rest."

"I'm not an invalid!"

"I know that. I need you better so that I can have someone to spar with, and not just with swords."

Later that morning I dropped by the library. Iksander and Balgichi were there. An unusually unrestrained Olaf welcomed me, tears running down his cheeks. Hanging onto a thread of his usual reserve, he clasped my hand and forearm, and I drew him into an embrace.

"Ulf, how can I ever thank you for sending me such a magnificent collection of books and manuscripts?"

"Well you may start by forgiving me for losing the spyglass you gave me."

"It was nothing but a trinket. What is important is that you're back. With a wife and now children. Oh, congratulations."

"Thank you, Olaf. Shouldn't you be getting on with cataloguing the items instead of sitting around and debating their merits with Iksander and Balgichi?"

"What has Boris been telling you?"

"Nothing that I would not have expected to hear about three overly wise old men."

"Ha ha. The three wise men, I like that. You know, we have much to discuss and talk about."

"You mean you three have not already done that?"

We laughed.

"I need to borrow Boris for a while."

"Why?"

"Because I need to send a message south to the Isle of Khortytsia and I need him to help me identify a trustworthy trader.

"The Isle of Khortytsia? Why? What is there?"

"Never you mind. If I told you I would have to kill you, or at the very least cut your tongue out."

"Very funny. Very well, you may borrow Boris."

Legend of the Last Vikings

"Thank you. Come on, Boris, let's go to the docks."

At the docks Boris used his old contacts and his new-found authority to find a trader returning late to Byzantium and I arranged for him to deliver a message to Bohdan Hetman on the Isle of Khortytsia, saying that the Grand Duke was interested in exploring an alliance with the Kozak and that I would meet with him at a place of his choosing in the spring. Although, I had the feeling that he would probably pay me a visit in Kyiv before the winter was over. This way he would have the advantage of surprise, which would minimise the risk of ambush.

When our mission at the docks was over, Boris returned to the library and I walked over to the barracks. Haldor was training a cohort of Kyivian infantry in battle manoeuvres, a difficult task to achieve in a quadrangle. Everything had to be done on a very limited scale rather than on the usually vast scale of a battlefield.

Surprisingly the whole crew was present and watching. Not surprisingly, because of the lateness of the season, those who wanted to return to the Viking kingdoms of the north had decided to winter over in Kyiv. Starting north now would have meant wintering in Novgorod, and I knew which city I would rather have wintered in. I offered the crew as a pretend enemy and we practised the move a few times before Haldor released them to practise their swordsmanship.

Over the next few weeks I divided my time between the library and rehearsals for the retelling.

I spent my mornings in the library. While Boris and his assistants laboured away cataloguing the thousands of new books and manuscripts, Iksander, Balgichi and Olaf continued to debate a range from Greece and Aristotle to Arabia and al-Khayyami's Rubyat.

I found I would have to refine my area of study. I had learnt a great deal over the years since I first met Olaf and had covered a great many subjects, all of which interested me. After discussing it with Lydia, it was she who suggested that I compile a works, cataloguing the feats of the great seafaring nations of the world. She knew that, coming from a seafaring nation, not only would this keep me interested but would be something I could understand and appreciate. And so I embarked on a research project in the now vastly expanded library.

In the afternoons the crew and I met in a disused storeroom. Using Ibn's book, we practised the retelling of our adventure. We soon decided that we would need a narrator. While the men could act out their parts, albeit rather ham-fistedly, none really had the ability to speak eloquently, not to mention that most were rather scared of speaking in front of a large audience. So we co-opted Olaf, who was overjoyed at gaining first-hand knowledge of our journey. I knew that it also made him feel a part of the adventure and the team. Serakh and Tsai-Ming sewed the costumes and took their parts at the appropriate times. During the third week we were surprised when Lydia and the twins, supported by Balgichi, Iksander and the midwife, appeared at the rehearsals. Everything came to a stop as everyone crowded around Lydia and the twins and I gave up trying to get rehearsals started again. Thereafter Lydia and the twins became a regular feature at our sessions. It was amusing to watch my wife trying to sew in between feeding the twins. In the words of our midwife, she could wield a sword like it was a matchstick, but came away from sewing with bloodied fingertips.

A week after Lydia's visit we had our final rehearsal and spent the next few days building a makeshift stage in the great hall of the court. Iziaslav was intrigued, but not at all put out by having to shift his court into smaller chambers.

Word had got out and about and anyone who had claim to rank or importance was vying for an invitation. Some had even travelled to Kyiv through the early winter snows for the event.

On the evening of the event, the whole hall was buzzing with anticipation. Iziaslav and his family were in the front row, and his court in the rows immediately behind. Palace staff packed the side aisles, some standing on boxes to see over the heads of those in front. A drum roll brought about an immediate silence, and the play commenced.

Over the next three hours the audience were taken from the sadness of losing a king and friend to the hilarious laughter as Sven chased Rat around the knarr. The emotions dived into the pits of despair at the mine and rose to the heights of excitement and romance at the Hidden Kingdom. It also covered the tedium of traversing the Taklamakan to Qocho and the anticipation and fear of our first meeting with the Lang Ren. The audience experienced the joy at finding Ingvar's mummified remains and the shock of seeing Lydia's aunt lying in that state. They experienced the pain of my wound, the amazing discovery of finding sharks' teeth in the middle of the Kyzyl Kum Desert, then the despair when the

Black Scorpions found us yet again. Again they were taken through the fear and anticipation of the night ride and the rage at losing Larz at Cherkassy, when we were so close to home.

At the end Lydia and the twins were a surprise request from the audience and she received a standing ovation when she walked onto the stage with one twin in each hip. On the spur of the moment I gave her a full kiss, which brought the house down.

Then Iziaslav stood and came forward. As he did, silence descended over the audience. He turned and faced them. "Tonight what we have seen has been a spectacle. If it were not for the fact that Ulf Uspakson, Haldor Snorreson and Ibn al Arslani were the three main characters, most of us would undoubtedly dismiss this as just another story. A fable from a far-off land. But then consider the first-hand account by a captain of the Kyvian Guard of the burial of an innkeeper and his family and the inn, which was burned to the ground on Ulf's command in Cherkassy only but a month ago. Then you realise just how much these men, and women, have been through. In addition, Ulf Uspakson has decided to make Kyiv his home…"

Applause broke out, which Iziaslav allowed to continue for a short while. Then he raised his hands, before continuing. "Ulf Uspakson, come forward."

Still wearing my Lang Ren elders' robe I broke from the players and walked forward.

He motioned Lydia and the twins forward as well. My heart swelled with pride as my wife and family came to stand next to me.

"Almost two hundred years ago, at the start of the Rurikidernas dynasty, a position was created which has, for a while, been void. It has been void because there was no one fit to bear the title and responsibilities. Until now. The position of Defender of the Realm requires that person to have absolute integrity, to have compassion, to be utterly trusted by the people he leads and above all to be absolutely trusted by his sovereign."

He paused to let the words sink in.

"Ulf Uspakson, I now confer on you the position of Defender of the Realm. Please kneel."

I knelt on one knee, head bowed before Iziaslav.

"Ulf Uspakson, I now appoint you Defender of the Realm of Rus. From now on you will answer to no one in the kingdom except me."

The audience applauded. The first minister came forward with a chain of gold medallions laid out on a red velvet cushion. Each medallion had a giant blue sapphire set in its centre. A medallion, larger than those on the chain, with an extremely large sapphire, hung from the centre by a number of links, forming a triangle. Each medallion was encrusted with fine gold filigree. Iziaslav took it off the red velvet cushion and hung the clinking chain about my neck. It weighed heavily about my shoulders. Still kneeling, I looked up straight into Iziaslav's stare. A moment of understanding passed between us. He extended his right arm and I kissed the ring of state on his third finger. He nodded and smiled and with the same arm bade me rise. The audience roared their approval.

Standing on his right, I bowed to Iziaslav and then bowed to the audience. I held out my right hand and Lydia and the twins came forward. Again the audience cheered loudly. The noise was so loud that the twins began crying. I kissed Lydia on the cheek, quickly whispering some instructions. She looked at me, initially without comprehension. Then realising what I had said, she curtsied to Iziaslav and exited with a crying baby on each hip. Iziaslav then returned to his seat and to thunderous applause the crew took a bow, and another and another. Eventually I called a halt to the encores, thanking everyone for their attendance and support.

Just as we were leaving the stage I caught sight of a blonde-haired man at the extreme rear of the room. Bohan Hetman had lived up to my expectations. I caught his eye and bowed my head slightly. He raised a hand in acknowledgement and slipped out of the room.

Immediately after the applause had died down, benches were rearranged and tables brought out. The crew and I mingled directly with the audience, receiving many slaps on the back. While this was going on the stage was dismantled and the head table laid out. I was rescued from a boring official by a page advising me that my attendance was required by Iziaslav at the head table.

I took my place and was soon joined by Lydia. She asked, "Did you know that this was going to happen?"

"No. Did you?

"No. It has come as big surprise."

"To me as well."

"What does it mean?"

"We'll have to wait and see."

"Ooh, I hate that."

"Hate what?"

"Waiting and seeing."

I chuckled and the first course arrived. Lydia was about to tuck in but I placed a hand on her wrist and she abruptly stopped.

"You must wait for the Sovereign to start."

Embarrassed, she blushed and replaced her spoon, glancing at Iziaslav, who smiled.

"I love it when you blush."

"Why?"

"It makes you seem all naive and maidenly."

"Oh it does, does it?"

"Yes it does. Not that you claim to be all naïve and maidenly anymore."

"And whose fault is that?"

"Tell me you didn't enjoy it?"

"This soup is absolutely delicious. I'll have to ask the cook for the recipe."

The rest of the evening passed off in a heady mix of wine and laughter. Later in the evening troubadours and acrobats entertained us. Long after midnight we stumbled back into the house.

Twice a week I was required to attend court. In the summer I was to tour the kingdom and deal with any insurgency that threatened the realm. In the meantime I set about creating a network of informers and agents. If the Black Scorpions could run such a network then so could I. I divided the work up between a few hand-picked men, Rat and Sven among them. I was saddened by Haldor's announcement that he would be returning to Norway in the spring. I would sorely miss my dear life-long friend when he was gone.

In my spare time, which was now considerably less, I continued my research on ancient seafaring nations. I came across an ancient Phoenician document, which turned out to be one of the first works Balgichi had sent Olaf.

Olaf, Balgichi and Iksander sat down to translate it for me.

Olaf provided a literal translation as he read, "It says that the Phoenicians sailed the seas of the world for trade. Hmmmm. Probably means the Mediterranean and the Pontus Euxinus and probably the Sea of Azov."

"I agree," said Balgichi.

"And I concur," said Iksander.

"Could we just get on with it, please?"

"Patience, my boy, patience," said Olaf, waggling a finger.

Iksander chipped in, "He's not a boy anymore. He's a man now. Has children as well, you know…"

Before Balgichi could start, I stopped him, "Alright, alright. I get it. You can stop now."

The grins on their faces were wonderful to see.

"The document, Olaf?"

"Oh yes. It mentions something about Brzl and sailing beyond the Pillars of Hercules to get it."

"What is this Brzl?"

"Not what, but where?"

"What do you mean where?"

"Well…"

Chapter 38

Epilogue

<u>Stockholm. 19 July, 2003 03:08</u>
The incessant ringing of the phone finally woke Professor Nils Christianson. With a sigh of resignation he lifted the receiver and said, "Ja?"

"Professor, it is Benni here."

"Benni? Benni? But you're in Afghanistan."

"Ja, Professor, I am."

"Benni, it is 3am in Stockholm. Please be quick. I have a long day planned for tomorrow and I want to go back to sleep."

"Ja, OK, Professor."

"Well?"

"Professor, we had a large earthquake here at Balkh today."

"So? Balkh always has earthquakes. It's what killed the city in the first place."

"It unearthed two perfectly preserved knarrs."

"Two what? Impossible!"

"No, Professor. I am standing right next to one, my right hand resting on the gunwale."

"So...Viking traders did make it as far as Balkh. And in knarrs."

"Knarrs, yes. But not the usual format for trading knarrs. These have extra rowlocks."

A silence followed Benni Johansson's statement. Benni was about to speak when he heard the Professor whisper, "Uspakson... So Snorreson's account was true..."

"Professor?"

"Benni, I am on the next plane out and you had better be correct."

"There's no question about it, Professor."

John Halsted
Maps

The Journey from Nidaros to Kyiv

NIDAROS

GRIPSHOLM

STARAIA LADOGA
NOVGOROD

KVIV

CHERKASSY

Sea of Azov

Pontus Euxinus (Black Sea)

Legend of the Last Vikings

The Journey from Kyiv to Lou Lan and Back

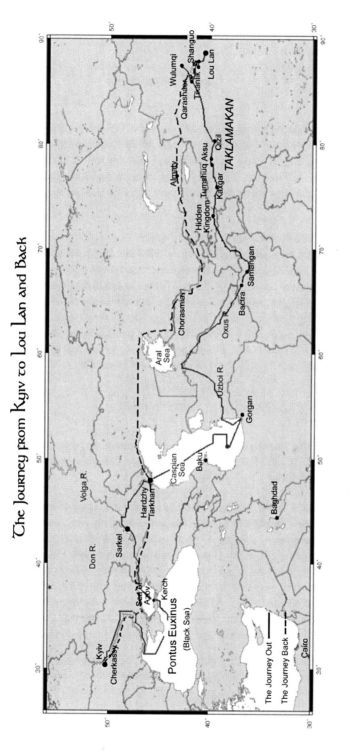

The Characters

Ulf Uspakson was as real as you or me. He did live a thousand years ago and was Harald Hadraada's marshal and died at the Battle of Stamford bridge defending his King. So while he was real, his role in this story is fictitious. Although he did have a wife and children in Norway, I have chosen not to give him any. But after a lifetime of being married to the state, why shouldn't Ulf find love?

"Ulf Uspakson stood in great esteem with King Harald; for he was a man of great understanding, clever in conversation, active and brave, and withal true and sincere. King Harald made Ulf his marshal, and married him to Jorun, Thorberg's daughter, a sister of Harald's wife, Thora. Ulf and Jorun's children were Joan the Strong of Rasvol, and Brigida, mother of Sauda-Ulf, who was father of Peter Byrdar-Svein, father of Ulf Fly and Sigrid. Joan the Strong's son was Erlend Himalde, father of Archbishop Eystein and his brothers. King Harald gave Ulf the marshal the rights of a lenderman and a fief of twelve marks income, besides a half-district in the Throndhjem land." Of this Stein Herdison speaks in his song about Ulf.

Ref:http://www.worldwideschool.org/library/books/hst/european/heimskringla/ HeimskringlaVolume6/chap36.html : Snorri Sturlson

Haldor Snorreson (or Snorrason) was also a very real person and served with Ulf and Harald Hadraada in the Varangian Guard, as well as when they returned to Norway.

"Haldor was very stout and strong, and remarkably handsome in appearance. King Harald gave him this testimony, that he, among all his men, cared least about doubtful circumstances, whether they betokened danger or pleasure; for, whatever turned up, he was never in higher nor in lower spirits, never slept less nor more on account of them, nor ate or drank but according to his custom. Haldor was not a man of many words, but short in conversation, told his opinion bluntly and was obstinate and hard; and this could not please the king, who had many clever people about him zealous in his service. Haldor remained a short time with the king; and then came to Iceland, where he took up his abode in Hjardarholt, and dwelt in that farm to a very advanced age."

Ref:http://www.worldwideschool.org/library/books/hst/european/heimskringla/ HeimskringlaVolume6/chap35.html: Snorri Sturlson

Balgichi, Serakh and Pesakh Simantov of Hardzhy-Tarkhan are all fictitious characters.

Barjik Chernetsov is a fictitious character, but would have been old enough to have served with Ulf as a young man when Yaroslav was Prince of Novgorod and later Kiev.

Although **Beket-Ata** did not play a significant part in the story, I feel it appropriate to mention him, as he was an Islamic monk who inspired and built the cross-shaped underground mosques which can be found today in the limestone near the Caspian Sea. I have used author's licence and have had him living some 700 years ahead of his actual time.

Big Sven is unfortunately a fictitious character. However no great leader is without a trusted lieutenant that they can lean on in times of need. Indeed, Ulf filled this role for Harald Hadraada.

Bijana Smedjrute, although fictitious in the book, is a real person and is still probably alive today. He was my neighbour and childhood friend when I was a boy in Durban, South Africa. His father, in true Norwegian style, was crew on the whaling fleet which used to sail out of Durban until the whaling station was closed in 1976. Because of his northern heritage and because he just happened to live next door to me his name came to mind when I needed a character for the book. Thanks B.

Bohdan Hetman, leader of the Kozak. It is thought that the early Cossacks called themselves the Kozak, and were formally formed in the twelfth century. It is then likely that their beginnings were sometime in the eleventh century. The term Kozak is indeed a Turkish word meaning free men, or men freed from bondage and slavery.

In time the Cossacks built their headquarters on the Isle of Khortytsia, the same island that the crew crossed at night not long before entering Cherkassy.

Bodhan was the name of the first recognised leader of the Cossacks and Hetman was their term for "headman", a convenient combination of words to name a character.

Cheng and the doctor **Cai Sui** are fictitious. However the cave complexes at Tumshuq and Qizil are on any good tourist itinerary of the Tarim Basin, as are the caves at Dun Huang. The Spring of Salt Tears is also a real geographical feature and the local legend is as I have written it.

Malik Shah was indeed a real person and did become the Sultan and ruled the Seljuk Empire until assassinated. Was Malik Shah ever governor of Gorgan? Unlikely, although it is probable that he would have visited the town at least once in his lifetime, as it has long been considered the capital town in the area with significant defensive walls.

It is even sadder to think of the ideological struggle that was to commence between Christianity and Islam within just a few years of the crew's visit to Gorgan. The whole struggle between the Christian, the Jew and the Moslem is made even sadder when you think that all worship the same God, albeit from different sides of the religious altar.

For the scholars who read this, I have made a logical assumption that in 1067AD the **Caspian Sea** would have been significantly larger than it is now. Indeed maps in the Mosaic Account have the Oxus River / Amu Darya flowing into the Caspian Sea. As such I have followed this logic and placed the town of **Gorgan** on the Caspian itself. If it was never on the Caspian then it was certainly reachable by ship, as it was the terminus town for the Swedish Viking traders in the Caspian from the late 700s onwards.

Grand Duke Valdimir was also a real person and succeeded his father **Yaroslav the Wise**. **Valdimir II Vsevelodovich** was also a real person and duke of Smolensk. However the complex succession arrangements left by Yaroslav only gave rise to an internecine civil war, which weakened the kingdom that Yaroslav had striven so hard to build.

Harald Hadraada, "the Hard One", was killed in battle by Harold Goodwinson's army at Stamford Bridge, only weeks before Goodwinson himself was defeated and killed by William the Conqueror at Hastings in also in 1066.

Their return to Norway in 1045 is also as I have described. Even accounts of the masses of treasure they brought back were true. **Queen Ellisif**, or Elizabeth, was indeed Jaroslav's daughter. Jaroslav had also married daughters into the royal families of France and Hungary. Detailed accounts of any of Harald's, Ulf's and Haldor's adventures can be found in any decent historical textbook. See also -

http://www.worldwideschool.org/library/books/hst/european/heimskringla/Heimskringla Volume6/toc.html : Snorri Sturlson

The battle of Stamford Bridge in 1066 signalled the end of the Viking age. It is this event that I use as the start of what was possibly the last great Viking adventure.

Ibn Rashid al-Arslan is a fictitious character loosely based on the famous Arabic writers of the time, namely Ibn Khordo Adbeh, who gave a very vivid description of the mannerisms and habits of Viking traders, as well as Al Maksidi and Ibn Fadlan, renowned Arabic travel writers of their time.

Iksander, Lydia, Kalas, Marsias and their families are all fictitious characters but were given names that would have suited a Hephthalite/Greek heritage.

Ingvar Vittfarne was also a real person and lived in Gripsholm, Södermanland, Sweden, born in about 1015AD into the Swedish Royal family.

Coins stamped with Central Asian and Arabic rulers continue to be unearthed in this part of Scandinavia, which prove the existence of trade with Arabia. However, trade withered when the Arabic silver mines became exhausted.

In approximately 1041AD, Ingvar went off in search of "Sarkland" and "Tavastaland" and never returned to Sweden. Ingvar travelled the Volga route, which lead into Hardzy Tarkhan (modern-day Astrakhan) and the Caspian Sea. Ingvar's last journey was ostensibly to reopen the trade routes with the Arabs. But to assume that he and his men were not intent on adventure, in my opinion, would be wrong.

Sarkland is thought to be modern-day Samarkand, which as most students of Central Asia will know, is a pivotal point on that most ancient of routes, the Silk Road, along which this story takes place.

I could find no reference to Tavastaland, and instead have used the legend of the Holy Grail, common to Buddhism and Christianity, as a reason for his journey.

Lin Ya is also a fictitious character, although a garrison commander at Qarashaher would most definitely have existed. At the time Qarashaher was the western-most border of the Kingdom of Qocho, strategically placed in the neck of a valley.

Lou Lan. When the great Swedish explorer Sven Hedin rediscovered Lou Lan approximately one hundred years ago, he described the city *"as if everyone had suddenly got up and left"*. When did this happen, who knows? The overnight abandonment of Lou Lan by the Lang Ren fitted neatly with Hedin's descriptions. Hedin also used **shotas** and donkeys or camels to carry ice for water on his many trips through the Tarim Basin.

Lou Pyi and **Cai Sui.** If you are a wordsmith, by now you would have realised that Can Sui and Lou Pyi are a play on the words *cannis lupis*, which is of course the Latin name for the wolf family. They are also fictitious.

Olaf and **Boris** are fictional characters.

Suwayd al-Khawalani is also a fictitious character. It would have been no coincidence that he would have been at Jerusalem when Harald and the Varangian Guard laid siege to the city in 1035. In 1036, after peace talks (*they were happening even back then*), the siege was called off and Harald, Ulf, Haldor and the Varangian Guard were ordered to retire just when they were preparing to storm the walls.

The Vikings were not the only traders on the Byzantium route. Finnish traders were also active on the route. **Yurii Vartinnen**, like Bijana Smedjrute, also a real person, is probably still alive and does hail from Finland. He went to school with me at Westville Boys' High, just outside Durban, South Africa. As with Bijana I needed a suitable name and he came to mind. Thanks Y.

Archeology, Cultures & Customs

Did the **Black Scorpions** really exist? Probably not. However, the story of a group of misguided individuals who did try to mix Buddhism, Zoroastrianism and Manichaeism is true. Legend has it that they did manage to hold this heady mix of religions and beliefs together—for a short time. However they were exiled to an uninhabited area of the Tarim Basin. They did have a multi-coloured, multi-segmented scorpion as their symbol. It is alleged that at one point their leader did manage to conjure a black scorpion out of the air in front of a king of a Tarim Basin city-state, which allegedly devoured the king! From this account I developed the idea of the Black Scorpions. It is even less likely that they or any similar group ever occupied the Maiden Tower at Baku. The Maiden Tower is real and was used by the Zoroastrians for a fairly lengthy period.

The Fortress at Sarkel did exist. The site is now submerged by the Tsimlyansk Reservoir.

The **Jewish Empire of Kasaria** did exist with its capital at current Astrakhan (Hardzhy-Tarkhan). Yaroslav's father did defeat the Kasarians in battle and did push them back as I described. He then used the captured Fortress at Sarkel on the Don River as a forward base, as did Yaroslav.

THE HEPHTHALITES
According to Procopius's *History of the Wars*, written in the mid 6th century, the Hephthalites:
"are of the stock of the Huns in fact as well as in name: however they do not mingle with any of the Huns known to us. They are the only ones among the Huns who have white bodies...."
Ephthalites was the name given by Byzantine historians and Hayathelaites by the Persian historian Mirkhond, and sometimes Ye-tai or Hua by Chinese historians.

In my research I uncovered the story of the Hepthalites, whom Xuanzang, the first Chinese monk to travel the Silk Road in 644AD, described as "fair skinned with large round eyes, who kept to themselves and did not mix with other tribes".

The Hepthalites lived and ruled Central Asia much as I described. Like Alexandra the Great before them, they even crossed the Hindu Kush and
411

conquered most of Northern India, ruling their empire from Bamyan and Balkh, both in current-day Afghanistan. In fact their rule in Northern India continued well after they had suffered defeat in Central Asia.

There is limited information on them and their legacy. The most complete account I found was in the UNESCO books, Civilisations of Central Asia, volumes three and four.

They came into power in between the end of the golden age of Buddhism and the rise of Islam.

Also, the phonetic similarity of the name Hepthalite and the name Japheth (Hebrew name "Yaphat Elohim le-Yephet"), one of Noah's sons, brother to Shem and Ham, enabled me to create a biblical link back to Japheth, son of Adam and Eve, whose full name was Yaphat Elohim le-Yephet, which to my ear has a ring of Hephthalite in it.

The fact that the Hepthalites did live on the plain of Ordos, had a woollen garment-weaving industry, were fair skinned, had large round eyes and the discovery of the Tarim Mummies, is more than coincidental to me. But I have no empirical proof of any the connections I have made.

Just as monasteries were carved out of rock and lived in, then why shouldn't the remnants of a lost race live in an underground city, a **Hidden Kingdom**? This is not as far fetched as you might think. If you have ever visited the Wieliczka salt mine near Krakow, Poland, you'll know exactly what I mean. Nine centuries of mining in Wieliczka produced a total of some 200 kilometres of passages as well as 2,040 caverns of varied size. The carvings in the rock are a sight to behold as well. The description of the chapel in the wedding was taken directly from the main hall in Wieliczka mine, which is now an underground museum. Crowned Heads of Europe, Goethe and Sarah Bemhardt have visited the mine. Because of its unique acoustics it is not uncommon for underground concerts to take place in the mine.

Another example is the ancient city of Petra, which for a time was a stop on the Silk Route.

Tunnelling through the Hindu Kush has been going on for more than two thousand years. In approximately 320BC Alexander the Great had pursued the people of this region only to have them suddenly disappear from his front and appear at his rear.

More recently the Allied forces have had a hard job trying to capture Osama Bin Laden. More than once, and not surprisingly, the myriad of caves used by the Taliban have featured in news reports as possible escape routes used by Bin Laden and the Taliban.

THE WEDDING CEREMONY

When researching the traditional ceremonies of Islam, Christianity and Judaism, I was pleasantly surprised at how rich in culture and tradition each one is. As such I let common sense prevail. What better way to please all the attendees but by having an element of each of the major three religions represented in the ceremony? Plus, who wouldn't want to be locked away for a whole week with his or her new spouse with absolutely no interruptions?

Lang Ren is the English pronunciation for the Chinese characters that mean Wolf People.

The exact location of **Shanguo** has never been established. As such I have used author's licence and placed it towards the western end of the Qurutagh Mountains.

Well preserved mummies have been unearthed in the desert regions of Chinese Turkestan around the towns of Cherchen and Loulan, and colloquially named **the Taklamakan Mummies**. The The Loulan mummies, from Qäwrighul near the town of Lou Lan, include the Beauty of Loulan (*surprise, surprise*) and a few other mummies including an eight-year-old child wrapped in a piece of patterned wool cloth and closed with bone pegs. The wool clothing from Loulan seems to be much less colorful (in much more neutral, earth-tone colors--though fading could have occurred), but it is no less impressive in its patterns and weaves. The Cherchen mummies are known for their degree of preservation (far better than most Egyptian mummies), their colorful clothing, and their Caucasian features. Many of the corpses are almost perfectly preserved, with their reddish-blond hair, long noses, round eyes and finely woven tartan clothing (usually associated with the Celts in Scotland), showing undeniably European racial traits.

City, Town and Place Names

Old — *New/Current*

Afrasiab — - Sacked and destroyed by Genghis Kahn in 1200s. A new city was built in close proximity and named Maracanda, later renamed Samarkand.

Aybāk — - Ancient Samangan, Afghanistan. Has ruins of a Buddhist cave monastery.

Hardzhy-Tarkhan — - Ancient Astrakhan, a major port on the Caspian Sea

Holmgard — - Novgorod, Russia

Korchev — - Kerch, northern end of the Black Sea where it connects with the Sea of Azov

Korsun — - Sevastopol, Crimea, Ukraine

Kyiv — - Kiev. Capital of the Ukraine

Miklagaard — - Byzantium, Constantinople, Istanbul

Tašqorgăn — - Kholm, Afghanistan

Tianxia — - also Tian Xia - China

Wulumqi — - Uighur/Hun spelling for Urumqi in the Uighur Autonomous Region of The People's Republic of China

River & Geographical Features' Names

Old — *New/Current*

Araxes River — - Syr Darya (darya = river)

Huang He — - Yellow River, China

Kaspian Sea — - Caspian Sea

Konqi He — - Konqi River

Ostersjoen — - Baltic Sea, known in Viking times as the East Sea, hence Ostersjoen

Oxus River — - Amu Darya

Pontus Euxinus — - Black Sea (Latin name as used by the Byzantines)

Sita Darya — - Ancient name for Tarim River

Uzboi — - Now a dry river channel from Aral Sea leading to the Caspian Sea. It was listed as a channel of the Oxus that flowed into the Caspian Sea in the Hebrew Mosaic Account.

Yenikale — - Tartar name for the Kerch Strait (connects the Black Sea with the Sea of Azov)

Equivalent Terminology, Mythical Beings & other bits n' pieces

Detinets   - Kremlin or local fort

Dolgthvari or Dori   - mythical Norse elves or dwarves

Ichigi   - Indoor slippers traditionally made and worn by Khazar women

Jinn   - Second lowest in the order of Islamic mythical magical spirit beings. The lowest being Jann, and the three orders above being Sheytans, Ifrits and Marids, the most powerful magical being.

Ousiako Dromon   – Greek galley consisting of two banks of rowers and taking its name from one company or 'Ousia' of one hundred men.

Svear   - Swedish

Werma   - Spirit being thought to frequent snowstorms and sand storms

Runic Names for the Seven Cataracts of the Oneiper River

1. **Essupi** (Supa): the Drinker or Gulper; or Ei Sofi ("Sleep not!")
2. **Ulvorsi** (homfors) Island-force
3. **Gelandri** (gjallandi), the Yeller
4. **Aïfor** (eifors, Aifur), the Ever-fierce, Ever-noisy, or Impassable, or (edfors), Narrow-force or Portage-force
   a. Rusfstain is one of its levels.
5. **Baruforos** (bárufors), Wave-force, or possibly Highcliff-force (varnfors)
6. **Leanti** (hlæjandi, leandi), Laughter or Seether
7. **Strukun** (struk, strok), the Courser

Old Norwegian Units of Measure

(used in this book)

Length

- *fot* - Foot, 31.374 cm.
- *landmil* - Old land-mile, 11.824 km.
- *mil* - Norwegian mile, spelled *miil* prior to 1862, 18000 *alen* or 11.295 km. Before 1683, a *mil* was defined as 17600 *alen* or 11.13 km. The unit survives to this day, but in a metric 10 km adaptation

Weight

- *pund* - Pound, alt. *skålpund*, 2 *merker* 0.4984 kg, was 0.46665 kg before 1683

- *skippund* - Ships pound, 159.488 kg. Was defined as 151.16 kg in 1270.

Nautical

- *favn* - Fathom (pl. *favner*), 3 *alen*, 1.88 m
- *kabellengde* - Cable length, 100 *favner*, 185.2 m
- *kvartmil* - Quarter mile, 10 *kabellengder*, 1852 m
- *sjømil* - Sea mile, 4 *kvartmil*, 7408 m, defined as 1/15 Equatorial degree.

--FINSK--

.

John Halsted

About the Author

JOHN HALSTED

"You're only here once. Make the most of it!"

John Halsted was educated at Westville Boys High, just outside Durban, South Africa, where he spent more time on the sports field, gaining honours for athletics, and in 1976 just managed to graduate. His lack of interest in academic school work led his teachers and parents to despair, while his coach rejoiced.

In the two years following high school he commenced national service in the South African Air Force and spent more time on athletics tours and having a good time, never fully committed to the defence of apartheid, as his Sergeant Major will readily testify. After completing his national service he used London as a base and spent the better part of eighteen months touring and cycling around Europe.

On returning to South Africa in 1980 he found a job as a shipping clerk and when the opportunity presented itself he transferred to Johannesburg, only so he could continue his athletics career. In 1982 he found himself managing a container depot. It was here that he was run over by a seven-and-half-ton forklift truck and his athletics career brought to a screaming halt – literally and figuratively. He spent three months in an orthopaedic hospital recuperating. It was also at this time that the Western nations applied strict sanctions against South Africa due the country's apartheid policies and the shipping industry all but died. Not long after leaving hospital he found himself out of a job and without any marketable skills. The easy times were over, he had to skill up.

In 1983 he found employment as an internal auditor with a major motor manufacturer. Searching for the ideal career he later transferred to the Accounts and Finance department. In 1985 he went to night classes and trained as a computer programmer later transferring to the I.T. department.

In 1986 he met his future wife Joy, a Kiwi Occupational Therapist, on assignment from the International Leprosy Mission, at Westfort Hospital, Pretoria. They married in 1987 and in 1988 moved to Auckland, New Zealand where they had their first two children.

In 1991 John and the family were transferred from Auckland to Wellington. In 1994 he moved in to project management, finally finding his ideal career which gives him the fun, the challenge and the variety he requires. Their third child was born in 1996 and their fourth in 1998.

In 1999 the family moved to England, the birth place of his Grandmother. In 2001 he made a poignant journey to Poland and Stalag VIII-C where his father was a PoW during WWII. Always relishing a challenge, in 2004 he cycled 500m/800km across northern Spain on the Way of St James and in 2006 he cycled 300m/480km from the Atlantic to the Mediterranean through France along the Canal du Midi.

In 2000 he started a part-time MBA at Bath University, which he successfully completed in 2002. On completion of his MBA he realised just how much time he had on his hands and commenced an in-depth personal study of Viking history (from which his family are allegedly descended). In his research he discovered Vikings who travelled East across Europe via the inland waterways to the Black sea and Caspian sea. Finding the action and adventure across Europe and along the Silk Route more interesting than family trees, it didn't take much to convert his research into an Historical Action and Adventure novel.

In 2006 he was stunned to find this inaugural novel was a finalist in the ForeWord Book of the Year awards in. He is currently researching and writing the sequel.

'IK Ltd.

J1B/76/P